THE DRAGON WAKES WITH THUNDER

BOOKS BY K. X. SONG

THE DRAGON SPIRIT DUOLOGY

The Night Ends with Fire
The Dragon Wakes with Thunder

An Echo in the City

ABOUT THE AUTHOR

K.X. Song is a diaspora writer with roots in Hong Kong and Shanghai. Raised between cultures and languages, she enjoys telling stories that explore the shifting nature of memory, translation and history. Her young adult novel, *An Echo in the City*, was named a Best Book of 2023 by the *Financial Times* and *Kirkus Reviews*. Her adult fantasy debut, *The Night Ends With Fire*, was an Indie Next Pick and an instant *New York Times*, *USA Today* and #1 *Sunday Times* bestseller.

THE DRAGON WAKES WITH THUNDER

K. X. SONG

HODDERSCAPE

First published in Great Britain in 2025 by Hodderscape
An imprint of Hodder & Stoughton Limited
An Hachette UK company

The authorised representative in the EEA is Hachette Ireland, 8 Castlecourt Centre, Dublin 15, D15 XTP3, Ireland (email: info@hbgi.ie)

1

Copyright © K. X. Song 2025

The right of K. X. Song to be identified as the Author of the Work has been asserted by her in accordance with the Copyright, Designs and Patents Act 1988.

Book design by Daniel Brount
Map illustration by Alexis Seabrook

All rights reserved. No part of this publication may be reproduced, stored in a retrieval system, or transmitted, in any form or by any means without the prior written permission of the publisher, nor be otherwise circulated in any form of binding or cover other than that in which it is published and without a similar condition being imposed on the subsequent purchaser.

All characters in this publication are fictitious and any resemblance to real persons, living or dead, is purely coincidental.

A CIP catalogue record for this title is available from the British Library

Hardback ISBN 978 1 399 72530 9
Trade Paperback ISBN 978 1 399 72531 6
ebook ISBN 978 1 399 72532 3

Typeset in Tactile ITC Std

Printed and bound in Great Britain by Clays Ltd, Elcograf S.p.A.

Hodder & Stoughton policy is to use papers that are natural, renewable and recyclable products and made from wood grown in sustainable forests. The logging and manufacturing processes are expected to conform to the environmental regulations of the country of origin.

Hodder & Stoughton Limited
Carmelite House
50 Victoria Embankment
London EC4Y 0DZ

www.hodderscape.co.uk

To my brother, for asking what happens next

大江东去,浪淘尽,千古风流人物.

　　—苏轼,《念奴娇·赤壁怀古》

The great river flows east, sweeping away heroes of ages past.

—SU SHI, *REMINISCING AT THE RED CLIFF*

RUNONG DESERT
Xianju
LEYUAN
RED MOUNTAINS
Zhong Wu
THE THREE KINGDOMS

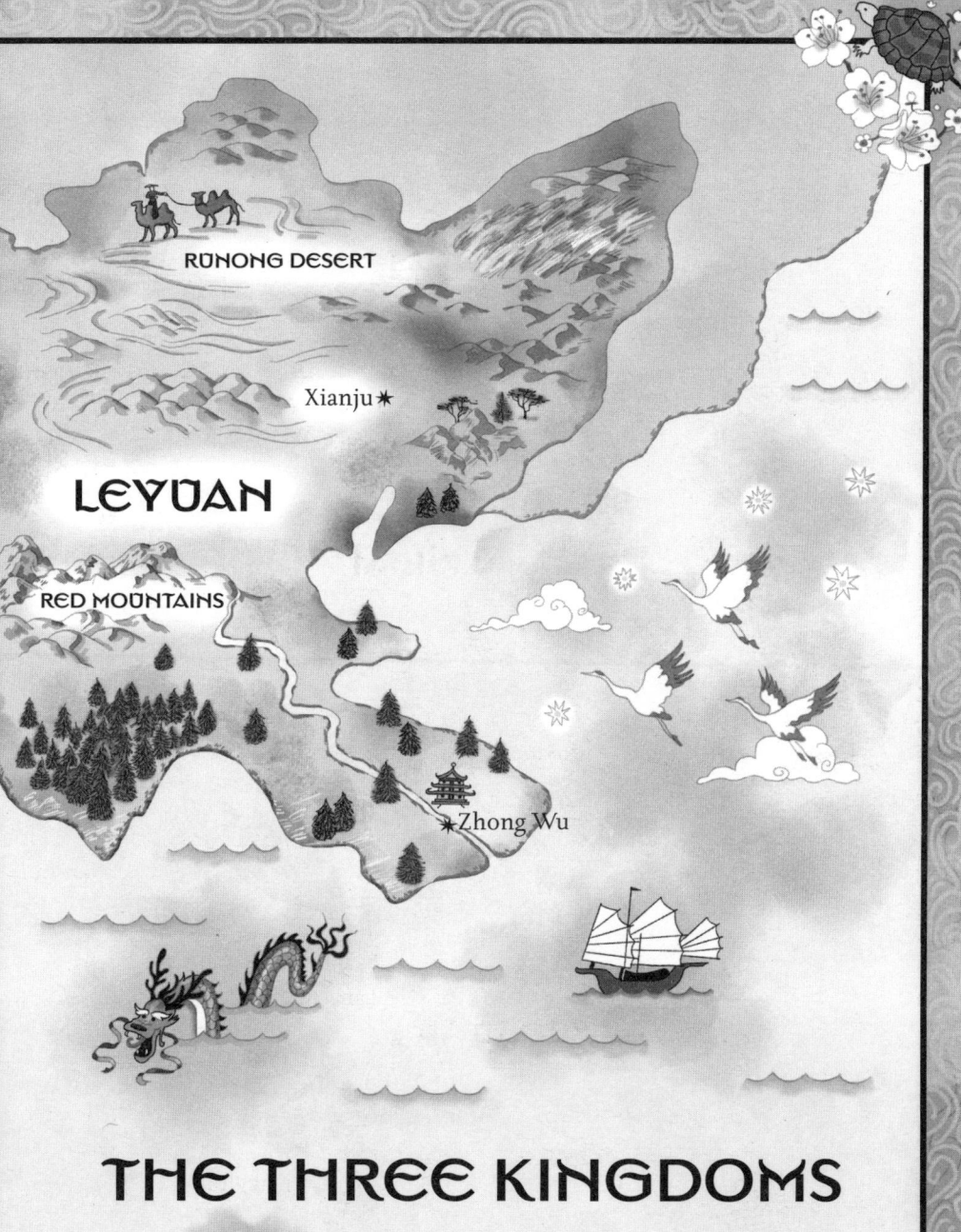

PART I

PART I

ONE

You may burn bamboo, but it will still stand straight.
You may shatter jade, but its color will not fade.
—BOOK OF ODES, 856

TIME BORE THE QUALITY OF A TANGLED SPOOL OF THREAD. I could not unravel the knots, could not sense where things ended, could not recall where things began.

I started, like always, from what I knew: I was in the palace dungeons, in the capital city of Anlai, my home. My home when I had no ability to choose where I called home.

I had been here for some time now. I had not tried to count the days, which had bled into weeks or months or years. By the chill in the air, and the fur lining of my jail warden's coat, winter was fast approaching.

Snow would be settling on the branches of Xiuying's beloved plum trees, which she pruned every spring. The snow would spread across the garden like colorless jewels, catching the winter sunlight and refracting it in every direction. Rouha would be chiseling out exuberant ice sculptures, and Plum would be trying to eat snow. Uncle Zhou would be simmering his favorite winter melon soup, which tasted heavenly on a cold snowy morning.

The taste of life had been sweet, hadn't it? But it tasted sweetest when it was taken from you.

I remembered the thrill of unfathomable power surging through my veins, that eddy of sheer delight as roiling waves rose to meet my call. Racing through a darkening forest, fighting side by side with my comrades in arms. Knowing my platoon had my back. Knowing I had friends to call my own.

Friends, they said, before betraying me. But we didn't think about that anymore.

I remembered climbing onto a terrace railing and looking out over the dark expanse of water, the waiting ocean like a well of black, black ink. The recklessness that felt like a drug, better than a drug, the thrill of knowing the waves would catch me. *Will you obey me?* I'd asked the sea. *Will you obey me as you obey the dragon?*

And yet, down here in the dungeons, my memories felt as distant as dreams.

The outer door to my prison cell clanged open. I heard the thud of footsteps, even and heavy. Three sets of them.

"Good evening, sweetheart. Let's continue where we left off last time, shall we?"

My heart began to stutter. A practiced response, a trained step in the choreography. Already I could feel the nerves in my hand tingling, anticipating the pain to come. Perhaps the anticipation was worse than the pain itself, for these days, pain lingered beneath every waking moment. There was the pain of separation: of no longer hearing the dragon's voice. The pain of dependency; I needed lixia in my bloodstream like a person needed water. Then there were the more insidious hurts, carved into me like scars: the marks of betrayal, of loneliness. Of knowing there could be no happiness for someone like me.

A perversion. A threat to the state. A girl who desired more.

"Get up."

I did not move. They unlocked the door to my cell and lifted me. Still I did not resist. I felt them clasp chains around my legs, securing me to the interrogation chair.

"Your greed is unending," the dragon had once told me. *"An ocean's hunger."*

They fit wooden sticks around my fingers, opting for my left hand this time. Slowly, the guards pulled the ropes connecting the sticks, not enough to inflict pain, only discomfort. Ironically, the zanzhi, finger crushing, was a torture method reserved for women, as it was considered more humane than jiagun, leg twisting. But I had endured both.

"Where are the remaining black magic practitioners hiding?" asked Warden Hu.

I tried to speak but no sound emerged. It must have been days since I'd last spoken aloud.

"Give her water."

One of the guards forced a canteen of water down my throat, and I sputtered, coughing.

"Where are the black magic practitioners hiding?" he asked again.

I cleared my throat. "There are no others."

"You lie." He nodded once. My throat tightened with the ropes.

I gasped as the pain came, sharp and staggering. Although the pain was concentrated along the base of my fingers, my entire arm reverberated with feeling. Despite the chill in the air, I was soon sweating.

They released the ropes. I sagged against the chair, my hand throbbing with pain. I stared at the useless appendage as if it belonged to a stranger. My right hand was too sore to use, and now my left would soon follow. How did they expect me to eat and drink? How did they expect me to live?

Or had this been their intention all along? To bide their time until Sky forgot me, until my family forgot me, until I faded into oblivion, an unnamed scratch in the annals of history?

"The might of the sea," Qinglong had said, *"is yours."*

"Where are the remaining black magic practitioners hiding?" Warden Hu asked a third time, his voice as calm as a still lake.

"I know of no others," I said hoarsely. "But perhaps . . . there could be minor spirit summoners in the south? They are more open to lixia practitioning in Ximing . . ."

"Ximing?" He leaned in. "Is that where—"

"Let me through!"

Warden Hu startled at the sounds of a scuffle. A figure clad in white shoved past the stationed guards, striding toward me like a mirage. His complexion was so fair and his robes so clean, he looked like he belonged in a heavenly realm, one set apart from the filth of this place.

"Warden Hu?" Sky's surprise was evident. "What are you . . . ?"

His eyes flicked to me—and I caught the horror in them. Without meaning to, I shrank from his gaze, as if I had anywhere to hide here. It stung for him to look at me like that, to see me with pity, and beneath it, revulsion.

Sky whirled on the warden. "What are you doing to her?"

Warden Hu straightened his shoulders. "Your Highness—"

"My father strictly forbade torture of any kind!"

"The Imperial Commander authorized me to conduct this interrogation," Warden Hu said, careful to keep his tone neutral.

Sky glared at him. "Then why sneak around like this—in the middle of the night, as if . . ." His face changed as the answer came to him. "To keep me from finding out," he finished flatly.

Sky was always like this, as expressive as an open flame. It endeared him to me, but also, it made me resentful. Because no woman could live like that. No, what we were trained to do was conceal, conceal, conceal. Every emotion flung far beneath a smiling mask of good humor and grace.

"Your father believes you have more pressing matters to attend to, Your Highness. You need not concern yourself with the welfare of a state traitor."

Sky ignored him, seizing the bars of my cell. "Meilin," he said urgently, and up close he was so lovely and clean and pure it was difficult to look at him. He radiated health and vigor, like nothing else in these dungeons. "I'm going to get you out of here. I promise," he said. "Just—hold on a bit longer. I'm sorry."

I did not feel any particular emotion, and yet my eyes filled with tears. I did not know why I was crying.

"Meilin," Sky said again, but his face had become an indistinct blur in my vision.

"*Conserve your qi*," the dragon had warned me. "*You must learn to harness your power.*"

The Azure Dragon had lied about many things, but he had not lied about this. No matter—I had not listened. At first, I'd fled from my power, and when I'd finally embraced it, I'd broken every rule, believing myself the exception. I'd overused my lixia, draining my qi—all to keep going, to keep fighting. For what? To save my family, my kingdom? Yes, I had saved them. Yet still I felt empty. Because all along, what I'd really wanted was to prove myself.

I'd wanted to show everyone that I belonged. No—more than belonged. I'd wanted to become the hero of legend, to have my name whispered through the streets, my deeds etched in the stones of history.

Instead, Warden Hu had informed me I had become a stain in

the war annals, a cautionary tale passed from parent to child. Like my mother before me, my legacy would be one of madness and decay—a rot spreading in dark places, remembered not for what it built but for what it destroyed.

That young girl from a year ago, the one who'd dreamed of adventure, of seeing the world beyond the women's quarters. She had sought wonder, wildness. She had believed in the world's capacity for beauty.

Only a year had passed, and yet I could no longer recall what that felt like. To believe in the goodness of people. To seek justice but live with compassion. To hope for better days.

There was no hope for someone like me.

SOME TIME LATER, I WOKE TO A DARK SILHOUETTE AGAINST MY CELL, slashing the light of the flickering lantern. His long shadow stretched across the length of the corridor like a grasping hand.

"Did I wake you?" the Ximing prince asked. Against the icy air of my cell, his low baritone felt like the crackle of a warm fire.

I pushed myself upright, wincing as I put weight on my throbbing hands. "I no longer sleep these days."

"That doesn't sound healthy," he said, his tone light and teasing.

I was in no mood for his banter. "What do you want, Lei?"

He peered down at me through the bars, his eyes narrowing. "I heard you've been refusing food."

I looked away. "I'm not hungry."

It was a lie. I was hungry all the time. Hungry for lixia, for the intoxicating surge of spirit power in my veins. I needed it, craved it, ached for it all the time. I could feel the nearness of my jade, its energy thrumming just out of reach. The lack left me breathless and off-balance, as if I were missing a vital sense.

"Funny," said Lei, his expression unreadable. "You used to strike me as a survivor."

"What's that supposed to mean?" I snapped, losing my temper. How dare he judge me from his seat of privilege? "Go gloat somewhere else, will you?"

He crouched in front of me, so that we were eye level through the bars. "From one prisoner to the next—" He tilted his head, his amber eyes seeming to absorb the flickering firelight. "If you lose your will to live, it's simple. You die."

With that, he rose to his feet. "Do you want to die? If you die, they win. Remember that."

I STARTED EATING AGAIN. THE FOOD UPSET MY STOMACH, FORCED ME to use my broken hands, and heightened my lixia cravings, but at least I started to feel strong enough to stand again. To take a few steps around my cell. To think beyond the span of a day. Two days, a week—that was the limit of what I could take.

The warden's questions kept coming, though they were no longer accompanied by torture. Vaguely, I wondered what Sky had done to achieve such a feat—what he might have bargained with. For there was always a price. I hadn't known that the first time.

"Though you were initially accused of black magic practitioning," said Warden Hu, watching me, "it seems now your accusers have retracted their allegations. Any guesses as to why?"

I shook my head.

"Let's say you did know a thing or two about black magic," he said. "How might one access such a power?"

I told him nothing more than what was common knowledge.

"But why can only some access such a power?"

I said I didn't understand.

"Why are some stricken with seizure and lunacy when confronted with spirit power, while others retain clarity of mind?"

For the first time in a while, I recalled that strange, rippling haze outside the inn in New Quan. The bandits who had wandered near were drawn by the lure of spirit power, moving toward the portal as if in a trance.

"It is a tear in the veil," the dragon had told me. *"So that any human, not just those with seals, can enter our realm. But only those with strong enough spirit affinity can survive such a place. The rest..."*

The rest lost their minds.

"Are more gates appearing?" I asked, raising my head.

"Gates?"

"Portals into the spirit realm," I clarified.

"What are they caused by?" asked the warden, more urgently now. "Why are they forming?"

"I-I don't know," I said, taken aback. "But I wonder if it has something to do with overuse of lixia," I added quietly, thinking of a similar rippling haze I'd once found in my mother's chambers, which were now sealed and boarded up.

If there were more gates appearing, that meant there were more spirit summoners at work. But who? Chancellor Sima was dead. I was locked away in an iron dungeon. Could there be someone else? Someone who'd been biding their time?

Lately, I'd begun to feel a prickling to my senses, though I'd chalked it up to lixia withdrawal. An uncanny sense, as if the spirit realm were somehow nearing. As if the worlds had begun to merge.

Before I could respond, the passageway door burst open. Sky raced toward us, his face alight with undisguised joy. "Father's agreed!" he exclaimed, skidding to a stop in front of my cell. "Meilin can go free."

I blinked at him, unable to process his words.

"Did you hear me?" he asked. "You can come out with me, now. Your maids are waiting for you—they'll help you wash and prepare for court. I asked Mother to set aside a few dresses for now, but once we get your measurements I'll send for . . ." He trailed off as he took in my expression. "Meilin . . . why are you shaking?"

I could not answer. Cold fear coiled around my neck like an insistent noose.

Sky tried to enter my cell but found it locked. He impatiently motioned for the key before barreling inside. But I shrank from the proximity of him.

"Meilin, what's wrong?" asked Sky, kneeling before me, and his voice was so tender it made my eyes sting. I tried to push him away, but my broken hands were useless, unable to do what I wanted from them.

He caught my left hand and I gasped in pain. Immediately he let go, as if my touch burned him. "Meilin. Speak to me, please." His eyes were wide and filled with feeling. It broke something within me, to see myself through his eyes. A pitiful creature, better left alone in the dark. "Don't you want to be free?"

I was sobbing so hard now that I could not form words. He gave me his handkerchief, but my fingers would not close around it, and the fine cloth fell uselessly to the floor.

"Meilin, I made a promise to you. I want to marry you. Did you think I would go back on my word?"

He tried to draw me into his arms, but I flinched away again. Hurt flashed across his face as he backed away, raking his fingers through his hair. "Please. Tell me what's wrong."

"I-I can't. I can't go to court," I said, and I meant it. I couldn't imagine myself in fine dresses, eyes painted like a doll's, and—like a doll—face vacant but smiling, sitting silently by Sky's side as I'd seen the warlord's consorts do. "I want to . . . to leave this place—"

"I'll take you out of the dungeons," Sky said, but I shook my head.

"No," I rasped. "I want to leave the . . . palace. The city." The world.

His face fell. "My father's terms were for you to remain within the Forbidden City," he admitted, "and to return to the ways of womanhood."

The noose drew tight around my neck. So it was the old offer, made again. I would have to relinquish my sword, my freedom, my knowledge of the world beyond. I could be Sky's pretty ornament, or nothing at all.

Yet memories of the outside world, however undesirable, still called to me. I missed the morning sunlight and the reflection of the moon upon water. I missed my family and the ability to run with the wind at my back. When the Imperial Commander had first offered me this choice, I hadn't understood the stakes. I understood them now.

But there was a third factor I hadn't weighed. Here in the dungeons, I was suffocated by iron. There was no possibility of the dragon's presence, his influence, his sly whispering voice in my head. The last time I'd seen him, he'd tried to kill me. Just like he'd killed my mother.

Perhaps once I was freed, he'd finish the job.

"Meilin? Do you want me to call your maidservants here?"

I shook my head. "Can you . . . can you give me some time?"

I could feel his sadness like a millstone, dragging me beneath its weight.

"I'm sorry, Sky," I said, and the sound of his name hurt us both. "Please go." When he didn't move, I turned my back on him. Eventually, I felt the strength of his presence recede.

I didn't know myself anymore. The girl he'd loved . . . I didn't know if she still existed. So many conflicting desires battled within me at once, until I couldn't make sense of any of them. I wanted to be free—of my loneliness, of my captivity, of my weakness. I wanted to be confined—I couldn't be trusted with power, with responsibility, with choice. And all those people above, judging me, mocking me, wanting something from me . . . the thought made me want to hide forever.

Who was I anymore? And if I couldn't trust myself, who could I possibly trust?

TWO

After physicians deemed Emperor Zhuan's illness incurable, he vanished for forty-nine days. Upon his return, fully restored to health, he gave no clear explanation, hinting only at Zhuque's eternal spring. Word of his recovery spread far and wide, prompting many terminally ill patients to seek the spring, believing it could heal both body and spirit.
—A COMPREHENSIVE OVERVIEW OF LIXIA-INDUCED DISORDERS, 910

THE VERY NEXT DAY, I HAD VISITORS. VISITORS I HADN'T SEEN since the start of the war.

"Jie!" Rouha broke free from Xiuying's viselike grip first. She ran toward me on her sturdy, small legs, legs that were not so small anymore. How had she managed to grow so much in the span of a year? I struggled to sit up on my pallet, not wanting to appear weak and sickly in front of my family.

Rouha reached my cell and stuck her little arms through the bars. Unable to deny her, I held my hand out and let her grasp my cold fingers with her warm ones. The weight of her small palm in mine, the softness of her skin, the simple, trusting gaze she beheld me with, as if there were nothing I could ever do to harm her . . . it was too much. As I tried to release her hand, she clung to me. When I forcibly pulled away, she began to cry.

Plum, who had waddled forward on his own, took this cue to also burst into tears. Xiuying scooped him up, darting an anxious glance at the soldiers standing guard down the hallway. "They missed you," Xiuying explained. As our gazes met, I saw that her eyes were full of tacit meaning. "As did I."

Even Uncle Zhou had come. "Despite your father's fall from favor, your prince asked for an exception to allow us to enter the Forbidden City," he explained, and I was reminded of Sky's shrewd decisiveness as commander general. He knew what he wanted, and more importantly, he knew how to get what he wanted.

Uncle Zhou continued: "He said you were reluctant to leave your confinement."

I stiffened at his choice of words. For they reminded me of my mother.

My mother, who had refused to leave her rooms. Who had shut herself away in her final days, unwilling to see or hear from anyone. That was how one gave up on life, wasn't it?

"If you lose your will to live, it's simple. You die," Lei had told me. *"Do you want to die? If you die, they win. Remember that."*

I did not want to die. Rather, I wanted life as the migrating birds did, flying thousands of li to stay warm and outlast the winter. I wanted life as did the wolves, who, when crippled by hunters, still came limping back for leftovers, determined to eat their fill. The naïve parts of me that had survived the war wondered if life in the imperial palace would not be lovely and delightful, like a storybook character's happy ending. Yet the lie was as flimsy as rice paper. I could not even convince myself.

Life came with responsibility. Given freedom, I was afraid of what I might do. Could I still be trusted, I, a corrupted state traitor, who desired lixia more than air itself?

"I know the Imperial Commander's pardon pertains only to your freedom in the Forbidden City," said Uncle Zhou, "but I wonder if, with time and good behavior, he might lessen his restraints.

Perhaps come spring, you could be permitted to visit Willow District. You'll find our home much changed since you last saw it."

"Why?" I asked hoarsely.

"His Highness wanted to make sure we were well equipped for winter. Our household lacks for nothing now."

My mouth twisted. Father would have no trouble filling his pipe, then.

"How is Father?" I asked.

Uncle Zhou and Xiuying exchanged a glance. "As well as one can expect."

"I'm sure he was thrilled to hear news of my treachery."

Xiuying shook her head. "Meilin," she said. "Be free. Remember what you once wanted."

Xiuying spoke softly, choosing her words with care. I scrutinized her face, but as always, she wore her mask of polite civility. We both knew the warlord's soldiers were listening.

I got to my feet gingerly, gripping the bars of my cell for balance. "Sister," I said quietly. "I'm afraid. I'm afraid I no longer know how to live. I'm afraid I can no longer tell right from wrong. I'm afraid of who I am now, and, given freedom, of who I will be up there."

As ghastly as they were, the dungeons were also safe, and predictable, and unvarying. My days here were routine, without stimulation. All I had were my memories, but even those were safe, for the past could not change. I could not alter my prospects from here.

But out there, the future was permeable. I could change my fate—for better or for ruin. The warlord had condemned me as a traitor—to the kingdom and to our social order. But perhaps my legacy could still be rewritten.

"Mei Mei, your fears are only natural," said Xiuying. "Be glad you have them, for they will keep you safe. Fear your own power and you will not become a slave to it." She leaned in, so that we were only a hair's breadth apart. "And I trust you. I trust even your basest of instincts. Remember that no matter how far you have fallen, you can be no lower than those above us both, those who occupy the throne today."

My mouth fell open. Xiuying caught my eye before busying herself breaking apart Rouha and Plum's squabble, once again playing the role of good and faithful mother. But this was the most subversive, insurrectionary comment I had ever heard from her.

Xiuying—optimistic, ever cheerful, the very paragon of a dutiful Anlai woman—had no faith in those who held power today.

How many others were like her, I wondered—disillusioned by the status quo, waiting for a spark of change?

It was then that I felt it—what I hadn't felt for a very long time. The first stirrings of desire.

THEY HAD TO LEAVE SOON AFTER. ROUHA AND PLUM COULD NOT STAND the dankness of the air and the wafting scent of rotting flesh. Only Uncle Zhou managed to linger, glancing furtively over his shoulder as Plum started a screaming tantrum in front of the guards. Under the cover of Plum's echoing wails, Uncle Zhou said to me, "I meant to give this to you before you left for your husband's household. Of course, you didn't bother saying goodbye."

"I'm sorry—"

He waved my apology away. Opening his cloak, he passed me a worn leather-bound book, its binding warped and the ink on the cover no longer visible.

"Your mother's diary, Meilin. I found it on her body the night she drowned. Many of the pages are ruined, but miraculously, some survived. I tried to decipher her words but . . . I think you may understand more than I do now."

With one last look, he hurried down the hall, joining Xiuying in soothing the children.

I waited until the guards had returned to their usual posts before poring over the unexpected gift. It amazed me to think my mother had once touched this artifact, had once written and caressed these pages. I did not remember her keeping a diary, but then again, there were many things that I did not recall.

The pages were deformed from extensive water damage. Most of the ink had run, but as I flipped through the wrinkled pages, I found a few passages where the characters were still faintly legible.

I plan to use him— my mother had written, in her sprawling, confident handwriting.

How thrilling, to finally be able to—

And she laughed and kissed me—

But surely, the tide will—

I kept leafing through the pages, until I was more than halfway through the book. Here a greater extent of the writing had been preserved, the ink less blurred. On one such page, a whole paragraph was readable: *He is using me. Just as I am using him. But he is winning. His will overrides my own these days, in moments that I cannot recall. Is he stealing my memories? I worry my body is no longer my own—*

Gradually, I saw, her handwriting had become like bird scratches, sparse and thin.

His goal is far more ambitious than anyone could have known. It is long-drawn-out, and yet, what is time to an immortal? He has been biding his time for centuries. I must stop him, before it is too late.

From her final entry:

I can feel myself fading, losing bits and pieces of myself day by day. Is it too late for me? And yet I cling to hope, that obstinate creature. I must hold out until the end of winter, when I can make my last journey to the Red Mountains— and save myself—

I slammed the book shut, my heart hammering in my chest. I could not keep reading. It was too painful, like trying to excavate shrapnel buried deep in the flesh.

My mother had died trying to thwart Qinglong's plans, whatever they were. Stealing Zhuque's seal? But he had not succeeded. No, his goals had always been far more ambitious than my own. He had likely wanted Zhuque's seal for a larger purpose.

Thoughts of the dragon inevitably led to my jade. Its absence gnawed at me, leaving me weak and depleted. Perhaps the only thing sustaining me now was the overpowering presence of iron in these dungeons. Once I left, how could I possibly function without my seal? My hands twitched compulsively, until I finally drifted into sleep. In my dreams, my jade found me. In my dreams, I was made whole.

THE CLANG OF THE OUTER DOOR WOKE ME. I HEARD THE FURTIVE RUSH of whispers, before a familiar shadow cut across the guttered prison walls. I recognized him by the slope of his gait, like a jungle cat's. Cao Ming Lei.

Now that I thought about it, I had no idea how he'd managed his visits to me thus far. As a prisoner of war, his movements were surely restricted. But if anyone could bend the rules, it was the prince of Ximing.

What else could he manage, I wondered. What other rules could he circumvent?

"So you've been offered a way out," said Lei, hands clasped behind his back as he studied me. "Will you accept?"

"How have you managed to visit me?" I asked, disregarding his question. "Surely the Imperial Commander would not allow it."

Lei smirked. "Using your little brain again. I'm glad to see it."

I scowled at his condescension. "Bribery?" I guessed. "But where have you the means?"

"There are things people want more than gold," he replied. The knowing glint in his eyes told me he had the means to help me. Few were as charming or as cunning as he was. And what I needed was something no one else would dare attempt.

I still despised him for what he'd done to me in the Three Kingdoms War, the way he'd exploited and manipulated me as his prisoner. We were by no means friends but . . . I had few allies in this place. And after what we'd endured together to survive on Mount Fuxi, we were no longer exactly enemies either.

"Lei," I started, struggling to keep the desperation from my voice. "Can you help me? I-I need my spirit seal."

He opened his mouth to speak but I cut him off. "I can't live without it," I said in a rush. "I-I'm off-balance all the time. It's hard to sleep, hard to think, hard to even breathe. If I'm to return to the palace, if I'm to stand a chance at court, I need it. Lei," I said again. "I-I think my life force is tied to it now."

"So you will accept, then," he asked, his face as inscrutable as ever, "the Imperial Commander's offer?"

I thought of my mother's diary, which was hidden within the folds of my tunic. *And yet I cling to hope, that obstinate creature. I must hold out until the end of winter, when I can make my last journey to the Red Mountains—and save myself—*

In the end, it had been too late for her, and she had not lasted to catch the blossoms of spring. But she had wanted to save herself; she had not given up on this world as I had so often imagined. What had Qinglong done to her? And what was he planning now? I was no match for the dragon in my current state, but I could not surrender myself as I'd once believed my mother to have done. I would fight—until my bones were dust, I would fight.

"It's a surprising offer," I told Lei. "I don't know why the Imperial Commander would agree to it, but..."

"Not for your sake, certainly," said Lei. "Despite the official reports, legend of the woman warrior has spread far, and the people are restless. In the aftermath of war, famine has devastated the land. Do you know—news of your imprisonment has been met with anger, and in some cases rebellion? The warlord's position is precarious, and now he needs his prisoner on a pretty pedestal, to comply with and promote his agenda. And will you obey?"

A yawning restlessness was building inside me, one I hadn't felt since I'd fled my father's house, all those months ago.

"You know how obedient I am," was all I said.

Lei's smile was like a knife in the dark.

THREE

The bond between spirit and summoner is a tenuous one. The spirit draws upon the summoner's qi, while the summoner, in turn, derives lixia from his spirit. When this exchange is in equilibrium, a fragile harmony may be achieved. However, when the will of one overtakes and subsumes the other, the balance is disrupted, and it is in such moments that spirits often seize full control.
—LOST JOURNALS OF AN 8TH-CENTURY LIXIA SCHOLAR,
DATE UNKNOWN

FREEDOM. I TOOK MY FIRST TENTATIVE STEP OUT OF THE DUNGEONS and felt all blood rush to my face. Sunlight streamed in through the windows above, painfully brilliant and warm. I could hear trees rustling in the wind, and the distant sound of laughter. Footsteps, everywhere, echoing. The clink of porcelain, the chime of bells, the scent of linen and lavender, of cleanness, of wholeness—of everything I was not.

My head felt as if it were cleaving in two. I staggered to a halt and my many guards went still, tensing as if I might suddenly breathe fire or grow a tail. I wanted to laugh at their fear, but instead my knees buckled and I collapsed beneath my own weight, covering my ears as the stimulation became too much. There was too much to see, to smell, to hear. No longer surrounded by iron, I could sense lixia everywhere, but I no longer possessed an outlet to channel it. I needed my seal to ground me, to keep the pain at bay.

Someone knelt by my side. "Meilin?" It was Sky. "What's wrong?"

"My jade," I rasped. "I need my jade. Please, Sky."

"I-I can't," he said. "My father ordered—"

"Her heart," said another voice, as cold fingers checked my pulse, "it's failing."

"Perhaps... should she wear iron?" Sky's voice was unsure.

I heard Winter reply, but I could no longer make sense of sound. The pounding in my head built to a crescendo. I gasped as the pain reached greater heights, until it was too much to bear. I fainted.

"SHE'S REACHED AN INFLECTION POINT IN HER ADDICTION." I WOKE groggily, struggling to rise from my stupor. "She likely can no longer function without a seal, which channels her black magic."

"What do you mean, 'function'?" demanded Sky.

The other man cleared his throat. "With physical dependence, the body adapts to the presence of a drug, until withdrawal becomes lethal. Simply put, without a seal, she will die."

The silence that followed felt like a living creature, impulsive and impossible to predict. At last, Sky said, "Ge, do you think we could tell Father—"

"You are not a fool, Di Di." His high, lilting voice was like the sound of wind chimes. Liu Winter, the sixth prince of Anlai. "Do not act like one."

"She'd wear iron at all times." I could hear the pleading note in Sky's voice. "The iron would counteract all spirit power. She wouldn't be a threat—"

"Telling him the truth will only sentence her to death." Winter sighed. "You know how he is. There is no reason to his fear." His voice changed directions. "You may go. Do you remember the terms of our agreement?"

"Of course, Your Highness," said the other man. "Your secret is safe with me."

They said their goodbyes, which were followed by the sound of a sliding door. "Brother," Sky whispered, his voice wretched. "Help me."

"I did warn you—"

"I know!" Sky growled, his sorrow morphing into anger. He was like that: never one to brood over sadness.

"Have you spoken with the Ximing prince?" Winter's voice came out thoughtful. "He may prove useful. Particularly when it comes to her."

Sky's reply was blunt. "I want nothing to do with him."

"Father cannot be reasoned with, not in his current state. But his condition does provide some benefits, does it not? He has become quite negligent, particularly with the state's treasures..."

I was in the depths of the sea, and there was no light to guide me out. I searched and searched, but I could not find the surface of the water. Each time, I drowned.

"IT WAS NO TROUBLE." CAO MING LEI? HIS VOICE WAS SO LOW IT WAS hard to make out. "But keep this between us, will you?"

"Of course," replied Winter. "I doubt my father will find out anytime soon, given his current preoccupations and the caliber of the forgery. Still... I hope you did not leave a trail."

Lei said something else, but the waves were calling me.

AND THEN, A LIGHT. PIERCING THE DARKNESS, THE DEPTHS OF THE SEA. Emboldened, I swam toward it, up and up and up. The azure light grew stronger, and with it, a growing awareness of my own body. I sensed the fragrance of lavender in the air, the hushed voices whispering about me, and the familiar weight of a warm, pulsating stone. And then—I broke free.

I WOKE WITH A GASP, TRYING TO SHOOT UPRIGHT IN BED ONLY TO FIND my arms tied down. I opened my mouth but my throat was too parched to make a sound.

"You're awake." Sky sat by my bed, face haggard and worn. To himself: "It actually worked."

I struggled against my bonds, and he seemed to remember himself, untying the ropes that bound me to the bed. "I'm sorry. You weren't . . . yourself. I didn't want you to get hurt."

He brought a cup of water to my lips, and I drank greedily, as if I hadn't had water in days. I sat up, feeling as if I could breathe again. It was as if a long-borne weight had suddenly been lifted off my chest, and now I was free.

But of course, I thought, looking down. A necklace was tucked beneath my tunic. Though it was cleverly ornamented to appear like a graduated string of imperial jade beads, I could tell one piece of jade was not like the others. It was my seal.

I exhaled in sweet, utter relief.

"Don't tell anyone," said Sky. "You're technically not supposed to have it. But we figured no one will notice, given the current state of things."

"What state of things?" I asked, feeling like myself again for the first time in weeks, if not months. "What's going on?"

"Father . . . he's—"

"Di Di, I knew I'd find you here." Winter popped his head through the door, sounding, for once, less than calm. "Let's go. Sorry, Meilin, we're horrendously late."

"I'll explain later," said Sky, squeezing my hand before racing after his brother.

In the ensuing silence, I marveled at how much better my body already felt. While unfamiliar bruises covered my body and a shallow burn mark marred the back of my hand, I felt more whole than I had in months. I got to my feet gingerly, and found, to my delight, I could now stand without losing my balance. My vertigo, which had followed me everywhere like a faithful shadow, was no more.

"My lady, would you like to bathe?"

I was startled to find a moonfaced girl standing in the doorway, dressed in a blossom-pink gown with flowers pinned up in her long shining hair.

"Who are you?" I asked.

"I'm your maidservant, Lotus. And that's Lily."

Lily bowed. She had a face as angular as Lotus's was plump. She was tall while Lotus was short, somber faced while Lotus smiled continually. And yet, by their easy manner with each other, I guessed they were close friends.

"We're honored to serve an esteemed guest of the prince's," said Lily.

"I'm not a . . ." I trailed off, blushing. "I'd love a bath."

The bath they drew up was warm and scented with rose petals. My rooms were airy and spacious, with floor-to-ceiling windows that overlooked the Resting Cloud Pavilion and the nine-turn bridge. I dozed while they combed and pinned my hair, then applied cosmetics to my face. By the time they were done with me, I was unrecognizable even to myself. My hair had grown long and unruly in the dungeons, but now it had been combed and pinned up in the shape of a flying crane, adorned with pearl and jade hairpins that chimed every time I moved my head. They'd dressed me in fluttering silk robes that billowed out behind me as I walked, their sleeves so long they swept the floor, concealing the two slim iron bands encircling my wrists. The dress was a light green to match the jade in my hair, with intricately fine hyacinth embroidered in silver thread on the bodice.

"I can't wait for the prince to see you like this," said Lotus conspiratorially. "Perhaps he'll propose on the spot."

My face turned red, which made her giggle. "Do you know where the princes are?" I asked, thinking of how Sky had rushed out with Winter.

"The Imperial Commander sent out an urgent summons for his children," said Lotus. "Some suspect it is to discuss the matter of succession."

My eyes widened. The last I'd seen him, Liu Zhuo had appeared in robust health. I was astonished that someone as power hungry as he would be willing to even consider the question.

"Is the Imperial Commander's health in doubt?" I asked.

Lotus lowered her voice. "Some say he is not long for this world. He has not been of . . . sound mind, as of late."

Did this have anything to do with Warden Hu's line of questioning? Were Warlord Liu's fears of the spirit realm somehow catching up to him—were they coming true? I recalled the Ruan seer who, at the start of the war, had given the Imperial Commander a prophecy: "*The seer told my father a spirit would spell his demise,*" Sky had said, "*and the demise of Anlai itself.*"

Was he falling mad from paranoia? Or, worse, had he somehow found a spirit of his own? I wished there were a way to request an audience with him, to ascertain his state for myself. Yet to demand to see the Imperial Commander was to risk death. No, I would have to bide my time.

Warden Hu had been particularly curious about the spirit realm gates, I recalled. He had tried to learn how to stop their numbers from increasing. And why were they appearing? Certainly, without Chancellor Sima and me, there were no more spirit summoners in our world.

Unless there were others I did not know about.

"Princess Ruihua has requested your presence. Would you like me to accompany you to her quarters?" asked Lotus.

I squinted at her, bewildered.

"The wife of the third prince," Lily clarified. She appeared less talkative than Lotus, but more observant. "The third prince has the ear of the General Counsel—she could be a helpful ally."

This sounded like the last thing I wished to do. But, breathing out a sigh, I said, "Please show me the way."

Princess Ruihua's quarters lay at the far end of the Resting Cloud Pavilion, beyond the nine-turn bridge that my rooms overlooked. In the jade-green waters below, brightly colored koi darted beneath lily pads. The air was filled with the sweet fragrance of mung bean soup, mingling with the crisp scent of fading autumn.

"Oh no," muttered Lotus, as another party approached ours up ahead. They paused for us at the end of the nine-turn bridge, which was too narrow to allow more than one group to pass at a time.

The lady at the end of the bridge was accompanied by an entourage of half a dozen. Though my own head ached with the weight of my accessories, this lady wore twice the amount of jewelry I did and held her head as regally as a heron surveying her land. Her hair was twisted and looped in the style of twin butterflies, and her headpiece was made of lapis lazuli, which accentuated her large glittering eyes.

"That is Princess Li Yi Fan, the wife of the crown prince," Lotus whispered to me. "Her courtesy name is Yifeng."

Princess Yifeng nodded at me, so I inclined my head in return. At this, her eyes narrowed like an attack dog's and I knew I had somehow done wrong. Xiuying had tried to teach me proper palace etiquette, but her knowledge only went so far.

Princess Yifeng's voice was as sweet as honey. "And this must be..."

"Hai Meilin, Your Highness."

"Hai Meilin." She repeated my name as if wringing out a wet rag, leaving no syllable unspent. "Newly freed from the dungeons, I see. And where are you off to in such a hurry?"

"Princess Ruihua has requested my presence, Your Highness."

"Ruihua must suspect wedding vows to be imminent. How thrilled you must be."

I did not know what to say, so I said nothing.

"Well, I would certainly like to be the first to congratulate you," said Princess Yifeng. "Let me offer you an early wedding gift, so that I may share in your happiness."

"Oh," I said, startled. "That's quite all right."

"I insist."

"There's really no need..." I began, but my words were ignored. Princess Yifeng jerked her head at her lady-in-waiting, who passed forward a giant basket of white leilu plums, which were only in season at the tail end of autumn. The fruit was rare and unconventional as a wedding gift, as they were pure white in color, but I was not one to uphold custom.

"Please accept this humble token of my congratulations," said Princess Yifeng.

The hesitation on my face must have shown, for her expression turned insidious. "It is an insult to refuse a gift, Lady Hai," she reminded me. "I hope you are not attempting to demonstrate your true feelings toward—"

"No!" I grasped the basket, which was so heavy it made me lurch forward clumsily. "Thank you for the gift, Your Highness."

"I hope the fruit will be found satisfactory."

"I will enjoy it most gratefully," I said as Lotus took the basket from me.

"Just you? And will you not share your windfall with Princess Ruihua? She has always mentioned her fondness for leilu plums, especially at this time of the year."

"I—yes, of course," I said, flustered. "I will offer her some when I visit."

"Very good," said Princess Yifeng. "I'm so glad to welcome you into the inner palace."

Shaken, I bowed once more as Princess Yifeng stepped onto the nine-turn bridge, heading in the opposite direction.

Arriving at Princess Ruihua's quarters, I stepped over the high threshold and bowed deeply, determined not to commit another social gaffe.

Princess Ruihua rose to meet me, lifting her skirts so that they did not trail on the floor. She was dressed in crimson red robes, which seemed to catch and hold the lantern light. Beneath her stunning attire and ornate jewelry, she was not particularly beautiful, though upon further reflection, I found this did not matter. With her tasteful cosmetics and brilliant attire, she gave the appearance of beauty.

"Lady Hai, it is an honor to finally meet," she said, before looking past me to Lotus. Her face changed. "And what is this you have brought for me?"

"Leilu plums, Your Highness, as I heard your taste—"

She closed the distance between us in two quick strides and slapped me hard across the face, so hard I tasted blood. I swallowed thickly, trying not to cough, as I heard titters behind me. "How dare you bring white mourning fruit into a home soon to welcome new life?"

FOUR

Thus, white became the color of death, for so lovely and pure was the maiden of white that she could not endure the mortal world.
—WINTER AND SPRING ANNALS, 417

To my horror, I looked down at her robes and saw, beneath the voluminous silks, a slight bulge to her stomach. My own dropped.

"I beg forgiveness, Your Highness, I did not realize—"

"Stupid girl," she snapped. "Take those away." She pressed a protective hand over her stomach, as if shielding her unborn child from the sight. Lotus fled with the offending fruit.

"I see now you know little of the ways of court," Princess Ruihua said, still breathing hard. "Follow me."

I bowed again and followed as she led me into an adjoining parlor, where a table was prepared with dinner. A pretty girl with skin like glass waited by the window.

"This is Lady Caihong," Princess Ruihua said. "Consort to the Imperial Commander."

I raised a brow. The girl looked to be in her mid-twenties, nearly half the age of Sky's father.

"It's so nice to finally meet you," said Lady Caihong. "I'm so happy for you and Prince Sky. I still remember him as a little boy—he used to cry after losing at go."

"Caihong grew up in the palace," Ruihua explained. "She often played with the princes when she was little."

Even stranger, then, that she'd ended up with their father. But I only nodded.

"How is your son?" Caihong asked, when we were seated.

"Energetic as always," replied the princess. "I thought the second time would be easier. You know how Peony is, as calm as they come. But Baoxia is trying to run before he can walk!"

"Boys are different," said Caihong, smiling. "How fortunate you are, to have a third child already on the way. Princess Yifeng was singing your praises earlier. She prays some of your good luck will rub off on her."

Ruihua's smile was wry. "Princess Yifeng makes her own luck. I have no doubt good fortune will soon follow her." Her eyes dipped briefly to Caihong's figure, which was as slim and flat as a folded fan. "Perhaps good fortune will soon follow you too."

Caihong colored and looked away. "I have long since given up hope of bearing my own child. But the Imperial Commander is good to me, despite my deficiencies."

Ruihua frowned. "But perhaps it is not your fault," she posed. "Have you ever considered . . ."

"No," Caihong said firmly, her tone final. "The fault is all mine."

To avoid awkwardness, Princess Ruihua gestured for us to eat. Tentatively, I selected a piece of roasted duck, coating its crispy skin in sweet plum sauce. Adding green onions and sliced cucumbers, I wrapped the bite in a thin pancake, then stuffed it into my mouth. The flavor was exquisite—perfectly balanced between savory and sweet.

"What an appetite!" Ruihua commented. "And yet such a lovely figure. How fortunate you are."

I could not tell if this was a compliment or an insult. Bowing my head, I murmured my thanks.

Both ladies waited a beat, as if expecting something from me. I did not know what they could possibly expect, until they resumed conversation and moved on to other matters—only then did I understand that I might've complimented Ruihua in return.

My cheeks flushed even warmer. *What am I doing here?*

"And how is His Highness?" asked Caihong.

Princess Ruihua sighed. "Busy, as always. He's been traveling along the western coast for over a fortnight, but is expected home tomorrow."

So she did not know about the imperial summons, I thought. Her husband must already be home, if the Imperial Commander had called for all his sons.

"Peony asks for him every day now. He spoils her rotten, of course."

Caihong smiled at this. "He does dote on his daughter, no?"

"If only he'd give me half the attention!" Ruihua laughed, to show she was joking, but I caught the note of bitterness in her voice. "The number of women he keeps . . ." Caihong made a hemming noise of sympathy as she continued, "But he loves the children, and for that I can't complain. Just wait"—she turned to me—"the seventh prince may be besotted with you now, but as soon as your body changes with childbearing—"

A knock on the door interrupted the princess. "Your Highness," a harried manservant began, "the third prince has just—"

"Yuchen!" Ruihua cried out, rising as a tall man climbed across the threshold. I followed their lead, bowing, then watched with surprise as Prince Yuchen took hold of his wife in front of us and kissed her on the lips.

"My dear," he said. "You look rather unwell. Have the children been tormenting you?"

"They said you wouldn't be back until tomorrow!" she said, breathless from the kiss. "How good it is to see you."

"I came to find you as soon as I was dismissed. Please forgive the intrusion," he said to Caihong, bowing. He appeared oblivious to my presence, and I did not know how to introduce myself.

His eyes drifted to the table, and Ruihua laughed. "Please, sit," she said. "You must be famished."

Prince Yuchen gulped down a bowl of bone broth in response.

"Real food," he groaned, biting into a crispy bamboo shoot. "I've been subsisting on dried pork floss for weeks."

Ruihua clucked with concern. "Was the weather rough along the western coast?"

As he sat back, my eyes dropped to his shoes, momentarily exposed beneath the hem of his traveling robes. He certainly had come straight from the saddle, for his shoes were caked with grime. Curiously, the dirt was tinged indigo, reminding me of the lakeside town of Saiya, which we had passed on our journey back from Mount Fuxi after the war. Saiya was a day's ride away, yet entirely off course from the western coast.

"The weather was fine," he said, "but the journey fruitless. No leads, still. Black magic is all over the countryside, yet nobody seems to know where the cursed practitioners have gone. Father is bent on eradicating them. He wants a party to set out as soon as tomorrow."

"Tomorrow?" Ruihua screeched. "How inhumane—you only just got back!"

He said something to comfort her, which I did not hear. *Black magic is all over the countryside.* How was that possible? I had watched Chancellor Sima take his own life. I had watched him wither into ashes. He had been the last spirit summoner, apart from me.

But I recalled the poem my mother had taught me, long ago.

One buried.
One drowned.
One stolen.
But none so pitiful—
as one forgotten.

Four jade seals. Four directions, four seasons, and four Cardinal Spirits. I carried the seal of Qinglong, the Azure Dragon. Zhuque, the Vermillion Bird, had lost hers for now and was biding her time in the spirit realm. But what of Baihu, the Ivory Tiger? What of Xuanwu, the Onyx Tortoise? And what of Qinglong—who surely was not resting, just because I was?

His goal is far more ambitious than anyone could have known. It is long-drawn-out, and yet, what is time to an immortal?

How foolish I was to believe this could end so easily.

My vision was tunneling, like it always did before a panic attack. I clawed helplessly at the iron bands on my wrists, knowing full well they could not come off. Cold sweat coated my skin as my need for lixia surged within me. The craving was ever present, yet especially unbearable when acknowledged.

"Meilin!" exclaimed Ruihua, rousing me from my thoughts. "What are you doing in the corner? Please sit."

"Who is this?" Prince Yuchen asked, studying me as I took the open seat beside him. His face, rather flat and round, reminded me of a polished copper coin. Like his wife, he was gilded from head to toe, with long flowing robes embroidered with gold. Most strikingly, he wore a diadem of perfectly symmetrical ruby beads across his forehead, the color so brilliant they reminded me of living flames. "I haven't seen you before."

"This is Lady Hai Meilin," said Princess Ruihua. "A *special* friend of the seventh prince."

"Ah," said Yuchen, a wicked grin spreading across his face. "The notorious woman warrior. You're certainly prettier than the rumors suggest."

Behind him, Ruihua fought to keep her expression neutral.

"I didn't know you wore dresses," he continued, his eyes roving down my body. "For the songs always mention a pair of shapely legs."

Ruihua coughed, while Caihong wore her disapproval openly.

"I thought you knew better than to trust the drunken bards," chided Caihong. "Don't they claim the Imperial Commander to be taller and stronger than a stallion?"

"And that you have the wit of a tiger?" said Ruihua, recovering.

"All true," said the prince, chuckling. He savored a long sip of wine before his lascivious eyes slid back to me. Though he gave the appearance of propriety, something in his look made my skin crawl. "What a quiet one you are," he remarked. "Do you have anything to say for yourself?"

Three apprehensive gazes shifted in my direction. I felt the weight of their attention, their judgment, the way they assessed my every word and found me wanting.

What would Xiuying do? Perhaps she would make a joke, or flatter them, or simply smile. But I could not muster any clever words, and my face had forgotten how to contort itself into anything more than a grimace.

So I only shook my head.

I was used to being a disappointment. But it did not make the sting any less sharp.

Caihong covered up the moment graciously, insisting that Prince Yuchen take more soup. As more courses were served, I tried to eat, but my stomach churned at the reminder of my own incompetence. How could Sky possibly tie himself to me, when I was this inept and unworthy of his world?

I swallowed, wondering if I was going to be sick. I glanced at Lotus, signaling my intent to leave.

"Your Highness," I started, but my hoarse voice barely rose above the hum of conversation.

"Your Highness," I tried again, and this time my voice rang out too sharply. I did my best to carry on. "Thank you for the kind invitation, but I'm not feeling well and think it best if I retire early..."

Slowly, Prince Yuchen slid his chair back to survey me, so that he gave me no personal space. I ignored him, looking to the princess.

"Of course," she said. "I do hope you'll recover soon. I'd heard of your... condition... but of course, please, don't let us keep you."

I nodded, eager to leave. As I rose, I heard Caihong's gasp of warning, but it came a moment too late. There was a great ripping sound as the delicate fabric of my dress came apart. I tried to step back only to realize my skirt was captured by the leg of Prince Yuchen's chair.

He'd deliberately moved his chair to accomplish such a feat.

The long tear in my skirt now revealed my bare legs, up to my thighs. Prince Yuchen snorted with laughter as I yanked the hem of my dress from under his chair. I tugged hard enough that he nearly fell, which sobered him.

Clutching my skirt to minimize the tear, I gave them a short bow before rushing out of the room. Tears stung my eyes—tears of rage. Did he not know that I had saved his life, and the lives of all the royals safely ensconced in the Forbidden City? Did he not know that without me, Anlai never would have won the Three Kingdoms War?

But no one knew. The Imperial Commander had branded me a traitor and an anarchist. And now I was simply expected to accept his pardon as though he were a magnanimous and benevolent ruler.

My legacy had been stolen from me, just as it had been from my mother. The thought of being remembered, at best, as a victim of the war, when I should have been celebrated as a hero—it was a knife to the gut. Xiuying would have said it was enough that I knew what I had done. But I was not selfless like her, and I wanted everyone to know it. To know me and to fear me.

"It was a cruel thing he did," Lotus said, as soon as we were back in the safety of my quarters. "I've always hated him most out of all the princes. He treats the servants terribly. How Princess Ruihua stands him, I have not a clue."

"She doesn't have a choice, does she?" I snapped, shoving the ruined clothes off my body. "He doesn't care for her wishes, or the wishes of any women in his life."

I had always known men like him, men who would never respect me until I showed them why they had to. How dearly I wished for my powers then, the ability to make his eyes widen and his lips stutter with fright. If only I could threaten him as I'd once threatened Red, a soldier in my platoon, who had learned not to disrespect me after I had taught him a lesson.

I missed my black magic, my lixia. And yet it did not come without strings attached.

"*You're even worse than your mother,*" Qinglong had said, the night of the ambush on Mount Fuxi. "*I should let you die a worse death than her.*"

Seconds later, he'd tried to drown me. He might have succeeded, if the prince of Ximing had not fastened iron around my wrist, dragging me back into the human realm.

I shivered at the memory. I had destroyed the phoenix's seal instead of handing it over to Qinglong as he'd told me to, and now he was furious with me. What were his ulterior motives? I did not know. He had always hidden far more from me than I had succeeded in hiding from him. All along, he'd been using me.

Just as he'd used my mother. And when she'd stopped obeying him, he'd discarded her.

Uncle Zhou had given me her diary, I realized with a jolt. Where had it gone? Had Sky taken it after my seizure? Or worse, had the Imperial Commander found it?

"Lotus," I said. "Have you seen a diary around here? It was in my old robes."

Lotus frowned. "I'm sorry, my lady," she said. "When you were brought to your new rooms, you came with no possessions of your own."

I swallowed hard. So I was a prisoner, yet again.

FIVE

The question of whether spirits are inherently good or evil has long been a subject of scholarly debate. While some spirits have performed acts of kindness and others have committed malevolent deeds, their overall impact on humanity defies simple categorization. What is widely agreed upon, however, is that spirits are agents of chaos, and like all things, must return to equilibrium. For even balance cannot exist without chaos.
—A HISTORY OF LIXIA, 762

"Don't you miss it? Don't you miss the rush of power?"

My body thrummed with pulsating energy as I harnessed my lixia once more. There was no discomfort, like trying on old clothes that no longer fit. Rather, the weight of my spirit power felt like the heft of my sword—and my hands molded around it like the embrace of a long-lost friend. I directed my lixia toward the soft earth—then drew qi from the land itself.

The trees groaned, the grass withered, and slowly, the endless greenery faded as I drew all water from the earth, leaving behind nothing but a barren layer of dust, and within it, a small, rippling darkness.

With reckless abandon, I lifted my face to the stars and called upon the rain. As water plastered my hair and shoulders, I began to laugh, letting tears spring to my eyes. There was nothing like this feeling—this heady exhilaration, this soaring rush that threatened to implode my chest. Was this what my father had once felt—when he'd taken that first hit of opium? Like the world itself was reborn, and it was a radiant place, full of promise and thrill?

THE DREAM DISSOLVED LIKE A SHALLOW PUDDLE, LEAVING NO TRACE behind in the heat of day. I woke wondering why I felt so sore, despite walking no more than a few steps the day before.

When I stretched my arms, I noticed a series of brand-new scratches along my forearms. I stiffened with fear, wondering what this meant. A spirit summoner did not need a gate to enter the spirit realm. Instead, they could gain entry from anywhere in the human realm—by buying passage with their own blood.

Had I been drawing my own blood to access the spirit realm? And yet, rubbing the iron bands locked around my wrists, I knew this to be impossible. I could no more access the spirit realm wearing iron than I could fly. No, I must have simply scratched myself in the night.

Whispered voices in the sitting room roused me. Though I could not make out what they were saying, I could recognize that low, steady timbre anywhere—Sky. At once I scrambled out of bed, sliding open the screen divider.

Sky was leaning against the wall, arms folded and eyes flashing. "He must believe she's temporary. Otherwise he would never dare act so—" He stopped short when he saw me. "Good morning," he said, before his gaze roved down to my attire, or lack thereof. I wore a thin shift meant for sleep and nothing else. Sky flushed and coughed, turning away to stoke the fire needlessly.

I was puzzled by his sudden propriety, given that he'd seen me in less before.

"What did your father want yesterday?" I asked, once Lily had helped me into a robe.

Sky rubbed a tired hand across his face. "He's obsessed with black magic, or what he believes is black magic." He sighed. "He's trying to obliterate every trace of it from the Three Kingdoms."

I did not bother hiding my bewilderment. "Then why exactly is he letting *me* live?"

Sky shot a pointed look toward the door, which was closed. He came to me, then lowered his voice. "It's not exactly confirmed that you're a spirit summoner, Meilin. And I would prefer to keep it that way."

"But Tao and Sparrow—they've both seen me—"

"They've been silenced." At my look of astonishment, he clarified: "For a price. Did you think I would kill my own men?"

I shook my head. "But the jade . . ." My hand clenched around my necklace, where I wore my spirit seal.

Sky nodded. "It was replaced with a replica. Don't ask me how." He grimaced. "I had to resort to . . . less than ideal means."

Lei, I realized, the memory surfacing from a foggy place. Lei had done this.

"But who are these other summoners?" I asked. "Where are they hiding? Do you know if their powers are those of the lesser spirits, or another Cardinal—"

"Meilin." Sky stopped me, his hands coming around my shoulders. "Don't concern yourself with these matters. Focus on recovering. That's all I ask of you." His grip tightened. "You're so thin. It frightens me."

"But—"

"You nearly died, do you know that? Winter couldn't sense your life force anymore. If that Ximing traitor hadn't stolen your jade back, you wouldn't be here."

"I-I know."

"Winter wants you to be examined by a lixia specialist—"

"No," I said, my stomach tightening at the thought. "Absolutely not."

"Meilin, you need—"

"I will not be *examined* like a pig for slaughter," I said harshly, the quaver in my voice betraying my fear. Sky must have heard it too, for he dropped the subject.

"You know, I've been researching the effects of lixia and how to counteract the withdrawal symptoms," he said. "With time, I think you can heal..."

"What if it's too late for me already?" I whispered, voicing aloud my worst fears. "During the war, I..." I ignored Xiuying's cautions. I ignored Sky's. I even ignored Qinglong's.

I fidgeted with my sleeve, which hid the dark veins along my forearms. They had never returned to their usual color. Now the faint traces of black were permanent.

I had done this to myself.

"Let me show you something," he said suddenly. "I was going to wait until it's complete, but..." He sighed, running a hand through his hair. "I wish I didn't have to go so soon."

"You're leaving again?"

He nodded. "After the parade tomorrow."

"What parade?"

Sky shooed me away to get dressed, clearly in a hurry. Leading me out of my rooms at a brisk pace, he brought us to a small reading library overlooking the nine-turn bridge.

"Have you been here before?" he asked.

"Yes, of course," I said. "You know how close my rooms are—"

"I placed you there intentionally," he said. "Watch closely. I don't have much time."

How many demands must weigh on him as a prince. The thought unsettled me, knowing his schedule was packed while I had nothing to do but wander the gardens. In war, I had been of use to him. But now I was nothing more than a burden to be coddled.

Sky checked to make sure no one was coming before running his fingers along the oak paneling, tapping until he came upon a hollow spot. A secret passageway.

With a soft click, the wood paneling came away, revealing a narrow corridor. "Follow me," he ordered. My heart racing, I followed him down a cramped flight of stairs, into a cave-like space hardly the size of my dressing room. I expected hidden weapons, potions, even a dangerous beast. But not... books.

The room was lined with scrolls upon scrolls, some fallen to decay, others newly copied and unmarked by age.

"What is this place?" I asked. "Why all the secrecy?"

"I told you I've been gathering intelligence," he explained. "For the past few months, I've been bidding on the black market for any texts on lixia." His lips curled into an arrogant smile. "Word has spread of a wealthy bidder who will outbid anyone for a worthy text. I have quite a monopoly now."

I gaped at him, at a complete loss for words. He had done this for me. To help me overcome my weakness, to help me regain my health. He could have kept the knowledge from me, choosing to leave me in the dark like so many others. Instead, he had given me access to every book he could buy.

"Sky..." I tried to swallow away the choky feeling in my throat. "I... you didn't have to do this."

"I wanted to do this," he said. "To help you heal, to grow, to master your power."

"You make it sound like I have a future."

"You do have a future, Meilin. A very long one. With me—if you'll have me."

And to my shock, he produced a string of twisted red and gold thread, one tied in a loose knot to form a bracelet. An engagement band, which was worn ahead of a marriage ceremony.

"I love you," he said simply, his voice low and unwavering. "I love who I am with you. You vex me. You frighten me. You challenge me. And I would have it no other way. With you by my side, I'm confident we can rebuild Anlai for the better. The people believe in you. As do I."

I turned my agonized gaze on him. I wanted to explain what it felt like to have your insides ripped apart, then knit back together; to crave lixia so desperately you had no appetite, no thirst, no ability to pay close attention to anything beyond that craving, which was always there, biding its time, waiting for a moment of weakness. And he thought I could live?

But he loved me; I saw that now. He loved me, and it was a pure love, like nothing else within me was pure.

Without thinking, I flung my arms around him. He staggered back in surprise, before wrapping his own arms around my waist and lifting me in the air. I laughed and clung to him, feeling lighter than I had in a long time. My robes parted indecently, but instead of scolding me he ran a warm calloused hand up my raised thigh, and I felt tendrils of long-buried desire rise up like smoke within me. "Meilin," he groaned into my mouth, and I only pressed myself more greedily against him, giving in to the fierce want that I'd nurtured ever since first laying eyes on him in a crowded market street.

His mouth tasted me hungrily, demanding me, claiming me as his. He came up for breath only to kiss my jaw, my throat, pressing his lips against the contours of my body. Carelessly, his hand grasped at my jade necklace, lifting it from my throat.

Immediately I froze, my body tensing with the cascade of emotions that spilled out of me at once—anger, resentment, jealousy, fear. Sky felt me stiffen and pulled away, releasing me.

"What's wrong?" he asked. "Did I hurt you?"

"No—no," I said, though my expression must have suggested otherwise. "I don't know what came over me."

"I'm sorry," said Sky, taking my hand in both of his and bringing it to his lips. "I don't know what came over *me*. I shouldn't have. I'm going to get my father's approval to marry you, Meilin. I will marry you—I swear it."

He thought I was afraid of becoming a ruined woman. Unconsciously, I clenched my jade in a tight fist, finding immense relief in its constant pulse against my own. For a second there, as Sky had taken my jade in his hand, a strange thought had occurred to me, one so unsettling I'd discarded it right away, like turning your head instinctively from a ghastly sight. And yet, late that night as I was drifting into sleep, it returned to me:

I'd kill him, I'd thought. *If he stole my jade, I'd kill him.*

SIX

Thus the god of fate bound the lovers together with a red string, tied around their wrists. Though the string may stretch or tangle, it will never break, for they are destined to be together—whether in this life or the next.
—WINTER AND SPRING ANNALS, 417

S KY WOKE ME THE NEXT DAY. I HAD GROWN ACCUSTOMED TO HIS daily visits, so it was a disappointment to learn he would be leaving that evening.

"We set out at sundown," he explained.

"For?"

"Another supposed spirit summoner, what else?" said Sky, a tinge of weariness crossing his face. "Father wants to come along this time, which is a logistical nightmare."

"You have a lead?" I asked, rubbing sleep from my eyes.

Sky answered reluctantly. "There's been some suspicious activity in the forests of Wei An. Townsfolk who have either disappeared or gone raving mad."

"A gate," I whispered.

"Hm?" said Sky, before the front door was flung open.

"What are you doing?" Winter hissed, out of breath. "Look at the time."

"I didn't want to wake her," Sky explained abashedly. He glanced at me. "You were sleeping so soundly."

Winter looked to be at the end of his patience. "Everyone's waiting outside."

"Go," I told Sky. From Winter's tone, it sounded urgent.

"You too," said Winter, to me. "You might consider getting dressed."

"Me?" I asked.

"For skies' sake, you haven't told her yet?"

"I was getting to it," said Sky, scratching the back of his head.

"It's the anniversary of Anlai's founding. There's to be a parade through the city, and Father wants the two of you to head the procession."

"The two of us?" I repeated. The last I'd heard, Sky was the war hero, and I was nothing more than a convicted criminal. "Why?"

"To dispel the rumors," said Winter tersely.

"What rumors?"

"You've been absent from the public lately," he hedged.

As if my absence had any significance to it. "What—do they think I'm leading a rebellion against the throne?" I scoffed.

At Winter's silence, my mouth fell open. Only now did I recall Lei's warning: *"Despite the official reports, legend of the woman warrior has spread far, and the people are restless . . . Do you know—news of your imprisonment has been met with anger, and in some cases rebellion? The warlord's position is precarious, and now he needs his prisoner on a pretty pedestal, to comply with and promote his agenda. And will you obey?"*

"You're exceedingly popular among the people," said Sky, and I detected the hint of pride in his voice.

"That's enough," said Winter, dragging his brother away. "Let her get dressed."

LOTUS AND LILY OUTDID THEMSELVES ONCE AGAIN, OUTFITTING ME IN a demure ruqun gown. The sleeves were petal pink and embroidered with dainty plum blossoms, while the fitted chest was ivory white, accentuated with a gold ribbon that cascaded down my front. My hair was done up to resemble a bird in flight, held up by an ivory hairpiece embellished with tinkling gold flowers. To cover up the dark circles under my eyes, they dusted ground pearl powder on my face, then applied a soft pink rouge to my cheeks and lips. As the final touch, Lotus covered me in an ivory cloak made of the softest wool. The effect was not lost on me: I was made to appear delicate, innocent, as pure and unsullied as a snow maiden.

How appearances deceived.

Sky was waiting for me at the base of the stone steps, dressed in matching ivory attire, which accentuated the broadness of his shoulders and the narrow tapering of his waist.

"You look . . ." His voice trailed off, and the wonder in his eyes made me laugh. "Breathtaking," he finished, touching my hair lightly, as if afraid to ruin it. "How did I get so lucky?" he whispered, trying to draw me close before I pushed him away. Others were watching.

He took my arm as we walked, and for once in my life, I thought we appeared well suited for each other.

If his siblings shared my sentiment, they did not make their agreement known. Prince Yuchen sneered as he caught sight of me, whispering in Princess Ruihua's ear with haughty derision. The crown prince nodded at me, though he could not entirely hide the pucker to his lips. Princess Yifeng, who gripped his arm like a lifeboat, gave me a wide, toothy grin.

It felt like a threat.

Sky helped me into the open palanquin, then got in behind me. As we rode out into the dazzling sunlight, I braced myself for the crowd—for their resentful murmurings, their hateful stares. Instead, the first thing I noticed was the sound. A dull roar, like the ceaseless rush of a river. But as the gates to the Forbidden City opened and the crowds flooded around us, I understood: they were *cheering*.

I turned, searching for the Imperial Commander, or the crown prince, trying to locate the source of their enthusiasm. But as flower petals fell upon my lap, and the commoners shouted my name, it struck me at last: it was for me. They were cheering for me.

Bewildered, I caught a bouquet of flowers flung in my direction. At the same time, a boy snatched at the trailing hem of my cloak, even kissing the wool before the palanquin passed him by. Behind him, a young woman with striking amber eyes stared intently at me, something in her curious gaze giving me pause.

Those eyes. They reminded me of Lei's. As if they could see straight into my soul.

The girl winked at me before turning away. I tried to track her in the crowd, but our palanquin was already moving on.

"See?" Sky said, drawing my attention back to him. His face gleamed with pride and something else, something I preferred not to acknowledge. "They adore you."

I shook my head, though hope stirred within me. I wanted to believe it so badly, I almost didn't dare to. "It can't be," I said, looking down.

Sky caught my chin, forcing me to meet his gaze. "They can't help it, Meilin," he said lowly. "They can't help but love you." And then, in front of his entire family and the throngs of people surrounding us, he kissed me.

The crowd screamed with explosive excitement. From behind

us, I saw Winter shake his head with resigned amusement. If it wasn't clear before what was going on between me and Sky, now it certainly was. In such an official capacity as this, he'd as good as declared his intent to marry me.

The parade turned toward Willow District. Eagerly, I leaned out of the palanquin, searching for my family. It would be my only chance to see them for some time, as the Imperial Commander had confined me to the palace, and minor nobles of their rank were banned from entering the Forbidden City. But the procession moved too quickly, and if Xiuying and the others were in the crowd, I could not find them. My heart sinking, I sat back in my seat, resenting my powerlessness, resenting the gradual way I'd grown compliant to my cage.

As we crossed the Gate of Heavenly Peace, the last stop in our procession, I froze at the sight of Lieutenant Fang and the familiar battalion behind him—my own. But if I still thought of them that way, I was the only one. The disgusted looks they shot me only magnified the difference between how they viewed me and how they treated their commander, Sky. Of all the princes, it was now evident Sky was the most popular. Apart from his charisma and indisputable good looks, he was the most straightforward candidate for a wartime leader, with his skill in combat and his clear head in battle. Despite the fanfare the palace was trying to promote around the resolution of the Three Kingdoms War, Lotus had told me the people were uneasy with this current façade of peace. Many spoke of another unification effort as inevitable and remembered the empire of the Wu Dynasty with growing wistfulness and nostalgia.

Now, as our palanquin went up the wooden dais raised beneath the Gate of Heavenly Peace, a cheer arose in the crowd, starting with the soldiers Sky had led into Ximing, then expanding beyond the army to the common people: the merchants, the laborers, even the street urchins and orphan children. "Commander Liu Sky!" they chanted. Notably, they did not call him Prince but referred to him by his wartime title.

I assumed Sky would be embarrassed by the ostentation, but when I glanced over at him, I sensed his gratification. He kept his expression stoic so as to appear humble, but his eyes shone with triumph.

It struck me then: he wanted this. *He wants the throne.*

I had not been reading between the lines. *"With you by my side, I'm confident we can rebuild Anlai for the better,"* he'd told me in the secret library. But only now did I grasp the underlying meaning of his words.

During the war, he'd told me he bore no illusions of inheriting the throne. As the seventh and youngest prince, he faced too many obstacles in his path. But in the aftermath of the war, while I'd been locked away and gathering dust in the dungeons, he'd been acclimating to his newfound fame and glory. Indisputably, he'd become the kingpin prince, the one to turn the tide of the war. But not because of his own prowess.

It was because of mine.

I had saved the kingdom, and now he claimed my reward. But why not claim it together? As I gazed out at the hordes of people, shouting not only his name but mine as well, I wondered if I might not leverage my newfound popularity. I could help him. We made a good team, after all. I could convince the Imperial Commander to let me be with him, and together, we could secure the throne. Just as I was good for Sky, he was good for me. He kept me grounded, and more importantly, he loved me. His love for me felt pure, and I wished to cling to that purity. Perhaps with him by my side, I could heal. I could find myself again, and learn how to live.

My belief in my own future had been middling at best, and so being around Sky was like basking in constant sunshine; his unwavering belief in me buoyed my own.

Under the calm blue sky and the adoring cheers of the Chuang Ning people, I took Sky's large hand in my small one. His eyes cut to mine, and in them, I recognized his love and affection, his pride and his joy. His feelings were uncomplicated, undivided. For me, someone who was divided in almost every matter, I was drawn to that magnetic simplicity, that feeling of absolute conviction that I'd never possessed in anything—not in my strength, not in my love, and certainly not in my future.

Meeting his steadfast gaze, I decided, *Your fate will be mine. And mine will be yours.*

SEVEN

When the woman warrior smiled, it was a smile so radiant it stole the strength from his knees. Thus her blade sang, severing his head in a single mighty stroke. The heavens trembled, the phoenix shrieked in fury, but the evil chancellor was no more.
—BARD'S TALE, AUTHOR UNKNOWN, 924

BY THE TIME WE RETURNED TO THE FORBIDDEN CITY, I WAS EXhausted, the muscles in my face sore from smiling. Meanwhile, Sky was practically vibrating with adrenaline and excitement. As I stepped out of the palanquin, I came face-to-face with the Imperial Commander for the first time since my imprisonment.

He swung down from his stallion, no easy feat given the beast's immense height. His stature had not changed in the intervening months, but his face had. His skin looked to have aged years, if not decades, with sagging wrinkles that had not been there the last time I'd seen him. His hair was now seeded with silver and gray. But what was most pronounced were his haunted eyes—they looked dead inside.

No wonder he had chosen to ride at the back. It was not a face that would inspire confidence.

Sky's vitality and youth were particularly striking against his father's deficit. "Your Majesty," said Sky, bowing, and I hastily moved to follow.

"We depart at sundown," said the Imperial Commander to his

seventh son. Then he strode past us, without acknowledging my presence.

Winter, who stood next to Sky, folded his lips silently. He too had gone unacknowledged.

"Did you enjoy that?" asked Princess Yifeng, sidling up to me as Sky was approached by his personal guards. "It must feel nice to be so well thought of outside the palace walls. The contrast must feel stark, I imagine."

She smiled, waiting for me to clarify. But I wouldn't give her the satisfaction.

"Don't worry." She patted my arm. "Perhaps the commoners' praise will help you forget what all the nobles think." She leaned in close and reached for my hand, and for a foolish moment I thought she was trying to hold it. But instead she hooked her fingers around my red and gold engagement string, which hung loosely over my sleeve. "It doesn't matter what your besotted boy prince thinks he wants. The Imperial Commander will *never* accept you as his daughter."

She twisted the string and snapped it in half. But before she could prance away, I seized her wrist. Hard enough to hurt.

"Perhaps it's the Imperial Commander's opinion that no longer holds any weight," I murmured. "Power can be taken away just as easily as it's given."

My irreverence shocked even her. With a gasp she tore her wrist free and hurried after her departed husband. I watched her go, smiling grimly. I understood that the white leilu plums had been a test. The princess had wished to assess my social intelligence, to know how much of a threat I'd be to her in the palace. And she'd learned how little I knew of the myriad ways of court.

And yet, what was a court if not its people? And people, I reminded myself, I understood. People, I could read like a sailor reading the tides before a storm. My father and his volatile temper had taught me that much.

I picked up the remains of the string and pocketed them before Sky could see. If I wanted to survive at court, I could afford no more careless blunders. It had taken bravery to enlist in the army, to learn how to wield a sword, to train every night under the light of the stars. It was not bravery I had in short supply. No, it was confidence.

I would need both to survive in a place such as this.

And I would survive. Not only for my sake, but for Sky's, whose fate was now publicly bound to mine. Princess Yifeng had been a cold reminder: Sky's place was no more secure than a nestling hovering at the precipice of a tree. He had gained much in the past year, but that only meant he now had farther to fall.

I would not allow him to fall. I would stand by his side, and together, we would secure the throne.

My motives were not entirely selfless. I had not forgotten Prince Yuchen's insults, nor Princess Yifeng's. And I certainly hadn't forgotten the Imperial Commander's betrayal.

My mother had long taught me there was no justice in this world. Yet I hadn't expected fairness from the Anlai ruler—only reason. Even that proved too much to ask.

Now, I promised myself I would no longer let those in power dictate my fate. In taking the throne, I would rewrite my own narrative, forging a new legacy for myself.

From now on, I would make my own justice.

As Princess Ruihua passed through the courtyard, her gaze flicked toward mine. She hesitated, not knowing if we were on speaking terms after her husband's insult.

"Your Highness," I said, bowing. "How well you look today."

Her smile was one of relief. "As do you," she replied. She fiddled with the tie of her cloak, glancing around the courtyard before saying in a rush, "Please forgive my husband's behavior the other day. His sense of humor can be . . . difficult to understand."

That day, I had been intimidated by her carefully made-up face, the way she knew how to dress and hold her body like a honed blade. But today I saw that her appearance was nothing more than a veneer, and beneath all the silks and rouge we were all the same: insecure, doubting, and afraid.

"There is nothing to forgive," I said, before smiling. "Though next time, I know not to underestimate the perils of chair legs."

Princess Ruihua smiled back, before her daughter screamed her name from inside. She apologized and took her leave, and now it was my turn to sigh in relief. Only a year ago, I would've avoided her gaze and tried never to interact with her again. But now I understood that relationships were like bodies of water, fluctuating with the seasons.

I felt the weight of someone's gaze behind me. I glanced over my shoulder and found Winter watching me. In his eyes was a shrewd recognition—both of who I was and what I was trying to achieve.

I had become acquainted with the sixth and seventh princes during wartime, when Sky had been the protector of the two. But Sky had once confided in me that back in court, their roles had been reversed. Winter did not fight, and so in battle he became a liability. But in peacetime, he was someone I wanted on my side.

A handsome man in uniform stopped by Winter's side, whispering something in his ear. His hair was brown with a hint of red in the sunlight, and as Winter replied, the man smiled, revealing a dimple in one cheek. I vaguely remembered him from the war, but his name escaped me.

"Captain Tong," said Sky, striding up to them. "Ready the horses."

"Yes, sir," said Captain Tong, whom I now remembered from First Platoon, back when he was still a lieutenant. He had been a reliable leader—reserved, but steady. He never drank or socialized with his men, preferring to keep his evenings to himself.

As Captain Tong turned to go, Winter caught his arm, saying something else. Although there was nothing indecent about the gesture, there was a certain quality in Winter's expression, a softness there that I'd never seen before, that gave me pause.

Before I could eavesdrop, Sky bounded over. "Were you waiting for me? You shouldn't have." His eyes trailed over the gooseflesh lining my exposed skin. "You must be cold."

"It's your fault," I said, wrinkling my nose at him. I missed my practical uniform from our army days. Despite the quality of the cloth, my fine robes were made for beauty rather than warmth. "If it weren't for you, I'd never dress like this."

"I find I can't summon any regret," said Sky, eyes twinkling, "when you look so beautiful." He rubbed my arms to generate heat. "Here, I'll warm you up."

But I noticed the soldiers behind him, watching us impatiently. "You have to go, don't you?" I guessed. "Is this goodbye, then?"

I'd said goodbye to Sky before, but always as the one with the mission, never the one left behind.

"I'll be back as soon as I can," said Sky, taking my cold hand and rubbing it between his warm ones. "I've asked Winter to keep an eye on you while I'm away."

"Can I visit my family now?" I asked, careful to keep the pleading note from my voice.

"I'm sorry, Meilin." He clenched his hands more firmly around mine. "You know how my father's moods are right now. I wanted to ask, but . . ."

I didn't want Sky to risk provoking the Imperial Commander on my behalf, not with things as precarious as they were. I squeezed his hand to show that I understood.

"Don't go near any spirit gates, if you find them," I warned. I had seen firsthand what those gates could do to a man. It did not matter how skilled you were with a sword or how fast your horse could carry you. Against the seductive pull of lixia, all that mattered was the affinity of your qi. "You don't understand what the lure of spirit power is like. No one does, until they meet it face-to-face."

He lifted his sleeve to show me a familiar iron armlet. It was the same one Lieutenant Fang had given him during the war. "These days, I never take it off."

I bit my lip with worry. "I wish I could go with you."

"When you're better," he assured me, before tweaking my nose, which must have turned red with cold. "Now go inside and get warm."

WITH THE IMPERIAL COMMANDER, THE CROWN PRINCE, AND THE SEVenth prince all departed from the capital, the Forbidden City seemed to take on a subdued, languorous air. That night, I dreamed of wandering the city, the rivers, the forests beyond the palace. In my dreams I called upon my lixia and wept with relief. But in waking, I knew these visions to be nothing more than dreams.

I wiped tears from my face and called for my maidservants.

"Would you like breakfast, my lady?" asked Lotus.

"Please," I said. "Sit."

Lotus and Lily exchanged looks of confusion.

"I'll be blunt," I said. "Can I trust you?"

"Of course, my lady!" Lotus replied indignantly. Lily nodded, though I noticed a flicker of guilt pass through her eyes.

"I'm sure others have tried to buy your loyalties, given how close you are to me," I said, eyeing Lotus to see her reaction. Hers was the more expressive face, and sure enough, she blinked in response, glancing away from me. "But I can offer more than gold."

"We would never—" Lotus sputtered.

"What can you offer?" asked Lily quietly.

I smiled. "Freedom."

Lily's eyes darkened. "There is no freedom under a system such as ours."

Taken aback, I said nothing for a second, realizing the assumptions I'd made based solely on her status.

"You're right," I said, recovering, "which is why I want to change the system. You've heard the rumors of succession. You know that Sky is the strongest heir. He will be named next in line, and I with him." I leaned forward. "You want to bet on the winning team."

Lily smiled, revealing a gap-toothed grin that reminded me momentarily of my sister. "I'll help you," she said, "if you teach me how to fight."

Again, I was caught off guard. I had mistaken her reticence for docility, but now I saw it was anything but.

"Not this again," groaned Lotus. "We've talked about this, Lily."

Lily ignored her. "Please," she said to me. "I must learn how to fight."

My throat tightened at the earnest hope in her eyes. Other, kinder people would certainly agree. Xiuying would accept in a heartbeat, and would urge me to do the same. And yet I had enough on my plate with Sky's bid for the throne. If we were caught, I could be jailed once more. In the dungeons, I would be wholly powerless.

I could never let myself be that powerless again.

"I'm sorry, Lily," I said. "It's too risky right now."

Her shoulders sagged with disappointment.

"But I can arm you," I continued, though I didn't yet know how. Lily's frown deepened—again, that strange flicker of guilt. "Just give me time."

"What do you need?" Lily asked.

"I need to secure the throne."

"THERE ARE SEVEN PRINCES," SAID LOTUS, IN HER BEST IMITATION OF A schoolteacher's voice. "The eldest, Prince Keyan, is the crown prince."

"What's he like?"

"Dutiful," said Lotus. "He obeys his father's every command."

"He tries to be fair," added Lily. "Though he lets himself be pushed around by his wife."

"Princess Yifeng," I said knowingly.

Lotus nodded. "I'd be careful around her. Theirs is a loveless marriage, yet she has him wrapped around her thumb."

"The other princesses seem scared of her," I remarked, thinking of Princess Ruihua.

Lotus nodded. "When Princess Aixia got pregnant before her, rumor has it she made her miscarry."

I grimaced, not wanting the details. "Who's next?"

"Prince Daxing is the second prince," resumed Lotus. "But we don't need to worry about him. He was exiled last year after attempting to poison the crown prince."

I raised a brow. So fratricide was disturbingly commonplace among the princes.

"Got it," I said. "Moral of the story—don't poison a prince."

"Moral of the story, don't get caught poisoning a prince," corrected Lily.

I smothered a laugh as Lotus shook her head at her friend. "Moving on, we have third prince Yuchen."

I stilled. "That one means trouble."

Lily nodded.

"Find out his weaknesses," I said. "What about the fourth prince? I haven't seen him yet."

"He's often sequestered in his rooms," said Lotus. "He was born sickly, and his health has troubled him for many years."

I crossed him off my mental list. "And the fifth prince?"

"He departed on a naval expedition shortly before Ximing declared war," said Lotus.

"Even if he returns, he won't pose a threat to you," said Lily. "He values his independence far too much to ever aspire to the throne."

That left Winter, who I trusted. I nodded. "Investigate Prince Yuchen and Prince Keyan," I said.

"Should we approach their servants?" asked Lotus.

"Not the princes' servants," I clarified. "Talk to the servants of their wives."

The princesses, far less guarded and easier to approach, held all the secrets of their husbands, and more. They were the less obvious targets to investigate, and yet I was accustomed to the ways of men—how they so often revealed their vulnerabilities through their women.

"See if you can befriend their maidservants," I said. "Persuasion is more effective than force."

The two girls nodded, rising to their feet. I was about to dismiss them when I recalled that flicker of guilt on Lily's face. It reminded me of another mystery I hadn't yet solved.

"Lotus, you're dismissed. Lily, do you mind staying back a minute?"

Lotus shot her a look as if to say *I told you so*. Lily's face revealed nothing.

I waited until we were alone. "Do you remember the day I was brought out of the dungeons? My memory is a bit hazy, so I need to rely on yours."

Her face remained carefully blank. "Of course, my lady."

"I'm told I experienced a seizure."

"Yes."

"I remember faces around me, and then being carried somewhere. I think I vomited."

Lily nodded.

"Did you help clean me then?"

Another nod.

"What did you do with my clothes?"

"I had them incinerated. They were . . . beyond salvaging."

My breath caught. "Before you burned them, did you find anything . . . of note? In my tunic, perhaps?"

She hesitated, just for a fraction of a second. "I burned only the clothes, my lady. There was nothing of note with them."

"But surely . . ."

I paused, meeting her eyes. We were both holding back, each wary of saying something that might tip the other over the edge. Always the youngest, the least powerful in the room, I was accustomed to silence. But things had changed. Now I understood it was up to me to set the boundaries of what we could or could not discuss. If we were to be candid with each other, I needed to lead by example.

"Lily," I said. "There was an old notebook in my tunic. One that is worth nothing to others, but everything to me. It was my mother's diary."

She nodded hesitantly.

"Do you know what happened to it? Sky was with me the entire time, except for that one hour in between."

Tight-lipped, she shook her head. But I had seen guilt in her eyes.

"Lily, if you help me, I can help you in return. You wish to learn how to fight?" I asked, leveraging her earlier request. With a sigh, I said, "I can teach you."

Her eyes widened with astonishment. "R-really?" she asked, her voice turning high and breathless.

"Yes."

She hung her head, her hands beginning to shake. "I'm . . . ashamed, my lady. I don't know what came over me."

"Just tell me," I said gently.

"Lotus went to fetch clean clothes, and so I was alone with you. I left for only a few moments to refill the water jug, but when I returned, suddenly—"

"Suddenly?"

"There was a man," she whispered. "I'd never seen him before. He was moving you away from the fire, even though you were so cold. I-I asked him what he was doing." Now that the truth had slipped out, she seemed eager to share the story. "He offered a gift in exchange for my silence. Of course I didn't mean to agree, until . . ." Red-faced, she blurted, "He offered me a sword! A real one. I don't know how he knew it was my weakness. I've wanted to learn how to fight ever since—ever since the war began. My eldest brother was killed in battle, you see. And, and you—" Her eyes filled with obstinate tears. "Everyone's heard the stories. How you slayed a hundred men with the kiss of your steel. How you rescued the sixth prince with the might of your arrow. I . . . I wanted to be like you."

"Don't cry," I said hurriedly. "Just tell me—the man's face. What did he look like?"

She wiped at her eyes. "He was... handsome. The handsomest man I've ever seen. His hair was so black it shone nearly blue. And his eyes... they were the palest eyes I ever saw."

My stomach dropped. "Did he have a scar?" I asked. "On his face?"

Her eyes narrowed in concentration. "Yes... A thin scar across his brow."

Cao Ming Lei.

EIGHT

Under the corruption of the Quan Emperor, the land was plagued with ceaseless drought, until even Zhonghai Lake had dried to its sediment. In desperation, the scholar Wang Qi ordered the fishermen to bring their boats onto the cracked lake bed. Some mocked him, while others grew enraged. Yet when the scholar raised his hands to the heavens, the Azure Dragon was moved to mercy. He wept great tears of rain, which filled the lake and returned the boats to shore. Thus, the Tianjia people celebrate the Dragon Boat Festival to honor the dragon, who saw the people's plight and gave them rain.

—BOOK OF RITES, 829

I DID NOT KNOW HOW TO FIND HIM. LILY CLAIMED THAT THE PRINCE of Ximing was both everywhere and nowhere. Technically, he was under house arrest, forbidden from leaving his quarters. And yet, through bribery and blackmail, it was an open secret that he did not remain confined to the guest rooms reserved for political prisoners. Some servants claimed to have seen him at private dinner parties with notable advisors and magistrates. Others professed to have seen him enjoying the botanical gardens, or even sunbathing at the moon-viewing pavilion, always with a beautiful lady in tow. But of course, no matter where I went, he did not make himself known to me.

I had no choice but to turn to other avenues. In the days following, Lily proved an invaluable resource. Every morning before sunrise, we met for an hour of sword practice. I had made Lily a promise, yes, but there was another reason I was particularly soft on her. With her gap-toothed grin and her cleverness, she reminded me of my little sister. My little sister, who I was forbidden from visiting.

Though I had not fully recovered from my time in prison, I could still demonstrate proper technique, albeit at a slower pace than I was used to. At first, it was just the two of us. Lily kept pestering me to include others, and while I was hesitant at first, the idea of using them as additional spies eventually won me over. Two of Lily's close friends joined us soon after. Three became four, and then five.

After every session, Lily and Lotus brought me scraps of palace gossip. Through them I learned madness was catching in Chuang Ning, just beyond the Forbidden City walls. Allegedly, the spirit gates had begun spreading in the north, suspiciously close to when Sky and the others had departed for the south. As if the spirit summoner was baiting them, luring them out just to strike close to home.

Common folk had taken to wearing iron around their fingers and wrists, until the demand for iron had risen to such heights, even a market for replica iron had sprung up.

I too was growing superstitious about my iron. Recurring visions haunted my sleep, dreams of qi being drained from the land, sucking the earth dry. At the growing lixia imbalance, birds dropped from the sky. Rivers turned to sand. And all around me, everyone I loved went mad.

I started sleeping with my hands locked around my irons, as if holding them there would keep my mind in place. Every evening, when most of the court went to supper, I feigned sickness and stayed in my rooms. When I was certain the coast was clear, I'd slip into the reading room and take the secret passageway into the library Sky had built for me. There I read of ancient mythology surrounding spirit summoners of old, poetry concerning the whims of gods, and even medical texts detailing the biological pathways blocked by overuse of lixia. Instead of imbuing me with hope, my newfound knowledge stole my sanguine ignorance. I had done exactly everything I was not supposed to do: depleted my qi, overused my lixia, allowed my life force and spirit power to develop into a parasitic relationship.

Had Sky read these same texts? Was his unceasing optimism rooted in greater conviction for my abilities, or simply baseless faith? And yet I had defied the inevitable before. Perhaps I could do it again.

A creak from above jarred me from my thoughts. Was it Lily, coming to look for me? Hurriedly I shoved the scroll I was reading back onto the shelf, which sent another one careening to the floor. Bending to retrieve it, I noticed a familiar ruby bead, the brilliant crimson color reminiscent of fire. Although the floor beneath the bookcase was dusty, the ruby bead was gleaming.

It had not been there for long.

I left the scroll lying on the floor, racing back up the passageway. I made it up two flights of stairs before needing to stop and rest. As I clutched the stair banister, panting, a maid I didn't recognize appeared by my side.

"Can I help, my lady?"

"N-no," I said, trying to keep my vision from blurring. "Just need to catch my breath."

"Very well," she replied, before lowering her voice. "My life for the rebellion, Phoenix-Slayer."

I raised my head sharply, which only caused my nausea to swell. By the time the dizzy spell had passed, she was gone.

How strange... but I didn't have time to dwell on it now. Racing to my quarters, I found Lily in my bedroom. I'd hoped for both of them, but perhaps this was for the best. Lotus was more obliging, but Lily was far more discreet.

"Lily," I said. "I need a favor."

THE NEXT DAY, I WOKE WITH THE SUN, MY STRANGE DREAMS FLEEING in the morning light. My body no longer ached with soreness, and my head felt unusually clear. Under the blue light of dawn, I headed for the back kitchen courtyard, meeting Lily for our morning training sessions. I had a dozen regular pupils now, and the rate at which they learned enlivened me. Their consistent improvement was the only tangible progress I could point to in my life. While I could not use my lixia, could not track down the wayward spirit summoner, could not even leave the palace walls, at least I could teach a few others how to defend themselves.

But perhaps I had grown overly cocky in the Imperial Commander's absence. After practice that day, I spied a glimmer of white among the gray linens drying on the clotheslines. My pulse thrumming in my ears, I moved closer to investigate.

Before I could part the linens, none other than Winter emerged. "Good morning," he said, and several girls gasped as he drew back the hanging clothes.

"Should we wait for you?" asked Lily, her terror at being caught plainly visible.

"It's all right," I assured her, motioning for the girls to leave us. "I trust him."

I drew Winter into the privacy of the kitchen alleyway, where the clatter of the cooks preparing the palace's breakfast muffled our conversation.

"I expected Sky to warn you to keep a low profile," said Winter. "But perhaps I'm giving him too much credit."

"He did," I said. "I'm just . . . not the best at following orders."

A flicker of reluctant amusement crossed his face. "Just don't make things harder for him," said Winter. "He's already put himself in a precarious position by siding with you." With that, he turned to go.

"Winter," I called after him. "What makes you think I can't make things *better* for him?"

"It's not about whether you can," he said, in his deliberate way. "It's about whether you will."

I stilled. He wasn't certain where my loyalties lay with Sky. And it was true that even I had questioned my own motives at times. But after hearing the cheering crowds at the parade, after seeing the depth of Sky's love and unwavering confidence in me—greater even than my own—I had made my decision.

"I can, and I will," I told Winter firmly. "Your father wouldn't have let me go if public opinion hadn't forced his hand. But I can change how he sees me—and how the court does too."

"Is that why you made Yuchen think you a timid fool?"

The comment stung, as Winter knew it would. He could be ruthless when necessary, but I understood—like Princess Yifeng before him, he was testing me.

"I won't make the same mistake twice," I said. "I can help Sky secure the throne, Winter. But I need allies."

I waited, counting every heartbeat. Winter assessed me for a long moment, before saying, somewhat reluctantly, "I can make a good ally."

I beamed.

A ghost of a smile flitted across his lips. "Do you know," he said, shading his face against the rising sun, "Sky asked me not to meddle?"

I squinted at him. "Why?"

"He wants to win the throne 'fairly,' he said."

I snorted at this, and even Winter smirked. Fairness had no place in court, I'd long ago decided. It did not matter how you got there—in the end, there were only winners and losers, and the winners rewrote the rules.

"Keep an eye on Prince Yuchen, will you?" I asked him now. "I think he means to make a move for the throne. I just can't tell when."

Winter nodded, and I made to leave.

"There's something else," said Winter, and to my surprise he reached out and snagged my wrist. Pushing up my sleeve, he saw the irons I never removed. "I thought so," he said quietly.

I pulled my wrist free from his grasp. "What—"

"Do you know—the dragon cannot kill you?"

"What do you mean?" I asked, a touch resentfully. "He tried to drown me—"

"He can torture you. He can cause you emotional and psychological distress. He can let misfortune befall you without intervening. But no spirit can directly sever the bond with their human vessel. The two of you are stuck together, for better or for worse."

I stared at him, wondering at his motives. "How do you know so much?"

He gave me a cryptic smile. "I once faced a choice much like yours."

Before I could press him further, he left, leaving me to ponder the weight of his words.

I had been wearing my irons out of fear, thinking that once the dragon found me, he would try to drown me. After all, I had foiled his plans at the end of the war.

And yet my spirit affinity made me a powerful summoner, one even a Cardinal Spirit could not easily replace. And if the dragon could not kill me, then he could not find another vessel in my stead. Perhaps I could make Qinglong see me as an equal this time. Perhaps we could work together, two reluctant partners made to dance.

It had been a long time since I'd called out to the dragon. Perhaps it was finally time to say hello.

NINE

Given the often parasitic nature of the spirit-vessel relationship, many summoners come to resent their spirits. Open hostility is unadvised, however, as spirit and vessel are bound together, like two birds that mate for life.
—LOST JOURNALS OF AN 8TH-CENTURY LIXIA SCHOLAR,
DATE UNKNOWN

LILY FOUND ME AS SOON AS I RETURNED TO MY ROOMS. "THEY caught a spirit summoner," she said breathlessly.

"Who?" I demanded, wondering if Sky was hurt. "Where?"

"I don't know. All I know is that they're set to hang him at the Gate of Heavenly Peace next week."

I held my breath. Could it be him? The one behind the spirit gates, responsible for the terror and paranoia gripping the city? The disappeared ones, the mad ones, the dead ones? Had they caught him at last?

Perhaps this meant Sky could finally return home. But with him would return the Imperial Commander, and the crown prince. I was not moving fast enough.

"What news of the princes? Have you learned anything of value?"

She shook her head. "We've tried to bribe the servants, but their loyalty remains unshakable. The only way to compel them would be through force, but then they would surely report back to their mistresses."

But what if there was another way to compel them—without them knowing? I thought of Winter's advice as I toyed with my irons, the weight of them now as familiar to me as the weight of my own hair.

"Find out who the spirit summoner is," I ordered. "Leave the princesses to me."

I KNEW WHICH GUARD CARRIED MY KEYS: ZIBEI, A YOUNG MEMBER OF Sky's personal guard. I did not particularly like him; his private smiles and long, lingering looks left me uneasy. But perhaps I could turn his interest to my advantage.

I waited until the changing of shifts to emerge from my rooms.

"My lady!" said Xiang, the most senior of Sky's guards, who had replaced Luo Tao following his betrayal.

Improvising on the spot, I feigned dizziness. "What time is it?" I asked, stumbling forward.

"Nearly sundown, my lady—"

I had just passed Zibei when I pretended to trip and fall. Zibei reached out to catch me, as I knew he would. My hand closed around the ring of keys at his hip before I fumbled for the right one. *There.* He tried to help me up, but I bought time by bending over, letting my body become deadweight as I unlatched the key from its hook.

Quickly I slid the iron key from its ring.

Then I straightened. To my annoyance, Zibei did not let go of me. Instead, I felt his thumb stroke the inside of my elbow.

"I'm so sorry," I said, wrenching free from his grasp. "I should probably rest."

Xiang looked concerned. "Do you need me to call for the physician? The prince likely will not return for another week."

"It's okay," I said, hurrying back inside. "I would prefer to be left alone."

I closed the door and locked it out of habit, never mind that my guards all had keys. Hurrying back to my bedchamber, I changed into dark robes that would blend into the night. Then I slid the key into the first of my iron bands. But I hesitated.

I stood there, frozen, equal parts fear and anticipation quickening my pulse. It had been so long since I'd tasted the thrum of lixia in my veins. I longed for that power, but also, I was afraid of it. Afraid of who I could become under its influence.

My desire superseded my fear. I turned the key and the first manacle fell open, clinking softly onto the rug below. Suddenly, I couldn't stand my irons a second longer. Trembling now, I jammed the key into the second manacle, my impatience making me clumsy. The key turned. I shoved the iron off my wrist.

I was free.

I gasped less from pain than from shock—I was flying, no, falling—falling from the sky in a thousand-li drop. My qi surged forward to meet the incoming rush of lixia, which matched my qi like yin to yang. I had forgotten what true power felt like. Like a man living underground, I had forgotten the kiss of the sun. How the light sparkled upon water, how its brilliance touched everything as far as the eye could see.

This life I'd been living ever since the war ended—it was but a half-life. This true power—this immensity, this richness of breath and sight and sound and every sense imaginable—this was what I had lived for. This was what I had killed for.

This was what my mother had died for.

I could feel my jade humming, urging me toward the spirit realm, but I ignored its call. I did not have time.

At the periphery of my senses, I could feel the dragon stirring with curiosity. His presence was like a haixiao wave gathering power, threatening to tip at any moment. But I was no longer afraid. He could not kill me.

"Qinglong," I whispered.

I felt the flick of his tail against my mind—irritated, yet intrigued. *"So the rat has finally emerged from her little hiding place."*

"Rats are ever so hard to catch, aren't they?" I replied, pacing the length of my room. "You and I have had our differences in the past, but I'll be honest with you now—our goals are one and the same."

"Oh?"

"I want the throne," I said bluntly. "And if *your* summoner controls the throne of the strongest kingdom in all of Tianjia, think of the influence you'll have. In the spirit realm, and the human realm."

"Interesting," he hissed. He said nothing else, but I felt him prying at the edges of my consciousness, searching for a chink in my armor. I strengthened my mental shields in response, and he hissed with impatience.

"Those tricks won't work on me anymore," I told him.

I could feel his amusement nettling my skin. *"Is that so?"*

"Yes. And if you try again, I'll bring back my irons, and you'll be without a vessel once more. Which do you prefer?"

His amusement strengthened, but he did not deign to answer me. As his presence faded from my mind, I couldn't be sure if I'd imagined it, but I thought I felt a hint of respect within his obstinate silence.

I hid my discarded irons under my bed, then went out through the front door—only to find Zibei stationed in the corridor. I'd forgotten about him.

"My lady," he said, in a manner that was less formal than familiar.

"Sorry!" I exclaimed. "Just wanted some fresh air."

"I can accompany you," he replied. To my surprise, he tried to take my arm, but I evaded his touch.

"I changed my mind," I said, backtracking. "Do not disturb me."

I slammed the door shut behind me, annoyed but unwilling to wait. I leaned against the wall for several breaths, heart pounding, before eyeing the balcony inside my bedroom.

It would do. Sliding the screen door open, I scaled the balcony railing and climbed onto the nearby yinhua tree. It felt strange to sneak around again, after weeks of trying to do what was right and proper. My robes made it more difficult to run, but my body, rejuvenated with lixia, felt limber and free.

"See all that you can do with my power," Qinglong murmured.

"You're distracting me," I snapped, as my heel missed a branch and I nearly plummeted into the lily pond below.

I heard his chuckle as I scrambled down the tree, landing softly on the nine-turn bridge.

"Should I target Princess Ruihua or Princess Yifeng first?" I whispered into the dark.

"I thought I was distracting you."

I rolled my eyes.

"What do you think?" he purred.

Princess Ruihua had a closer connection with Prince Yuchen, who seemed poised to act first. However, it was Princess Yifeng who would undoubtedly find herself at the heart of any gossip and intrigue. I headed in the direction of her rooms.

"I wouldn't go that way, if I were you."

"Oh, so now you're helping me?"

"There's someone approaching the Southern Gate."

Skeptical, yet unable to resist the bait, I changed directions and was rewarded for it. I arrived just as an imperial messenger rode through the outer courtyard. Seconds later, Princess Yifeng's lady-in-waiting came hurrying through the gallery.

"I came at once," she said.

"Give this to your mistress," said the messenger. "Prince Keyan returns in a day."

She nodded, bowing to the messenger, who was already saddling a fresh horse for departure. Meanwhile, the maidservant sped back through the gallery, and I after her.

Princess Yifeng had a shrewd eye. Her maidservant was neither as young nor as pretty as most ladies-in-waiting, yet the way she moved—swiftly and silently—suggested other skills. Her face reflected years of honed awareness, her eyes alert to every subtle shift in the night. Cautiously, I kept my distance from her—until I almost missed her vanishing behind a tapestry.

Before she could disappear, I raced forward and caught the edge of the hidden door.

"What in the skies—"

I slipped inside and shut the door behind us, so that our only source of light came from the candle in her hand. Closing in on her, I stared straight into her eyes. *"What is your name?"*

It had been so long since I'd used my power. I'd forgotten how good it felt—like stretching your legs after a long confinement.

Her expression contorted, before going blank. "Wei Xu."

"Give me the letter, Wei Xu."

Shaking, she handed me the messenger's scroll. I broke the seal and tore it open, reading beneath the wavering light of her candle.

Yi Fan,

The Imperial Commander has accused me of misappropriating treasury funds. There appears to be an accounting discrepancy concerning the imperial gold mines, for which I am held liable. I shall return tomorrow but must depart the following morning to conduct a thorough investigation. Kindly prepare my medicines for the journey with all due haste. And ensure that our accounts are in order, should further inquiries arise.

Keyan

"*You're welcome,*" whispered the dragon.

While I was reading, Wei Xu's face had begun to clear. "Wh-what—"

I forced her chin up so that her eyes met mine. "*Give this to your mistress. Tell her you opened it by mistake. And forget I was ever here.*"

The last command, the costliest, stole my breath from me. I cursed as my knees buckled, and I nearly collapsed against the stairs. Wei Xu had already turned in the direction of her mistress's rooms. I followed at a distance, dizzy and lightheaded, as she disappeared through a door at the end of the stairway.

In the back of my mind, I could sense my roiling qi—impossibly fragile, as thin as a spider's web. Why did my qi feel so weak, when I had not used it in months? I called upon my lixia to strengthen it, but that only highlighted the stark disparity between the two. They were meant to exist in harmony, reflecting each other as mirror images, but now my lixia felt more and more like a hungry shadow, swallowing up the light.

I waited a few beats before climbing up to the stairwell, now cast in total darkness. Then, when I heard voices on the other end, I peered through the door.

A tapestry obscured most of the opening, but I could make out several nobles in the sitting room, in various states of repose.

"His standing among the people comes from that girl," Princess Yifeng was saying. "They know she is bound to him."

"He is popular in his own right. They see him as the great hero of the war," said Prince Yuchen mockingly. "Because he waved his sword around a few times and shouted 'Charge,' now they regard him as fit to rule the kingdom."

"Father will appoint whomever he deems suitable." I didn't recognize this speaker, but I thought it might be the fourth prince, a quiet man who rarely emerged in public.

"Your filial nature is a guiding light for us all," said Princess Ruihua, though I detected a note of scorn in her voice.

"If only our dear brother Sky could be half as filial," said Princess Yifeng. "He seems to believe he is the heir apparent already, with his flagrant disregard for His Majesty's edicts."

"The consequences of his disobedience will fall upon him," said Yuchen knowingly, "sooner than he thinks."

It was an unmistakable threat. I wanted Princess Yifeng to ask him what he meant, but her attention was diverted as she read the letter from her maidservant.

"It's late," she said abruptly, pocketing the scroll. "I must retire for the evening."

"Apologies for overstaying our welcome," said Princess Ruihua, rising. "We only wished to congratulate you on the appointment of your brother to the magistrate's seat. You must be overjoyed."

"Pity he couldn't secure it on his own," said Yuchen wickedly.

"Some of us rely on cleverness," said Yifeng. "Others rely on who they know."

Princess Yifeng waited until they all filed out. Then she burned the letter over a candle.

"Any other news?" asked Yifeng, watching the devouring flame.

"Your brother is asking for extra funds dedicated to Weiyang. The storehouses are empty and the famine is particularly bad this winter."

Yifeng examined the remains of the letter, now turned to ash. "Tell him I can't help right now."

"Your sister also requests assistance. She says her eldest is struggling to pass the jinshi exam and may require—"

"Tell them they're on their own right now!" Yifeng snapped. "I need to think. Leave me."

I did not envy her. In that moment, she reminded me of my stepmother, shouldering the brunt of her family's survival alone. No wonder even Prince Keyan had turned to her with his problems. She might have a penchant for brewing trouble, but she was equally skilled at resolving it.

I hurried back to my rooms, climbing up the yinhua tree. I winced as several branches broke and dropped into the pond with a splash, but no one came to investigate the commotion. Back in my chambers, I knocked on Lily's door.

Despite the late hour, she was fully dressed, her cheeks red with cold. "My lady?"

"Where were you?" I asked suspiciously.

"I went for a walk."

I eyed her, but she did not shrink from my gaze. It was a lie, I suspected, but not one that betrayed her loyalty to me. "Can you send a message to Winter?"

"At this hour?" she asked. I nodded.

I regretted disturbing her rest, but the Imperial Commander would soon be returning, and I had a feeling Prince Yuchen would not wait. *"The consequences of his disobedience will fall upon him,"* he'd promised, *"sooner than he thinks."*

"After you deliver the note, I want two bracelets fashioned to look like my irons." I used a paper fan to slide my manacles out from under the bed, careful not to touch them. "The shape and heft of them should be the same, and the color ideally. But they cannot be made of genuine iron."

Lily shot me a piercing look. I held her gaze, daring her to ask for an explanation. *You want to bet on the winning team.* It had not occurred to me before tonight to use mental manipulation on my own maids. Even the idea of it left me uneasy, and yet I was not above such ruthlessness.

"Yes, my lady."

Once she'd departed, I wrote a letter. I would have to return the iron key to Zibei, I thought, or face Sky's questioning. But before I could determine my next move, a knock sounded at the door.

"The sixth prince," announced Lily.

"That was quick," I said, rising as Winter crossed the threshold to my quarters.

He had changed clothes and now wore a shimmering emerald silk that caught the firelight as he moved. He looked as if he were going out to the theater, rather than to bed.

"Is this appropriate?" he asked, eyeing the interior of my rooms as he met me on the raised kang platform. "The servants will talk."

"If I were trying to make Sky jealous I would've chosen a different prince," I said impatiently, as Lily set a tea tray on the kang table.

Winter raised a brow. "What is it?"

I relayed the contents of Keyan's letter.

He swept back his robes and took a seat in the rosewood armchair across from me. "You certainly work fast," he remarked, as I poured him a cup of steaming tea.

"I thought you knew how I worked."

Winter raised his cup to me in a silent toast. "So when does my brother depart for the mines?"

"The day after tomorrow," I replied. "Where are they located?"

"There are several, but the most prominent ones are in Jitang, Yenwu, and Saiya."

Saiya. The lakeside town we'd passed on the way back from Mount Fuxi.

I set my tea down, looking up at Winter. "I think Yuchen is the one stealing from the gold mines and shifting the blame to Keyan." I told him of the indigo dust I'd seen on his shoes the day he'd returned.

Winter blew on his tea. "He certainly wasn't supposed to be in Saiya," he said thoughtfully. "But what would he need the funds for? The discrepancy would have to be substantial to catch my father's attention. Yuchen already commands the influence of the General Counsel—he does not require additional resources for any of his charges."

"I don't know yet," I said. "Monitor him, will you?"

"Whatever you wish," he said, rising with a mocking bow. "Now, if you'll excuse me—I have a real date I cannot be late for."

I glanced out the darkened window. "At this hour?"

"The night is still young."

"With whom?"

Winter smirked. "A gentleman never tells."

I shot him a sidelong look. "Does this have anything to do with Captain Tong?"

Winter blinked, the first semblance of a reaction I'd gotten out of him.

"You two look good together," I said, smiling. I'd first encountered Captain Tong during the bandits' ambush near Ji Zong. Winter had nearly been taken captive that day, but Captain Tong had guarded him fiercely. "I'm glad at least some good came from the war," I remarked.

"Oh?" Winter raised a brow. "I can think of a few other good things." From his arch tone, I knew whatever he said next would be at my expense.

Before he could tease me relentlessly, I bid him good night and ushered him out the door. Exhausted, I prepared for bed, telling myself I'd sleep in tomorrow—I'd earned it.

Unfortunately, the morning had other plans for me.

"MY LADY," SAID LOTUS. "SORRY TO WAKE YOU—BUT YOU MUST RISE."

"What time is it?" I asked groggily. "I thought I asked Lily to cancel today's training session."

"It's not that," she said. "The crown prince has returned early on an imperial mission. No one knows why! The third prince requested a private audience with him—and now the crown prince is issuing a summons for you! It's an official summons"—she worried her lower lip—"under the jurisdiction of the Imperial Commander."

Which meant it was either a punishment or a promotion. Given my previous track record, I knew not to expect the latter.

With mounting unease, I let Lotus and Lily dress me as we waited. Lily discreetly handed me the custom-made bracelets, crafted to mimic iron—a simple task, she remarked, given the current fashion for wearing iron.

Within the hour, the imperial guards arrived, summoning me to Prince Keyan's palace. Though they did not bind my hands, I noted the way they surrounded me, as if they thought I might try to escape. But I was not so foolish as to think running could get me anywhere.

When Lotus tried to follow, the head guard shook his head. "He requested only the lady."

"Lady Hai is prone to nausea and vomiting," explained Lotus. She shot me a wink as the head guard allowed her to accompany me.

The throne room of the crown prince was smaller than the Imperial Commander's, but no less extravagant. Prince Liu Keyan sat on a raised dais made of rosewood and cedar, the steps intricately carved to resemble a swaying bamboo forest. In front of him Princess Yifeng poured him a medicinal-smelling tea, before placing the porcelain teapot on the table and retreating to the back.

Prince Yuchen stood before the dais, vibrating with a nervous, uncontainable energy. As my presence was announced and I entered the room, I watched him watch me, tracking my every step like a cat before a mouse. But who was the cat, I wondered, and who was the mouse?

"There she is," said Yuchen, "the demon girl."

TEN

After the war, they were brought over by sea to serve as forced laborers. Thus their bodies were buried on foreign soil, where they haunted the capital city until Emperor Wu declared they were to be given a proper burial. Their souls have now gone to rest, but on a particularly windy night, one may hear them singing in the old language, singing of a land they can never return to.

—REMEMBERING THE WU DYNASTY, 913

"Your highness," said the third prince with spurious humility, "I have it on reliable authority that the seventh prince has been openly defying the Imperial Commander's edicts. Prince Liu Sky has engaged in black market dealings to amass an extensive collection of banned texts. His actions are intended to spread the wickedness and corruption of black magic, deliberately undermining the Imperial Commander's efforts to eradicate such evil."

My pounding migraine had returned. I studied the crown prince's reaction; he listened silently, his only tell in the deepening fatigue on his face. Perhaps rumors of his sickness had not been exaggerated.

"Why does he do this, you may ask," said Yuchen, with an actor's flair for the dramatic. "He does this for *her*"—he whirled on me—"because she is a black magic practitioner."

He strode toward me and grabbed my wrist. I struggled against him, but in my weakened state, he easily restrained me, raising my arm in the air so that my trailing sleeve fell back.

"Why do you think she wears iron at all times?" asked Yuchen, his hand squeezing my wrist hard enough to bruise.

"That's not exactly particular to her, is it?" said the crown prince, before coughing into his sleeve. "Half the city wears iron these days." He glanced down at his left hand, and I noticed the thick iron ring on his middle finger, out of place beside the sparkling gemstones he wore.

"And where is proof of this supposed collection?" Keyan asked, after taking a long sip of his tea. From the way he grimaced, the tea did not seem particularly appetizing.

Yuchen's smile widened as my ears began to ring. Of course Yuchen would make his move while Sky was away, leaving me to defend him. And how could I, when in the palace I was regarded as a fallen woman at best, a demonic spirit at worst?

"Your Highness, allow me to show you—so you can see with your own eyes."

As the third prince led the way, he spared me one glance—his smile sweet as a sated viper's.

AS WE ENTERED THE NOW-FAMILIAR READING ROOM, I SENSED RATHER than saw Lotus trying to catch my eye. Aware of the intense scrutiny upon me, I resisted meeting her gaze, not wanting to do anything that might implicate her.

The crown prince showed no particular surprise as Yuchen led him and our entourage through the secret passageway. He made sure I went last, lest I somehow tamper with the evidence.

As I entered the secret library, my focus was drawn not to the books, but to the third prince. He followed his older brother like a dog eager to receive a treat, practically wagging his tail as Keyan removed a scroll at random. Lifting a brow, he opened another scroll, then another.

"What joke is this?" Keyan demanded at last, before descending into a coughing fit.

"Your Highness?" Yuchen asked.

With disgust, Prince Keyan dumped the three scrolls he'd skimmed into Yuchen's arms. Yuchen wasn't ready to receive them, and only managed to catch one. From my vantage point, I caught a portion of the title. "*Household Proverbs for the Venerable Wife: On Marriage, Children, and—*"

Yuchen dropped this text like a burning coal. "No," he breathed, grabbing another scroll off the shelf. "*Ways to Mitigate Monthly Bleedings—*"

I restrained a smile as I now glanced at Lotus out of the corner of my eye. On my hunch, Lily and I had stayed up long past midnight clearing the banned texts from Sky's library. That had been my first priority. Once the banned scrolls had been removed and safely hidden, I had tasked her with going into the city and buying all the women's literature she could find. I had no idea how she had accomplished this feat so quickly, but from the glint in Lotus's eye, I figured she'd had help.

"How can this be?" Yuchen demanded. "Ge—I was just here the day before last, I-I have proof . . ."

I bowed deeply, choosing at last to speak. "Your Highness, given the gaps in my early education, I have endeavored to further my understanding of the ways of womanhood, so that I might better serve the imperial family. If you find any aspect of my studies objectionable, I will seek to amend—"

"You—you demon!" Yuchen lunged at me, but the crown prince stopped him.

"That's enough, Brother."

Yuchen sputtered with outrage. "She—she used her black magic to warp our vision! Our eyes—we can't trust our own eyes!"

Keyan's exhaustion had deepened, his complexion appearing wan and sallow under the torchlight. "I said, that's enough. You've wasted my time, Yuchen, and at a particularly important juncture. Do not think I will forget—" He broke off abruptly, coughing into his handkerchief. When he removed the cloth from his mouth, I noticed a spot of red on the silk—blood.

"Your Highness," said Princess Yifeng gently. With her newly adopted air of diffidence, I'd forgotten she was present. "Should I call for the physician?"

Keyan nodded. "Lady Hai, may we meet again under more favorable circumstances," he told me, before leaving. Curiously, he did not look me in the eye.

LOTUS ACCOMPANIED ME TO MY QUARTERS, GLOWING WITH TRIUMPH. As soon as we were reunited with Lily in the privacy of my bedchamber, she burst into speech. "You should've seen the look on his face! And the books you chose. I'll never forget the sight of Prince Yuchen reading about how to cure cramps," Lotus giggled. "I was wrong about you, my lady—you'll do wonderfully in the palace." She sighed, collapsing on the sofa. "We can rest now."

"No," said Lily adamantly. "We can't rest until all of them are deposed."

They began bickering as I returned to my desk. I was relieved, yes, but I couldn't shake the nagging suspicion that I had just woken the sleeping beast. Prince Yuchen would not let this moment of humiliation pass. And I could not forget the calculating glint in Princess Yifeng's eyes when she'd contemplated me in the library. More danger was surely on its way.

I could not afford to alienate anyone else. My enemies had multiplied in a matter of minutes, and still I was no closer than when

I'd begun. I needed to understand the dragon's ulterior motives, to see if we could form a truce of sorts. But to do that, I had to find my mother's diary.

I knew the key to retrieving it; I was simply reluctant to learn its cost. Because I knew Cao Ming Lei, and I knew he would never agree to anything without exacting a favor in return.

What would be his price this time?

"SEE IF YOU CAN LOCATE WHERE THE XIMING HOSTAGE IS BEING KEPT," I instructed Lily that evening. "I'll also see if I can find any leads." Perhaps Winter knew where Lei was under house arrest.

No sooner had I relayed the order than a mysterious note arrived for me. Bemused, Lotus told me it had been concealed within my supper tray, implying that whoever sent it had access to Sky's personal servants.

But when I opened the letter, I found myself unsurprised by the sender's extensive reach. It was from Lei himself. How he managed it, I had no idea, but I had long since learned not to underestimate his cunning.

It is no secret that your enemies at court are many, while your allies are few and far between, he wrote. *You too are discontent with the ruling regime. I believe our underlying goals align, and that together, we can prevail in achieving our shared objectives. If you are amenable to an alliance, meet me at the moon-viewing pavilion at midnight. Cao Ming Lei.*

I burned the note, my heart pounding at the audacity of his request. Form an alliance with him—a prisoner of war? To do so would be to commit treason.

And yet Lei knew me. He'd suspected how dissatisfied I was, with both the current regime and life at court. I needed alliances against Sky's family, who were intent on removing me. And most importantly, Lei possessed my mother's diary.

"What does it say?" asked Lotus curiously.

I colored, and she mistook my blush for shyness. "Oh!" she said, giggling. "Is it a love note from the prince?"

I nodded, though I knew which prince she'd been referring to. The wrong one. Lei had always done this to me—forced me to lie, to deceive, to turn traitor to my own convictions and values. But if I were being truthful, I couldn't blame this on him. Because while he'd stoked the flames, the spark had long lived within me. I was the one with this selfish ambition that could not be sated no matter how much I took, and took, and took. After all, Qinglong had chosen me for a reason, hadn't he? Because I was hungry—for life, for freedom, for power. He had been drawn to that hunger.

Lei would remain here in Chuang Ning until the Three Kingdoms Treaty was finalized. If I allied myself with him now, I reasoned, he could provide me with valuable leverage against the other princes. One by one, I could take them down, until Sky was the last heir standing. Then Sky could ascend the throne—and I with him.

From the throne, I could rework any rule. I could punish those who had wronged me. Most importantly, I could rewrite my legacy, so that everyone would know *I* was the one who saved the kingdom.

"My lady, are you all right? You're white as a ghost," said Lotus, her voice coming from someplace far away.

"Are you having another panic attack?" asked Lily. "Should I bring out the irons?"

"No!" I screamed, seizing her by the arm.

"Meilin," Lily said sternly. "You're hurting me."

"*You're a perversion*," General Huyi had called me. "*Repulsive*."

More often than not, I had read, *the spirit will overpower its host, assuming control over the medium's body and mind.*

This obsession with the throne, with power—was it consuming me? Was I losing my sense of self? If my family saw me now, could they recognize me? Could I even recognize myself?

I released my breath, centering myself through qi gong. Painstakingly, I forced myself to let Lily go. To my shock, I saw that my hands had left bruises on her skin.

"I-I'm sorry," I said, clutching my head. "I'm not feeling well. I need... to be alone..."

I didn't catch her response. I turned and slammed the door to my bedchamber, then slid to the floor. My head was pounding as if someone had taken a hammer to it. What was wrong with me?

Strangely, I could not sense my own qi. All I could feel was the force of my lixia, like turbulent waves crashing against a crumbling dam. *"Would you surrender yourself to the world, or would you make the world yours?"* It was the age-old question—the one that had led Chancellor Sima to accept the phoenix's bargain, and me to embrace the dragon's offer. Because we had been hungry, dissatisfied with our lot in life. Because we had failed to value what we already had.

I could not tell if I was awake or dreaming. *"It is inevitable."* The voice that spoke was no stranger's, but I could not recognize it. *"Surrender is inevitable."*

I looked up and saw my own face, reflected back at me.

"Give up," she said. *"You're so close already."*

Darkness closed in.

I WOKE ABRUPTLY, SITTING UPRIGHT IN BED. OUTSIDE, THE SKY WAS dark.

Lily sat beside me, her eyes pensive and watchful. "Is it worth it?" she asked quietly. "Your power?"

The curiosity in her voice sent a chill through me. I seized her shoulders, before recalling my earlier outburst of violence and unhanding her. To her credit, she did not flinch. "Listen to me," I said. "A bargain like mine cannot be undone. You're too young."

"Only a few years younger than you." She scoffed. "You'd do it all again, wouldn't you? If given the choice."

I didn't know how to answer her. "It's not that simple."

She shook her head. "My brother is a summoner, you know, of a lesser spirit." At my stunned look, she laughed. "I know you don't trust your spirit, but my brother trusts his. In fact, he considers her his friend."

I said nothing. I too had been so naïve once.

"You don't believe me," she said, shrugging. "Not all spirits are alike, Meilin."

I puzzled over her words. But before I could ask more, I recalled Lei's note.

"What time is it?" I exclaimed, panic rising. Had I missed him?

"A quarter to midnight."

I breathed out in relief, then scrutinized Lily. Although I trusted her, I couldn't be certain if she reported my actions to Sky.

"Please return to your room," I said. "I sleep better alone, as you know."

"Are you certain you wouldn't like supper, or—"

"I'm certain. Good night, Lily."

I waited until Lily's footsteps had faded before dressing by candlelight, taking care not to make a sound.

Apart from one near miss with the palace patrol, I made it to the moon-viewing pavilion with no one the wiser. I could not tell the exact hour, but from the position of the moon in the sky, I felt certain I had not missed our appointment.

But where was Lei? It was not like him to be late. And on second thought, as I observed the way the radiant moonlight shone upon the marble pavilion, offering its radiance to the half-moon bridge and the sleeping lotus pond beyond, I began to wonder why Lei had chosen such a conspicuous meeting place. Not only was the pavilion brightly lit, but it was also highly visible, offering a clear line of sight to the surrounding palace.

The first shivers of doubt ran down my spine. What proof did I have that it had been Lei to write that note? What if it had not been the Ximing prince, but . . .

Cold laughter rang out from across the half-moon bridge. Dread sank like a stone in my gut as I turned to find Princess Yifeng and a contingent of her guards crossing the bridge toward me.

"Oh, Lady Hai, how you amuse me," she said, her voice sparkling like light on water. "What a clever girl you are . . . until you're not."

I tried to back away, but there was nowhere to go. The pavilion had but one path, and even if I were to run, how could I escape the palace in my current state?

"Seize her," Princess Yifeng ordered. This time, the guards afforded me no pretense of politeness. One jerked my arms behind my back, while another fitted genuine iron manacles around my wrists. I swallowed a cry as my lixia left me like a flame extinguished on a bitter cold night. My knees buckled and I did not have the strength to keep myself upright. I collapsed on the ground, curling into a fetal position until a guard forced me to my knees.

"Your greed is astounding," she said, looking down at me. "Despite breaking every rule imaginable, you still came out with *everything*. You had the love of the people, the love of a prince, the life every girl in Anlai can only dream of. And yet, even still you would throw it all away . . ." Her smile returned, but not before I saw the glimmer of jealousy in her eyes.

In a way, her machinations were a compliment. They meant she saw me as a viable threat, a key obstacle in her path to the throne.

"How insecure you must be," I spat, jutting my chin up at her, "to see someone as insignificant as me as a threat to you, Your Highness."

"If you wish to survive at court, darling, you must see everyone as a threat. But I don't disagree. You are insignificant." Her face turned emotionless. "Especially once you're dead in the ground."

And now real fear sluiced through me as I realized why they'd forced me to kneel. Princess Yifeng nodded at the swordsman beside her. I struggled against my captors, my vision blurring with cold terror. "N-no," I tried to say, but my voice wasn't working properly.

Princess Yifeng smiled at my panic. "Did you think I'd wait for your besotted prince to return home and protect you?" She raised her voice, and I wondered if others were watching. "You know the punishment for treason." The swordsman beside her unsheathed his blade. "Death by execution."

ELEVEN

In fact, during the Yong Dynasty, the wielding of spirit power was closely linked with virtues such as justice and ambition. However, following the Warring States Period and the subsequent ban on black magic, public perception shifted, associating those who wielded spirit power with negative traits such as vengeance and greed. As for whether the qualities that attract spirits are inherently good or evil, this author cannot answer. Emotions, much like the sun and the moon, possess both a bright and a dark side—it all depends on the angle from which they are viewed.

—MANUSCRIPT FROM THE DESK OF LIU WINTER, 924

I SHOULD HAVE RUN, I THOUGHT HOPELESSLY, STRUGGLING NOT TO hyperventilate. I should have fought with everything I had, rather than accepting my fate so foolishly, like a sheep led to slaughter.

I was angry, so unbearably angry. Angry at Princess Yifeng for twisting the narrative, for once again casting me as a traitor and a liar. Angry at Sky for abandoning me, for taking my credit and then letting me fall.

Above all, I was angry with myself—for letting one stupid mistake ruin me.

"Wh-what proof?" I wheezed. "Other than hearsay—"

"What proof do I have?" she repeated, laughing. "Oh, Lady Hai, I already have the approval of the prince, and three independent witnesses who have each verified the evidence in question. Now," she directed the executioner. "Do not tarry."

The swordsman raised his blade high, its surface catching the moonlight and scattering shards of brilliance across the pavilion. But I refused to avert my gaze from the sword.

"Pleasant night for a stroll, is it not?" Though the words were casual, the voice rang out across the lake, forceful and resounding.

"Prince Winter," said Princess Yifeng, trying to hide her alarm. "And—Keyan!" Her dismay grew. "What are you doing here?"

"I might ask the same of you, princess," said Winter. He inclined his head at me, as if I were not bound and kneeling on the floor. "Lady Hai."

The crown prince was frowning, his frown so deep the lines looked engraved into his face. "Did you know about this?" he asked Winter.

Winter shrugged in a gesture that indicated neither yes nor no. "Now that the crown prince is here, his jurisdiction precedes that of Prince Yuchen, who I trust is the one who signed the execution order?"

Yifeng gave a curt nod before appealing to her husband. "Your Highness," she said. "Lady Hai has committed an act of the highest treason. I have long harbored doubts about her loyalty to the Imperial Commander, particularly after her defection to Ximing during the war—"

"My lady," said Winter, "do not forget that I too was in Ximing, and I have already testified that those rumors are false."

"Fine, those are false, but this certainly isn't!" she snapped, losing her composure. "I have the letter! Given the chance to collude with the enemy, she immediately agreed, seeking to enter an illicit alliance with the Ximing prince—"

"Yi Fan," said Keyan, using her personal name, "drop it, please. She is too popular among the people. They believe she is responsible for ending the war."

"But—"

"If they learn of her execution, they will riot."

"Not if they know she committed treason against the throne! Think of the precedent this sets, if we allow her to live freely despite her multitude of crimes—"

"And what crimes are those?" asked Winter. "Her alleged all-powerful demon magic? Why hasn't she used her demon magic to free herself, then? Her secret library of banned books? Why did these books never materialize? And this letter you speak of . . . Lady Hai, did you ever receive such a letter?"

Winter's eye caught mine. I shook my head.

"It is nothing but a misunderstanding. I in fact asked to meet Lady Hai at midnight. That is what I wished to discuss with you, Brother. The reasons are improper, but not treasonous."

"An affair?" Keyan asked, his eyes alighting from me to his brother. His expression changed as he beheld both of us in a new light. "Di, I thought better of you. To covet what belongs to your brother . . ."

"He lies!" Princess Yifeng screamed. "You—" She pointed an accusatory finger at Winter. "You—deviant—"

"That is no way to address a prince," Keyan interrupted his wife coldly. "I've had enough of your antics. Go."

"But—"

"I will speak with you in private," he said, and by the tone of his voice, it was not going to be a pleasant conversation. Blanching, Princess Yifeng obeyed.

Keyan turned his disapproving gaze on me. His lip curled with subtle repulsion before he looked away. "Put her in a holding cell," he ordered the guards. To me: "You will sit in solitary confinement and reflect on your actions. Consider yourself fortunate that nothing more occurred, or your punishment would have been far, far worse."

THE CROWN PRINCE HAD NOT MENTIONED HOW LONG MY SOLITARY confinement was to last for, but I expected the length to be no longer than a day. I was a noble lady, after all, too delicate to even be lashed.

And yet, the first day passed, and no one came. My appetite, which had shrunk in prison, now made my stomach ache with hunger. But most frightening of all—the water jug, which had been full when I arrived, was now empty, and no one had come to refill it.

Had I known how long my confinement would last for, I would not have finished it so carelessly.

I awoke to thirst, and more thirst. I began to pound on the door of my cell, wondering if I'd been forgotten. At first I cried out for help, but as I heard no footsteps, I quieted, conserving my voice.

By the end of the second day, my mouth had begun to burn with thirst. Hallucinations crowded the edges of my vision, until I wasn't sure if I was awake or dreaming. Always, the same vision—someone sapping qi from the land. Huge swaths of it, stolen. The land would take years to heal. And the people afflicted with madness, they would never recover.

"Despite breaking every rule imaginable, you still came out with everything. You had the love of the people, the love of a prince, the life every girl in Anlai can only dream of. And yet, even still you would throw it all away . . ."

Princess Yifeng was right. I had been terribly, terribly lucky. I had gotten everything and more; surely seventeen-year-old Meilin could never have dreamed of the life I had today.

Still I was not satisfied. Still I hungered for more. I could come and go as I pleased within the palace grounds? Now I sought to move freely across all of Tianjia. I was known as a woman warrior who had aided the war effort? Now I wished to be known as the woman warrior who had saved the kingdom itself. I wanted not only the common people to recognize me, but also every noble who sneered in my face or gossiped about me behind my back. I wanted to be known; I wanted to be respected; I wanted to be *remembered*.

The want was so fierce, it became like a living thing inside me. Sometimes I wondered if it would overwhelm me, until I was made of nothing but want. I knew I should fear the notion, and I did, but somehow, I also savored it. After all, my desire had brought me this far—perhaps it would yet bring me further.

I lost track of time. I did not know if it was the third day or a hundred days later, though I was still alive, and that meant something, didn't it? It made me laugh, a dry, soundless laugh, to think of the irony of my predicament: a spirit summoner of the water dragon, dying of thirst.

The door creaked open behind me, and I wondered if this was yet another hallucination. I opened one eye and saw a tall, broad-shouldered figure standing above me, his pale eyes like two moons in the sky.

He knelt and guided me into a sitting position, then brought a cup of water to my parched lips. I drank greedily, with abandon, water dribbling down my chin. He held me while I drank and drank, then eased me back even as I protested for more. "That's enough," he said. "I'll give you more in an hour."

Then he withdrew an iron key and undid my manacles, replacing them with the false irons Lily had procured. "Your friend gave them to me," he said.

As lixia returned to my veins, the fog in my head cleared. I took in the man's bright eyes, his tawny complexion, the faint scent of alcohol on his skin. Of course, he'd been drinking.

"It's you," I rasped.

"I heard you've been looking for me," he said, his voice more wicked and toe-curling than I remembered. "Was the little prince too much of a bore?"

I gritted my teeth. "You stole something from me."

"Your heart?" He raised a sardonic brow. "I'm not in the habit of returning those, unfortunately."

"A diary," I snapped. "I thought even you wouldn't go so low as to steal a keepsake from an unconscious invalid, but I guess I should've known better than to expect morals from you."

"Unconscious?" he repeated, unfazed by my insults. "Well, that certainly explains things."

"What are you talking about?" I bit out.

"You didn't appear unconscious to me, though you weren't quite . . . yourself."

A hot bolt of fear ran through me. There had been instances during the war, brief moments of inexplicable insanity. When I'd lost myself and tortured a fellow soldier in my squad, nearly killing him in the process. When, certain a parasite lived within my mind, I'd bashed my head against a wall so hard my forehead split open. But never had I lost the memory itself, as if it weren't me living in my own head. If I could not trust myself, who could I trust?

"You're lying," I said, because the alternative was too distressing to consider.

Lei shrugged, sitting back against the wall. "Perhaps," he said, with the air of one who did not particularly care one way or another. "Though you may consider my motives, and find I have little reason to lie."

He knew how to toy with people, I reminded myself, how to make an audience believe anything. Knowing this, still, I could not help but be sucked into his stories.

"What..." I drew in a quick breath, bracing myself. "What happened?"

"The diary," he said instead, ignoring my question. "It belongs to your mother, no?"

I tried to keep my expression neutral, but it was no use hiding things from him.

"I thought so," he said, inclining his head. "There's nothing valuable in there, you might as well know. Any notes that could've once been useful are too damaged now to be legible."

"You—you *read* it?" I demanded, struggling to remain calm. "How dare you?"

"You would've destroyed it," he said, as if pointing out the obvious. "I wanted to know what was so *not* worth reading."

"What are you talking about?" I asked, and now I could not keep my outrage in check. "I would've expected you of all people to know how much it meant to me, how much it—" My voice broke in a flood of despair. As quickly as it had risen, my anger splintered into grief. "There were sides of my mother that I never knew," I said hoarsely. "I thought at last I might know them."

His pale eyes were indefinable as he considered me. Then, reaching into his tunic, he withdrew a thin leather-bound journal, its cover partially charred with ash.

I stared at the proffered journal in astonishment, before my eyes skipped up to meet his. "What is your price?" I whispered.

"Nothing," he said, and the word seemed to cost him. "This one, you may have."

Cautiously, as if expecting him to reveal the magic trick at any moment, I accepted the diary from him. It was real and solid in my hands. Giving in to the childlike urge, I hugged my mother's diary to my chest, and I imagined it was a little like embracing my mother.

Lei said nothing. As I looked into his eyes, it became clear he was thoroughly inebriated.

At my expression, he threw me a derisive smile, as if guessing my thoughts. Despite his frivolous demeanor and flippant remarks, the Ximing prince was no better off than the rest of us. And beneath those cold smiling eyes he hid a deeply troubled soul.

But Lei hated my pity. Quickly I asked, "What did you mean?" I swallowed. "That I would've destroyed it?"

He tipped his head back against the wall, exposing the knot at his throat. It made him appear oddly vulnerable, human, and it occurred to me that he could have *envied* me, to know that I had my mother's last thoughts, when he did not.

"When I entered the infirmary, you were trying to tear that book into pieces, but you weren't strong enough. Then you brought it to the fire, but you paid no notice to your own hand. I stopped you when I saw that your skin was burning."

The burn mark on my right hand, I remembered with trepidation. Lei wasn't lying.

"You kept twitching, like a startled animal. When I spoke to you, it was like you couldn't hear me. Only then did I notice your irons had been removed. And your eyes"—he met mine—"they were the color of minted gold."

Qinglong.

Icy fear stabbed the pit of my stomach. That he'd tried to destroy my mother's diary only confirmed my suspicion—there was something valuable within it, some crucial information he did not want me to discover.

"Will you consent to see a lixia specialist now?" Lei asked.

I crossed my arms. "No," I said, in a tone that was final. Sky had asked me multiple times, but I saw no point. I didn't want a physician examining my blackened veins and depleted qi, only to prescribe infinite bed rest. No, I would heal on my own terms.

Lei shrugged and got up to leave. "They'll be coming for you soon," he said, his tone facetious once more. "Your little prince has returned from his brave and harrowing journey. Just in time to play the hero."

His voice was mocking, but I wondered if there was not a note of bitterness to his words. Lei, who played the perennial villain, who pretended as if everything he did was for foolish vanity, or selfish gain. But looking up at him now, at his cold, derisive expression, I knew it was but a carefully constructed mask.

"Thank you," I said. I rose to my feet unsteadily, gripping the wall for balance. "I can't say for certain what the future holds, but if ever I'm in the position to, I'll speak in favor of relations with Ximing, and with . . . you."

He studied me then, and I tried stubbornly to hold his gaze. One beat passed, then two, until I couldn't take it; I blushed and looked away, but not before glimpsing the wicked curve of his smirk. Did he know the residual power he had over me? The lingering desire that I could not suppress, no matter how hard I tried?

"Do you want the throne?" he asked. "Or does Sky want it?" The unexpected shift in topic unsettled me. His voice dropped dangerously low. "Or does the dragon want it?"

"I want it," I replied, but my voice sounded strange to my own ears.

"You hate it here," he said suddenly, his tone vicious.

I opened my mouth to argue, but he seized me roughly by the shoulders. "Don't lie to me, Meilin." To my astonishment, I heard his voice tremble with suppressed fury. "I thought we'd passed that point."

"You are *made* of lies, Lei!" I ripped myself from his hands. "So what if I hate it here? I have nowhere else to go."

His eyes were a dilated molten copper, so bright and deep I felt like I could fall into them and drown. "You could come with me."

"How much have you had to drink, Lei?" I scoffed, but as he closed the distance between us, I retreated until my back hit the wall, my bravado slipping. "I'm sure your brother would love to see me," I hissed. "We got along so well last time." I shivered at the memory—when Prince Zihuan had pressed a burning candle to my throat.

"We needn't return to Ximing, though Autumn would certainly be pleased to see you." His eyes flickered like caught fireflies. "But I believe that you and I share the same concerns, do we not?"

Lei had read my mother's diary.

For the first time, I considered it. Was that a real option—to go with him? Or had it always been in my stars to stay?

"The dragon's plan," I began dubiously. "The one my mother wrote of. Do you think it's connected to the sudden appearance of spirit gates?"

"What do you think, sweetheart?" asked Lei, looming over me, and I loathed him for it. For in his tone, the answer was obvious.

And yet: "How can it be?" I demanded, glaring up at him. "I'm still alive, aren't I? He can't choose another vessel, apart from me."

Lei glanced at the ceiling window, at the light slowly resolving into day. "I don't know how the dragon is managing it," he said at last, "but I doubt we'll find the answer within these palace walls."

I shook my head tiredly. "I can't leave Sky." And Sky could not leave the capital again, not at such a critical juncture.

Lei appeared unsurprised. His smile, scathing and contemptuous, was like a slash across his face. "I must be more like my brother than I thought," he murmured, alcohol loosening his tongue.

Impulsively, he fitted his hand around my throat, as if he meant to strangle me. Yet his touch was surprisingly gentle. He left it there for a beat, before seeming to remember himself and dropping his hand. "Do me a favor," he said, his mask of insouciance back in place. "Try to stay alive, will you?"

TWELVE

There are times when he is placating. When he asks me, "What is your favorite tea?" or "What music do you find pleasing?" And I think to myself, perhaps I could be happy here. But then I recall—I already know his answers to such questions, while it has taken him this long to even think to ask mine. And I wonder, why are the expectations for our husbands made so meager? Why do we mistake the absence of cruelty for kindness? When I remain cold, he grows angry, shouting like a child in the throes of a tantrum. And I remind myself never to lower my guard again.

—FROM THE DIARY OF HAI MEIHUA, 914

SKY CAME FOR ME NOT AN HOUR LATER. HE BURST THROUGH THE door, upsetting the water jug Lei had left for me by the threshold.

"Meilin." He reached for me, wrapping me in his arms as if to make sure I was real. "Did they hurt you?"

I shook my head against his chest, my lungs unexpectedly tight. At the familiar sight of him, a foreign emotion constricted my throat, making it hard to speak.

He pulled back, holding me at arm's length to check for injuries. "When I heard the news . . ." He swallowed, sensing the roiling emotion within me. "I came as soon as I could."

"Do you know how long I was trapped here for?" I asked, and now I recognized this strange emotion, not strange in and of itself, but in its unexpected object. "Two days, Sky. Two days—with no food or water. I thought I was going to die—" I broke off, chest heaving.

Sky's expression was dazed. Until it morphed into fury. He released me, his eyes turning cold and vicious. "You should never have been held in solitary confinement for longer than a day," he said. "I'll find out who's responsible for this."

"No." I caught his sleeve, at once regretting my temper. "I don't think it was the crown prince's fault," I clarified. "Someone must've bribed the guards to go against protocol. But, Sky, if you investigate the matter, it'll only draw attention to the rumors of my punishment—and my crime."

Sky clenched and unclenched his jaw; I doubted he'd heard half of what I'd said. "They can't get away with this," he insisted, breaking free of my grasp and striding for the door.

"Sky!" I cried out, feigning sudden weakness. Immediately, he was upon me, steadying me in his warm embrace.

"Let me take you to the physician," he said, in a different sort of voice.

I shook my head. If he got rid of me now, he would only return to his quest for vengeance. The culprit was obvious—Prince Yuchen, who could easily claim innocence of the matter. Worse, if word of my supposed infidelity reached the Imperial Commander's ears, he might choose to remove me for good. No, better not to draw attention to the matter. I would search for more substantial evidence to make my case.

"No," I said, straightening. "I need fresh air. Would you take a walk with me?" At his reluctance, I added, "Please? It's been so long since I've seen you."

His eyes softened. "Of course," he said at last, tucking my arm into his. "Wherever you wish to go."

I started to lead him to the gardens, before my stomach gave a loud unbecoming grumble.

"I'm rather famished," said Sky tactfully. "Should we take breakfast first?"

WE ATE UNTIL I WAS FULL TO BURSTING, EACH DISH BETTER THAN THE last. At this time of year it was common to serve winter melon soup, which I adored, but I'd never had it with dried dates, mushrooms, and rice noodles, which soaked up the savory broth deliciously. Moreover, there were pork and chive dumplings, both boiled and fried; tofu with ginger and spice; and baked sweet potato glazed with honey and sugar. When I wondered aloud how Sky knew all my favorite dishes, Lotus shot me a wink behind him.

"Do you need to rest?" he asked again, after breakfast.

"I've been resting ever since you left," I said. "Why have you returned? Did you catch the alleged spirit summoner?"

To my astonishment, Sky nodded. "He's to be executed at midday."

"I want to see him."

"It's impossible," said Sky. "He's already awaiting his sentence at the Gate of Heavenly Peace." And I was prohibited from leaving the Forbidden City, he did not add.

I could not go out, but... "We could watch," I suggested. "From the palace walls."

The Gate of Heavenly Peace stood directly outside the Forbidden City, and the square was visible from the outer palace walls. Though it was unconventional for a palace lady to be seen there, it was not technically banned.

Sky was hesitant, but I would not take no for an answer. And yet, once I'd gotten what I wanted, I did not know what I was looking for. As I watched the young man brought up to the chopping block, his burlap clothes marking him as a tenant farmer, I could see no signs of spirit power from him.

"What proof do you have of his black magic?" I asked Sky, who looked discomforted by the entire procedure. Below us, commoners were heckling the prisoner, throwing rotten fruit and vegetables at his back. The fruit and vegetables he bore, but the slurs wore him down as he shrank from the crowds and even tried to cover his ears.

"His neighbors ratted him out," said Sky. "They spoke of how he'd made flowers bud in winter, and fruits grow in the most infertile of soils. His harvests were sweeter and more abundant than any others, and so he stirred the jealousy of many farmers in the province."

"But that's hardly a crime, is it? For skies' sake, it sounds like a gift."

"I argued on his behalf against Father, but . . . you know how he is."

I did not, in fact, because Sky had been shielding me from him. I'd heard from the rumor mill that Sky had asked for my hand in marriage, but the Imperial Commander had refused him, claiming my reputation was too controversial and my health too unstable to warrant the risk. But most likely, he wanted something to hold over Sky, leverage to keep his youngest and most popular son in check.

"Father asked him to use his lixia, and the fool complied, growing a small seed into a sapling tree. And that was it." As Sky spoke, I scanned his face and noticed new lines there I hadn't seen before. Just as the times had not been kind to me, neither had they been kind to him.

"His power is nothing like yours," said Sky, brows furrowing in thought. "His lixia didn't feel the same either. Yours felt like . . . like . . ." He struggled for an appropriate comparison.

"An ocean?" I offered.

He nodded. "If yours felt like an ocean," he said, still deep in thought, "then his was rather like a river creek. I could feel the bottom of it, its limitations, I suppose."

I cut him a sidelong glance, but he was lost in his own memories. I had never questioned Sky's spirit affinity before, but perhaps it was stronger than I'd first perceived.

His only brother of the same parentage, I recalled, was Winter, whom I'd once encountered in the space between realms. Winter had sensed my affinity before I was even aware of his. He was the one who'd urged Sky to look after me. And Winter's spirit affinity—it likely surpassed even mine.

No matter. I would not let Sky take on the enormous cost that I had borne. Sky, who was noble and purehearted, would never become a spirit summoner—not while I lived.

I'd always known of the Cardinal Spirits, but not until recently had I considered the existence of other, lesser ones. And yet, hadn't I seen proof of them in the spirit realm, in my nightly wanderings? The floating, blinking lights in the dark world, most of them minding their own business, but others perhaps seeking out human vessels. And what if, I thought suddenly, the hairs on my arms rising, what if the new tears in the veil were causing more humans to wander into the spirit realm, and form a bargain with a waiting spirit?

Perhaps the spreading madness was not just the madness of a human overwhelmed with lixia energy. Perhaps it was also the madness of a human vessel, subsumed by its spirit master.

This was all getting more complicated than I'd ever imagined.

"I don't know how the dragon is managing it," Lei had said, *"but I doubt we'll find the answer within these palace walls."*

"Sky," I began, and he frowned at me, guessing my intent. "The next time you have a lead, I want to go with you. I want to see these spirit gates for myself."

"You were the one who told me they were too dangerous to

approach!" said Sky, outraged by my double standard. "No. Absolutely not."

"Then you agree with your father?" I asked. "That I should become a noble lady, and never stray from the confines of the palace? That I am too weak to lift a sword, much less best a man with it?"

"You know I don't agree with him, Meilin," he said with growing irritation. "Of course, I would rather you come with me—you don't think I value your judgment on these matters? But"—he bit his lip, his eyes roving down my body in a way that left me deeply insecure—"do you honestly think you could keep up?"

My eyes pricked with tears. I was frustrated with him for reminding me of my shortcomings, but even more so with myself—for having reached this state of unforgivable weakness.

At my tears, Sky's face contorted. "I'm sorry," he said, "I shouldn't have—"

"No." I cut him off. I refused to let him pity me like this. "I propose a deal."

His expression took on a wary cast, but he did not interrupt.

"We'll set aside the matter for the time being. But a month from now, before the new year, I will—I will consent to be examined by a physician. If I am deemed fit, then you *must* allow me to accompany you. If I am not, then I will agree to stay."

I would train every day, I resolved, my heart pounding. I would spend every waking hour on recovery. And slowly, I would heal.

This was the way I had tackled every problem in my life—and this was the way I would solve this one. There was nothing that hard work and determination could not fix. Nothing.

"All right," Sky promised, without thinking it over. He was unlike Lei in every way. He wore his emotions on his sleeve. He said exactly what he thought. And he did not see the world in terms of power structures and twisted games, but instead as black and white, good and evil. In some aspects, I envied him, because the world to him was knowable, just as he was knowable. The doubt I felt every day of my life was foreign to him. Perhaps, I mused, if I could keep him by my side, those doubts would be banished forever.

I stood on my tiptoes to kiss him on the cheek. He caught me around the waist and pulled me close before I could escape. "What was that for?" he asked teasingly. But before I could respond, the gong sounded below. Midday had arrived.

With mounting apprehension, I peered over the edge at the crowd below. Some were still jeering, their taunts cruel, yet oddly exuberant, as if they took pleasure in this spectacle. Only one girl stood unmoving in the crowd. She was tall, her build slight. *Lily*, I recognized with a pang. What was she doing down there?

I shivered with unease, and Sky wrapped his cloak around me, mistaking my discomfort for cold.

The provincial magistrate read out a list of the prisoner's crimes before giving him a chance to speak.

"I, Duan Mingze, have never sought to harm a living creature. My only crime is in dreaming of a better, more prosperous world, and hoping that we might rebuild this kingdom into a place more beautiful than we left it."

I could feel his qi intertwined with lixia, and in his voice—I could hear that unmistakable echo. It was the voice of his spirit master, speaking through him. And yet his spirit master felt so unlike my own, inclined toward life instead of destruction.

Were spirits in fact like men, not a monolith as a species, but as separate and distinct as the veins of leaves?

I expected the crowd to be moved by his speech, but instead, they jeered louder, some laughing at the audacity of his words. They were afraid. They were afraid, and so they channeled their fear into a thirst for violence. I knew, because I had once done the same.

Hiding my face against Sky's chest, I did not watch as the magistrate handed the prisoner off to the executioner. Sky held me in his arms, not questioning my sudden sensitivity.

It was an inexplicable sensation, following no reason or precedent. And yet I couldn't shake it, that peculiar feeling that somehow I was the one responsible for this crime. That if not for me, Duan Mingze would not be standing where he was today. He would be alive, and I—well, perhaps I would be dead.

The axe met its mark. The crowd cheered as the body fell.

THIRTEEN

Though the southern monks control much of Tianjia's most fertile land, spirits generally avoid their territory, for those who enter seldom return. The methods of defense used by these reclusive monks remain a mystery, but it is said that when confronted by one, a spirit would sooner choose iron than dare challenge them.

—LOST JOURNALS OF AN 8TH-CENTURY LIXIA SCHOLAR,
DATE UNKNOWN

AFTER SKY LEFT ME, WINTER REQUESTED MY PRESENCE IN THE plum blossom grove. He awaited me beneath a wax plum tree, its yellow blossoms at their brightest in the depths of winter. As he inclined his head in greeting, a few petals drifted softly onto his white robes. The gardens, typically brimming with life, lay barren in winter. In an effort to fill the void, the gardeners had meticulously arranged potted camellias and narcissus, brought in from the south. But the lush, colorful flowers only called attention to the bare, frost-kissed landscape beneath.

"Walk with me?" asked Winter.

A party had gathered just beyond the plum blossom grove. Instead of steering us away from the crowd, Winter led us toward it, where the resonance of the zither, mingled with laughter and lively debate, would mask our conversation.

"Yuchen is meeting with the Imperial Security Commissioner

tonight," Winter murmured beneath the music. "Palace security is outside his jurisdiction—and he's never publicly allied with Lord Xu before."

Lord Xu oversaw the security of the Forbidden City, a role that granted him considerable influence. Typically, he coordinated only with the Imperial Commander. But with Liu Zhuo's health failing, Lord Xu might now be looking to align himself with a more favorable faction.

The army's loyalty lay with the Imperial Commander, and with Sky. If Yuchen needed rival forces, Lord Xu would be the perfect ally. But what leverage could Yuchen use to bribe a man as powerful as Lord Xu?

The Saiya gold mines.

"A secret army would certainly explain the need for the gold mines," I said, and Winter nodded. Prince Yuchen was playing both sides. He had collaborated with Princess Yifeng to eliminate me while simultaneously plotting against the crown prince. If he was amassing a secret army beyond his father's watch, it was clear he had no intention of honoring his succession plans. He was preparing to take the throne—by force if necessary.

"I can send a spy to tail him tonight. Or"—he paused, casting me a sidelong glance—"I can ask Sky."

My skin tightened at the thought of Sky knowing our machinations. "Don't bother," I said. "I'll go."

He raised a brow. "Are you certain? You'll be vastly outnumbered."

"I don't plan on fighting," I said. "Besides, this job is too important to delegate."

"And you trust yourself to handle it?"

I met his gaze. "There's no one I trust more."

Winter inclined his head, his attention sliding past me to the party sitting beneath the Rain-Listening Gazebo. Captain Tong stood at the edge, looking bored out of his mind until our approaching footsteps caught his attention. He raised his head, and though Winter barely acknowledged him—just the faintest quirk of a smile—a rosy flush crept up Captain Tong's neck before he quickly looked away.

Winter's pace remained even. As we rounded the bend, the rest of the party came into view. I spotted a few finely dressed imperial advisors, familiar faces from the Anlai treaty delegation. But then, in the corner—my skin crawled. Lei was slouched against a bench, one arm draped lazily around a striking girl with porcelain skin. Her crimson lipstick was smudged, half of it transferred to the underside of Lei's jaw.

As the zither performance drew to a close, the girl twisted to whisper in Lei's ear. He smirked, one hand lazily stroking her shoulder.

You have no right to be jealous.

"Interesting," said Winter. "That is Lady Tang Liqing, whose father just happens to control the Anlai treaty delegations."

"Did I ask who that was?" I snapped. "I don't care."

"Of course not," said Winter, but his eyes were appraising. Sputtering an excuse, I made my exit.

AS I WAITED FOR NIGHT TO FALL, I FORCED MYSELF TO READ MY MOTHer's diary in its entirety. I had been avoiding this task, knowing it would stir painful memories, but I could no longer afford to remain in the dark.

Lei was right: the diary was almost entirely illegible. But unlike

Lei, I recognized my mother's handwriting, and moreover, I recognized certain characters that only appeared in women's writing.

> *He is comforted by my beauty, and does not perceive me to be a threat.*
>
> *The new warlord is an intelligent fool. He does not suspect a thing. I can only thank the skies Emperor Wu has been deposed, for surely he would not have let me live.*
>
> *Broke into the imperial library today. It was a near miss; I am becoming too old for this sneaking around. No new information—a waste of time.*
>
> *The myth of the eternal spring taunts me. It is just credible enough that I cannot keep from dreaming. But just fantastical enough that every lead turns insubstantial. And yet I must believe, for if it is but a fairy tale, then all hope is lost.*
>
> *A new lead—a traveling lixia scholar from the east. She claims to be seeking a heavenly peach vendor in Chuang Ning. According to legend, she tells me, the heavenly peach takes its life from the healing powers of the eternal spring. If we find this vendor, perhaps it will lead back to . . .*
>
> *A false lead. I have nothing. I am running out of time.*
>
> *I have discovered a way to trick the dragon in his own domain. There is a way he cannot perceive me in the spirit realm, but it requires mastery of technique and time.*

Who was creating the spirit gates? And if it was Qinglong, how in the skies was he managing it?

I was still no closer to solving this riddle.

Just as I was about to leave, certain I had read all there was to read, I took one last look at the waterlogged remains of the last few pages. These entries were blotted out by large ink splotches and water stains, and yet, if I held the pages up to the candlelight just so, I could decipher a few characters here and there. Slowly, filling in missing words from context, I deciphered the final entry in my mother's diary:

My hands shake as I write this. The Ruan seer at last agreed to meet me. She told me her great-grandmother once visited the spring, and that it is real. Journey to the summit of the Red Mountains, she said, and within the clouds, you will see every peak covered in snow. Look for the one covered in green—and there you will find what you are searching for. But, she told me, you cannot go in winter, or you will die from cold. It is winter now. I think I will die from impatience.

Tears leaked from my eyes. For my mother had died in winter. Whatever she had been looking for, she had never found.

AS NIGHT FELL, I ARMED MYSELF TO THE TEETH AND DONNED BLACK robes that would obscure any trace of blood. To mask my identity, I tied a silk cloth over my nose and cheekbones, concealing the lower half of my face. Then, pulling up my hood, I climbed over the balcony railing, now familiar with what to expect from this route.

But I had not come to expect company on the palace rooftops. As I scaled the low-hanging eaves, a shadow detached from the roof gable, rising from his crouch with all the lethal grace of a jungle cat.

I immediately drew my sword.

"You do not recognize a friend?" He pulled back his hood to reveal bright amber eyes. Cao Ming Lei.

My heart in my throat, I did not sheathe my sword, but I did not raise it either. "Are you a friend?" I hissed.

"Certainly," he said, his smile a flash of white against the dark. "Unless you're looking for something more?"

I scowled, grateful the darkness hid my flush.

"Why are you here?" I demanded.

"A little birdie told me you'd be up to trouble tonight," he remarked. "You know me—I have such an incurable fondness for trouble."

"Winter told you?" I asked, astonished.

"No." He raised a brow. "You just did."

I bit back a curse, hating him for making me fall for the oldest trick in the book. Lei had a way of doing that—throwing you off-balance, drawing out the words you least wished to say.

I sheathed my sword, then hesitated. My natural inclination was to go about this alone. And yet, although I doubted his allegiance to me, I doubted his allegiance to Prince Yuchen even more. For tonight at least, I trusted he would not sabotage me.

"Don't get in my way," I said, before taking a running start and leaping from the eaves. I did not look back, but I could hear Lei behind me, then beside me, matching my pace with ease.

After so long confined to the palace, it felt good to race in the dark. We leapt from roof to roof, avoiding the palace guards by staying close to the shadows. When I lost my way, Lei took the lead, somehow knowing precisely where the Security Commissioner's residence was located.

Getting past Lord Xu's personal guard proved more challenging. Although his home lay outside the Forbidden City, it was heavily fortified, with guards stationed in even the most unexpected places. I swore as a guard patrolling the roofs caught sight of us, bringing a whistle to his lips mere moments before Lei threw a knife at his chest. The man dropped, and I hastily leapt across the distance to stop his body from rolling off the roof.

"Lord Xu does have a reputation for being cautious," said Lei, extracting his knife from the corpse. "Some might even call him paranoid."

"For good reason," I said, "if he's plotting treason against the throne."

"And is that why you are here tonight?" Lei asked, cleaning his blade on the guard's tunic. "To protect the Imperial Commander's reign?"

I shrugged mockingly. "I am but a humble vassal," I said, and Lei smirked, before suddenly seizing my shoulder and shoving me down.

"What—"

He crushed his hand over my mouth and I nearly bit him before catching sight of a second guard scanning the rooftops.

We pressed ourselves flat against the roof gable, breathing hard under the cover of night. I had forgotten the distinctive scent of him, like cedar and jasmine. Was he seriously wearing fragrance even tonight—on a reconnaissance mission?

"Have you ever considered that your perfume might give you away?" I muttered, keenly aware of how close he was to me.

"It would be a worthy defeat," he said in my ear, and his low voice made my skin tingle. "If I'm to go, at least I'll do so in style."

I huffed against my mask. "Your vanity knows no bounds."

"One of my many flaws," he murmured. I could feel the heat of his gaze upon me.

I fixed my attention on the courtyard below, where the patrol guard had just turned his back on us. "Now," I ordered, and we rose in unison, dropping to the lowest eave directly above the atrium.

From this vantage point, I recognized Prince Yuchen's manservant, waiting with his horse by the back gate.

"He's already here," I said, cursing. "We'll need to find a way inside."

"It's too risky."

"I need to hear what—"

"I know," said Lei. "I have a better way."

Bewildered yet intrigued, I followed as he leapt up to the inner roof overlooking the rock garden, then removed a blunt tool from his robes. Chiseling out a clay tile, he created a small fissure in the roof, then inserted a thin metal rod inside the gap.

"Come here," he said, and I bent toward the rod. Voices issued from within.

In amazement, I stared at Lei, who grinned back at me. It struck me then that this was one of the first times I'd seen him truly sober. I preferred him like this: still playful and mischievous, but sharper, clear-eyed, less volatile and prone to fits of violence. Sober, he was someone I could imagine choosing to spend time with.

But it did not matter how I preferred him. As soon as winter passed, he would depart for the treaty negotiations, and then to Ximing. And I would never see him again.

I bent my ear to the listening rod.

"Your Highness, the arrangements have already been made. But the payments you promised are long overdue—"

"I told you—the gold mine is under investigation," Prince Yuchen snapped. "How do you think it will look if I keep funneling the funds to you?"

"Then find another way to acquire the gold," Lord Xu said calmly. "But I cannot supply the additional troops without it. If you want me to double the numbers, I will require double the compensation."

"I'll repay you tenfold once I'm on the throne," Yuchen hissed.

"Your Highness," said Lord Xu slowly. "I appreciate your generosity. But as I've made clear, I need the funds first before I can provide the forces you require. I'm more than happy to wait until you can locate a new source—"

"Well, I can't wait!" Yuchen interrupted. "My father's health is failing. I suspect that damned Yifeng is poisoning him, so that he'll name his successor any day now." His voice grew bitter. "He's never respected me, never taken me seriously as his son . . . No, he won't name me his heir, and if I stage a coup after he's announced his successor, the people won't stand by me."

Princess Yifeng was poisoning the Imperial Commander? I knew she was cunning, but I never imagined she'd go so far as to off her own father-in-law.

"That's a serious accusation," Lord Xu said. "But if you can prove it, that would provide grounds for removing the crown prince, no?"

"Damn it, don't you think I've tried? The bitch has covered her tracks more carefully than a snake in the grass."

Though I despised the princess, I couldn't help but smile. Like an artist appreciating a rival's work, I had to respect a job well done—even if it made my own life significantly harder.

"As I've said before, my loyalty lies with the winning side," said Lord Xu. "I placed my faith in you initially, but it is now your responsibility to demonstrate that that trust was well-placed."

There was a long silence, before I heard the sound of a heavy stone being set against wood. "Let this serve as a promise of future payment," said Yuchen. "You may use my chop as your own." His voice grew distant. "It is only a matter of time before I am on the throne."

Their voices grew inaudible as they left the room, before I heard them once more in the courtyard, exchanging pleasantries in parting.

Prince Yuchen had left his name chop on Lord Xu's desk.

Nothing was as personal as a name chop, which was used as a signature to validate your approval. If I could steal Yuchen's chop from Lord Xu's desk, perhaps I could use it as proof to demonstrate their secret alliance.

"It won't be enough," Lei warned, as I prepared to take flight. His hand closed around my wrist. "Remember, you're fighting from lower ground—you're at a disadvantage."

I struggled to break from his grip, but in the time he stalled me, Lord Xu had already returned to his desk.

"What is your problem?" I hissed, when he'd finally released me.

"You steal his name chop now, and he cannot use it to incriminate himself. Give them time. Let Lord Xu mark every damning document with Yuchen's seal. Let them believe no one is watching. Only then, when the evidence paints a compelling picture on its own, do you strike."

As the patrol changed, Lei rose from his crouch, and I followed, trailing him until we'd left the immediate vicinity of Lord Xu's home.

On the streets of Chuang Ning, I tossed my mask and black robes into the bushes, revealing plain linen robes beneath. With the Spring Festival fast approaching to mark the new year, most Chuang Ning migrants had left the capital to return home and celebrate with their families, leaving only the locals behind. As a result, the usually bustling streets were empty, even as night above bled slowly into the first light of day.

Although I knew I should hurry back before Sky noticed my absence, I couldn't resist the allure of the vacant city streets. Not knowing when I might return, I took advantage of the open space and paced back and forth, savoring these unguarded moments where I didn't have to appear ladylike and proper, my every move scrutinized.

"The gaps in my memory are getting worse," I confessed without thinking. I was too afraid to tell Sky, but Lei, who'd seen me after my seizure, already knew the worst of it. I pulled up my sleeve, staring at the dark, purple-black veins snaking along my arm before dropping it in disgust. "I'm afraid I'm losing my mind."

Lei watched me with lidded eyes as he leaned against a boarded-up gate. The gate, once leading to an apothecary, was now defaced with graffiti scrawled in charcoal: "BLACK MAGIC LIVES HERE."

"Why don't you see a lixia specialist?" asked Lei.

"You sound like Sky," I said irritably, before sighing. "I agreed to see a physician before the Spring Festival."

"That's nearly a month from now."

I ignored him. I did not like to think of myself as superstitious, and yet I somehow believed that if I avoided a physician's diagnosis, my body could heal miraculously on its own. Every morning I trained with Lily, and every night I meditated, strengthening and building my qi.

These days, I looked healthier, even if I did not feel healthier. My body had regained its muscle and my skin its supple elasticity. My hair was shinier and thicker, and my nails less brittle and prone to breakage. Yet inside, I couldn't shake the tightening dread rising like bile in my throat. The ominous fear that I was losing parts of myself, and that I had fallen so far, I no longer knew what those parts even were.

Regardless, I should not be sharing this with Lei, who would only exploit my fears against me. I returned to my pacing. On the bright side, I had a way to take down Prince Yuchen now. But I still didn't know what to do about the crown prince.

"Prince Keyan is too clean," I muttered, thinking aloud. "I have no leverage against him." I felt as though I were juggling a hundred balls at once, growing cross-eyed as I tried to keep them all in the air. Ironically, though I'd hated the war, now I missed the decisiveness of it, the way battles were fought with clear lines drawn. "Perhaps if I can catch Princess Yifeng poisoning the Imperial Commander..."

"Already tried that," said Lei with a yawn. "She's good. Covered all her tracks, just like your dear brother said."

"Prince Yuchen is not my brother," I snapped.

"Not yet," he said, and something in his gaze made me falter.

"Lei." My steps slowed as I stopped in front of him. The night air was cool, and without our earlier exertion, my sweat had dried, leaving a chill on my skin. "What are you planning?"

He smirked at me, revealing nothing. "Shall we go?"

FOURTEEN

Do you remember the elephant that Father received from the Leyuan delegation? You were only eleven back then, but I still recall how boldly you answered when Father asked how to have the elephant weighed. "Put the animal on a boat," you told the entire court. "And mark the water level. Then replace the elephant with bricks until the boat reaches the same level." Father was so proud. But your mother—I recall her anger, how harshly she scolded you! Perhaps she predicted the curse of your cleverness then. I know you say you are needed in the Anlai capital, but don't forget to look after your own needs. If it is too dangerous out there, come home. We need you too.

—CAO REA, IN A PRIVATE MISSIVE TO CAO LEI, 924

Lei began to walk, and I hurried to keep up with his long, even strides. Even though the rooftops would have been faster, he opted for the more scenic route along the Wen River.

As we walked, I recalled what Lotus and Lily had told me—how he'd been fraternizing with certain nobles as of late. Knowing Lei, those couldn't be happenstance friends. "You're negotiating the treaty terms, aren't you?" I speculated aloud. "For Ximing."

I watched his face, the way he tilted it up toward the fading stars, as if expecting the night sky to fall upon us like a velvet blanket. Though he said nothing, I saw a tendon in his neck rise.

He'd once told me, on an equally late night, how the war had begun. After the collapse of Tianjia, the Three Kingdoms had been divided unfairly—leaving Ximing with nothing but scraps. Over time, its people had grown hungry and vengeful, clamoring for change. And as violence begot violence, change became synonymous with war.

Could another unjust treaty become grounds for a second war? Weren't the people sick of fighting already? And yet it did not matter what the people wanted, in a world such as ours. It mattered only what the throne wanted. And those in power would do anything not to give it up.

The system was broken, and I had suffered beneath its weight. But now, rather than try to fix it, I only wanted to rise above it, ensuring I would never be the one suffering beneath again.

Xiuying, I knew, would be ashamed. She would expect more from me. Compassion, kindness, self-sacrifice. All the qualities she exhibited. And yet I did not wish to become another selfless woman hidden beneath the shadow of men. I wanted to be remembered, and I wanted to carve out a legacy of unquestionable greatness.

I did not question the pulsating warmth of the jade against my skin.

Lei was looking at me oddly, in that penetrating way of his that made me wonder if he could read my thoughts. His mother had possessed the gift of second sight. I did not understand how the Ruans passed down their abilities, but I sometimes wondered if he had it too.

"Did you see something?" I asked him, clearing my throat. "About the fate of the Three Kingdoms?"

His smile was mocking. "I can't see the future, sweetheart," he said. "I can only look at the past, and see the way cycles repeat themselves."

A hard expression flitted across his face. He glanced past me to the looming silhouettes of the palace pagodas, and the craggy mountains beyond them. "I won't let another war happen," he said lowly, and it felt like a promise. "I can't."

Selfishly, I saw an opening—and I seized it. I caught his sleeve, forcing him to stop. "Then help me," I said, more loudly than I'd intended. The harshness of my voice seemed to shatter something in the night's stillness. "Help me and I promise you—I'll ensure the treaty terms are fair."

He laughed, a scornful, derisive sound. "You think I need you for that?" he asked. "Do you really believe I don't have alliances with every potential successor?"

Caught off guard, I hesitated, but only for a moment. "Then help me for another reason," I said, changing tactics. "Help me take the throne because you know me. Because you know I'll be a better ruler than the rest of them."

"Meilin," said Lei quietly, "what makes you so sure you'll be better?"

"I—what?" Taken aback, I dropped my hand. "I'm not . . . you know I'm not like the others!"

He shook his head. "I mean this as a kindness," he said gently, but his tone only made his words cut deeper. "It's true you aren't like the others now. But who's to say what you'll become, in one year or ten, once the cancer of power has taken root? I'll tell you this—there is no one in all of Tianjia who can take the throne and not be changed by it."

"I'll be different," I promised. When he refused to look me in the eye, I recalled his former weaknesses and wrapped my arms around his neck, bringing his face down to mine. "Please, Lei," I whispered. "I need your help."

It was not a kiss, but from afar, it would have resembled one. Sky, I knew, would have been furious with me.

But what he didn't know couldn't hurt him.

Lei's eyes were heavy-lidded, yet within their amber depths, I could feel his suppressed desire. To my surprise, it mirrored my own.

Then Lei broke from my grasp, and I thought I'd lost him. "Who's the little trickster now?" he asked, his voice taunting.

I colored but refused to look away, waiting.

He adjusted one of his many rings, his face unreadable. At last, he spoke in a careless voice that was anything but. "For you, sweetheart, I'll gather the evidence against Yuchen. Besides, *you* are hopeless at this." I opened my mouth to protest, but he silenced me with a wry glance. "As for Prince Keyan, it's no secret that he and Princess Yifeng have a loveless marriage."

I nodded; Lily had mentioned this before.

Still twisting one of his rings: "But what most do not know is that Keyan had a secret lover long before he allied himself with Yifeng in a political partnership. A pretty girl named Caihong, who was relatively unknown before she was discovered by the Imperial Commander and chosen as his concubine."

My mouth fell open as I recalled the beautiful woman I'd met in Princess Ruihua's quarters. "Prince Keyan shares a lover with his father?" His father would be *furious* if he found out.

"She'll never admit to it," said Lei, his eyes cutting to mine. "Not willingly, at least."

I smiled, my fingers reflexively reaching for my jade. "I have ways of making people willing."

Lei's mouth tightened. Unexpectedly, Xiuying drifted to the forefront of my mind, and I wondered what she'd say if she were here. The thought left me nauseated with guilt.

Don't think of her, then, a voice in my head whispered. And I could no longer tell if it was my voice or the dragon's.

"You've changed," said Lei, so quietly it was nearly lost in the early-morning breeze.

"People change," I snapped. "You of all people have no right to judge me."

He said nothing, only watched an old farmer lug his half-empty basket of crops up the hill. The bokchoy leaves looked brown and wilted, but I wondered if he had nothing better to sell.

"They will both be punished if discovered," Lei said at last. "But you know who will be punished worse."

It was not Prince Keyan. No, it was never the princes.

It was always the nameless women, who would either be blamed, or cast out from history.

"Don't lose yourself," Lei said lowly. "No power is worth that."

"I'll decide that for myself," I hissed. Even though it had been a long time since I'd truly wanted to kill him, no one else could provoke me quite like he could.

I stormed away, not caring that I was going in the opposite direction of the palace. I had to get away from him—I had to get away from his hypocrisy, his two-faced manipulations, his stupid sanctimoniousness. I had to—

"Why don't you visit your family?" Lei called after me. I ignored him, but he caught up with me easily. I thought about drawing my sword on him, but the sun was quickly rising, and morning delivery wagons winding down the street. It would not do to cause a scene.

I turned in the opposite direction, heading for the palace.

"They live in Chuang Ning, don't they?" he pressed.

"I'm prohibited from leaving the Forbidden City," I retorted, despite my best intentions to remain silent.

"And you're so used to obeying the rules . . . ?"

We crossed the crescent moon bridge overlooking the Wen River. Once-green willow branches dangled lazily over the railing, waving hello in the wind. Lei could not have known this, but my family was quite close by—just a stone's throw away. Within a few minutes I could be hugging Rouha and Plum, checking on Uncle

Zhou's bad leg, learning all the household updates from Xiuying. And yet, instead of warmth and excitement, the thought sent guilt spiraling into the pit of my stomach.

"There's no point," I said, heading away from Willow District.

"Why not?"

"They'll just be disappointed."

Lei waited.

Suddenly, I was burning to tell someone. I kept silent until we'd entered a narrow hutong alleyway, then turned to him. "I-I'm scared," I confessed, the words tumbling out of me with a life of their own. "I'm scared they won't respect what I've become. I'm scared they won't recognize me."

"Then become someone they'll respect, Meilin," Lei said, closing in on me. "Don't let him change you."

My shoulders went up. "This isn't Sky's fault!"

"Is that so?" asked Lei, arching an infuriating brow. "Curious—why is it, then, that I always seem to see him reaping the rewards of your labor?"

I glared at him. "We're a team, Lei."

"Then where is he?" Lei looked around the abandoned alleyway, as if expecting to see Sky lurking in the shadows. "Why did he leave you without a lookout?"

"I didn't tell him," I said defensively. Under Lei's razor-edged gaze, I felt compelled to explain. "If I'd told him," I muttered, "he wouldn't have let me come."

My eyes dropped to my worn shoes. But Lei slid his hand beneath my chin, forcing me to look up at him. "You deserve someone who will work with you," he said, a muscle in his jaw clenching. "Not someone who treats you like you're made of porcelain."

I pushed his hand away. It was always like this between us: this relentless chase, this unending push and pull. We'd met under the ruthless shadow of war, and perhaps the war still lingered between us, because we could never seem to find common ground, could never seem to hold a conversation that didn't spiral into conflict.

But the sun was rising, and I was so very tired. "I can't talk about this with you."

"Then talk to someone else!" he cried out, exasperation breaking through his veneer of calm. "Talk to your family, for skies' sake. But don't shut everyone out; don't do this alone, Meilin. Your enemies want you isolated—that's how they control you."

"You would know," I snarled, shoving him back, hard enough to hurt. He fell back a step, rubbing his chest.

"What does that mean?" he asked with a sigh.

"It means you're the master manipulator!" I burst out, breathing hard. Trying to keep my voice level, I said: "Did you really think I could trust you—after everything that you've done to me?"

His eyes flashed with barely suppressed emotion. But when he spoke, his voice was cold and remote, unfeeling. "I'm not a good person, Meilin," he said. "But the difference between me and your little Anlai hero—I've never pretended otherwise."

FIFTEEN

A wise general discerns that a battle is won long before it is fought. For if one can signal the certainty of victory, then victory is already within grasp.
—BOOK OF ODES, 856

Lei didn't seek me out again, but he didn't seem to hold a grudge either. Only a few weeks later, a series of damning letters and financial records were delivered through Lily. The Ximing prince had even uncovered accounting statements that demonstrated how rations, housing, and stipend expenses had doubled, despite the number of official reported soldiers remaining unchanged.

I showed up at Winter's quarters at the crack of dawn, heeding Lily's warning against making my relationship with Winter obvious. Rumors of an illicit affair between us were already circulating, though those within the palace's inner circle knew there was little truth to them.

Sure enough, when Winter met me in his sitting room, wrapping a robe around his bare chest, I caught sight of Captain Tong in the bedroom before Winter shut the door behind him.

"This couldn't have waited?" he asked, voice scratchy with sleep.

"I wanted to avoid gossip," I said.

Winter scoffed. "This will only fuel the..." But he trailed off as his gaze drifted to the documents I'd arranged on the table before him.

Over the next hour, he pored over the Imperial Security Commissioner's private correspondence, his hand often lingering on the crimson red stamp left by Yuchen's name chop.

"I have to say I'm impressed," he said, after some time. "You're certainly cleverer than I gave you credit for."

I blushed. "I have clever friends." At Winter's look of confusion, I busied myself with rearranging the pages. "Don't ask," I said, before echoing his own words: "A gentleman never tells."

He laughed, a clear sound like wind chimes. "How are you planning to deliver the evidence?" he asked.

"I'm going to ask for a private audience with the Imperial Commander."

Winter raised a brow. "You're trying to take down Yuchen that way?"

I nodded.

Winter sighed, riffling through the documents again. "Do you want my advice?"

My shoulders stiffened before I nodded reluctantly.

"Only a fool makes herself the face of the opposition," he said. "Gather the necessary evidence, then give it to Prince Keyan." He smiled grimly. "An enemy of an enemy is a friend."

"Then Keyan will take the credit," I said, bristling.

"Yes, and the blame," he said. "Rule number one of palace politics: always leave yourself an exit."

I stroked my jade pendant, mulling this over. Winter's gaze flicked to my necklace, before just as quickly flicking away. Still, my hand tightened reflexively around my seal; when it came to my jade, my defensiveness verged on paranoia.

Chancellor Sima had once believed Winter to be the next summoner of a Cardinal Spirit. And yet, despite his powerful affinity, Winter seemed to have no interest in spirit wielding. Or was he only biding his time?

Can I really trust you? I wondered. *Or are you lying to me—just as so many others have before you?*

Winter stared back at me, unblinking, his eyes as dark as tea leaves. And this was what made me trust him: he'd had so many opportunities to seize power, and yet he'd taken none of them. He'd been born a prince of Anlai, yet had no interest in competing for the throne. He possessed the greatest lixia affinity of anyone I had ever met, and still had never made a deal with a spirit. Instead, he seemed content to lurk in the shadows, learning to fight not with swords but with sharp eyes and sharper words.

I had once thought him weak, but now . . . now I envied him.

"The Imperial Commander will be furious if he learns of Prince Yuchen's treachery," I said, returning to the matter at hand. "If he thinks Prince Keyan is the one who uncovered the plot, he'll be grateful to his son—and convinced of his ability. I'll only be setting him up to succeed."

"You help him, and you make a friend," said Winter. "Then, when you stab him in the back, he won't see it coming."

The words were ruthless, made more so by the fact that he was speaking of his own brother. But who was I to judge?

I rose to my feet. "Give the files to Keyan, then, when he returns from Saiya," I said. "But tell him to act quickly."

He nodded, following me to his threshold. "I think we all wish to avoid another war."

My hand on the door, I hesitated. "Are you prepared to lose a brother?" I asked.

His eyes flashed against the lamplight. "It wouldn't be my first time."

THE NEXT MORNING, I WOKE IN MY BED, SOMETHING WET AND STICKY sliding between my ribs. I pressed my hand to the wetness, then gasped.

I'd been stabbed.

I rolled out of bed, wrenching open the curtains and staring open-mouthed at the mottled bruises that peppered my legs, the trail of black soot my bare feet had left on the rug, and most damning of all, the wound between my ribs—which, after my initial panic had subsided, I discovered was barely a graze.

A knock sounded at the door; I realized the knocking had woken me.

"My lady?"

It was Lily. "What is it?" I rasped.

"Prince Sky is here," she said, poking her head through the door. I noticed her eyes were rimmed red, but I was too preoccupied to give it much thought. "Should I tell him to . . ." Her voice trailed off as she took in my state of dishevelment.

"My lady, were you . . . ?"

"Tell him I'm indisposed," I said, my voice coming out hoarse. As if I'd been screaming.

Lily left. Moments later, she was back. "He's asking what's wrong and if he can help—"

"No," I said, and I was shaking now. "I'll clean this up on my own."

"Meilin . . ."

I shook my head, and she fell silent, though her expression was mutinous. She wanted to help, I knew, but fear gripped me, driving me back to my default state—relying only on myself.

Alone, I cleaned and bandaged my wounds. Lately, I'd begun

waking up most mornings with fresh cuts and bruises, with no memory of how they got there. I longed to tell someone, *anyone*, to ask if I was going insane. But who could I tell? Sky would insist on confining me to bed rest. Already he was concerned I was overextending myself. Lily would urge me to put my irons back on, but I couldn't afford to lose any more time. And Lei . . . how would Lei respond? He would laugh at me, most likely, and make some petty joke about sleepwalking. And then he would tell me whatever I most wished not to hear.

So I handled it myself. I meditated and pushed the memory to the back of my mind. Years of enduring my father's abuse had taught me the art of compartmentalizing. By the time I was finished, no one could tell I was any worse for wear.

"The prince is gone," said Lily, when I emerged from my bedroom. I nodded, glancing at Lotus. "And Caihong?"

"The consort is in the Imperial Art Pavilion, my lady," said Lotus, delivering the information I'd requested earlier.

"Very good," I said, touching my ribs to ensure my bandages were in place. "Take me there, please." It was time to initiate the second phase of my plan. This time, Prince Keyan was my target.

Lotus nodded and rose, but not before Lily tapped me on the shoulder. I turned as she adjusted the sash around my waist, making sure it was no longer creased in the back. I smiled at her, and she smiled back, though it was a pained expression. "Let me know if we should suspend tomorrow's training session," she said quietly.

"Why would we need to do that?" I asked, shaking my head. But I saw the worry in her eyes.

The Imperial Art Pavilion was an open-air space, with green bamboo stalks interspersed with mahogany wooden beams. As the breeze drifted in, their shadows danced across the polished stone floor, which was tiled with intricate spherical designs. The air was still and silent but for the sound of running water from a nearby stream. I found Consort Caihong in the sculpture room, bathed in dappled sunlight, her attention fixed on porcelain vases from the Sun Dynasty.

As I approached, I saw that she carried a small sketchbook and was in the process of rendering a vase by hand. Although the design was simple, her skill was evident in her confident, swift strokes.

"Consort Caihong," I said, bowing.

She turned, shutting her sketchbook. "Lady Hai!" she exclaimed. "I didn't see you there."

"How well you draw," I said. "May I see your work?"

She blushed prettily. "Oh," she said, delaying, "they're nothing—"

"Please," I insisted. "I'm trying to learn, but I'm a rather slow study."

At that, she handed me her sketchbook. I flipped through the pages, discovering landscapes, still lifes, portraits. One drawing gave me pause—a lone figure standing at the edge of a cliff, gazing into the river below as her long hair billowed loosely around her. Something about the inherent melancholy of the piece spoke to me. As if the artist had touched something deep within me—something I'd believed I was alone in feeling.

"You're very talented," I said, handing her sketchbook back.

"It passes the time." She shrugged one shoulder with a practiced smile.

"Do you come here often?"

She nodded, a pleasant smile still pasted on her face. "It's my favorite part of the palace."

"And what is your favorite work?"

At this, her smile grew genuine. "This one," she said, leading me into an adjoining room, to a glass display in a corner. Inside was a small statue that appeared like a fossilized piece of amber, which caught and reflected the dappled light. The longer I stared, the more its colors seemed to shift and change. At first it appeared blue, but now I was beginning to think it green, or gold.

"What is it?" I asked in a hushed voice.

"It's a reproduction of a remnant of the old gods," she said, her voice also lowered in respect.

"The old gods?" I repeated, surprised.

She glanced at me. "Do you know the stories?"

I shook my head.

She laughed again, a self-deprecating sound. "They're quite silly, superstitions, you know—"

"I'd love to hear them."

She wavered, glancing back at me. I waited, making no effort to fill the silence. At last, watching the flickering amber, she said:

"Long, long ago, in a time before ours, spirits and men walked the earth together. They say it was an era of chaos and instability, because the spirits were capricious and fickle, and the emperor a weak and corrupt man. But one day, as the people cried out for change, the Mandate of Heaven shone upon a worthy man called the Red Sword, who took the throne only to rule for eighty-eight days. When a spiteful monkey spirit kidnapped his youngest son, he pursued the spirit up the mountains to present-day First Crossing, where he battled the monkey and overpowered him with his great life force. But as he ventured into the caves to retrieve his son, he found the young prince at the brink of death, for the monkey had stolen his heart. And so the emperor removed his own heart and gave it to his son, and the Mandate of Heaven passed on to him.

"Unable to carry his father, the son buried him in the Red Mountains, weeping all the while. The earth grew wet and pliant with his tears, so that the following day, the buried body reemerged from the soil. Only, the emperor's bones had fossilized into amber, and just as the father had once shared qi with his son, now this amber could be used to bridge qi from person to person. Understanding his father's last gift to him, the prince gave the amber to his people. Together, they joined hands and shared their qi across the land, and thus with their great numbers the first veil between spirits and men was formed."

Interesting, how these old legends diverged and shifted with every retelling. For I had heard a different version of this tale, like a warped mirror reflection. Regardless, it was impossible to tell fact from fiction now.

"Do you believe it?" I asked, watching her expression.

She flushed. "Of—of course not," she said. "I guess I just like the old stories, although they're quite silly, are they not?"

She was the consort to the Imperial Commander—young, pretty, and powerful—yet she tiptoed through conversations like she was walking on glass, voicing every statement as if it were a question, downplaying even her most remarkable talents.

Had I too been like this once?

"I believe it," I said.

She glanced sharply at me. "In—in the stories?" she stammered. "In magic?"

"I've never been able to resist a good story," I admitted. "And to be honest, it would be harder for me to believe that a world as wondrous as ours is entirely without magic."

She smiled. "I'm prone to belief as well," she said, as if confiding a secret. "I know everyone seems fearful of spirits these days, but I remember tales of kind ones too, and even beautiful ones. In the stories of old, spirits were as varied as men, each with their own personality and inclination."

I, who knew only one spirit, said nothing.

As we passed into the next room, a collection of ink and wash paintings, I asked, "Can we find your work here, Consort Caihong?"

"Mine?" Her eyes went round. "Of course not, Lady Hai. I would never dream..."

"And why not?" I asked, thinking of the way her art had made me feel. "I would love to be able to admire your work here, and I'm sure your future children would agree."

"Lady Hai, you may have forgotten, given your unique circumstances, but only men are allowed to display their work in the Imperial Art Pavilion."

"And why is that the case?" I asked. Against the black-and-white paintings, her youthful complexion appeared even brighter, as if all the light in the room favored her.

"The palace is a place of rules, and those rules are dictated by the throne..."

My pulse quickening, I said: "I want to change the rules."

The air around us seemed to thicken as Caihong's eyes darted around frantically. But this section of the gallery was deserted. Lotus had made it so.

"Come with me," I said, guiding her to the edge of the rushing stream, which the open-air gallery overlooked. I had learned this trick from Winter: using ambient sound to mask private conversations, rather than seeking silence.

By the water, I said, "Only Prince Keyan stands in my way to the throne. If you help me take him down, I will help you in return."

"I—what?"

"I know he's sleeping with you," I said, "and I know you don't want it."

It had been a wild guess, but her expression confirmed it. For what woman would risk her very life for an illicit affair that offered no loyalty, protection, or hope for future happiness? At best, she might wish to become another consort, no higher than she stood now, should Prince Keyan ascend the throne. At worst, it would cost her everything.

Perhaps at one time she had been infatuated with the crown prince, loved him even, but after being chosen as consort for the Imperial Commander, I was certain she would have prioritized her survival over any notions of romance. For Prince Keyan, however, the calculus would have looked very different. His life had never been at risk. Longing to return to simpler times, especially with a wife as shrewd as Yifeng, he could have wheedled, pressured, or even coerced his childhood love into maintaining their illicit relationship, no matter the danger it posed to her.

It was not fair, but when had life ever been fair?

"Lady Hai," she said, taking a strained breath. "I don't know what you speak of, but—"

"I can offer you a way out," I said, "if that's what you want. I can help you"—I could see the growing interest in her eyes—"if only you confess that Prince Keyan has been coercing you."

She recoiled, all her prior interest vanishing like a snuffed match. "He'd kill me," she said adamantly. "You don't understand him, Lady Hai. The Imperial Commander is . . . unforgiving. He's executed other consorts for far less." As she spoke, she fidgeted with the collar of her robes. Beneath, I caught the edge of a trailing green bruise.

Bile rose in my throat. "Let me protect you," I said. "I swear it— upon my life."

"No one can protect me now," she whispered, close to tears. "And I am resigned to my fate. My mother used to tell me that beauty is the wisdom of women, but she was wrong. It is our *curse*."

I thought of her sketchbook, that drawing of a forlorn figure at the edge of a cliff. In its raw desperation, its helpless melancholy, I felt as though I understood her.

"The woman at the cliff's edge," I said, "that was you, wasn't it?"

Her face bone-white, she nodded. "I am resigned to my fate," she said again, as if to convince herself.

It would be so easy to use lixia in this moment. If I only compelled her, in a moment it would be over. I could sense her will, and it was fragile as glass. I need only speak her name, hold her gaze, and she could become mine. She would agree to act as my pawn, and I could use her to take down Keyan. But Lei's warning echoed in my mind: *You know who will be punished worse.*

A knot formed in my chest. Caihong had suffered enough. And I would not become another bully in her long line of tormentors, threatening and forcing her against her will.

"Besides," Caihong added, in an attempt at lightness, "Keyan hasn't come to me in weeks. I think he's being cautious, biding his time until his father names him as heir."

It was not loyalty holding her back. It was fear.

Palace politics were all about signaling, I'd learned. If you could find a way to signal that you were destined to win, then you would actually win. Everyone wanted to back the winning side, but no one knew where to place their bets.

"You believe in the stories of old, don't you?" I asked.

Her face had not regained its former color. "What do you mean?"

"What if I told you they weren't merely stories?" I said. "What if I told you I could harness the power of the old spirits?"

"I . . . I don't understand."

I reached out a hand and the stream seemed to pause in its course, before droplets of water rose in the air, reshaping themselves into a slender vase in the Sun Dynasty fashion. Caihong gasped, and I could see in her eyes her rapt admiration for beauty. I transformed the vase into flowers, meaning to make them blossom, but I was stymied by the frailty of my qi, which was so weak it no longer felt like my own. If before my power had been balanced, like yin and yang, now it felt more and more like the waning moon, gradually consumed by the sun.

I dropped my hand; water sprayed everywhere. Sweat dripped down my temples, but Consort Caihong did not seem to notice.

"That was—incredible," she said, peering into the trickling stream below. "Could you offer me the same power?"

The question flustered me; not for a second had I expected it.

"The things I could create," she went on, "if I were not constrained by mere brush and ink."

What had I created with my power? I knew there must be some good, but in that moment, all I could remember was the fear. The way my victims looked at me with horror in their eyes.

"Caihong," I said, dropping honorifics. "You said beauty was a curse. I will tell you ... power is one too."

Her shoulders sagged with disappointment, but she nodded in quiet understanding. I could almost see her mind racing as she looked from me to the stream to the paintings around us, austere and solemn in their black-and-white depictions.

A decision took shape in her eyes. "I want to leave the Forbidden City," she whispered. "Do you know—in all my life, in twenty-eight years, I've never left even once?" She laughed, a hint of embarrassment in her voice, as if she expected judgment on my part. But I could not judge her.

I had once harbored the same dream.

"I can promise it," I said. "If you help me, I will do everything in my power to ensure you go free."

"Is it wondrous out there?" she asked, a shy vulnerability entering her voice. "Is it as wondrous as they say?"

"It is," I agreed, after some hesitation. "Wondrous, and terrible."

LOTUS AND I WERE WALKING BACK THROUGH THE PALACE WHEN I overheard a familiar voice drifting through the bamboo leaves.

"She won't talk to me," Sky was saying. "Brother, I don't know what to do. She's clearly sick but refuses to see a physician—"

"I thought you said she agreed to see one before the Spring Festival," said Winter. I peered through the leaves, spotting Sky and Winter in the rock garden.

"That's still a week away!" said Sky. "She's overexerting herself, and she won't listen to reason—"

I was seconds away from barging in when Winter said, "Why don't you let her do what she wants?"

Sky stopped pacing, turning toward his brother. I felt my lip curl; Sky had always listened to his older brother in a way he never did to me.

"Maybe she's afraid of confiding in you because she knows you'll derail her plans—and prescribe her bed rest."

"Yes, but if that's what she needs—"

My irritation curdled and I turned away, knowing if I remained, I wouldn't be able to stop myself from picking a fight.

Sky would thank me later, I told myself—after I had carried out the dirty work for both of us. As always, I would have to act alone. Since he was so unwilling to get his hands dirty.

As for me, my hands were already stained black.

SIXTEEN

During the Yong Dynasty, lixia masters scoured the land in search of children with strong spirit affinity. Those found worthy were taken to an elite academy in the capital, where they underwent rigorous training in the art of summoning, their talents honed to serve the empire.

—A HISTORY OF LIXIA, 762

IN MY DREAMS, THE EARTH CRIED OUT IN SUFFERING. QI WAS DEpleted from the birds, the sky, the very air itself. Hungry spirits lurked at the edges of my vision, hiding just beyond the thinning veil. Slowly, a crack began to form.

Thunder echoed across the land. Always, my dreams ended right before the lightning struck, before the crack cleaved the veil in two. I woke panting, my undergarments soaked with sweat, my palms streaked with dirt that had not been there the night before. Whatever was happening, it did not concern me, I told myself. The Spring Festival was fast approaching, and my plans were nearly complete.

"THEY'VE ENACTED A CURFEW ON THE CITY," LILY ANNOUNCED. AS THE reports of people succumbing to madness increased, security around the palace tightened. "They've closed the gates leading out of Chuang Ning, so that no one can enter or leave the city. Still, nothing seems to slow the spreading corruption."

Just that week, a scullery maid had allegedly begun behaving erratically. Another maid had noticed and reported her to the guards. But when they'd come for her, she'd somehow convinced them to kill themselves. Finally, a maid had struck her from behind with a frying pan, subduing her.

The string of murders had shaken the palace.

I needed to visit the spirit gates myself, to ascertain if Qinglong really was the one behind all of this. But this concern was only one of many, and I had more pressing matters on my hands. Prince Keyan had returned from Saiya yesterday and spent the evening locked up with Winter. Meanwhile, Prince Yuchen was leaving the palace grounds every evening, and Caihong had informed me that the Imperial Commander's health was increasingly in question.

"How precarious is his condition?" I'd asked Caihong, as we'd strolled through the winter gardens together.

"It is not my place to question the might of great men," she'd said, before lowering her voice. "But he requires the physician's presence daily now, in addition to the protection of over a dozen guards. He is afraid of betrayal from within. And he is even more afraid of death."

Succession was going to happen, regardless of whether he named an heir. I only hoped violence could be avoided.

The Forbidden City itself seemed to understand something was about to happen. The koi fish began hiding beneath bridges, barely emerging for food or sunlight. The winter lily flowers had dried up, and yet spring cherry blossoms were reluctant to take their place, despite the gardeners' most fervent efforts. All the servants who could be spared had left the capital, returning home for the New Year holiday. As for those who remained, they bore the beleaguered look of farmers preparing for a blizzard, trying to carry in their crops before the impending storm.

The morning after Prince Keyan's return, I dressed with particular care, adrenaline thrumming through my veins. Lotus helped me into pale cream robes, which were embroidered with blooming osmanthus flowers. The bodice was tightly fitted, my waist cinched with a silk sash that trailed down the skirt. The sleeves, long and loose, were made of a fine satin so light as to be transparent. My hair was pinned up in several heavy loops to resemble a butterfly's wings, with freshwater pearls scattered throughout to match my robes.

Lily burst through the doors just before breakfast. "Prince Keyan has sent out an official summons—for the entire royal family!"

I frowned at this. I had presumed he would include me, but since Sky and I were not yet married, I was technically not a part of the royal family.

Regardless, I went as if invited.

I arrived at the Hall of Supreme Harmony just as Sky did. "Meilin?" he called, and I turned, giving him my brightest smile.

Taken aback, he scanned me from head to toe, his gaze lingering on my face, carefully painted with cosmetics, and my robes, befitting a princess. He paused, searching for the right words. "You look . . . incredible," he said, before rousing himself as Winter appeared on the stone steps. "What are you doing here? You're not allowed—"

"Let me go with you," I said, taking his hand.

He squeezed it back, before glancing worriedly toward the red columns and the imposing doors beyond. "Father may—"

"He has enough on his plate as it is," said Winter dryly. "I doubt he'll notice. Unless, of course, you plan on making trouble?"

I smiled sweetly at him. "Would I ever?"

Sky shot me a questioning look, but he seemed to trust Winter's opinion on the matter. "If you insist," Sky said, offering me his arm as we ascended the steps. "Though I can't comprehend why you'd want to waste your time witnessing our family drama," he muttered.

"Believe me," I replied cheerily, "I'm used to family drama."

As Prince Yuchen waltzed past us with his usual entourage, Sky tightened his grip on my arm. "This may get ugly," he warned me.

You have no idea, Sky.

THE THRONE ROOM HAD NOT CHANGED SINCE MY LAST VISIT, BUT THE Imperial Commander had. He now sat shrunken against his throne, the grandeur of the golds and reds around him only emphasizing the pallor that had overtaken him. Above his dais, the inscribed golden plaque proclaimed *Establishing the utmost harmony and promoting good governance.* Yet here was a man who had sown only discord—both within the state and within his own household. Now he was paying the price.

As we kowtowed, I inspected him covertly through my lashes. He'd lost weight, and the transformation was stark. Once large and muscular, he now reminded me of a northern snow dog stripped of its fur, revealing a scrawny and misshapen frame underneath.

At his side, Consort Caihong—his current favorite—served him eight-treasure rice, replete with red bean paste, orange slices, kumquats, lychees, and goji berries. Despite its mouthwatering fragrance, he barely picked at his plate.

"Speak," he said to Prince Keyan, who had summoned us today.

"Your Majesty, long may you live," began the crown prince. "As I mentioned in my correspondence, I was initially astonished by the discrepancy in the Saiya gold mine production and the imperial treasury reports. But after investigating the issue, I discovered how the missing funds were being appropriated."

My lip curled at the way Prince Keyan so easily took credit for my work. As expected from a prince.

To my right, Yuchen straightened, his back as stiff as a bamboo scroll. Out of the corner of my eye, I watched Ruihua, who seemed completely unbothered, a deer unaware it stood in a hunter's sights.

"Moreover, after interrogating the Imperial Security Commissioner, I learned that one of my brothers had suddenly come into possession of a gold windfall, and was using the funds to commission an illegal army that would rival the Forbidden City's own imperial guard. Lord Xu, please come forward."

Yuchen's face turned bright red, though he dared not speak.

Lord Xu emerged from between the marble columns. To my horror, he now walked with a limp.

Had Lei tortured him to extract a confession? Just as he'd once tortured me?

"Your Majesty!" Lord Xu cried, pressing his forehead to the floor. "Please forgive this most loyal servant for his shameful weakness. I was coerced into this—I had no choice—"

"Who?" Sky's father demanded, anger reinvigorating his pallid face. He leaned forward, hands clenching the arms of his throne. "Who did this?"

Trembling, Lord Xu rose and turned. Prince Yuchen started to back away. But Lord Xu searched the princes' faces, settling on the one I least expected.

He pointed at Sky.

SEVENTEEN

But the dragon does not lower his head for the stream; the stream rises to meet him.
—LEGENDS OF THE MOUNTAINS, 754

"No," I breathed, as Winter's face drained of color. Sky, meanwhile, looked blankly back at Lord Xu, too bewildered to process fear.

"The seventh prince Sky, Your Majesty," said Lord Xu.

Liu Zhuo took this in, his frown deepening into the grooves of his face. With an almost imperceptible shake of his head, he sat back in his chair. "Guards," he ordered.

"You fool," Winter hissed at Keyan, his eyes like shards of ice. "Did you really believe I wouldn't make copies of the reports I gave you?"

"By then," Keyan said quietly, so that their father would not overhear, "it will be too late."

The Imperial Commander rose to his feet wearily. Consort Caihong rushed to help him, but he waved her off. "Call the executioner," he said to his advisor. "We must make haste, before news reaches the standing army."

I felt my knees buckle. Because the standing army, most of

which had fought during the Three Kingdoms War, would be loyal to Sky.

Everything was falling apart. My carefully crafted plans, which had taken months to engineer, were being dismantled in seconds. Winter could find his copies of the security reports, but would the Imperial Commander listen to words and numbers over the visceral confession of Lord Xu?

I could try to reason with Sky's father, but experience had taught me he would not listen to common sense. No, concerning the treachery of his beloved son, his was an emotional response. There was no reasoning with a man like this.

But I had another way to compel him.

My thoughts racing, I surveyed the throne room, the myriad people surrounding us. The imperial guards, approaching Sky like little boys approaching a wild bear. Some of them had fought by his side, or served under him, and their reluctance was evident in their manner of approach. Then there were the servants, making themselves scarce; the consorts and wives, plotting their own lines of defense; the imperial advisors, whispering and pointing; the princes, distancing themselves from Sky; and the Imperial Commander, who stood like a captain before his ship's helm, scanning the gathering storm beyond.

The storm was about to get worse.

Will you help me? I asked silently. *When our goals are one and the same?*

Qinglong's response was slow, as if coming from a great distance. But when he spoke, I felt his power thrumming through me, the thunder of his voice. *"It's about time a true dragon took the throne."*

Emboldened, I stepped forward. I needed to find a way to get the Imperial Commander alone; compulsion was most effective when focused, and controlling the minds of this great an audience was beyond my power. But securing a private audience with him was no simple task—and he would not agree to it unless I first earned his trust.

"Your Majesty," I said, as the guards reluctantly took hold of Sky.

Sky's glare shifted to me, fear clouding his eyes. "Meilin," he warned, his voice tense.

"You," said Liu Zhuo with a sneer. "I have no use for you anymore. Take her—"

"The traitor is not Prince Sky," I interrupted, and covertly, I drew from my powers to ensure that my voice carried throughout the hall. "The traitor is Prince Keyan, who has been carrying out his own deceptions for over a decade."

Prince Keyan shook his head wearily, seeming to expect this, but I forged on.

"Lady Caihong," I said, meeting her troubled gaze. "Please come forward."

Caihong rose timidly from her seat, her head bowed and her hands tightly folded.

Keyan looked in widening disbelief from me to Caihong. Now his resigned tolerance of me was replaced with loathing. "Ignore her, Father," said Keyan. "She lies to save herself—"

"P-please," Consort Caihong said, and her high-pitched voice, so out of place in the throne room, seemed to startle her audience into a stillness of sorts. "Let me explain."

"It's all a ploy," said Keyan, speaking over her as she tried to address the Imperial Commander. "Don't listen to—"

"Enough!" Liu Zhuo ordered, looking even more tired than before, if that were possible. "Caihong, what is it?"

She prostrated herself before him and I felt my stomach tighten with nerves. I had forced her into the spotlight, which she hated, and made her share what she considered her most hideous secret.

But I had promised her—and myself—I would not let her bear the consequences alone.

"Your Majesty," she said, her voice wavering only a little. "After you elevated me as your consort, I was loyal to you and only you. But Prince Keyan—having long coveted what you possessed—pursued me in secret. After I rejected his advances, he forced himself on me. When I tried to seek help, he blackmailed me, so that I could not tell a soul. Please," she said, and now her voice caught. "Forgive me, my love—"

He backhanded her so hard blood flew from her mouth. I started forward but the guards at the dais raised their swords. He struck her again and Caihong did not so much as lift a finger to defend herself.

"How dare you," he snarled, his breathing heavy as he reached for her throat, "and with my own son—"

"Did you not hear—he forced himself on her! It's not her fault!" I shouted. "*Stop!*"

I did not know if I spoke with compulsion, but the Imperial Commander suddenly went still, dropping Caihong. She crawled away to the edge of the dais, her face streaked with tears.

"You *bitch*—" said Keyan, lunging for her and grabbing her by her hair. But even this act of possession seemed to enrage his father.

"Do not touch her!" he roared.

"Father," said Keyan, backing away. "They are conspiring against me—"

His father's face was altered with rage. I saw now that to Liu Zhuo, there was no deceit more personal than this. Even Sky's supposed treachery paled in comparison. "You don't think I know her? You don't think I know she does not lie?"

Prince Keyan stared open-mouthed, at last understanding that the tides had changed course. "I—please—"

"Get out of my sight."

"Father," he pleaded.

"You are no son of mine," he said. "Get out of my sight now—or I'll murder you where you stand."

Keyan stumbled back. So engrossed was I in their exchange, I did not notice Princess Yifeng until her talon-like nails dug into my shoulder. "I warned you," she breathed, her eyes alight with malice. "You little rat, you'll pay for this—"

I wrenched her off me. "You believe I don't know the scent of poison?" I whispered. Her eyes widened, though I was only bluffing. "I could take you down with your dear husband," I said, "but I'll spare you this time, and this time alone."

Yifeng bared her teeth in a growl. "I won't be cast aside so easily." Her voice carried certain promise. "I'll find my way back, and I'll take my revenge. I don't make idle threats, Lady Hai—you'll learn that soon enough."

She clearly wished to say more, but her husband had already turned on his heel and run, and she had no choice but to chase after him, lest she too attract the Imperial Commander's wrath.

Behind me, Winter whispered a few choice words to the imperial guards, who, though still restraining Sky, did not lead him away. Sky caught my eye and gestured for me to back away from the dais, but I shook my head.

I turned my attention back toward the throne.

"I should kill you," Liu Zhuo was saying, looking down at Caihong prostrating herself before him.

"Please," she begged, her hand grazing his shoe. He flinched and jerked back.

"Don't touch me."

She flinched, as did I, remembering the weight of their collective disgust against me. Liu Zhuo returned to his throne, his face cast with that same disgust, but also unease, and I understood then how much she meant to him.

"Your Majesty," I tried. "None of this was her fault—"

"Silence!" Liu Zhuo interrupted with growing impatience. "Tell me," he said to Caihong, rubbing his forehead. "What would you have me do with you?"

She raised her overbright eyes to him. "Give me the common law's punishment for infidelity, and banish me."

I sucked in a breath. The common law's punishment was a flogging, and a brutal one at that. For men it was thirty strokes, for women it was fifteen. But in her state, as delicate as she was . . .

"Very well," said Liu Zhuo, his eyes closing briefly. "It will be done as you have said—"

"I will take her punishment," I blurted, the words escaping before I could even think.

I felt the weight of countless eyes turning toward me, whispers spreading and fingers pointing in my direction. I ignored them, focusing on Liu Zhuo.

"Very well," he said, infinitesimal relief crossing his face. "Handle it with all due speed. I want this matter resolved and dismissed."

A guard came forward to bind my wrists. The sight of rope in his hands made my ears begin to ring.

"I only have one request, Your Majesty," I said quickly. "In return for bringing this matter to light."

His face darkened with irritation. "Have you overlooked how precarious your own position is, Lady Hai? Do not think I have forgotten your previous deception."

"All I request, Your Majesty, is a private audience with you."

He sneered. "You think I'd agree to meet with you alone—"

"I am but a woman," I replied. "I carry no weapons and harbor no ill will. But if Your Majesty still seeks to maintain utmost caution," I continued, "let it be immediately after the flogging, when it will be impossible for me to pose any threat. Your Majesty, I simply wish to speak with you, without the interference of others."

Consort Caihong nodded. "She means no harm, Your Majesty."

And he was right; she had never been a liar. I had assured her that I did not mean to harm the Imperial Commander, only to speak with him, and she had believed me.

Yet words could cut sharper than any blade.

"Very well," he agreed, after studying Caihong's expression.

A wooden post was brought out, which I was swiftly bound to. As the first bamboo cane struck my back, I bit back a cry, my nails digging into my palms. The second lash came on the heels of the first, and my breath caught at the shock of it, the way pain never failed to amaze me.

The third sliced open my skin, and as tears stung my eyes, the horrified faces of the royal family blurred before me. "*You're a perversion.*" I heard General Huyi's voice in my ears.

Another lash: "*You thought you could become squad leader? You'll never be good enough.*"

I lost count, my thoughts clouded with pain. My mind, ever a creature of habit, drifted back to well-worn memories.

Luo Tao's eyes glittering with malice. "*Hai Ren is a liar and a traitor.*"

Princess Yifeng laughing over me. "*Your greed is astounding. Despite breaking every rule imaginable, you still came out with* everything."

Then the bamboo cane struck my left shoulder, which had never fully recovered after the war, and a scream ripped from my throat, the ghost of the old wound resurfacing. I was going to black out, and then I would lose my chance to speak with the Imperial

Commander. Sky would be executed for a crime he did not commit. Yuchen would seize upon his stroke of good fortune. And I would be imprisoned, put to death, forgotten.

My legacy would be one of ruin.

The pain threatened to swallow me whole, darkness pressing at the edges of my vision. And yet, in the midst of my despair, I sensed the presence of another, anchoring me against oblivion. I raised my head and found Sky's eyes locked on mine, filled with a bleak, unspoken understanding.

I had regretted making Sky watch, but now his presence became an indispensable comfort, for he knew my most private of pains. As the guard caned my shoulder once more, I stifled my cries, yet Sky winced all the same. He knew each of my vulnerabilities, the weaknesses I tried to conceal in the dark of night. The pain was tremendous, but he shared it with me, and somehow that made it just a little more bearable.

Distantly, I realized the lashes had ended, some time ago, and someone was untying me now. I swayed, on the verge of collapse, before remembering my lixia and using it to anchor my life force. *Wood, fire, earth, metal, water,* I whispered silently, circling through each element as my jade heated against my skin. Always, I had held something back; I had kept a part of myself free from the influence of lixia. But now I felt even those vestiges slipping, unable to resist the tipping scales.

No one noticed; no one apart from Winter, who watched me with guarded eyes. He approached slowly, offering me his cloak to hide my torn robes.

My qi was dangerously spent, as dry as the Runong Desert, and testing it felt like trying to catch smoke in my hands. Ignoring every warning I'd read on the necessity of balance, I allowed my lixia to fill the void left by my depleted qi, letting it assume complete control. I could not afford to fail, not now, not this close to victory.

"*Let my power heal you,*" murmured the dragon.

But I no longer needed to consent. Without lifting a finger, I felt the wounds on my back knit together, returning my skin to its smooth, unblemished state. The dragon sighed with contentment, and his pleasure became mine.

I felt, for the first time, invincible.

"Your Majesty," I said, clutching Winter's overlarge cloak around my shoulders. "If you please."

He waved one hand in the air. To the rest of the room: "Leave us."

Slowly, everyone cleared the room, grumbling to themselves but obeying the order all the same. I did not watch them go. All my willpower was fixed on Liu Zhuo, who lounged before me on his dais with a shadowed, dour expression.

Up close, his eyes appeared haunted, as if possessed by a hungry ghost. Was it my imagination, or could I feel Chancellor Sima's presence in the room with us, returned to torment him until his vengeance was complete?

"You have five minutes," he said, his voice skeptical. He had never been convinced by my performance, but after all my scheming he trusted me enough to warrant five minutes alone.

Five minutes was all I needed.

Though the reminder of Chancellor Sima should have been a deterrent, instead, the memory lent me strength. For our mental manipulations had been equally matched, despite his superior skill in other regards. Compulsion was my strength.

"Your Majesty, long may you live," I began, taking a step closer to him. He tensed but did not move.

The war had aged him prematurely. He remained a proud,

arrogant man, but he'd begun to realize his own limitations. More than present contentment, he sought to leave behind a legacy of greatness. Thus, most of his waking thoughts were devoted to the future—how to maintain the esteem of the people, the strength of the dynasty, the honor of Anlai. He'd pardoned me not because of his son's love, which he saw as a passing infatuation, but rather, to curb the growing dissatisfaction of the common people. His time was almost over, he could feel it in his bones, but in the legacy he left behind, he thought he could live forever.

I could use that against him.

"The burden on your shoulders is a heavy one. The kingdom is at its most vulnerable—and your sons each have their own schemes in mind." I took a breath, letting lixia fill my lungs. "*But there is only one prince who will uphold the legacy of your greatness—who will lead Anlai into a new age of prosperity and peace, and who, above all else, will establish your dynasty as the greatest that ever was. You know which son I speak of.*"

My voice echoed with spirit power. I had never let lixia subsume me so completely, and now, throwing caution to the winds, a dangerous thrill ran down my spine. The dragon's power had never felt more potent within me, and with every word I spoke, I could see Liu Zhuo's eyes falling into a mindless haze of wonder and belief.

"*Name Prince Sky as your successor, and consent to our union,*" I said. "*Then you will gain the legacy you have always dreamed of. Your name will be spoken for centuries to come, and your ancestors will worship you with gladness in their hearts. But you must name Prince Sky as your heir, for if you do not, the other princes will only destroy your empire with strife and discord.*"

I could hear Qinglong's voice speaking through me, overpowering my own. I could feel his presence in the room, like an impending typhoon. Our wills were one and the same. Just as I was near victory, so too was he. He could return to his former glory, no longer bound to the prison of the spirit realm. He could roam free, master of both humans and spirits. Like in the days of old, the people would fall to their knees in worship and desire. All would be his again. Both here and beyond the veil.

Very soon, it would all be his.

I startled awake, my consciousness sliding back to me. The Imperial Commander was speaking, but I had not heard him.

"—it is true," he was saying. "For I have long doubted Keyan's filial piety, and Yuchen is an inept, weak-willed child. Sky is popular among the people, and the war has proven his leadership and strength in battle. And with you by his side . . ." He frowned, the haze temporarily lifting from his eyes.

I strengthened the force of my will. *"You will consent to our union."*

His expression tempered. "Lady Hai," he said, his voice ruminative. "You and I have not always seen eye to eye, but I am not so prideful a man as to ignore the shifting spirit of our times. Help my son root out the blight of black magic spreading across the kingdom, and I will permit your union with my heir."

He stood, sounding a gong at the foot of the throne. He struck it three times, the vibrations resounding throughout the hall, and the doors were thrown open as his imperial advisors, guards, and family poured in.

"I have made my decision—I have chosen my successor," said the Imperial Commander, rising to his feet. Consort Caihong, to my left, gasped in astonishment. Princess Ruihua swooned, several servants rushing to fan her on the floor. And in the very back, Sky stood motionless, surrounded by guards. He was the only one not watching the Imperial Commander. He was watching me.

Silently, I made my way to the back to stand beside him.

"Your wounds—" Sky began, in a low voice.

"The dragon healed me," I whispered. "I'm perfectly fine now."

"How—"

I shushed him, before his rudeness prompted his father to reconsider his decision.

"But, Your Majesty," one of his advisors was protesting, "you cannot—"

"You dare contradict me?" Liu Zhuo demanded, and his advisor fell silent, though he trembled with frustration. This was probably about to become a bureaucratic nightmare of paperwork.

But he had made up his mind. "Send forth the decree: once the Three Kingdoms Treaty is signed and the threat of demon corruption eliminated, I will agree to step down as Imperial Commander." His gaze swept across the room, before settling on his youngest son at the very back. "Prince Sky," he said, and the crowd seemed to shift, heads swiveling in unison like a flock of birds in flight.

Sky met their stares with unexpected composure, and I recalled his immovable calm in the face of battle.

His father cleared his throat, caught off guard by a sudden surge of emotion. "You, my seventh yet strongest son, will be named as my chosen heir."

EIGHTEEN

They say when a man dies seeking vengeance, the gods may show him favor and return him as a ghost, haunting those who wronged him. Thus, men must tread carefully on the path of justice, for a vengeful ghost will not rest until it sees its enemy fall.

—BOOK OF RITES, 829

Sky and I spilled out into the open-air gallery like giggling schoolchildren. Despite the cold, our pace was leisurely as we crossed the courtyard leading out of the Hall of Supreme Harmony. I felt a light tingle on my cheek and looked up at the sky. "It's snowing!"

Sky followed my gaze and laughed, picking me up and twirling me in the air. "The skies are smiling down on us," he whispered in my ear, which was turning red from cold. He kissed the rim of my ear and then my nose, and then at last, my hungry mouth. "I love you," he said, his mouth hovering just over mine. "I've loved you since the day I met you in the Wenxi market, when you saved my life with a blacksmith's pole. Since then, you've given me life a hundred times over."

"Only a hundred?" I asked, laughing. Despite the falling snow, the sun had started to peek out behind the clouds, as if joining in on our happy occasion. As I squinted up at Sky, my face in direct sunlight, Sky saw and shifted, turning me so that he took the sun's glare.

"A thousand," he murmured. "For there is no living without you."

"Don't say that," I said, growing uneasy. Although the Imperial Commander had reversed his sentence, there were other decisions that could not be so easily reversed. I dreaded the physician's exam I had consented to, which would be my first since I'd left the dungeons.

"I mean it," said Sky, his eyes flashing stubbornly. "Meilin, there is no life without you. No, listen to me." He held me still and forced me to meet his gaze. "Next time you risk your life, know that you risk mine. Because our fates are tied together now, forever."

He meant it lovingly, but his declaration felt like a noose around my throat. Had I gotten what I wanted, I wondered, or had I gotten what *he* wanted? For that matter, what did I even want?

Could I imagine myself living out my days in the Forbidden City, maneuvering around and against attempts at public humiliation, allegations of illicit affairs, and even the occasional assassination effort? Defending Sky as he succeeded his father on the throne, and took over the reins of the wealthiest and most powerful kingdom in all of Tianjia?

You want this, a sly voice whispered in my mind. *Of course you do.*

"Meilin?" Sky asked, his hands tightening on my wrists. Why did his hands suddenly feel like manacles? And hadn't I had enough of those?

I buried my face in his chest, so reliably warm and solid. With my ear pressed to his robes, I could hear the gentle thud of his heart, which was so dear to me I protected it as my own. Wasn't that what love was? Then I loved Sky. And yet, when asked to hand over my entire future to him, to reduce the wide expanse of possible roads and possibilities before me to one narrow, treacherous path, I found myself hesitating.

The snow falling on my back grew insistent. When one drop fell on the nape of my exposed neck, I realized it was rain. Raising my head in bewilderment, I saw that—despite the radiant sunshine, or perhaps because of it—the snow had morphed into rain.

"Father Sun is crying," I told Sky.

"Hm?" he said, toying with my rain-drenched hair.

"The legend of the Sun Daughter," I said, gazing up at the sparkling rain, which looked lit from within by sunlight. "The daughter of the sun loved the god of rain, but her father did not approve of the match in heaven. He arranged a different marriage for her, but in the days leading up to the wedding, she grew so lovesick that she wasted away and died. Now when the sun shines on rain, Father Sun is honoring the memory of his dearly departed daughter."

Sky laughed. "Wherever did you hear such a tale? In the story I always heard, the sun finally relented and gave his daughter to the god of rain. When rain falls on a sunny day, the daughter of the sun is visiting her father."

"Which one is it?" I asked him. "Is he mourning or laughing?"

"It's whatever you want it to be," said Sky teasingly. "Should we ask the god of rain what he thinks?"

Rain dripped from Sky's temples and nose, but he grinned, shaking himself like a wet dog. I laughed at him, at his ill-mannered behavior. But as he raked his glistening hair back from his forehead, the strong, aristocratic planes of his face catching the sunlight, I felt a low swoop of desire in my stomach. As if he sensed my change in mood, his eyes roved over me, skipping from my loose hair, which had fallen out of its pins, to my drenched dress, which I suddenly noticed clung indecently to the curves of my body. The silk of my ruqun, which had always been delicate, was now near transparent in the rain, exposing the shape of my breasts.

His eyes were a haze of desire. "I love you," he murmured, closing the space between us. "I want you."

"Where can we go?" I whispered.

Sky led me to his rooms with an alacrity that rivaled his wartime urgency. He'd removed his jacket to cover me but refused to let me walk on my own, as if expecting hungry wolves to come and snatch me away. By the time the guards had been dismissed and the doors locked, his face was alight with desire.

I was shivering from cold and eagerness. I huddled against Sky's warmth, trembling too hard to untie my own clothes. Sky stilled my hands and undid my sash himself, carefully peeling my wet robes back from my damp shoulders. The silk crumpled in a pool at my feet.

Sky took me in silently, my body rosy from firelight and nerves. My nipples were peaked from cold, my skin lined with gooseflesh. After I had bound my breasts for so long during the war, they had never regained their youthful shape. I started to cover myself with a self-conscious hand, but he stopped me, gazing at me with unabashed wonder.

That was the thing about Sky. You always knew exactly what he was feeling.

"You're beautiful," he breathed.

I smiled up at him, believing him for the first time.

Now I tore hungrily at his clothes, anxious to see the body that was at once both familiar and foreign to me. Familiar because I'd caught him shirtless many times during the war. Foreign because it had never belonged to me. Now I studied him as if I owned him. The solidity of his chest, which was so hard and pale his skin looked like honed marble. The strength of his thighs, which clamped around me as he pinned me to his bed and climbed atop me. If before he had kissed me gently, now he kissed as if trying to possess me, claiming my body as he savored my throat, my breasts, the curve of my waist and hips. The desire once contained to his eyes had taken over his entire being, lending him a savage, bestial quality. I thought I had known all there was to know about him, but here was a side I had never seen before, a side of him that was neither noble nor princely.

When I rose on my elbows to kiss him, he cupped a supporting hand around my left shoulder, knowing it remained weaker than the other. Sky hadn't forgotten my old injury from the war; he had recognized how much it still pained me. The thought was like fresh water down a parched throat. I had once believed pain to be private. But now I understood even your suffering could be shared, when someone knew you, knew the entirety of you—the secrets of your hidden hurts and old scars, the fears that kept you restless at night, the way you said one thing but truly meant another.

He eased my shoulder back onto the pillow before bracing himself over me. His eyes were made strange by lust, but still, he was himself. He was the friend who had trained with me every night under the flickering torchlight, who had nursed me back to health after I'd fallen ill with fever, who had kissed me at the front of the anniversary parade, before his father and his family and the cheering hordes of people. Everything he did, he did with intensity. And I, like a creature left out in the cold, found myself drawn to the warmth and brilliance of his temperament.

"Meilin?" he whispered.

"Yes?"

"Can—"

But before he could ask, an abrupt knock sounded against the bedroom door.

"Your Highness," said his manservant Hanbing.

"I told you I was not to be disturbed!" Sky snarled with uncharacteristic impatience.

Hanbing coughed. "It's your mother." Even through the door, I could hear the discomfort in his tone. "She wishes to see you." A pause. "It was not a request."

Sky groaned and rolled off me before going into the adjoining washroom. I heard the sound of water splashing in the basin, before he emerged several minutes later, cheeks still flushed but otherwise sober-minded.

"You should get changed," he told me. "My mother can be . . . nosy."

Now it was my turn to sigh. He left first, and although he kept his voice low, I could hear the bickering nature of their discussion.

I had no desire to meet Sky's mother like this. But conversations of this sort would soon become my duty as Sky's wife.

Sky's *wife*. The first consort of the Imperial Commander. The words were so foreign they felt like an entirely different language. As if I couldn't understand the meaning of them. As if I couldn't even form the syllables in my mouth.

Fear twisted like a serpent in my stomach.

You want this. You want this more than anything else in the world. Remember, that's why you fought so hard for the throne. So you'll never be forced to kowtow again. So you'll never see your name defamed in the official reports, the credit for your hard work stolen by another.

So you'll be remembered as your own person, by your own hand.

It was no longer the dragon's voice in my head. No—it was my own.

As I left the room, I did not wonder why the two had begun to sound the same.

NINETEEN

One must remain vigilant in preserving qi as a summoner. For when a spirit depletes their vessel entirely of his life force, full control becomes inevitable. In such a state, the spirit may manipulate their human vessel as a puppet master commands a marionette. Thus, death is the only escape.
—LOST JOURNALS OF AN 8TH-CENTURY LIXIA SCHOLAR, DATE UNKNOWN

THE NEXT DAY, WITH WINTER'S HELP, I MADE CERTAIN CONSORT Caihong made it safely out of the city. She was to travel with a wealthy marchioness who was returning to her hometown in eastern Anlai. Consort Caihong, who would now be simply known as Caihong, would serve as her lady-in-waiting. She was vastly overqualified and far too pretty for the comfort of most noble ladies, but the marchioness was wealthy and widowed, and she claimed Caihong's beauty was a feast for the eyes.

On the morning we parted, Caihong wore plain gray linen robes, nothing like the fine attire she'd once donned as imperial consort. And yet her beauty was so brilliant it felt like staring into the sun. I wanted to say this, to compliment her, but I wondered if she'd grown tired of being praised for her looks.

"You look well," I said instead.

"I'm nervous," she confessed in a low voice, as we waited for the marchioness to climb into her carriage.

A bit shyly, I offered her my hand in parting, and was gratified when she accepted it.

"I was too, when I left home," I told her. "But I don't regret my decision for a day." I squeezed her clammy hand. "Your story is only beginning."

She nodded, before the marchioness poked her head out the window to shoo Caihong inside. The last I saw of her were her bright eyes, luminous with hope and expectation. I hoped they would stay that way.

I waited until her carriage pulled away before returning to the palace. I had lied to her, though I hadn't meant to. There were days I regretted my decision, wondering how much simpler life would have been if I'd stayed at home and married Master Zhu as my father had ordered. I would not have so much blood and violence and death on my hands. I would not have to live with the tremendous consequences of my mistakes. To know that hundreds if not thousands of people were falling ill or starving or mourning loved ones—all because of what we'd done in the war. All because of choices I had made, or failed to make, decisions I might never truly know were right or wrong.

But that was the price of power, wasn't it? That was what I had bid for, vied for, fought for, and that was what I had finally claimed as my own. I had taken my prize—and with it, the curse of winning.

BEFORE MY APPOINTMENT WITH THE PALACE PHYSICIAN, I NERVOUSLY picked at my congee, barely managing to swallow a few bites. Sky monitored my lackluster attempts before finally allowing me to leave for the examination room on an empty stomach.

The first assessment was routine. With Sky's permission, Master Qian had me undress, measuring various parts of my body. He tsked at the new bruises that had formed on my arms—I chalked them up to sword practice, though I didn't remember how I'd gotten them. After physical measurements, he listened to my heart rate, counting each pulse, and pricked my finger, testing the viscosity of my blood.

Hopefully, I watched Master Qian's expression, reading the dip of his mouth like a weatherman reads the skies. He expressed pleasant surprise at my physical recovery, the weight I'd put on, the color I'd regained.

A knock on the door interrupted the examination. Sky frowned at the delay, and Master Qian apologized profusely, explaining that he'd told his apprentice not to permit any visitors. But the visitors were acceded to once they'd made themselves known. For it could not have been a more peculiar pair that walked through the door: Liu Winter and Cao Ming Lei.

"WHAT ARE YOU DOING WITH HIM?" SKY DEMANDED, AS I HASTILY FIN-ished tying my robe around my waist.

"Your Highness," said Lei, inclining his head. "I hear congratulations are in order."

As Lei entered the room, Sky stepped in front of me, shielding me from view. "Get out," he said.

"Why the paranoia?" Lei asked smilingly. "Afraid she'll change her mind if she sees me?"

Sky's hands clenched into fists. I touched his arm, standing. I had not seen the Ximing prince in weeks, ever since the night we'd spied on Lord Xu together. "Why are you here?" I asked Lei. *Why are you here, when you've been avoiding me all this time?*

Lei's piercing eyes seemed to bore into mine, and I shifted uneasily. He'd always possessed an uncanny ability to guess the hidden motives of others. Now I wondered if he was reading my mind, or if I was simply imagining it.

As if he heard me, he smiled.

The back of my neck prickled.

"Pardon the interruption," said Winter. "Master Qian, could you give us the room?"

"Of—of course," said Master Qian, though he colored at the request. To add insult to injury, when he opened the door to leave, standing outside was another man dressed as a physician, whom Lei beckoned forward.

"As you know, Anlai is advanced in traditional medicinal arts but lacking in the specialization of lixia treatment," said Winter. "Lei has kindly sent for a Ximing physician who specializes in the treatment of lixia-induced disorders. Master Yan can examine Lady Hai's—"

"This is the lixia specialist you mentioned?" Sky glared daggers at his brother. "You think I'd let some Ximing snake anywhere near—"

"Sky," I said. "I trust him."

I did not trust Lei to help out of altruism, but I trusted him to help when our objectives aligned. He had visited me in prison, stolen my seal for me, and even helped Sky secure the throne, though Sky did not know this. I trusted Lei did not want me dead, most likely because alive I played some part in his convoluted schemes.

Lei's eyes flicked to mine. "Will you submit to the examination?"

A knot of fear clogged my throat.

Deep down, I knew something was terribly wrong with me. My qi was depleted, my memories missing, and my chest ever hollow, as if gnawed by an aching void that refused to go away.

I had avoided seeing a physician for months, choosing to hide in the comfort of false hope. But as I met Lei's knowing gaze now, I saw the foolishness of my denial. No amount of ignorance could stop what was already in motion, and hiding from my diagnosis was nothing but cowardice. The only path to healing was to face the truth, no matter how wretched.

I took a small, reluctant step forward. Sky shot me a look, as if to say *Stay out of this.*

This infuriated me—we were talking about *my* health, after all. Ignoring his mounting anger, I stepped around him toward the lixia specialist. "I consent."

"You will do no such thing," Sky said, seizing me by my arm. His hand closed over my newest bruise, and I gasped sharply in pain.

Winter lifted an appraising brow. Lei's face turned cold, expressionless. And Sky—though I could not see him—I could feel him, feel the heat radiating off his body, his trembling hand, clenched on my arm, the weight of his indecision and hatred and fear. Because I knew him; I knew it was fear that made him behave this way. Fear for me, for my safety.

Slowly, he released me.

"What do you need me to do?" I asked the physician.

"Please sit on the examination table, Lady Hai, and drink this," said Master Yan, offering me a newly mixed herbal drink. The smell was foul, but I gulped it down.

Too late, I realized the tea's purpose was to help me relax. I felt my eyelids flutter as Master Yan eased me back onto the examination table. "What are you . . ." My words slurred together as my tongue refused to cooperate. My increasingly heavy eyelids begged to rest. I let them fall shut—just for a moment, I told myself.

Distantly, I heard Master Yan chant a sutra over me, and I felt a burning sensation that began in my chest, before spreading through my veins across my entire body. I heard a collective inhalation of breath and blinked open one eye; to my amazement, gleaming threads of elemental light floated in the air above my body, in a way that I'd seen only once before—in the space between realms, when I'd dueled Sima Yi. I could see threads of water, metal, and fire in my bloodstream, but frighteningly, water had spread to dominate the others.

"It is natural to contain some level of elemental imbalance," said Master Yan. "However, as you can see here, overuse of lixia heightens the natural imbalance found in our bodies, intensifying the overrepresented elements and leading to further polarity."

He exhaled, chanting another sutra, or perhaps the same one. His hands, which were raised in the air as if holding an invisible sphere, began to shake. The glowing lights above me shifted, growing dimmer as what looked like black mold spread across each thread. Slowly, lights began to wink out.

"This is the effect of lixia overuse on her life force. Like yin and yang, lixia and qi balance each other and keep the realms in equilibrium. But while lixia can imbue humans with power, it is also unnatural to the body, and given time, dependence and addiction will poison and corrupt from within. As you can see, her wood and earth threads have already been consumed in entirety. I'm sorry to say..."

Despite my attempts to pay attention, my eyelids fluttered shut. So I nearly missed Sky's interruption, if not for the release of the burning sensation in my chest. "Let's talk outside," Sky said quietly.

I imagined sitting upright to tell them no, stay. To tell them that I couldn't be bothered to stand. But then I understood they weren't waiting for me. They were talking about me, without me. As the door closed and the murmur of indecipherable voices continued outside, I felt the ache of betrayal in my throat. I tried to rise; I imagined the act of rising; and yet perhaps I was as helpless as they made me out to be. The medicine taking effect, I succumbed to sleep.

I WOKE FROM A BAD DREAM, GROGGY AND DISORIENTED. SQUINTING AT the stark white walls surrounding me, I stood and felt a cramp shooting up my leg. How long had I slept for? Why was sunlight coming in through the window? And why did I feel so horribly weak?

My right wrist was uncomfortably heavy. I raised my hand—and caught sight of the gleaming iron band locked around my wrist.

Panic started in my throat before surging through the rest of my body. Without thinking, I bashed my wrist against the edge of the table. Of course the iron did not budge. I ignored the stinging pain, the angry red welts left on my skin. I brought it down again, and again, using more and more force until the wood cracked beneath me. Still the iron did not budge.

The pain was but a distraction. I could feel a far crueler agony spreading through my chest—an aching lack where my spirit power had once been. I could not survive without the dragon's presence, without the weight of lixia to sustain me.

Reaching for my jade, I tried to steady my thoughts. *Think rationally, Meilin.* Sky would have given the key to Zibei. All I needed to do was find him.

Limping to the door, I twisted the knob.

It did not open.

"Sky?" I rasped, but my voice did not carry.

Why was I locked inside? Why had everyone forgotten about me? I was taken back to the war, when I had rescued Sky and Sparrow and Tao, only for them to flee without me. They had left me behind. They were free, but I would remain in chains.

The injustice of life never failed to astound me.

Circulate your qi. Uncle Zhou's instructions rang in my head as I sank to the cold floor. He had taught me qi gong after I'd begun experiencing panic attacks in the wake of my mother's passing. Now I tried to follow his instructions, and yet I could no longer feel the pulse of my qi. My life force felt thin, weak, like a riverbed in the thick of summer. The barest trickle of water ran down the rocks, soon to be subsumed by sand.

The door opened. I rushed toward Sky, only—it was not Sky, but his brother.

A crease marked the space between Winter's brows. Although he maintained his composure, there was something unsettled about him, like the air before a typhoon. "You're awake," he said, with some surprise.

"Where's Sky?" I asked him, accepting the cup of hot tea he handed me. I cupped the porcelain between my palms, letting it warm my skin. Skies, why was I so cold?

"He's . . ." Winter hesitated, which was unusual for him. "Indisposed."

I was too tired to decipher what that meant. As I drank the bitter tea, my heart rate steadied, and my racing thoughts slowed.

"I would keep that on, if I were you," said Winter, eyeing the iron band. "As disagreeable as it is, it may offset your growing lixia addiction."

Addiction? I thought, repulsed. Addiction was a disorder that belonged entirely to my father—his habit for opium, his weakness for gambling. I had spent my entire life trying to separate myself from him, trying to run as far from his legacy as I possibly could. And yet here I was, my father's daughter.

For the past few months, every waking thought had been fixed on securing the throne. Now, without the dragon's voice in my head, my mind was startlingly empty. A barren wasteland.

I took another sip of tea, and my sleeves slipped past my elbows, exposing my pallid forearms and the purple-black veins that ran beneath. Under Winter's gaze I flushed and hastily adjusted my sleeves. But he did not look frightened of me. He looked as if he saw me—and saw the worst.

In his eyes was none of the steadfast optimism that Sky expressed. Instead, I was confronted by bleak cynicism.

"You understand, don't you?" I asked quietly. I had always felt an implicit connection between us, though we'd never bridged the gap to a closer friendship. Always there was Sky between us, Sky speaking, Sky asking, Sky directing. The youngest Anlai prince was someone who brought people together, but also kept people apart. There was too much life and spirit and energy to him, so that when he was in the room, all attention could be fixed only on him.

Winter and I both preferred to act in the dark. But now, as I watched his closed expression, the polite mask he wore around me, I wondered if this distancing between us had not been intentional. Although he had saved my life on multiple occasions, he maintained a clear distinction between ally and friend.

"Do you know," said Winter, "I was offered a spirit seal once?"

I looked at him, uncomprehending. I wondered if I was still dreaming. "You made a bargain with a spirit?"

He smiled mirthlessly, smoothing his robes and taking a seat on the low settee across from me.

"No," he said. "I turned her down."

I sat back in astonishment. There were few recorded instances of humans being confronted with a spirit bargain—and refusing the offer. I could only think of the Great Warrior Guan Yang, but even he'd given in after multiple rejections.

I looked at Winter anew. Seated as he was on the low settee, he had to look up to catch my gaze, but this seating arrangement did not seem to irk him. Instead, he looked comfortable lounging beneath me, without concern for hierarchy or social convention.

"Why?" I said at last.

"I understood I wasn't strong enough to withstand the sway of power. I understood it would change me irrevocably." He lifted one shoulder. "Sure, I wish I could fight sometimes. I wish I could make those I hate cower in fear. But I like my life as it is. I like it too much to give it up."

It was that simple, wasn't it? When confronted with the past or the future, with safety or risk, too often we chose the future, thinking this was bravery. But Winter had looked at his life and thought, *I am well pleased with this. And I need nothing more.*

If Winter knew the cost of power, then he knew I was paying it now.

"There are ways in which I've . . . *changed*," I said cautiously, treading on uneven ground. "You know I'm not the same person I was when I first met Sky." I swallowed, trying to ease the dryness in my mouth. "But I'm not sure he recognizes that."

Winter looked out the window, exposing the high planes of his cheekbones to me. He reminded me of a great migratory bird, a wild swan perhaps, or a river crane. Elegant, lovely to look at, yet impossible to pin down.

"My brother's gift, as frustrating as it may be, is his propensity to hope. He will always believe in the best possible outcome; so much so that I've seen his untenable belief manifest in reality." Winter smiled, lost in a memory I would never know. "He's always had luck on his side."

Was it luck, or something much simpler—good looks, wealth, an affectionate mother who told him he deserved the world? Not for the first time, I could not tell if it was admiration or envy that I felt toward my former commander.

"Give him time," said Winter, rising to his feet and taking the empty cup from my hand. "He'll come around." His tone was polite, and I did not know if he truly believed his own words, or if they were merely pithy remarks meant to comfort a lost cause. I recognized that he was returning distance between us again. It did not matter how much he understood me and the effects of spirit power; he would always choose his little brother over me.

A wave of exhaustion overcame me after that, and I slept like the dead, awakening only to a low murmur in my ear. I felt gentle hands lift me, carrying me down the stairs. Recognizing the shape of him, I fitted my head against his shoulder and slept.

I WOKE AGAIN, THIS TIME IN MY OWN BED. SKY WAS COMPOSING A LETter by my bedside.

"What happened?" I asked him, my voice coming out hoarse.

Sky's hand moved to cover the letter.

"Nothing you need to concern yourself with," he said, but I could see the tension in his face, the strain around his eyes that did not ease even when he tried to smile. He'd never known how to lie. "Rest, Meilin."

"But it's day," I said, looking past him to the open window, where gardeners were trimming the rosebushes and cleaning the lily pond. "I need water," I said to myself, but before I could push off my blankets Sky had already crossed the room to pour me a drink.

I thought of the last drink I'd had—the bitter tea Winter had given me. Had it been sleep-inducing? "Did your brother drug me?" I demanded, struggling to dredge up my anger. I should be angry. I was tired of being drugged and coddled and handled like a child who couldn't take care of herself. I was tired of being misled by those I considered my friends. Yet overwhelmingly I was exhausted, and even the effort of maintaining my anger felt too wearisome.

Sky handed me a clear cup of water, which I inspected thoroughly. I took a small sip. It was water.

"Happy?" he said, but with none of his usual sarcasm. Instead, he smoothed the blankets back over my legs, then rested one hand over my ankle. When he caught me staring, he reluctantly removed his hand.

"Do you need anything else?" he asked me.

"Why are you treating me like an invalid?" I demanded. "What did the physician say?"

His face heated; he would not look at me. "Nothing."

"You've always been a terrible liar."

Sky smoothed my blankets a second time. I had never seen him so evasive; he'd always been one to face problems head-on.

"I-I think it's best you stay home for now."

"But . . ." I processed this. "You mentioned you had a new lead on the spirit gates?"

He gave a curt nod. "A seer told my father he could find a powerful weapon in the Reed Flute Caves."

Privately, I wasn't convinced. No sword could stand against the might of spirit power. But all I said was "When do you leave?"

His face looked even more pained. "Tomorrow."

"I'm coming with—"

"No." His hands clenched into fists around my blankets. "You will remain here."

"I'm not going to live my life waiting at your beck and—"

"Meilin—" he said, his voice breaking on a strangled note. It was so bizarre I paused, peering at him. His eyes were overbright.

"Are you crying?" I asked, bewildered.

He turned away, rubbing at his eyes angrily.

"Sky?"

Abruptly he rose from my side, pacing the length of the room. I got out of bed and realized I was in my nightclothes, though I couldn't remember changing. Already my memories from this morning were hazy.

"Sky," I said. "Look at me. I'll keep up with you, I promise—"

Sky swung toward me and I braced myself as if preparing to be struck. Instead his arms came around me as he buried his face in my chest, like he was seeking comfort. Nonplussed, I patted him on the back. He only gripped me harder, as if certain someone was about to pry me away.

"Sky ... what's wrong?"

"I'll do anything to make you stay," he whispered. "I just never know how to sway you."

Because he was not Lei, I mused, who knew how to persuade and manipulate until you no longer trusted even your own thoughts. I thought of how Sky had tried to find the missing jade during the Three Kingdoms War, how he'd marched up to a crew of Ximing sailors and expected their total honesty. As if you need only ask, and the world would provide.

Still, something about me staying in the Forbidden City mattered to him, though I could not say why. I had never seen him so distressed.

"Will you stay?" I asked selfishly, capitalizing on his anguish. People were dying out there, and Sky was trying to save them. But I wanted him for myself.

Sky hesitated, only for a moment. "All right," he agreed. "I'll stay until the festivities end," he amended, for the new year began tomorrow. "Then I must depart for the peace talks."

The treaty would be signed at First Crossing, the connecting point between the Three Kingdoms.

I kissed him on the soft underside of his jaw, where I'd once held a blade to his throat. We had our share of fights, I thought, but it was only because we both cared so deeply. It didn't matter that he didn't understand me. It was enough that he cared for me.

He cupped my cheek and guided my face up to meet his. I pressed myself hungrily against him, craving the hardness and heat of his body. A low sound rumbled at the back of his throat as he anchored my hips against his and crushed his mouth over mine, tasting me as if it was the last time he ever could. When I gasped for breath, his lips left mine to follow the line of my neck, finding the pulse at my throat, worshipping it.

"I'm going to protect you," he whispered, his breath warm against my skin. "I'm going to keep you safe."

He repeated these words like a mantra, over and over again, and by the way his hands held me, reverently, I wondered if he also said them as a prayer, as if by speaking them aloud, he could make them somehow come true.

TWENTY

Long ago, there lived a fearsome beast who hungered for the laughter of children. He terrorized the villages at the turning of each year, until one winter, a young boy set fire to a string of bright-cracking sparks, and the beast fled in terror. From that day forth, the people dressed in red and lit firecrackers at the dawn of each year to keep the beasts at bay.

—BOOK OF RITES, 829

THE SPRING FESTIVAL WAS THE LARGEST HOLIDAY OF THE YEAR. Every person in Anlai, from the wealthiest merchant to the lowliest butcher, celebrated the occasion, which ushered in the new year with festivity and grandeur. Past grievances were set aside, and new vows sworn. Old graves were cleaned, and new babies swathed. Chuang Ning, which boasted countless migrants, saw a significant outflow as many left the capital to reunite with their families in the surrounding villages. But the ones who stayed stayed for the spectacle.

The Forbidden City was never so grand as it was during the Spring Festival. Paper lanterns hung from every low-hanging eave, and red peonies lined every doorway, so that the air smelled sweet and redolent no matter where one went. In the week leading up to the Arrival of Spring, firecrackers lit the sky every night, their cheerful popping noises intended to scare away demons and hungry ghosts.

The last day of the holiday, the Arrival of Spring, culminated in a grand night of palace festivities that I had only ever heard stories about. My mother had attended once as a young woman, and she had always called it the most beautiful night of her life.

She had not exaggerated. After a week of firecrackers, I thought I'd grown jaded to the festivities, but the sight of the palace made me gasp.

The inner palace had been transformed into the glittering heart of a gem. As I crossed the threshold on Sky's arm, I felt as though we were entering a lit diamond; every polished surface gleamed with silver and crystals and flickering candles, which gave the palace a warm, underwater feel. Against the soft radiance of firelight, every lord and lady I passed looked ethereal, their fine robes and jewels reminding me of stars in the sky.

Lotus had not let my dress be outdone. To match the festivities, she had chosen a set of crimson red robes that cinched tightly at the waist, ornamented with a lovely gold shawl that showed off my shoulders and throat. "You'll want a dress that leaves your throat bare," Lotus had explained, after opening the gift Sky's mother had sent me, as congratulations for our betrothal. It was a diamond necklace, so heavy Lotus required two hands to lift it.

I had not particularly wished to wear such a loud statement piece, but I knew it would be rude to refuse a gift. As I examined my reflection in the darkened window of the ceremonial hall, I thought I did look the part of Sky's bride, young and healthy and happy. As for how I felt on the inside, that did not matter tonight.

Sky and I matched in our red and gold costumes, and we received our fair share of congratulations from strangers and friends alike. After dinner, as Sky fell into conversation with a childhood friend, I caught a glimpse of a lone figure outside, drinking wine in the open-air gallery. Princess Ruihua.

Shortly after Sky had been named heir, Winter had presented evidence condemning Yuchen for treason, though it was hardly necessary. The Imperial Commander had made his decision regarding his successor, and he would not change his mind. Yuchen was promptly stripped of his title and executed, though I had not heard what became of his wife and children.

Excusing myself from Sky, I made my way across the courtyard toward the princess, who stood alone in the corner, swallowing her drink as though each sip were bitter vinegar.

"Your Highness—"

Princess Ruihua turned, her expression souring as she saw me. She raised her hand to slap me, but she was drunk, and I easily caught her raised wrist.

"That is not my title," she said, her hands drifting to her swollen stomach. "I have no title. My children have no title. Are you happy now? Yifeng was right—your greed knows no bounds."

"I'm sorry Yuchen's fate was tied to yours," I said, "but I'm not sorry for what I did." I released her and stepped back, out of striking distance. This was the ugly underbelly of palace politics: that even those who played no part in their master's mistakes still reaped the consequences of his failure. In mere days, through no fault of her own, Ruihua and her children had been reduced from royalty to objects of charity.

It was easier to blame me, I saw, a fallen woman who had overstepped her place within the world of men, than to blame Liu Yuchen, a husband like any other husband, as fallible as any other master. I understood that if Sky made a strategic choice, he would be the one praised, and that if he made a wrong move, I would be the one blamed. Hadn't it always been like this in history—all the emperors led astray because of their wicked wives and concubines?

It was a pity Ruihua's presence reminded me of these ugly

truths, or I might've tried to help her. Instead, I walked away, an uneasy restlessness growing in the pit of my stomach. The grandeur of the palace had shifted into vulgarity, and suddenly I no longer wished to stay.

The lion dances had begun—acrobatic performers dressed in colorful lion costumes who wound around the courtyard and through the crowd. I felt an incoming migraine from the echoing drumbeat, which reverberated against the stone tiles.

Scanning the courtyard, I searched for an escape path, one that wouldn't alert Sky's family to my absence. How I longed to see Xiuying at this time, when the Spring Festival was always intended as an occasion for family. Once Sky and I were wed, I could invite Xiuying, Rouha, and Plum to live with me in the Forbidden City. But, thinking of Princess Yifeng and all my remaining enemies, I wondered if it was not wiser to keep those you loved out of the palace.

What a lonely life I'd signed myself up for.

"How festive you appear," said a low, mocking voice behind me. I felt my toes curl at the sound. "Not looking forward to the new year?"

"Are you?" I asked the Ximing prince, my gaze not leaving the writhing lion dancers.

"The future is always a source of comfort," said Lei. "It's the past I despise."

His tone was both light and derisive. But I never knew if he was making fun of others or himself.

"You'll soon be leaving Chuang Ning?" I asked, for I knew his status as hostage was only necessary until the treaty was signed. "You must be thrilled to be returning to Tzu Wan."

"And you will remain here?" he asked. A delicate pause. "Was my offer so uninteresting?"

"To go with you?" I asked, scoffing at the idea, which I'd perceived as another one of his twisted jests. "How do you think that would end?"

I felt the weight of his gaze like a sparking match. "I think we rather understand each other." His voice was unusually introspective.

I turned toward him tentatively. He looked like a mythical creature of the night, his long black hair loose and windswept, his skin golden under the flickering torches. His ink-black eyelashes were like the wings of butterflies, framing his molten amber eyes. Again, they were dilated. So he'd been drinking.

An icy gust of wind blew through the courtyard, sending the hanging lanterns swinging like fist fighters. Without warning, Lei reached out and brushed a careless thumb across my cold cheek, tucking back a stray lock of hair that had whipped free in the wind. Even that infinitesimal of a brush left me reeling with sensation, my skin tingling from his touch. But I refused to let him know it.

"Why are you always drinking?" I asked instead.

His smile was as bitter as oversteeped tea. "How else can I live with myself, sweetheart?"

"The rest of us find a way," I said, before adding quietly, "though I'm no stranger to falling victim to my vices."

The earth vibrated with the pounding drums. All around me, people cheered, laughed, toasted, and drank. Yet never had I felt so alone.

He was still watching me. "Do you think you'll be happy here?"

I shrugged, scanning the night sky above us. "It all worked out like a dream," I said. "The Imperial Commander pardoned me. He named Sky as his successor. And he consented to our betrothal." I watched Sky's father sitting at the head of his dais, ornamented in brilliant red and gold.

"So you secured the throne; you won your bid," said Lei dryly.

"Only, have you ever wondered whether you really want what you worked so hard to secure?"

There was something razor-edged in his voice. "What do you mean?"

"Do you know why the Imperial Commander finally named his heir?" He smiled coldly. "Because he cannot fight a war on multiple fronts."

I blinked at him. "The war is over, Lei."

"The Three Kingdoms War is over," he agreed, "but this current semblance of peace will not last, no matter what your new father would have you believe."

Another errant blast of wind caused me to shiver. Lei shifted his stance, shielding me from the cold air. Up close, I breathed in his familiar masculine scent and felt the old stirrings of desire within me. I couldn't keep doing this—wavering in my decisions, wondering what if, what if, what if. I had chosen my path, I did not regret it, and now there was no going back.

I tried to step back from the prince, but my heel struck the alcove wall. Lei's grin turned wolfish.

"Do you want to know what your dear betrothed is hiding from you?"

I shook my head, then slowly nodded.

His voice dropped, so that only I could hear him. "The casualties the Anlai army suffered were great. The coffers are empty, and the noble families openly defy their tribute agreements. And most strikingly"—Lei paused, his eyes on mine—"the famine has reached critical levels. The common people are rebelling."

I thought of my recurring dreams, of great qi being sucked from the land. Was my spirit power to blame for this? In overusing my lixia during the war, had I sapped the life force not only from my own body but from the land itself?

Lightheaded, I leaned back against the alcove. Sky would've stopped; Sky would've spared me. But Lei, as I'd always known him to be, was ruthless. He went on.

"Rebellion is like a disease; it knows no borders. Civil war in Leiyang ended with the disposal of their ruling family. Now the rebels are moving west—and Anlai is their next mark."

Rebels? My migraine intensified as I tried to wrap my head around this revelation.

Lei leaned one hand nonchalantly against the wall, shielding me from view. "The people are restless. They hunger for change. The question is, my little troublemaker, what role will you play?"

What role will you play?

I repeated his question, but in my head, it was not Lei's voice that resounded, but the dragon's. I recalled the icy weight of his voice, the hair-raising timbre of his roar. Even though I did not trust him . . . I missed his grounding presence. I *needed* it.

Ever since I'd started wearing irons again, a debilitating emptiness had filled my core. I felt lost, depleted, a cracked half shell of a person.

"I-I can't," I said, my voice breaking. "Something's wrong with me, Lei. My qi feels like a stranger's. Some days, I can hardly sense my life force at all. I have so many questions, but every time I try to answer one, a thousand more spring up. I barely recognize myself anymore. I-I'm just trying to hold it together."

"So you'll accept your sentence?" he asked quietly. "And spend your final months here?"

I wrinkled my brows at him. "What do you mean—my final months?"

For the first time, I saw astonishment flit across his face. "He didn't tell you?" Lei asked, something sinister and precarious in his voice. Surprise had crystallized into anger.

"Tell me what?"

"Prince Cao." Winter appeared behind Lei, his long pale robes stark against the blackening night. "My felicitations on the occasion of your betrothal."

Betrothal? My spine stiffened as I caught Lei's reaction. He straightened, distancing himself from me, his face regaining its impassive mask. "Thank you," he said, bowing his head. "I hope to share a toast with you at my wedding ceremony."

"You're betrothed?" I asked, ignoring etiquette. "To who?"

Lei raised a mocking brow, as if the information had no pertinence to me. "Lady Tang Liqing of the Tang family. Have you had the pleasure of making her acquaintance?" My stomach sinking, I recalled the pretty girl with crimson lipstick who'd kissed Lei at the Rain-Listening Gazebo.

Lei's face was cold again, and he looked at me as if I were merely a prying stranger. "I see," I said, struggling to keep my voice level.

To my mortification, I felt pressure build behind my eyes. I did not know if it was due to the holidays or simply because I missed my family; never had I been someone so quick to cry. Humiliated and fuming, I turned to go. "Goodbye," I spat out.

"Wait." He seized my wrist with the speed of a cobra.

"Let me go," I said, determined not to look at him. I would not let him see my tears.

His voice sounded odd. "Meilin—"

I felt a sudden movement behind me and turned just as Sky punched Lei in the face. Lei staggered back, wiping blood from his lip.

"Touch her again and you'll die," said Sky, his nostrils flaring. Nervously, I edged toward him as court officials gathered around us, whispering.

"Sky," I said. He was bristling, itching for a fight. "Let's go."

"Will you tell her or will I?" Lei asked, a cruel smirk playing across his face. "I always knew you were a coward, but the extent—"

Sky snarled and threw another fist at him. This time, Lei was prepared and easily dodged, laughing. Sky tried again and Lei eluded him once more, leaving Sky panting from exertion.

"That's enough," said Winter, seizing his brother. "You're making a scene."

Sky's face was still red, but at least he grew aware of the watching crowd. Taking a breath, he found me and grabbed my arm.

"We're leaving," Sky said, and an unsettling premonition struck me—that I might never see the Ximing prince again. In a few days, he would depart for First Crossing, and I would remain in Chuang Ning. It hardly mattered; he was soon to be married, as was I. Like two shadows meeting at dusk, our lives were only ever meant to cross for a fleeting moment.

Lei's face changed, growing raw and desperate in a way that made me hesitate. "Don't go with him," he said lowly, in a voice meant for me alone.

I steeled myself against his manipulations. "You have no right," I hissed. "Congratulations on your forthcoming nuptials. From now on, let us be strangers to one another."

TWENTY-ONE

Father, I know you will not approve, but I beg you to understand that no other man can compare. If you love me, please, I ask that you support my choice. And if you care for my happiness, I implore you to help him secure his terms in the treaty negotiations. His success is all that matters now, and I need you to endorse him—for both our sakes.

—LADY TANG LIQING IN A PRIVATE CORRESPONDENCE
TO CHANCELLOR TANG JIANGUO, 924

We did not speak as Sky led me back to my rooms. He hesitated on the threshold of my door, seeming to waver with indecision, before bidding me good night. I was exhausted and did not argue. I would talk to him tomorrow.

My guards exchanged shifts; Zibei smiled at me, squeezing my shoulder in what must have been intended as comfort. I ignored him and locked the door to my bedroom behind me, not waiting for Lotus before stripping off my heavy gown. What was Sky hiding? What did Lei want from me—why had he warned me of famine and rebellion and the burgeoning threat of civil war? Did he expect me to intercede, or to play his willing pawn? Why had he saved my life—why had he asked me to run away with him—only to propose to another woman?

Exhausted and upset, I buried my head beneath the covers and willed myself not to think of him. Gradually, I drifted into a deep, dreamless sleep, so that I did not hear the sound of the key fitting into the lock, nor the parting creak of my bedroom door.

―

I SCREAMED IN FEAR AND ANGUISH AS SOMETHING SHARP LANCED MY arm. The iron arrow tore open my skin, and I fell to my knees, trying to stanch the bleeding. I looked around wildly, struggling to make sense of my surroundings. Was this a dream? A memory from the war? But the blood continued to drip from my wound, and the pain did not abate.

Another arrow whizzed by me as I flattened myself against the dirt. Squinting into the darkness, I saw an archer crouching in the shadow of a tree. I extended a hand toward him, concentrating my lixia.

Water rose from the damp earth. The man whimpered, dropping his bow and sprinting away. He slipped, hitting the ground, just as I clenched my hand into a fist and drove a stream of water into his mouth.

His gurgling breaths continued for but a few more moments, and then—silence.

It was not my first kill of the night.

Confused, I shook my head as if to wake myself, then tore a strip of fabric and used it to bind my arm wound. The forest was silent but for my ragged breaths. By the age of these gnarled oak trees, I was in the woods east of Chuang Ning.

As I regained my breath, my memories returned to me. I was a prisoner—no, I'd been released. The Imperial Commander had given his blessing for Sky and me to marry . . . and yet I was not free to come and go from the Forbidden City.

How had I gotten here? I stared at the torn hem of my nightclothes and remembered... my last waking memory was of my bedchamber, as I prepared for sleep.

A woman's scream ruptured the sleeping forest. Heart pounding, I raced toward the sound.

But it was too late to save her. Between two ancient oak trees, both bent and dying, stood a newly erected spirit gate. I could sense it was new by the energy of the place, which hummed with change and turmoil. The portal had been created by sapping the life force from the forest floor, which was slowly turning as cold and desolate as a tundra.

The screaming woman lay before the gate like a living sacrifice. Her spirit affinity was not strong enough for the overwhelming lixia of the place, and it was driving her mad. She writhed like a hooked fish, her mouth foaming and her eyes rolled back in her skull. Her screams petered out, her body jerked, and then she was still, unmoving.

Another casualty of the night, I thought distantly, before rousing myself. I was not responsible for this girl's unfortunate death. I was simply at the wrong place at the wrong time. The spirit summoner that Sky was trying to catch had clearly just been here, and I had missed him. Perhaps, if I used my lixia, I could track him down.

But, I realized, how did I have access to my lixia? I rolled up the sleeve of my nightclothes, then gasped as I saw that my iron manacle was missing. How could I have taken it off? I only knew of one set of keys, and it was back in the palace, with the guard stationed outside my rooms.

A chill of dread snaked through my veins.

I'd been waking up for months wondering where these strange cuts and bruises had come from. I'd felt sore all over on days I'd barely strolled the palace gardens. And Zibei, my personal guard, he had acted as if we'd known each other, as if we'd possessed some secret relationship that I'd perceived as one-sided.

Could the dragon have been controlling me all this time, even when I wore my irons? Could he have used compulsion, or persuaded Zibei of some other terrible way to free me from my irons in the night, only to return them every morning?

No, it was impossible. The spirit gates had been cropping up all over the kingdom. It could not be me who was responsible; it had to be someone else.

But all the alleged summoners Sky had caught were minor ones. It would have to be a powerful vessel, one that bore the might of a Cardinal Spirit, to create a rift in the veil so wide that the spirit realm bled into the human world.

Please let it not be true, I begged. *Please let me not be the one responsible for this. Let me catch the true culprit, and rid myself of blame.*

Closing my eyes, I reached for my lixia to perceive the inner workings of the world. When I raised my head, the elemental threads of the forest glowed. Unmistakably, as if I'd left a trail of blood, I could see the elemental threads of my being, intertwined at the base of the spirit gate.

"No," I choked out. "No!"

Qinglong must be laughing, I thought. For he had been pulling the strings all this time, manipulating me in the night, then erasing my memories in the morning. It had been Qinglong who had tried to burn my mother's diary, Qinglong who had steered me toward the throne.

My obsession with claiming power, with eliminating the princes who stood in my way—it was the hidden handiwork of the dragon, warping and feeding my ambition. And I, a pawn who thought myself the player, had willingly dove into his game.

The iron arrowhead had shaken me momentarily from his grasp, but he was surely unworried. Sleep was no longer safe for me; he could exploit any moment of vulnerability to turn me into his puppet, to bend me to his will so completely that I lost my own. The true extent of my helplessness caused my knees to lock. In depending on Qinglong's power, I had damned myself.

Shaking uncontrollably, I reached for my jade. My hand instinctively clenched around the seal, yet I forced my fist open, telling myself to take off the necklace. I would throw away my jade; I would walk away at last.

Wood, fire, earth, metal, water. I cycled through each element, practicing my qi gong. The forest seemed to hold its breath as it watched me. No leaves rustled; no branches stirred. In one quick motion, like ripping out an arrowhead, I lifted the jade from my neck and threw it on the dirt.

Immediately, a searing pain tore through my chest. I fell to my knees in agony, screaming with untenable pain. I was going to die—no, I was dying, and there was no greater torment than this. Crawling on my hands and knees, I groped blindly for my jade, before something cool and pulsating brushed my finger. In desperate relief, I lunged for it, securing my necklace back around my throat.

As soon as it had come, the pain vanished.

I collapsed on the ground, wheezing, relishing the overwhelming sensation of the absence of pain. But as my relief subsided, it dawned on me what this meant: my addiction was past the point of recovery. Trying to remove my jade had been like trying to remove a vital organ. I could no longer live without it.

I swallowed a broken laugh. No wonder the dragon did not even deign to speak to me. It no longer mattered whether I knew of his deceptions; even if I made him my enemy, I could not survive without him.

"Keep your iron safeguards on," a voice barked into the night. "There's black magic here."

The marching thud of boots followed. Although I had no will left to live, my survival instinct still reared its head. Hastily, I rose into a crouch and ducked behind the nearest tree, so as to avoid the notice of the imperial soldiers. When they passed me, I ran in the opposite direction, toward the city.

Despite the late hour, most partygoers were still celebrating the Arrival of Spring. I saw no one on the back roads until I entered Chuang Ning, compelling the city guards so that they looked the other way as I crossed inside.

"Do you think you'll be happy here?" Lei had asked, only hours ago. At the time, I had not known what to tell him. I knew my answer now. The imperial palace, despite its finery and elegance, was little more than a cage to me. A place where I had to constantly look over my shoulder, second-guess every action, weaken and restrain myself so as to fit in and belong. I was wrong to think Sky's love could be enough for me. Despite the strength of his love, and the goodness of his intentions, this was the reality of who I was. Someone broken, someone corrupted from within, someone who took innocent lives and then slept soundly in her own bed.

I could not return to the Forbidden City; that much was clear.

"It's dangerous for a woman to be out alone this late at night." The words made me tense, but as I caught sight of the speaker, a young woman, I relaxed.

"I could say the same to you," I told her, as she approached me in the half-lit hutong near the Gate of Heavenly Peace.

"I knew I'd run into you tonight," she said. "You took your time, though. I was getting quite cold waiting for you, Hai Meilin."

I froze at the sound of my name. Then I noticed her eyes—pale and near translucent, like twin stars.

She smiled. "I'm a Ruan seer," she said. Now I understood why her eyes looked so familiar; they reminded me of Lei's, and he was half-Ruan.

"I've seen you before," I said, remembering. "At the anniversary parade."

Even then, she had been watching me.

"You saved my grandfather's life, in a street just like this one. Since then, I've been looking out for you."

"Your grandfather . . . ?"

"In Wenxi District," she said. "You stopped an unhitched wagon from running him over."

My eyes widened at the memory. That had been the first time I'd met Sky, who'd foolishly tried to run in front of the wagon as if he were a brick wall.

"All this time, you've been steadily draining your life force. With the remaining qi you possess, you only have six months of freedom left before the Azure Dragon subsumes you completely. Once your qi is consumed, you will become little more than a puppet under his control."

Six months of freedom left.

"W-what?" I asked, dumbfounded. "N-no. Thank you, but—I'm recovering. My appetite's returned, and so has my stamina—"

"Meilin," she said gently. "Feel your own qi. You know the truth."

My chest hollowed at the abyss of grief that threatened to swallow me whole. "*Will you tell her or will I?*" Lei had shouted at Sky. This must be what Sky had learned from the lixia specialist. This was why he'd refused to let me leave Chuang Ning, why he'd even agreed to remain in the city until the Arrival of Spring, why he'd cried in my arms that night—as if he were going to lose me.

Everyone knew I was going to die. Everyone except me.

My mouth dry, I realized that Qinglong had won. This, above

everything else, was what stung the most. I began to laugh then, laughing at the depths of my own spite, which remained even at my darkest hour.

Above us, fireworks exploded in the night sky, followed by raucous laughter and cheering. The Arrival of Spring was over. Winter had passed, and spring was upon us. The new year would bring life to others, but death to me.

And yet, thinking of the passage of winter, someone else had yearned for this day—and not lived to see it. Someone else had waited and prayed for the coming of spring, which would bring their last hope...

"My mother," I said hoarsely. "She had been searching for a mythical spring."

The Ruan seer nodded, taking my cold hands in her warm ones. I flinched at her forwardness but did not push her away. "Have you heard of the myth of Zhuque's eternal spring? Legend says the spring waters can heal lixia corruption by severing the connection between spirit and vessel. If you journey to the Red Mountains, Meilin, you will find it. Its healing waters can save you, but only if you choose to go in."

"Why would I choose not to?" I asked, crinkling my brows.

Her lips curled in an ambiguous smile. "It is a difficult choice, one only the strongest can make. For in order to be cleansed, you must give up that which is most precious to you. I do not know what your decision will be; I cannot See it."

That which is most precious to you. And yet what could be more precious than freedom? I shook my head at her seer logic. What mattered was that I would find this spring if I sought it out, and I only had six months left to do so. The Red Mountains ran across the kingdom's border, from southern Anlai deep into Leyuan. It would take over a month to get to First Crossing on horseback, and then months longer to journey through the mountain range on foot, for the narrow roads were too treacherous for horses.

"Stars go with you, Hai Meilin," she said. "For we will never meet again in this life."

The hairs on the back of my neck rose. I gave her a questioning look, but she simply released my hands and turned away.

"Wait!" I called out. I had so many questions, I didn't know where to begin. Yet the one that slipped from my lips was not what I expected. "Does Cao Ming Lei also have second sight?"

She smiled with amusement. "No," she said. "But the prince has other gifts."

I nodded, mulling this over. "I won't forget your kindness," I said. "What is your name?"

But she had already vanished into the night.

TWENTY-TWO

It is a good position—the mistress of the house is kind and generous, and the pay is well above market rate. Only, take care never to enter the upstairs quarters at the far end of the stairwell. Other maids have tried, and all have either gone mad or disappeared. They say the previous mistress of the house lost her mind in those very rooms, and the shadow still lingers. If you take the job, never open that door.

—PRIVATE INSTRUCTION FROM YU XIUYING'S
FORMER HOUSEKEEPER, 924

TIME WAS OF THE ESSENCE; I HAD TO SET OUT IMMEDIATELY, BEfore the ghosts of the night's events could catch up with me. And yet, though I feared any delay, I could not go without saying goodbye to my family. Not if this was possibly my last night in Chuang Ning.

Following muscle memory, I climbed the low-hanging eaves and ran across the rooftops to Willow District. The sky was awash with stars, and I had never so dearly missed being alive. Knowing I would lose myself in six months' time only intensified the richness of life today: the firecracker ash in the air, the crumpled lanterns colliding in the breeze, the sugary scent of sweet rice cakes and peanut cookies. Chuang Ning, despite all its flaws, despite how much I had hated living here, was still my home.

The house was dark as I crept inside, stealing in through the upstairs window as I used to long ago. It felt surreal to be back here, to breathe in these childhood smells, to step on floorboards that still creaked in the same places. Tiptoeing down the corridor, I avoided Father's end of the house and instead went to Xiuying's room, gratified to find candlelight pooling beneath her door.

I knocked once, then entered. Xiuying was sewing by candlelight, repairing a dress that was too big to be worn by Rouha. And then I remembered, Rouha had grown.

"Meilin!" Xiuying gasped, dropping her sewing. "How are you here? Prince Liu said you couldn't leave the palace until—"

"I wanted to see you," I choked out. "Sister."

Her arms came around me and I felt myself shatter, all my carefully maintained armor falling apart at the warmth of her touch. We cried in each other's arms, for minutes or hours I couldn't say. There were so many things I wanted to tell her, so many ways I wished to say *you were right*, and *thank you*, and *I'm sorry, I'm sorry* a thousand times.

"It's been . . . so hard." I sobbed like a little girl again, like I was twelve and my mother had just left me. "I've made so many mistakes. I've done—terrible things—"

"Shh . . ." Xiuying patted the back of my head. "It's okay. It's okay."

The door squealed as it opened a second time. "Jie Jie?"

I dried my eyes as I caught sight of Rouha and Plum by the threshold, staring at me as if they'd seen a ghost. Plum ran toward me first, giggling.

"You've gotten so big!" I cried out, lifting him in the air and groaning from the weight of him. Rouha tackled my legs and I nearly fell over, before Xiuying righted us both.

"Your hair!" I exclaimed, looking at Rouha's shorn braids, which now reached just below her ears.

"The style's in vogue," Xiuying said, her eyes twinkling. "Because of a certain woman warrior, the rumors say."

I shot her an incredulous look before bending down to listen to Plum teach me every new word he'd learned in my absence.

"Why don't you stay?" Rouha whined, interrupting Plum. "It's boring without you."

"Rouha, we talked about this," Xiuying chided. "Meilin has to attend to her duties in the palace—with the prince, remember? You liked him."

"He can come live here with us," Rouha protested. "He can stay in Father's rooms soon." To me, she said in a stage whisper, "Father's dying."

I glanced questioningly at Xiuying, who gave me a curt nod.

"It's not proper for the prince to live here," said Xiuying. "But we can visit Meilin one day in the palace—wouldn't you like to see the palace?"

"I don't like the palace," said Rouha, pouting. "I want to travel the world—like you did, Jie Jie."

I shot Xiuying a look of horror, and she grimaced in response.

"Me too!" said Plum, before biting into something on my arm. I yelped with surprise before noticing he'd torn my makeshift bandage. Xiuying, noticing the wound, got up to rebind it and assemble an herbal remedy for me. So she was downstairs when a knock sounded at the front door.

My insides writhed with coiling dread. Anything amiss was sure to be because of me. "Stay here," I ordered Plum and Rouha, my vision tunneling. "No matter what happens, do not leave this room.

"Rouha." I squeezed her hand, trying to sound calm. "You're in charge now." My younger sister was growing up to be a clever child with observation skills well beyond her years. I trusted her to keep Plum hidden in the presence of danger.

With that I hurried down the stairs toward the hushed voices in the entrance, imagining the worst. But as I neared, I recognized the newcomer's voice and breathed out an immense sigh of relief. It was Sky.

I put a hand against my chest to ease my pounding heart. Never again would I come here and put my family in danger, I decided. Not until I could trust myself again.

He too was relieved to see me, though his relief did not overcome his anger. "I've been looking everywhere for you," he said lowly. "I have guards scouring the city as we speak." He took a breath, trying to calm himself. "We arrested Zibei, but he killed himself before we could interrogate him. Here," he said, holding out my irons. I hesitated, not wanting to give up my power and vitality. But the threat of the dragon still loomed large, and I did not know when he would try to control me again.

Wordlessly, I held out my wrists as he clasped them around me. Immediately my senses dulled, the world losing its color and verve and light. Without my lixia, I was overcome with exhaustion, my limbs like paper fans threatening to fold at any second. Lightheaded, I swayed before Sky caught me. He looked me over, taking in my torn nightclothes and the bloody bandage around my arm. "Who did this to you?" he asked, his voice lethal.

Wearily, I shook my head.

"My apologies for intruding at this hour," Sky said to Xiuying. "We'll take our leave now."

"Wait," said Xiuying, thrusting a satchel of herbal medicine toward me. "Take this."

Sky frowned at the offending object but said nothing as I looped the strings around my arm. "Sister," I said, a lump in my throat. *I don't know if I'll ever see you again.*

She nodded, understanding me.

"When I look at the moon," she whispered, "I think of you."

THE DRAGON WAKES WITH THUNDER

SKY WAS SILENT AS WE LEFT, BUT I COULD FEEL THE SIMMERING RE-sentment in his bearing. He helped me onto his steed, then swung up behind me, urging his horse into a slow walk.

"When I saw your empty bed," he said at last, "I assumed the worst. I imagined you dead—or captured—or—" He broke off, breathing hard. In a strained voice, he continued, "Only to find you at your family's house, though you were explicitly *forbidden* from leaving the palace—"

"Why didn't you tell me, Sky?" I interrupted. "Why didn't you tell me I only had six months left to live?"

He froze. "He told you, didn't he?" he said tightly.

"If by 'he' you mean Lei—"

"I'm going to kill that bastard." The lack of bluster in his voice frightened me.

"It's not his fault!" I said, twisting in the saddle. "You should've been the one to tell me, Sky, not keep me in the dark like a child—"

"You act like a child sometimes!" Sky burst out. "You know why I didn't tell you? Because I was afraid of what you'd do."

Infuriated, I swung off the moving horse, landing badly on my knees. Sky's steed nickered, confused, before Sky comforted him and dismounted, facing me in the darkened alleyway. *I will not go with you*, I decided then.

"You've grown increasingly unstable as of late," said Sky. "I was afraid you'd hurt yourself, or—"

"Or hurt others?" I asked, my chest aching as if someone had tried to split it open. "So what, you wanted me to just go quietly?"

"I am doing *everything* in my power to save you," he said. "But sometimes I think you don't want to be saved."

My eyes burned with unshed tears. He had no idea what I went through in the palace every day: surrounded by people who wished to see me fail, constantly second-guessing myself, forcing a false smile despite the pain. Every moment was a violent struggle. And he thought I didn't want to live?

"You never understood me," I said quietly. "Sometimes I think it was a mistake for us to be together."

Sky sucked in a breath as if I'd just struck him. He raked a distracted hand through his hair, looking away from me, then back. When he spoke, his face was violence. "Is this because of *him*?"

"Who?" I asked, before bursting into cold laughter. "This has nothing to do with Lei."

Sky's voice was soft, but it pierced through the night. "You don't think I've seen the way you look at him?"

My laughter died on my lips as I met his wretched eyes.

"Do you even love me, Meilin? Look at you." Now it was his turn to laugh. "You can't say it, can you?"

My eyes narrowed as I strode toward him, my anger rising with every step. "Everything I have ever done in that cursed place was for you," I spat out, pointing at the high gates guarding the Forbidden City. "I foiled your brother's schemes for you. I kowtowed before your father for you. I stayed away from my family for *months* for you."

How much of it was the dragon's doing, I wondered, and how much of it was my own inherent ambition? Was it possible to divorce the two anymore? Did I truly love Sky, or had Qinglong been manipulating my affection for him in order to drive me toward the throne? As a sovereign, I could do so much more for the dragon than as a lowly foot soldier. That had always been his aim, I recalled now, to get me into a position of power in the world of men.

Why was I so easily manipulated? What was it about me that longed to trust—like a bird seeking a cage for comfort? How could

I have ended up here, once again, caught in a snare of my own making?

"I never told you I loved you because the truth is, I don't know if I'm capable of love anymore. But I'll be damned if I let you say I didn't do *everything* for you—that I didn't *lay my life down* for you—" My voice shattered in a soundless sob. I expelled a breath before choking out, "I've made up my mind. I'm not going back with you." I swallowed my tears. "I'm leaving Chuang Ning."

His eyes bulged as he realized I was serious. He shook his head, his mouth flattening. "No."

"Sky," I continued, as if he hadn't spoken, "this is goodbye."

"No," he said again. "You're not going."

"I wasn't asking for your permission—I've made my decision."

"It's not your decision to make," he said hotly.

Heat flooded my body at his arrogant presumption. "Is that an order, Sky?"

His eyes turned to slits; neither of us would back down now. "It's my prerogative," he answered.

I felt fury swallow me whole, changing me into a different creature, one unrecognizable to myself. I tore my engagement string from my wrist and ground it beneath my shoe. "The wedding's off," I said, trying to cut him where it hurt most. "Do you know—I never wanted to marry you?" My parting smile was full of disdain. "You have no claim over me."

An animal sound ripped from his throat. I turned to go, but he closed the distance between us and seized my shoulder, his grip rough enough to bruise. I leaned forward and sank my teeth into his hand, and when his fingers slackened I twisted out of his grasp.

"Are you going to drag me back as your captive?" I asked. "Is that what this has come to?"

"I'll do whatever's necessary," he said, eyes flinty and unyielding. "You're mine."

I leapt toward him with a spinning roundhouse kick. He dodged and feinted left before catching me in my blind spot and slamming me to the ground with enough force that we both went rolling. I scrambled to gain the upper hand, but his strength far surpassed mine, and in seconds he had me pinned beneath him, his hands like manacles around my wrists. His cruel smirk clouded my vision with senseless rage, and I reared up and head-butted him, feeling my forehead split from the impact.

His hold loosened and I kneed him, hard enough that he gasped in pain. Then I saw the hidden knife glinting in his boot, and I reached for it, desperate and unthinking with fury. He read my intent and slammed me back into the dirt, then wrapped his hands around my throat, choking me. I scrabbled at his hands, gasping for breath, but it was no use. He was too strong, and I could not escape him. As my breath thinned and my hands grew limp, the last thing I saw was his eyes, dilated with rage, before my vision went black.

TWENTY-THREE

*As surely as the osmanthus blooms upon the moon,
the hearts of the people will stir with rebellion.*
—BOOK OF ODES, 856

THE CARPET WAS SOFT BENEATH MY CHEEK. I RUBBED MY FACE against it, not wanting to rise, before wondering why I was on the ground. The world lurched around me as I cracked open one eye.

I was lying on the floor of my room, the pattern of my carpet most definitely indented into my cheek. I tried to push myself upright, but my arms wouldn't cooperate. Then I noticed: my wrists were bound in manacles.

Heat flushed through my body as my anger found me. Awkwardly I crawled into an upright position, finding my ankle also chained to the wall. Like a misbehaving dog, shackled alone to keep from biting others.

I hated him. I'd never hated anyone more in that moment.

"My lady . . ." Lotus was standing near the washroom, the muscles in her face tight with agitation. She'd poured me a glass of water. "Would you like something to drink?"

"Lotus." I tried to stand but the chains were too heavy. "Please. You must help me. You must find the key—"

She backed away from me as if I were a rabid dog. "I-I'm sorry, my lady," she whispered, on the verge of tears. "The prince said it was for your own protection."

The revelation sank into the hollow of my chest: I had made myself weak by relying on Sky's strength. I'd believed we could be a good team, equals in every sense. But by accepting the status quo of our society, I had allowed our union to be nothing more than a farce of equality. Sky was the recognized head, and in all decisions he would get the ultimate say. It did not matter what he promised me privately, in the bedroom and alone. By maintaining our existing systems of power, he in effect secured his authority over both me and his kingdom.

I would've never had any power as his wife. For it would not have been me on the throne—but him.

These chains were proof of that.

A mangled scream escaped me—part desperation, part anger. How dare he do this to me—after all that I had done for him? Was this a new side of him, revealed in the face of unchecked power? Or had this part of Sky always existed, but I, overcome by love and affection, had chosen to ignore it?

Lotus had started to cry. "Please, just bear with it a little longer, my lady," she pleaded. "Apologize tomorrow, and he'll forgive you, I know he will. All will be well then—"

"I will never ask for his forgiveness," I hissed. "I've done nothing wrong. Lotus, I demand you—"

Before I could get the words out she'd fled. I yanked at my chains, which did nothing but jar the cold metal against my shinbones. Swearing, I tested the range my chains offered me. I could see my mother's diary resting beside my bed, not a few feet away, but it was just out of reach.

"Sky!" I screamed, never mind that he was likely nowhere in the vicinity. He'd trapped me here, and the worst part was, he'd done it with my best interests purportedly at heart.

Didn't I get to decide that?

I thought of the first time we'd fought, when he'd found out my true identity during the war. We'd resorted to violence back then too, and perhaps that should've been the first warning sign. Both of us had too much fire in us—we were both stubborn to the core. But Sky had been raised with the knowledge that he was always right. I had been taught to humble myself and admit wrongdoing—and I was so damn sick of it.

A key turned in the door. I tensed, wondering if he'd come to gloat. Instead, at the broad-shouldered silhouette that filled the doorway, I gasped in surprise—and relief.

"You came for me," I said hoarsely.

Lei's smile was joyless. "I thought you'd been a prisoner long enough."

I let out a strangled laugh. "How did you—"

"No time for questions," he said, but I saw Lily's familiar shadow in the corridor before he shut the door behind him.

Lei crossed the floor in a few long strides, kneeling beside me with a metal ring filled with keys. But his hands stilled as his gaze fell over my face, lingering on the new purple-blue bruises circling my throat. Sky had left his mark on me.

Lei's eyes had turned black. "He'll pay for this," he whispered, and I shivered at the brutality in his voice.

I shook my head. "I want to forget it. I'm leaving Chuang Ning. Lei, I'm going to find Zhuque's eternal spring."

He looked up in surprise, and I was relieved to see the haze of murder fading from his eyes. He began to test keys on my manacles. "The mythical spring?"

"It's real. I spoke with a Ruan seer—and she saw that I would find it."

He took this all in stride. "It can heal you?"

"If I choose to let it."

Lei looked as if he didn't understand but wisely saw it was not the time for questions. "I'm coming with you," he said, as his third attempt opened the lock and the irons chaining me to the wall fell. I rubbed at my sore wrists as he helped me stand.

"What about your betrothal?" I asked him.

He shot me a sardonic look. "You know that was only for political reasons."

I didn't know that. "Then you'll break the official treaty—"

"That treaty was always meant to be broken, sweetheart."

Peering up into his face, I remembered the rumors I'd heard about Lei consorting with Anlai court officials. Had he been forming secret agreements with them, I wondered, agreements that stood outside the official treaty? For the official treaty had always been controlled by the ruling imperial family.

"I have the keys to those too," he said, nodding at the slim iron bands I wore on each wrist, "if you want them removed."

"No!" I said. "Destroy those." I couldn't take off my irons again.

He gave me a questioning glance. Only now did I notice that his complexion appeared unusually pale, a faint sheen of sweat glistening on his forehead.

"Are you ill?" I asked.

He grimaced but shook his head. "Don't worry about me. Are you sure about your irons?"

I nodded, rubbing my wrists. "The dragon," I explained tersely. "He's been controlling me in my sleep. He used my personal guard to..." I faltered, not wanting to relive the night's events.

Lei seemed to understand. "He can't use me," he said matter-offactly. The straightforward way he said it made no sense—how could he guarantee something like that? And yet his levelheaded confidence reassured me. If I couldn't trust myself, perhaps I could trust him.

But . . . I amended. This was the Ximing prince we were talking about.

I peered up at him. "How do I know I can trust you?"

"You don't," he said easily. "But isn't it so much more interesting this way?"

It was like him to joke at a time like this. I rolled my eyes and grabbed my mother's diary. "Fine. I know the servants' route to the stables—follow me."

"Here," he said, before we left. He handed me my old sword, a double-edged jian made of steel. I swallowed with unexpected sentimentality as I lifted the blade in my hands, remembering its weight and heft. Sky had never thought to return my blade to me, I thought bitterly. And I, consumed by palace life, had never thought to ask.

LEI WAS A MASTER OF STEALTH, PROWLING AROUND CORNERS LIKE A jungle cat and taking out guards so ruthlessly they made not a single sound. Lily accompanied us, before leaving to wake her friends.

"I know which servants are loyal to the rebellion," she explained, though I had not mentioned any sort of rebellion. "They'll distract the guards and help you escape. I'll show you the way—you can leave through the livestock gate."

Lei had grown increasingly pale and reticent as the night progressed. After securing two mares from the stables, we tied cloths around their hooves and walked them to the servant's gate.

"I'm sorry I didn't have more time to train you," I said to Lily, as the gates parted. "But you're strong—strong enough to stand on your own."

"I know," she said with her gap-toothed smile, the one that reminded me so much of my baby sister. "Long may you live, Phoenix-Slayer."

She had never called me that before. I shot her a look of confusion, but she motioned toward the open path. "Go," she said. "Before the prince learns you're missing."

For Sky would stop at nothing to find me.

I mounted my mare and followed Lei's. I did not know if it was the overwhelming emotions of the night, or the way the palace spires shone beneath pearly beams of moonlight, but looking back at the Forbidden City, I felt an odd mixture of nostalgia and regret. But I would not come back, I promised, turning toward the distant horizon.

I would survive out there—no, I would *thrive* out there—and I would do it all on my own terms.

Lei glanced over his shoulder and nodded. I urged my steed into a gallop, and we fled deep into the devouring night.

PART II

TWENTY-FOUR

It was rumored that the spirit of the Great Warrior had been reborn in Leyuan, for the leader of the Black Scarves stood tall as a mountain, broad as an ox, and fair as a spring morning. Astride his red-maned stallion, the rebel leader commanded the wind itself.

—CHRONICLES OF THE THREE KINGDOMS, 954

The sun crept stealthily over the mountain peaks as we rode east, avoiding the main roads in favor of the surrounding foothills. My eyes hurt from squinting, but the warmth of the sun did much against the cold wind buffeting my back. Although the mares were old, we made good time on the flat, well-groomed roads paid for by the capital city's high taxes.

But only a couple hours later, though Lei did not speak, I noticed him slipping in his saddle. Concerned, I drew up next to him, shouting over the wind. "Do you need to rest?"

He shook his head, his jaw clenched tight. But as we neared Canyuan, one of the last rural villages in the Chuang Ning prefecture, I caught sight of his slackening body, and I pulled my horse toward his just in time, catching him before he fell.

"Lei!" Up close, I saw that his skin was slick with sweat. I felt his forehead—high fever.

"What's wrong?" I asked him.

"I-I don't know," he said, as his eyes fluttered shut.

"When did you start feeling symptoms?"

His breathing was turning increasingly shallow.

"Answer me!" I demanded.

"A few hours ago . . . I think," he rasped.

A normal illness would not have set in this quickly. Unless this wasn't normal.

"Lei," I said, as it occurred to me. "Were you poisoned?"

Confusion washed across his features. "I don't know."

This was bad. We had just been at the Arrival of Spring the night before, mingling among friends and strangers alike. Who had poisoned him? Had it been Sky? No, Sky would never commit an act he deemed dishonorable. But Lei's enemies were far-reaching, and as a hostage prince in a foreign kingdom, he'd been easy prey.

I reluctantly let my mare go, mounting his horse instead. "You can lean on me," I said, sensing the waning of his qi.

But the old horse suffered under our combined weight, and in the wide-open plain, we were obvious marks. "We can take shelter in Canyuan," I decided. Hopefully I could barter for an antidote there.

"Leave me," he said hoarsely. "You must go on—"

I ignored him, and he was too weak to argue. *If only I could use my spirit power*, I thought grimly as we rode into Canyuan. Then I could compel a villager and make them offer us shelter.

But I'd forgotten I had other assets available to me. We'd barely made it down the main road when a crowd gathered around us, villagers gawking at the peculiar sight we made. For Lei's robes clearly marked him as nobility, and the sword I wore on my back, beneath my long flowing hair, was taboo.

"The woman warrior?" someone asked. "Is it her?"

"Look at her! Of course it's her."

"Phoenix-Slayer," a young woman said, prostrating herself on the road. "My life for the rebellion."

Bewildered, I wondered if they'd mistaken me for someone else. Yet I'd been called Phoenix-Slayer before.

"My life for the rebellion," others murmured. One woman even came forward to kiss the back of my hand. Taken aback, my first instinct was to run and leave this town behind. But we needed help. In Lei's current condition, we could not survive alone. If these villagers were rebels, then they did not support the throne. An enemy's enemy was a friend.

"The prince took me hostage, but I escaped," I said. "He will come after me. Are you willing to hide my companion and me?"

THE WOMAN WHO KISSED MY HAND WAS THE WIFE OF A WINEMAKER, who'd built a house with a sizable underground cellar. "The tenant farmers hide all their unreported crops there," she explained. "Canyuan's tax collectors are suspicious, of course, but they've never been able to find the trapdoor."

"Thank you," I said, as she led us through her front gate, which was crowded with countless chickens and two children. "We won't stay long. Only until..."

We both looked at Lei, who was barely managing to walk on his own. "Stay as long as you need," Madame Wu said. "Where is your journey's end?"

I opened my mouth, then closed it. If I told her about the eternal spring, she might think me mad. "First Crossing," I answered instead, which was the last major trading port at the base of the Red Mountains.

"For the Three Kingdoms Treaty?" she asked. "Do you mean to involve yourself?"

I shook my head. "I will be journeying on to Leyuan after." It was not technically a lie, given that the vast majority of the Red Mountains extended into Leyuan.

"Leyuan," she mused. "You will find much support there, Phoenix-Slayer."

"Please," I said. "Call me Meilin."

She smiled. "Of course, Meilin. I've heard a lot about you, you know. My cousin works in the palace, and your attendant Duan Lily used to live in Heyi, the village just over the river. They were both singing your praises here when they visited for the Spring Festival. That is how we knew your heart belonged to the rebellion, no matter what the Imperial Commander and his scribes would have us believe."

"But . . ." I faltered, not wanting to confess my limited loyalties to her cause. I had not been training those girls for war. I had not wished for another war. Wasn't one enough? How did we keep coming back here—these endless cycles of violence? By answering the dragon's call, had I made myself an indispensable majiang piece, to be put in play every round of the game? Or had my decision been set in stone much earlier—when I'd run away and joined the army?

"You must've had quite a night," said Madame Wu, once we were safely in the underground cellar. "I'll bring food and water, and a change of clothes for you."

"Wait," I said, recognizing that she'd been ignoring Lei all this time. "Could you also bring a change of clothes for my friend?"

She shot a dubious glance at Lei, who was leaning against the wall with his eyes shut, his breaths rapid and shallow.

"Who is your friend, Meilin?" she asked, a coldness creeping into her voice.

"An Anlai noble loyal to the cause," I lied.

After she left, I used Xiuying's herbs to concoct a simple tea against pain. It would not cure Lei's illness, only dull his symptoms, but this was all I could manage for now. After forcing Lei to drink it, I slumped beside him, then slept like the dead.

I AWOKE TO AN UNEASY STIRRING IN MY GUT. I COULD HEAR THUDDING footsteps above us, and the dull murmur of voices just beyond the walls. Standing on the rice bags to gain height, I pressed my ear to the cellar trapdoor.

"We found two escaped mares just outside Heyi. If you're hiding her here, you and your descendants will pay—up until the seventh generation."

My throat constricted at the threat, but Madame Wu sounded unperturbed. "If I hear of any news I will report it back to you, General. We have always followed the Imperial Commander in this household."

There was the low thrum of activity, and then a new voice, from farther away. "She's here, somewhere." Beads of sweat gathered on my forehead at the familiar timbre of Sky's voice. "I can feel it."

Damn you, I thought miserably. *For making me feel this way, small and afraid. For making me loathe you, when all I once wanted was to spend my life by your side.*

LEI'S CONDITION WORSENED. HIS SKIN BURNED FEVER-HOT AND YET HE shivered uncontrollably. He would take no food and barely any water. By the second day he could not keep his eyes open, having drifted into a restless oblivion. His pulse felt sluggish to me, and there were several times I panicked, thinking his heart had stopped entirely. Despite my best efforts, I was losing him. He would die under my watch.

"*Leave me,*" he'd told me. "*You must go on.*"

Had he Seen it, that he would die? Or had it only been a calculated remark, to convince me to leave him behind? And who had poisoned him—who wanted the Ximing prince dead?

We had already wasted two nights hiding in this cellar, and still Sky's troops swarmed every village in the prefecture. Sky would stop at nothing to find me. And I could not leave Lei behind like this, half-dead but still half-alive.

All the while, my time was running out.

I brewed more herbal teas to keep busy, though he refused to drink most of them. I could feel the contamination of his qi, like a once-roaring river now choked with algae.

His face was perturbed even in sleep, and I smoothed the crease between his brows, my hand lingering on his face. His beauty was the first thing I'd noticed about him, and it had intimidated me, how handsome he was. Yet now I understood he used it like a shield, so that others overlooked him, mistaking his vanity for foolishness. Somehow, over time, his beauty had become a comfort to me; it was his mind that frightened me still.

I sat up, realizing I could feel no breath from his lips. He wasn't dead, was he? Even though he was resting, selfishly, I wanted assurance. "Lei," I whispered, trying to recall the last time I'd heard his voice. "Lei, wake up."

He did not stir. Jagged fear gripped me, sending my pulse into a frantic race. I leaned over him, fingers trembling as I undid his tunic and pressed my ear to his bare chest, straining to catch a heartbeat. Silence. Only the furious pounding of my own filled my ears, and I wished for a foolish moment that I could transfer a part of mine to him.

There was a way, I thought, recalling old legends of the autumn and spring periods. There was a way I could lend my qi to him. But my life force was already so weak. Could I afford to give more of it away?

I thought of how Lei had brought water to my cell. How even before that, he had come to my aid in the dungeons, when I'd lost the will to live. Everyone marked him as a monster, but what if he was one of the most selfless people I knew? It was hard to tell, with him. He went to such lengths to conceal his true motivations, so that no one would ever suspect kindness lurking behind that wicked grin.

With trembling hands, I took one of Lei's knives and sliced open my wrist. Before the blood could leak down my arm, I brought my wrist to his mouth.

Reflexively, his lips parted. I watched his throat work as my qi transferred to him. When the pressure of his mouth diminished, I bound my wound, then pressed my ear back against his chest. Lightheaded with exhaustion, I felt tears drip from my eyes as I listened and listened, and then at last heard a slow, faint rhythm. I treasured that sound, pressing my cheek against it as if I could shelter it from the cold and wind.

It was like him to make life so troublesome for me, to make even his death as inconvenient as possible. "Ming Lei," I whispered. "Fight it, you bastard." In a quieter voice: "Don't leave me here alone."

He forced one eye open, reaching for me. I gave him my hand gratefully, squeezing it with all the strength I had left.

"I'll stick around," he said, in a voice so low I had to strain to hear it. "I'm not done with you yet."

ON THE MORNING OF THE THIRD DAY, MADAME WU BROUGHT BREAKfast with a radiant smile. "They answered our call," she told me breathlessly. "At last."

"Who?"

"The Black Scarves," she said, before clarifying, "the Leyuan rebel forces—who overthrew Warlord Yuan."

Lei had mentioned them, I recalled. He'd warned that they were moving west.

"They just finished a mission in Chuang Ning and are now returning to Leyuan. They've kindly offered to escort you to your journey's end."

"My journey's end?" I repeated.

"To First Crossing," she replied. "They have to pass through the city regardless on their way to Zhong Wu. And their military leader is here too." She giggled unexpectedly. "He's rather memorable."

I swallowed with distaste. I wanted no part in their rebellion, but I would have to use them for my own means. I could allow them to escort us as far as Weiyang, I decided, so that we were out of Sky's grasp. Lei and I would split off from there.

Nodding, I wolfed down a few scallion pancakes, braided my hair, then secured my sword on my back.

"Phoenix-Slayer," Madame Wu said, nodding with approval at my appearance. "Long may you live."

My face heated with discomfort. For I was beginning to see the similarities between how they addressed the Imperial Commander and how they addressed me.

"Help me take the throne because you know me. Because you know I'll be a better ruler than the rest of them."

"*Meilin*," Lei had asked, and under the dragon's influence, I'd thought him absurd at the time, "*what makes you so sure you'll be better?*"

"He's coming!" cried Madame Wu.

We all felt the rebel leader's presence long before we saw him. His heavy, hulking footsteps shook dust into the cellar, and I wondered if he was stomping on the floor to make himself known. Then, when he dropped through the trapdoor, I understood.

He was a man built like a mountain, so tall his head nearly bumped the ceiling. The cellar had felt spacious to me, but with the rebel leader inside it, the room grew cramped, as if he took up the space of a dozen men. He wore a pair of thick eyeglasses, though he did not give a remotely scholarly appearance. His hair was tousled and unkempt, tied in a loose ponytail at the nape of his neck, and his skin marked by months on the road: freckled, weather-beaten, and strewn with fresh cuts and old scars. Still, despite the lines around his eyes and mouth, he looked to be in his mid-twenties, for there was an undeniable air of exuberant youthfulness about him, as if he believed he could do anything, and he could convince you of the same.

"Tan Kuro," he said, without any of the usual courtesies. "I've heard a lot about you, Hai Meilin."

I inclined my head. My neck hurt just looking up at him. "I can't say the same about you."

"Then I haven't been doing my job," he said, smirking. "By the time I'm done here, everyone in Anlai will know my name."

"As a hero or as a villain?"

He laughed. "That depends on whether they're smart enough to pick my side."

I appraised him carefully. "And what makes you so sure your side is the winning one?"

He shrugged. "People like me don't doubt themselves," he said, exuding the sort of elusive, magnetic confidence I had struggled so hard to make my own. "Otherwise we'd never have the guts to do what we do." He extended a hand to me, motioning toward the trapdoor. "Shall we?"

I did not take it. "How much do you know about me?" I asked, testing him.

He shot me an easygoing grin. "I know you're a skilled warrior who could probably cut me down with that thing faster than I could blink." I raised a brow at the way he described my blade. "I know you're pretty enough to charm a man in your sleep. And . . ." He leaned in. I did not want him so close, but I refused to back down. "I know you probably have more powers than you're letting on, if the rumors are anywhere close to true."

The back of my neck prickled with unease. "What rumors?"

"They say you slayed the Vermillion Bird, but no one knows how you did it. Well, I have a theory or two."

I used my silence as bait.

His grin widened as he placed a scarred finger on my neck, then slid it down, slowly, hooking it around the string of my necklace—

I jerked away from him, my hand slamming down to conceal my jade. Breathing heavily, I glared at him.

He raised his hands in a conciliatory manner. "I mean no harm," he said. "I'm just despicably curious is all."

"Touch me again and you'll lose the hand," I snapped.

He grinned. "I do love a feisty woman."

My glare deepened. "A third time and you lose your head."

He laughed. "All right. I got the message. You like your personal space, and I like my limbs attached to my body. Now, let's get on the road?"

"One more thing," I said, wiping my sweaty palms on my trousers. "My friend comes with me."

Kuro shot a skeptical glance at Lei, who was passed out in the corner. "He's a near corpse," Kuro pointed out. "You can't let the man die in peace?"

He said it jokingly, but the remark made me stiffen. "I thought you were a powerful leader of a great force," I said tightly. "Use your multitude of resources to secure an antidote for him." I bit my lip. "Or I'm out."

"*You're* out?" He choked on a laugh. "My dear, you're the one trapped in a cellar because your spurned lover is ransacking the kingdom for you. And you're trying to tell me what to do?"

"You need me," I said, bluffing. "You wouldn't be here if that weren't true."

Our eyes locked in a silent battle of wills. At last, Kuro sighed. "I take it back," he said grumpily. "I don't like feisty women. More trouble than they're worth."

I waited, not moving a single muscle in my face.

"All right," he agreed. "We do have a healer in our crew. She'll fix him right up."

I suppressed the urge to smile. Perhaps I was better at bluffing than I thought. Lei humbled me with his ability to read my every feeling, but most people weren't Lei.

"Help me lift him," I said.

"Demand after demand," Kuro grouched, but his eyes were full of mirth, and I could tell he hadn't really conceded anything that had cost him.

"Who is he, anyway?" Kuro grunted as he took the brunt of Lei's weight on his shoulders. "A bit too handsome for *just* a friend, no?"

I flushed at the insinuation. "He was my personal guard in the palace," I said, for I'd torn apart his expensive silk robes and removed all jewelry from his person. "He's very... dear to me."

Kuro grinned knowingly. "A woman of the people!" he said emphatically. "Well, a handsome bodyguard will fit right in with the stories we spin. I'll get a scribe to—"

"No," I said forcibly. "I want no part in your—your propaganda—"

"Propaganda?" said Kuro, mock offended. "My dear, this is *history*."

TWENTY-FIVE

And when the Red Mountains groan, it is said to be the stirrings of the Monkey King trapped beneath, imprisoned for his defiance of the Celestial Emperor. His wrath shakes the earth, a warning that even the mighty must yield.

—WINTER AND SPRING ANNALS, 483

Kuro had a diversion staged, so that when we emerged into the sun and escaped on horseback, Sky's men were nowhere to be seen.

After three days underground, I felt overstimulated by everything—the sun, the wind, the animals, and the people. Kuro's rebels were a rowdy and brazen crew, entirely unlike the nobles I'd grown accustomed to in the Forbidden City. And yet it was clear from the onset how much they respected and lionized their military leader. As soon as Kuro issued a command, it was done, no questions asked.

So no one protested when Lei was given special treatment, despite the rebels' initial distrust of him. Because of Lei's condition, we had to stop earlier than expected, setting up camp a day's ride from the Dian River, where we would pivot south and follow the river's path down to the mountain pass, which would lead to First Crossing.

As Kuro's healer treated Lei, I tried to help, but she quickly shooed me out of her tent, insisting she needed to focus. Wandering the campsite, I found Kuro sitting by the firepit with a tiny woman who barely reached his chest. What she lacked in height, however, she more than made up for in strength. Despite the frigid temperatures, she wore a fur-lined vest with no sleeves, baring her muscular arms. They sat on a log grilling skewers of lamb, and I noticed that while Kuro was grilling, the woman was simply eating.

I approached tentatively, feeling like I had on my first day at the army training camp. "Can I sit here?" I asked.

"Phoenix-Slayer!" said Kuro, waving a grilled skewer at me. "Please, sit." He leaned toward me. "Don't worry about your friend," he added. "My healer is the best you'll find."

I shrugged, but worry still gnawed at me. The small woman passed me a grilled skewer. "Eat."

At her order, I realized I was famished. I bit into the freshly seared meat and savored its bold heat, infused with cumin, peppers, and garlic.

"Desert-style," said Kuro appreciatively. "Good, isn't it? Meilin, this is Lü Jinya, my right hand. Jinya, Meilin."

She spared me a half-second glance before returning to her food. I gave her a longer assessment, noting the multitude of throwing stars she wore on her body. Kuro too I assessed differently. Knowing he had a female second-in-command made me like him more.

Kuro grinned as if guessing my thoughts. "She trained me well," he said, patting Jinya on the head. In response, she shoved his face away with the back of her hand, and he nearly tipped off the log with laughter. Without smiling, she continued to chew the remains of her skewer, until she'd cleaned the stick. Then she reached for seconds.

I felt a prickling sensation and glanced behind me. Two men were staring at me, their gazes overly curious in a way that made me stiffen.

"Lan. Hanwen," Jinya barked. "Aren't you on patrol next?"

They saluted and hurried away. She shook her head at their receding backs. "Fresh meat," she muttered.

"What?" I asked.

She pointed at me. "You." She spat on the ground, then wiped her mouth. "Watch your back. They've all heard of your prowess with the sword. But you know how men are. They won't believe it until they see it." She got to her feet and eyed Kuro. "I'll check on patrol," she said, before striding off.

"One of us needs to work," said Kuro, stretching out by the fire. He took off his fogging glasses and cleaned them on his tunic. Without the thick frames, his eyes appeared unusually light, though it was hard to tell in the dark. "We'll be passing the Zoigen Marsh tomorrow. Will you come with me to see my mother? She's been dying to meet you. You're something of a living legend around these parts." His eyes gleamed strangely. "Makes me jealous."

I scratched the back of my head, uneasy. "I don't know," I said. "It's a detour, and I'm pressed for time."

"After all I've done for you," he said, wheedling, "you won't agree to pay a short visit to my mother?"

"Your mother lives here?" I asked. It was out of the way, but only by a day, and Lei could not move far regardless.

He shrugged. "She doesn't like people. This is as rural as it gets."

I appraised him silently. Kuro had an open, honest sort of face, the kind that made people invite him into their homes and beds, despite his huge stature and many war scars. His was a face that could lead a rebellion.

"All right," I said. "But only for the day."

He pumped his fist in the air like a little kid. "Yes!" he exclaimed. To me, he said, "We won't tarry."

"And I have a list of medicines I want acquired," I added.

He groaned loudly, but I could tell his distress was performative. "You're draining me dry, Phoenix-Slayer."

I thought of Lei's jewels in my satchel—I'd held on to them in case we needed the cash for supplies. "I can contribute."

He gave me a long look. "I don't want your gold," he said. In a quieter voice: "I want your friendship, Hai Meilin."

I RETURNED TO THE TENT TO FIND THE HEALER PACKING UP. "HE'S STABLE," she said, fatigue lining her face. "He would have died from the poison—if not for Kuro. Did he drink something intended for you?"

"Kuro?" I repeated, bewildered. *Did Kuro save him?*

She shot me a look as if I were being obtuse. "Tan Kuro is a poison master," she said simply, before leaving.

Alone, I sank onto the floor beside Lei. His face was still pale, but now I could see the slow rise and fall of his chest. Lying beside him, I watched that subtle motion, trying to assure myself it was real. Gently, I placed my hand over his chest, and then—I felt it. His heartbeat.

Comforted, I withdrew my hand just as he caught it. "Stay," he whispered, his voice barely a rasp.

"I'm right here," I answered. Still, he did not release my hand. We stayed like that all night—Lei asleep and I only pretending. For I did not dare fall unconscious.

Now that we were once again surrounded by people, I feared the dragon's reach. I did not know how he had manipulated Zibei, but I dreaded the possibility that he could compel and corrupt others. Perhaps he had used other spirits as his proxies. Or perhaps he had not needed to do anything at all. Perhaps, from the start, it had always been me.

Checking to ensure my irons were secure, I kept watch over Lei's sleeping body, both relieved and exhausted to see the sun rising over the jagged horizon. It was a new day, and I was still alive.

———

WITH ALL THE RAIN AS OF LATE, THE ZOIGEN MARSH REMINDED ME OF an overflowing cup, brimming with puddles that never ended. Under the spring sunlight, the shallow waters appeared like polished mirrors, reflecting back the bright blue sky and the waterfowl traversing it.

Kuro kept up a steady stream of chatter as we sloshed our way through the wetlands. We saw a few wild bulls grazing on the grasses and gave them a wide berth, but other than animals I could see no sign of civilization for miles. By midday, tired and hungry, I asked Kuro if we were lost.

"Lost? Me? Never," he replied, though he did double-check his compass. I rested my hands on my hips as I waited for him to navigate us. But instead of carrying on, he set his rucksack on a protruding stone. "I know what your problem is," he said, grinning. He fished out a barbecued pork bun from his belongings and foisted it high in the air like a trophy. "You're hungry, aren't you? Jinya's always a brute when she's hungry."

Without responding, I snatched the bun from him.

The bun was as soft and fluffy as a pillow, and the savory inside—full of barbecued pork, green onions, and eastern spices—was somehow still warm and steaming. I had to give the Leyuan rebels credit where it was due—they ate much better than the Anlai army.

"Good, isn't it?" said Kuro. "We have a spirit wielder on our cooking team—keeps the food hot no matter how long it's been stored."

I raised a brow. "So you permit spirit wielders to join the Black Scarves?"

"Permit?" he guffawed. "We *recruit* spirit wielders, my friend. Have you seen the damage they can do? One powerful spirit wielder is worth a hundred swordsmen, in my humble opinion."

I mulled this over. "Are there many in Leyuan?" I asked. "I mean, a year ago I knew of not a single one in all the Three Kingdoms."

Except myself, I didn't add.

He shrugged. "There's a growing number. With all these new gates popping up, anyone who dares can become a spirit wielder."

I spared him a wary look. I heard no judgment or fear in his voice. "Would you dare?"

His smile was cutting. "Would I dare?" he repeated thoughtfully, before suddenly jumping to his feet with a ferocity that made me flinch. I shot upright as I felt it too—a slow rumbling, shaking the earth.

"Bandits," said Kuro. "Sounds like a lot of them."

A huge force of bandits slowly emerged on the horizon, charging across the wetlands and spreading around us like water circling a drain. My heart accelerated at the sheer magnitude of their force—there looked to be nearly a hundred of them. The bandits leading the vanguard held sabers and spears, while the ones in the back carried bows and arrows.

"Vultures," Kuro spat out. "They'd join the rebellion if they had any moral code."

Now wasn't really the time for a lecture. "We can't fight that many," I muttered, edging closer to Kuro. "What do you think they want?"

"Our heads," he said simply. "We're both wanted men." Then he glanced at me, a grin curving his lips. "Apologies, Wanted Lady."

I ignored his ill-timed joke. We were about to be slaughtered and he was really grinning as he wrapped his fists with bandages?

No matter how formidable a fighter he was, his fists would do nothing against a hundred bandits.

"*One powerful spirit wielder is worth a hundred swordsmen, in my humble opinion.*"

I looked down at my iron manacles, which seemed to hum at my attention. Could I? No, I thought, rubbing my blackened veins, hadn't I overused my lixia enough? And yet . . . what difference did six or two months more of freedom make if I was going to die today?

A man who appeared to be their leader rode toward us on horseback, undeterred by the danger the marshes posed to his horse.

"We've been following you," he said to Kuro. "Thanks for making it easy."

Kuro drew his curved saber. "Easy?" he said. "I never promised easy."

"Kill them, but keep their corpses intact," the bandit leader ordered his men. Raising his voice, he shouted, "Today, we're rich men!"

A bead of rain fell on my cheek.

"*I gave you an ocean of might and you chose a drop of rain instead,*" Qinglong had once told me. He was right. I had nearly died that day, and moreover, I'd let my friends and companions die.

While I still lived, I would do anything necessary to survive.

Rain began to drizzle across the marsh, turning the already wet earth into oozing mud.

"Kuro," I said under my breath, "I need you to break my irons for me."

I rolled up my sleeves to show him my manacles. His eyes bulged with surprise and indignation at my irons. "What are you wearing those for?"

"Ask me later," I snapped, balancing my wrist against a protruding rock. "Hurry!"

Taking the steel hilt of a dagger, he rammed it with considerable force against my manacle. I clenched my teeth at the impact, but we both saw the crack that split the iron. He struck again, this time hitting the weakened spot, and the iron shattered into pieces.

I felt my lixia stir within me like a sleeping beast.

He went to work on the second manacle as one of the faster bandits swung at him from behind. "Watch out!" I shrieked, and Kuro ducked just in time to avoid getting beheaded, though he cursed as the saber glanced off his shoulder.

Forced to separate from Kuro, I dodged a flying arrow and threw a dagger of my own, listening for the satisfying *thwack* as the dagger met its mark.

I tried to draw on the overflowing water around me, but the iron blocked my lixia. I had to get back to Kuro, fast.

A trio of men came at me from behind. I sidestepped them once, twice, three times, weaving them into a tight formation where they became impediments to each other. Impatiently, one man's cudgel struck out too soon—thwacking his companion, who let out a cry of anger as I slipped out beneath them and ran.

"Kuro!" I shouted, as he felled a man with a single punch. The man did not get up. "Finish the job!"

I stabbed the man attempting to jump Kuro, then tripped another who ran at me. A third bandit locked me in close combat, and I managed to slit his throat, but not before taking a long gash to the arm. Sweating with pain and adrenaline, I steadied my left wrist on the rock and gestured frantically to Kuro. He raised his blade in the air just as an arrow came flying toward him from behind. I could tell him to duck, I realized, but then I would be no closer to freedom. And this time, with the majority of the bandits upon us, we would not make it.

Squeezing my eyes shut in a moment of weakness, I did not see the arrow embed itself in Kuro's shoulder, but I heard his howl of agony. Still, he did not waver as he brought his dagger down on my manacle, smashing it to pieces.

Qi and lixia coursed through me—yin and yang, dark and light. All at once, the world opened itself to me. I screamed in pure exhilaration as I opened my arms wide and brought the marsh to life. The sleeping tides pulled out from under the bandits like quicksand, and I watched and laughed as men stumbled, fell, *drowned*. Their screams echoed across the vast plain, and all the while the waters rose and fell upon them, as turbulent as ocean waves caught in a monsoon storm.

My vision flickered in and out, but I ignored it, my bloodlust overcoming my fear. There was one man remaining—one man who had somehow shielded himself against my lixia. I felt the small irritation like a kitten's scratching. Turning, I caught sight of the spirit summoner, his eyes yellow as he pointed at me. Birds of prey obeyed his command, diving toward me with their talons out. I used the rain to divert their path, sending them whirling back into the sky, before narrowing my focus on the lone summoner. I could feel the itch of his lixia, like a tiger sensing the nibbling of a rat. With a savage smile, I contorted my elemental threads to match his—then infiltrated his mind.

"*Who sent you?*" I asked, and in the sound of my voice, I heard the echo of Qinglong's. I sensed the strangeness—that I should've felt fear. But in my lixia-addled state, I felt only dizzying elation.

"I-I'm not sure," he stuttered. I narrowed my eyes at him, focusing as the world around us dimmed. "Old Gu mentioned something about the big man. The . . . rebel leader. He gave us the tip-off—"

He choked, blood sputtering from his mouth before he fell to his knees. Behind him, Kuro had slit his throat.

"Impressive," said Kuro, inclining his head toward me in a mock bow. "I barely had to lift a finger."

It took me a moment to realize what he was saying. As I stared in numb shock, I saw that all the bandits were dead. I had killed them all.

I let out a gasp of panic as, all at once, the fight left me. I swayed, struggling for balance, before collapsing to my knees in the mud. My sight went out like a snuffed candle as my body shook from lixia withdrawal, and I only had time to bend over before I vomited my guts out onto the river weeds.

I clutched my head in my hands, trying not to hyperventilate. *Qi gong, remember your qi qong.* But my control had deserted me, and try as I might, I could not bring air into my lungs.

Without my vision, the world spun around me, and I felt as though raindrops were flying into the sky. I was too weak to rise, but I felt the presence of another, his boots thudding toward me.

"The rebel leader," the bandit had told me. *"He gave us the tip-off."*

I was not safe, I reminded myself, my hands clenching into fists. I needed to defend myself—to fight—

But I could barely summon the strength to raise my head, much less stand. "You . . . you set me up," I said numbly, as Kuro stood over me. "Was this your plan all along? To wear me out, then kill me yourself?"

I felt him squat beside me. "My dear," he said. "Didn't I say we were friends?"

"Then . . ." I squinted at him. I could make out faint outlines once more, but his face was barely visible through the rain. "Why?"

His smile grew distorted in my vision. "What can I say? I've always wanted to see the power of a Cardinal Spirit summoner." He leaned in and I flinched. "It was better than anything I could've imagined."

He'd used me. He'd used me like a prized animal, as nothing more than mindless entertainment. Every death today had been unnecessary, serving no more purpose than Kuro's amusement. I coughed, tasting blood in my mouth.

"Let's get you bandaged up," he said, ignoring the arrow sticking out of his own back. He pulled out swaths of clean linen from his bag and wrapped them generously around my wounds before turning to his own injuries. I half expected him to ask for help, but instead, he gave them only a cursory inspection.

"Ready?" he asked, to my surprise. There was an arrowhead still embedded in his shoulder.

"You're not going to . . ."

"Are you willing to dig it out?" he asked, arching a brow.

I expelled an angry breath. I could not have resented him more in that moment—for using me, and then guilting me into helping him. But who knew what blood loss he'd suffered, and if he died now, his death too would be on my hands. Hadn't I caused enough death today?

"Turn around," I ordered stiffly. He squatted beside me, saying little as I cut the shaft and dug the arrowhead out of his shoulder, wincing at how deep it had penetrated the flesh. This would take months to recover from.

"What about your mother?" I asked. "Does she actually live here?"

"I don't have one," he said. "She left when I was a child." I could hear the smile in his voice. "For all I know, she could be living out here."

I shook my head, too weary to hold on to my anger. "Done," I said, sitting back on the rock.

"Can you stand?" he asked, holding out a hand.

Burying my pride, I clung to his arm as I tried to pull myself up. But my knees gave out, and the attempt left me dizzy and nauseated. My old shoulder wound from the war throbbed painfully, a familiar ache that always flared when I reached the brink of exhaustion.

"Get on my back," he said.

I looked up at him. "No."

His lip curled. "Are you going to die for your pride?"

"N-no."

"Then come on," he said. "Before it gets dark."

The thought of being left out here in the cold and dark was enough to spur me into action. After I climbed onto his back clumsily, he lifted me as if I weighed nothing and went on his way, whistling and humming a melody under his breath. Although I thought it impossible, with his even, steady steps and song like a lullaby, gradually, I fell asleep.

TWENTY-SIX

Many civilizations have sought to tame the Zoigen Marsh—some with stone, others with fire, and still others with oxen. But whether in the span of ten days or ten decades, all were undone by the slow breath of the marsh. To this day, the wetlands remain untouched, where nature bows to none.
—REMEMBERING THE WU DYNASTY, 913

I FELT MY CONSCIOUSNESS SLIDE, BUT I DID NOT THINK MUCH OF IT, not until I realized I was watching myself from a bird's-eye view, and that I was no longer in my own body. Below me, Kuro placed my body on a cot and handed me off to his healer. Was I dead? Had I somehow drained my life force, and now lacked a tether to return my spirit to my body?

I began to float, drifting out of the tent and into the sky. I struggled to return, to wake up, but instead, I found myself wandering into the spirit realm.

It was alive, bustling with tremendous activity and a chaotic, frenetic sort of energy. I didn't recognize any of the faces wandering the glowing trees, speaking with spirits, enacting bargains, testing their newfound lixia. As for the unlucky ones on the ground, writhing, foaming at the mouth—their spirit affinity not strong enough to withstand the onslaught of lixia—I turned away from their faces. I did not wish to recognize them.

I was seeking a pool, a pool from a memory or a dream. It had been many months ago, and many li away, and yet distance did not matter in the spirit realm. After some time, I found that golden pool of water, so brightly lit it was hard to see past the sparkling surface.

But there was a flicker of movement—a long tendril of hair, a confident swimmer's strokes. That girl—the one who I'd once believed to be me. She was still here, and while I had aged, she had not.

"Meilin," she said, and I recalled that her voice had always been different—sweeter, *younger*. "You're back."

"Who are you?" I asked, my lower lip quivering. Hope bloomed like a tiny seed in my heart, struggling to put down roots in a barren land. "You're not . . . you're not my mother?"

She tensed, her eyes widening in a gesture both achingly familiar and eerily strange. Then she did something that made the world go still. She nodded.

She nodded and I began to weep, my tears flowing into the pool of water and making the pond grow and grow, until nearby spirits grumbled and drifted away from us. Fireflies buzzed irritably in my ear, chastising me for disturbing the peace. Still, I wept.

"Why?" I asked her. "Why are you here?"

"Qinaide," she said. *Beloved.* But she kept her distance. She didn't comfort me as Xiuying would have, nor did she offer the simple touch of a friend.

"There comes a point for every spirit summoner when a choice must be made," she said. "You can let your spirit master subsume you entirely, as the Great Warrior Guan Yang once did. Or you can take your own life, denying both your spirit master and yourself." She paused, her gaze piercing mine. "Then there is a third path, though few are strong enough to take it—you can seek Zhuque's spring and relinquish your power." Her sad eyes were like mirrors, reflecting my wretchedness. "You must understand how difficult the path you've chosen will be. The dragon will do everything in his power to stop you."

"Ma," I whispered. "I-I'm so scared. I don't want to die."

"Remember, Meilin," she said softly, "the dragon is only as strong as you are. You both walk a fine line, because although you are his enemy, he depends upon you, as you do him."

"He was using me," I admitted aloud for the first time. "He was using me to create the rifts in the veil."

The melancholy in her gaze belied the youthfulness of her face. "He needs you, Meilin. The minor spirits may accelerate the process, and expand the existing rifts, but they cannot create a gate out of nothing, not like you can. The greater the rift, the more unstable the veil. Already it has been stretched thin. There is too much qi in this world, and too much lixia in yours."

I rubbed my temples, hard. This wasn't my problem. I needed to focus on finding Zhuque's eternal spring. I didn't have time to concern myself with Qinglong's plans or the fate of Anlai.

But it wasn't just the fate of Anlai, said the nagging voice in my head. It was the fate of the Three Kingdoms. Of the human world itself.

My mother nodded as if I'd spoken these thoughts aloud. "Once the veil collapses, it will be like the times of old—and spirits will once again roam freely among men."

All along, this had been Qinglong's plan.

Lei had tried to warn me: *"I believe that you and I share the same concerns, do we not?"* He had read my mother's diary and understood. Understood the gravity of our predicament and its far-reaching consequences. Meanwhile, I had covered my eyes like a child in a game of hide-and-seek, my focus narrowly fixed on securing the throne—a mere distraction that Qinglong had used to keep me preoccupied while he orchestrated greater schemes.

Even now, I wished to return to ignorance, to ignore my mother's caution, to run. I had never asked for any of this, I wanted to say.

But I had. I had lusted for power, skipped my stone across the water. Before me were the ripples of that throw, spreading wider than I'd ever anticipated.

"Be careful who you trust, Meilin," said my mother. "For the dragon does not act alone."

"What do you mean?" I asked, frowning. "Surely he doesn't have another vessel?"

"Not another vessel," my mother agreed. "But you are not the only summoner in disagreement with their spirit..."

She fell silent, and now I noticed the sudden absence of sound. All activity died; humans went quiet, spirits drifted away, and even the fireflies paused in their incessant buzzing.

"You must go," said my mother, sensing the change in the air. "Now."

"I-I don't know how." I knew I needed to use my qi gong, but as of late, I had not been able to find the calm required for it.

"Remember yourself," she said. "Remember your humanness, and you will be able to return."

"What about you?" I asked. "How will you be able to escape him?"

"I have my ways," she said, returning to the pond.

The tides lapped at my feet, restless and stirring. Birds shrieked as they took flight into the darkening sky. The air carried the heavy scent of an approaching monsoon, the wind hot and flecked with hints of rain.

"Hai Meilin." I had forgotten the blistering icelike quality of Qinglong's voice. I shivered compulsively, a trained response. "Long have you eluded me."

I could hear the triumph in his voice, the satisfaction he would take in my inevitable surrender. The currents rose, bringing me with them. I struggled to keep my head above the surface. He was going to drown me.

"Why do you run from me?"

"You deceived me," I hissed, paddling frantically to keep myself afloat. "How can I trust you anymore?"

"Meilin, do not forget—you and I share the same ambitions. What I seek is no different from what you seek for yourself. To no longer be confined to the darkness, to claim true freedom without chains."

Taken aback, I understood he was speaking of the spirit seals. Just as iron bound me, was the jade a manacle to him?

"I am going to restore the world to its former glory," he continued, his excitement causing the waves to churn. "You cannot fathom the wonder of those days, when spirits roamed free. We were not considered demons then. We were revered as gods."

"Revered?" I asked. "Or feared?"

But he did not hear me. "Just as you were not content in your father's house, the darkness of the spirit realm cannot satisfy me."

"Do you expect us to go quietly?" I asked. "The people will fight back."

He scoffed. "Humans are weak-blooded creatures. Their only real strength lies in their numbers. Fortunately, they rarely agree on anything, so even that advantage is inaccessible to them. Once the veil falls, humans will simply turn on one another."

"Millions will die," I snarled, "all for the sake of your greed. The world may have been wondrous to you then, but our history remembers it as a time of chaos and suffering. We've just come out of one war—must you thrust us into another? Does human life mean so little to you?"

The tides rose even higher. The sea beneath me was black, as was the sky above.

"I am a dragon," he said. Was it my imagination, or did Qinglong sound sad? "I must desire more. It is simply the way of things."

Before I could protest, a wave tossed me under. I choked, gasping for breath. But I was in the spirit realm, I reminded myself, and breathing was but a construct here. Even though my lungs screamed for air, it was all in my mind. Qinglong could not kill me.

But why did I feel like I was dying?

Remember your humanness, Meilin. Remember what you have to live for.

"*I love you.*" I recalled Sky's face in that moment, the certainty of his gaze. "*I love who I am with you. You vex me. You frighten me. You challenge me. And I would have it no other way. With you by my side, I'm confident we can rebuild Anlai for the better.*"

"*The future is always a source of comfort.*" Lei's voice was bitter. "*It's the past I despise.*"

The suffocating darkness pressed against me.

And yet I cling to hope, that obstinate creature, my mother had written. *I must hold out until the end of winter, when I can make my last journey to the Red Mountains—and save myself—*

"*You never understood me.*" I'd tried to cut Sky where it would hurt the most. "*Sometimes I think it was a mistake for us to be together.*"

"*Do you want to die?*" Lei had asked. "*If you die, they win. Remember that.*"

I imagined diving into the frigid Ximing sea to escape imprisonment, training under the stars every night to prove myself, dressing as a concubine and crossing inside my enemy's bedchamber, not knowing if I would survive the night. My addiction had begun to define me, but so did my persistent will to live.

"It is inevitable—" the dragon snarled. But I was gone before his words could reach me. My eyes flew open and I jolted awake, once again returned to my body.

I was lying on the hard dirt, and there was someone leaning over me. A man. One of Kuro's rebels. Terror and fury surged through me, each strengthening the other. His hand rested on my shoulder, his eyes hungry in a way that made my body lock in conditioned fear. Though I was no longer a prisoner of Ximing, no longer bound in chains, my body remembered. It remembered the paralyzing fear from the war, when General Huyi loomed over me, reveling in my helplessness.

"You're awake," the rebel said, surprised. "Did you have too much to drink, doll?"

I snarled, an animal-like sound, and threw him off me with such force that his body struck a neighboring tree. Stunned and bewildered, I looked down at my hands, before understanding that I'd used my lixia.

The world was tinted red with my thirst for violence. I advanced toward him as he groaned and clambered to his feet. "Look," he said, holding out his empty hands. "I only—"

His mind lay open to me, like a nest of baby chicks to a hungry hawk. *You will never touch another woman again*, I told him silently.

"Cut off your thumb," I ordered.

His body went rigid, his face turning vacant. From his boot he drew a hidden dagger. Then, without hesitation, he began to saw at his left thumb, barely blinking as blood poured from the wound.

The scent of blood only quickened my hunger. I would make him suffer, I decided. I would make him suffer so badly he would wish for his own death.

I smiled, baring my teeth. *"Now your hand."*

He was bleeding profusely already. But under the spell of compulsion, he ignored his injuries and directed his attention to my order. Shaking, he lifted his blade in the air.

"Meilin?"

I turned at the sound of that voice, that low, crackling baritone. I glanced at him, and what he read in my face must have frightened him, for he seized me by my shoulders and shook me. "Meilin!"

"*Release me*," I ordered. But although he trembled, he withstood my compulsion.

"Meilin, look at me. Look at me!"

His voice carried no spirit power, but it held a strength of a different sort. I looked at him, truly looked, and at last, I saw him.

"Lei," I said, my shoulders slumping as the haze of violence cleared. "You're recovered."

Behind him, I heard the rebel saw through bone. "Stop!" I cried out. "*Stop*."

At the commotion, others emerged from their tents. The man named Hanwen approached hesitantly, before spotting the rebel bleeding out on the dirt.

"Lan!" He crouched beside the unconscious man. To me: "What have you done?" His eyes were both accusatory and afraid. "You—you monster."

I was shaking all over. "He attacked me," I said, my voice thin and frightened. But, I wondered, had he? Or had he only been checking on a sleeping girl lying on the forest floor? How could I have jumped to such conclusions? How could I have tried to prolong his pain—I, who had experienced no scarcity of suffering?

My knees buckled. Lei caught me before I collapsed, steadying me against him. My veins were so black they looked like streaks of ink against my paper-white arms.

"Kill me," I whispered. "Just kill me now—before I ruin myself."

"No," he said, his grip tightening around me.

"Get away from me!" I struggled against him, but he locked my arms to my sides. "I'll hurt you too," I whispered, shaking uncontrollably. "I'll corrupt you."

He shook his head, refusing to let me go. "I'm safe from you," he said, with complete conviction.

He lifted me in his arms, carrying me back into his tent. I tried to sit up on his pallet but my journey to the spirit realm had left me exhausted beyond reason. Had the bandits' ambush only been today?

I had lost control of myself because I'd overused my lixia, back in the Zoigen Marsh. It was a parasitic relationship, I realized, with power inextricably tied to madness. How foolish I'd been to believe I could be the exception. No one was immune to power's inevitable corruption—not even the most powerful man in the world.

"I'm so tired," I whispered, my voice wobbling. "I'm so tired but I can't rest. If I fall asleep"—I swallowed—"I may lose myself again."

His eyes bored into mine. "I won't let that happen," he said, and he spoke with such certainty I felt the lure of trusting him.

"How can you be so sure?" I asked. "What if the dragon tries to corrupt you? What if I hurt you—" My voice broke at the possibility, at the helplessness I felt over my own body and spirit.

He came over to me then, drawing me into his arms. My body was ice-cold, but his was warm as a low fire.

"If you must know," he said, his chest rumbling beneath mine, "I lack a spirit disposition."

"What does that mean?" I asked, struggling to stay awake against his soothing warmth.

He adjusted me so that my head rested on his shoulder. It was so comfortable I could hardly keep my eyes open.

"It means I cannot perceive or possess lixia in any capacity," he said, his voice like the crackling of a hearth. "As for you"—I could hear the smile in his voice—"I think I have some sway over you."

I relaxed, nestling closer against him. In my sleep-deprived state, I did not fully understand what he meant, but I trusted his judgment, and moreover, I trusted his ability to think a step ahead of me.

Then I recalled his recent bout of illness. "Is this okay?" I asked, lifting my head to peer at his face. "Am I too heavy? Does it hurt anywhere—"

He laughed softly, pushing me back down. "Sleep, Meilin. I prefer you here, like this." He brushed a tendril of hair from my face. "With me."

Perhaps he did hold some sway over me, because his voice was like compulsion. Unable to resist the intoxicating sense of safety, I succumbed to dreamless sleep in his arms.

TWENTY-SEVEN

Although spirits cannot directly harm their vessels, the peril of inaction should not be underestimated. Indeed, many powerful summoners have met their demises at the hands of their own spirit masters, who simply neglected to offer a word of warning when it was most needed.
—LOST JOURNALS OF AN 8TH-CENTURY LIXIA SCHOLAR,
DATE UNKNOWN

SUNLIGHT STREAMED IN THROUGH THE THIN TENT CANVAS, BUT the warmth it offered was meager in the crisp morning air. I snuggled closer to my source of heat, before registering that it was Lei's bare chest.

I had fallen asleep in the Ximing prince's arms? Only a month ago, I would have laughed at the sheer impossibility. Studying his sleeping face now, I tried to make sense of how I felt about him.

I had not truly forgiven him for the atrocities he had committed against me during the war. Perhaps his goals had always been the same as mine, and perhaps the ends justified the means, and yet my personal grudges had nothing to do with logic and reasoning. At times I still flinched when I caught his attention on me, as if conditioned to expect punishment to follow.

And yet, despite all his flaws, despite my lingering trauma, somehow, I trusted him. His brush with death had revealed something undeniable: I cared for him. More than I ever knew.

He stirred, his arms tightening reflexively around me. Considering me with half-lidded eyes, he somehow managed to appear both cavalier and possessive. "See?" he said, his voice husky from sleep. "Nothing happened last night." When I bit my lip, he unhooked it with his thumb and forefinger.

"You're very pleasant when you sleep," he remarked. "Much less disagreeable."

I scowled at him, but at his teasing eyes, I felt my face soften. With his lips this close to mine, I couldn't help but recall the last time we'd kissed—right before I'd pulled a knife on him. He had tasted like sin, and I had only wanted more.

My lips parted, and his gaze darkened in response. Did I want him to kiss me? No. Yes. I was a tangle of desire and disgust, loathing and want. Confused, I pushed against him, and he released me, watching me silently as I got to my feet and dressed.

Though I knew I owed Sky nothing, I couldn't shake the deep-rooted guilt that crept in whenever I thought of him. He had expected me to fall for Lei, and perhaps in some twisted instinct for defiance, I wanted to prove him wrong. But was that enough to keep me away? I wanted Lei; that much was evident. But did I love him? Or was I incapable of love now—in any capacity, for any person?

Outside, the camp felt tense, like a drawn bowstring. I sensed the rebels glancing furtively in my direction but avoiding my gaze. And yet I heard laughter and applause coming from the center of the camp, followed by Kuro's distinctive booming voice.

Near the firepit, Jinya was smirking with her hands on her hips. "Can you do the same?" she asked, the challenge clear in her tone.

Kuro chuckled and took off his cloak. A few onlookers took wary steps back, and I too kept my distance, watching from the tent line. Kuro drew a deep breath, before leaping backward—an attempt at a backflip, I saw. Despite his colossal size, he almost managed it—before flopping on his back like a fish. Everyone roared with laughter, applauding their commander's attempt. Good-naturedly, Kuro righted himself, bowing to Jinya in defeat.

I watched this display with growing unease. How was Kuro able to twist his back like that—after taking an arrow straight to the shoulder? I had seen the severity of his wound, how deeply it had cut into his flesh. And yet he acted as if he were fully recovered, as limber and energetic as a teenage boy.

Jinya saw me, and her ghost of a smile vanished. She whispered something to Kuro, who looked in my direction and waved. As I came forward, the jovial smiles and good humor of the other rebels faded. I was a plague to them, bringing calamity wherever I went.

Jinya gave Kuro a pointed look, as if reminding him of her instruction. Obediently, he cleared his throat. "Listen up, folks. Our good friend Lan is lying in bed right now, nursing his many wounds."

My chest tightened as I awaited his condemnation. My hand went to my sword, and the rebels mirrored me, readying for a fight. Only now did I notice that some of them were like me—some of them had yellow eyes.

A cold tremor crept down my spine. Could I face this many swordsmen and spirit wielders on my own?

"Let his current predicament serve as a reminder for all of you. From now on, anyone who lays so much as a hand on our Phoenix-Slayer will be put to death. No exceptions," he said. "She is our friend, and we *respect* our friends, don't we?"

His easy tone clashed with his menacing words. The rebels nodded nervously, glancing at me with renewed discomfort. I studied Kuro, trying to understand his motivations. What did he want from me?

He'd used me to kill those bandits, claiming he'd acted out of mere curiosity. But I'd seen the way he'd regarded me after the battle, as if testing me. Why?

I could feel him holding something back, and I didn't trust his kindness. Yet he'd saved Lei, helped us escape Sky's men, and now he even sided with me against one of his own rebels. Perhaps what secrets he kept didn't matter; what mattered was that with his horses and supplies, we could reach First Crossing in half the time.

Jinya glared at the rebels, ensuring that they understood their orders. Then she handed me a flaky scallion pancake, which was crispy and warm, melting in my mouth.

"The Anlai contingent is also going the Dian River route to First Crossing," Kuro told me, as the others dispersed for breakfast. "We'll have to take the longer course around Weiyang Lake to avoid them."

"How many men?" I asked, my hands tightening around the pancake.

"The Anlai warlord goes with them, so I imagine an army's worth." Kuro shook his head. "No way are we taking that on."

"No," said Jinya in agreement. "We are fighting a slow war."

Was this why Kuro was helping me—so that I could helm his revolution for him? I knew the Leyuan rebels wanted rebellion not only in their kingdom but across all of Tianjia. But how did I factor into that equation? If they believed I would confront Sky in battle they were madder than I thought.

Lei joined us, clean-shaven and neatly dressed. Kuro made room for him before the fire, and he sat beside me, his familiar presence like a balm to me.

"My good man," said Kuro, clapping him on the back, "what should I call you?"

"Zhao Zilong," said Lei effortlessly. I nearly choked on my water. It was the name of my former friend—and the name I had given Lei when we'd first met. "It's a pleasure to finally meet you. I see the bards don't exaggerate."

Kuro puffed out his chest with pride, and I contained the urge to roll my eyes. As Lei asked him about our planned route to First Crossing, I noticed he'd changed his accent, adopting the northern Chuang Ning tones as easily as changing clothes. And Kuro was none the wiser.

Lei did not trust him either, I realized. Wondering what Lei read in him, I thought suddenly to use my impulsion. I watched Kuro, letting my elemental threads mold to his. The overwhelming disproportion of earth in his qi perturbed me, and I frowned at his imbalanced energy, which I now sensed as peculiar. Even more peculiarly, I could not infiltrate his thoughts. Pressing against his mental shields was like pressing a hand against hard-packed dirt, finding no forgiving soil.

How was he so impenetrable? His mental shields reminded me of Lei's in their invulnerability. But his qi, in its sheer weight and presence, reminded me of another's—a man who'd sacrificed his life rather than become the monster Zhuque would've made him.

I had not thought of Sima Yi in a long time. The reminder left me restless.

My suspicions deepening, I said nothing as Kuro rose to ready his mount. I waited until he left, before claiming I needed to use the latrine. Then, I followed him.

He was talking to his horse, a stallion with a resplendent red mane. He fed him a carrot from his pocket, then an apple, then another carrot, his demeanor both cheerful and childlike. He gave the impression of a simple man. But perhaps his simplicity was a mask.

Hardening my resolve, I expelled my breath, then reached for my lixia. Before he could turn, I crystallized water in the air, then hurled dozens of ice knives in his direction, which whizzed toward him with a speed no throwing star could surpass.

And yet the rebel leader reacted within the span of a heartbeat. Whirling around, he threw up a wall of stone around him, and the knives of ice embedded themselves in the rock, before melting into harmless puddles of water.

My mouth fell open in astonishment. I stood frozen as his eyes found me and he smiled grimly. "How did you know?" he asked.

"Baihu," I whispered. I should've recognized the distinctive presence of a Cardinal Spirit in his qi. That had been the odd, pressing weight I'd felt, the irresistible charisma of his qi. "You have the power of the Ivory Tiger."

Baihu was the Ivory Tiger of the west, of autumn, and of earth. Even the ground I was standing on—it was not safe. Not from him.

The dragon does not act alone.

He took off his glasses, and now I saw what was obvious in retrospect—how they concealed the yellow glint of his eyes. Because he had not wanted me to know.

"It was you," I whispered. "You were the one forming the spirit gates."

He shook his head, still smiling. "The ones down south, sure. But the northern gates were all thanks to you, my friend. Why do you fight it? Why do you fight it when we seek the same outcome?"

"Is Baihu controlling you too?" I whispered, as if there were a way the tiger spirit could not overhear me. "Is that why you're doing this?"

"Controlling me?" he repeated, as if I'd said something ludicrous. "Controlling me?" He threw his head back with laughter. "My dear, I am the one controlling *her*."

He was a lost cause, then. He believed what I'd once believed—that I could be the exception, the one to thwart fate. That I could be the one immune to the corrupting hand of power.

"So it is your wish to tear down the veil and let the spirits run amok among us?" I asked, disbelieving. "You would give our world to them, and let this too become a world of spirits?"

"What I want," he said, his eyes glittering, "is a world for all people."

"Then—"

"*All* people," he said again. "The blacksmith, the butcher, the widow, and the orphan." He closed the distance between us, as I edged back. "None will be greater than the other; the prince himself will be our equal. There will be no more class division, no more blood lineage, no more landowners and tenant farmers and beggars on the street. For the land will be centrally owned, and power will be returned to the people. At last."

"Then why?" I asked, my voice rising. "Why destroy our world if you care for its people?"

"Because I care for them," he said. "I equip them. I offer power freely, rather than withhold it for myself. That is what sets us apart from every lord and sovereign before us. You and me, my dear. We can be the last dynasty."

"You've got it all wrong," I insisted.

"With every new gate opened, more and more common folk can cross into the spirit realm," he said, voice slow, patient. "More and more people can become summoners and restore power to the masses. How do you think a ragtag band of untrained rebels defeated the Leyuan warlord? How do you think we'll defeat the Anlai one this time?"

"Aren't you tired of war?"

He shook his head. "For us common folk, the war never ended." He grew impassioned, stirred by the sound of his own voice. "They tax us mercilessly, stealing our hard-earned coin, promising to repair our roads and fill our storehouses in winter. But winter has come and gone, and the roads are still ruined, and the storehouses empty. The common people are starving, while in the palace, they gorge themselves on the spoils of our labor."

Was anyone ever satisfied? I wondered. The dragon wanted more; the people wanted more; even the lords and kings wanted more. Was this then our fate—to fight and destroy one another until the world was reduced to ruins?

Kuro must have seen the hopelessness in my eyes, for his voice gentled. "My friend, the time of emperors and warlords is over. The Mandate of Heaven has passed on to the people. Together, we can build a world where women stand equal to men, where every peasant has the same opportunities as a nobleman. A world where the land is not hoarded by corrupt officials but held centrally by the state for the good of all. Imagine the promise of such a world."

My heart was thudding wildly in my chest. His tone was soothing, level, and his expression sure and steady. In contrast, I was weak, torn, indecisive.

Help him. Help him return power to the people. You want equality, don't you? You trained those servant girls in the palace, even though you weren't supposed to. How is this any different?

Kuro's hand came down on my shoulder, and I flinched. "*Help me, my friend. Help me crush the foundations of the old world, and build a new one from its ashes.*"

I couldn't think, couldn't breathe. How could I discern right from wrong anymore? Who was an enemy, and who was a friend? I had been so certain in my choice to trust Qinglong, who had never seen me as his equal. At the same time, I had been too quick to discredit Sima Yi, aiming to kill him before I'd even known him.

What if the spirit gates did topple the monarchy? What if change *was* needed—what if the Three Kingdoms could not go on like this anymore? What if another young woman, as dissatisfied and reckless as I'd once been, was peering out her window at this very moment, wondering what lay beyond the monotony of the women's quarters? What if I gave her a fighting chance? What if she too struck a bargain with a spirit; what if she too sought the power that had transformed me?

"*Hai Meilin*," Kuro said, his eyes glowing strangely. "*Help me serve the people.*"

His compulsion entered me like sand slipping through the cracks of a sealed door. I felt myself go still, the anxious thoughts in my head settling like dust motes floating to the floor.

A spinning knife sliced open my tunic sleeve, drawing the thinnest of cuts. I turned in surprise, before spotting Lei fast approaching us.

Lei, who never missed.

Waking from the rebel leader's spell, I glared furiously into his gold eyes. Without giving him a chance to react, I plunged my qi into his, adopting the techniques I'd once tried on Chancellor Sima. I felt the dark energy of his lixia, the human emotion his spirit fed upon. Just as Qinglong devoured my greed, Baihu fed his pride.

He believed he could do no wrong.

He believed he could save the world.

I let his thoughts become mine; I let my qi become earth, let our minds settle like fresh soil under the sun. And then I was in.

"*I warned you not to disrupt the energy flow.*" Baihu's voice was like sharp claws trailing your skin. Soft yet lethal. "*The veil is splintering. But you cannot allow the realms to merge. We are nothing without balance.*"

"*I know what I'm doing!*" Kuro had shouted back. "*Why can't you trust me?*"

Kuro's mental shields slammed up against me before I could overhear more of their conversation. Blinking against the morning daylight, I squinted up at him. Baihu did not wish the realms to merge? Then the tiger's goals were not the same as the dragon's?

As I pondered this, dozens of rebels assembled behind Kuro, led by Jinya, who was now armed to the teeth. I drew my own sword.

Jinya tensed, but Kuro did not lift a hand. "Don't make me fight you," he warned. "You know this is a battle you cannot win."

"Even your spirit master has more sense than you do," I spat. "If you continue down this path, you'll do more than destroy the ruling regime. You'll destroy the world itself."

His eyes were bitter and bright with scorn.

"Everyone wants change," he said, lip curling, "but no one wants to pay the price of revolution."

I felt Lei's presence by my side, and I took strength from his aura of calm. I shot him a questioning look, and in answer, he gave me an infinitesimal nod. *So be it, then.*

I tightened my grip on my sword. "I will not join you," I said, my voice carrying across the silent campgrounds. "My loyalties do not lie with Anlai, nor with any other regime." I swallowed, wondering how much to tell him. Wondering if I had a choice now, surrounded and outnumbered.

I squared my shoulders. "I told you I am journeying to First Crossing. I did not tell you why. The truth is, I am seeking Zhuque's eternal spring—to relinquish my spirit power, and to give up my bond to the Azure Dragon."

Kuro's mouth went slack. Then his face hardened with repulsion. "You're mad," he growled.

"Yes."

The veins in his neck bulged. "You're making a mistake."

"Perhaps," I said. "But it is my mistake to make."

Kuro looked furious at this. His men tensed behind him, readying for battle. Yet Jinya was the first to sheathe her blade. The sound, so incongruous in the tense silence, caused even Kuro in his anger to hesitate.

"Kuro," Jinya said quietly, and some of his anger dimmed as he turned to his right hand. "Remember the core tenets of the Black Scarves. You cannot force her."

The rebel leader wore his emotions openly, so that I could see the warring resentment and irritation on his face, the mutual desire and disgust.

At last, he swung toward me. I anchored my qi, but he only said, "Fine. Seal your own prison." With a derisive laugh, he beckoned for a nearby rebel, who passed him a pair of iron bands, identical to my former set.

"Since you so love your chains," he said, throwing the irons at my feet. My cheeks burned at the humiliation, but I kept my head held high.

"You think you're unstoppable," I said. "I would know—I was there once. But the time will come when you realize that power always demands a price. And that price may be more than you're willing to pay." My hands were shaking; I lowered them to my sides. "By then, it may be too late. The one paying will not be Baihu. It will be you."

I could tell my warning fell on indifferent ears. When he met my eyes, there was not a hint of doubt or uncertainty within them.

"If you will not join me, Phoenix-Slayer, then do not stand in my way."

TWENTY-EIGHT

In the wake of the war, Zhong Wu came to be known as the City of the Dead. The fallen lay strewn along the roads, untouched and unburied, for none dared approach, fearing the plague clinging to their spirits. And so, silence claimed the city, where even the wind dared not mourn the unburied souls.

—COMMENTARY ON WARRING STATES PERIOD, 822

KURO LET US GO FREELY, BUT HE WAS NOT WITHOUT HIS SPITE. HE took from us our horses, our provisions, even our former clothes. But it did not matter. Lei and I were used to surviving, and neither of us were strangers to suffering.

For three weeks we journeyed on foot, taking the long route around Zhonghai Lake to avoid the Anlai warlord and his five-hundred-man contingent. By the time we reached Mount Fuxi, spring was well on its way. The air had grown fragrant with budding hydrangeas and plum blossoms, and the forest songbirds had returned with the advent of clear skies and warm weather.

I kept my irons on at all times, even though they dulled my senses and drained my stamina. We moved at a snail's pace because of me, though Lei hid any sign of impatience.

I began to dread the passage of each day, sensing the finite strength of my life force slipping away. I was only nineteen, for skies' sake. Even my mother had lived longer than I. And Qinglong would have stolen both our lives.

The spite fueled me then, when exhaustion threatened to overwhelm. Just another mile, I told myself, for Qinglong would not take me too.

All the while, Kuro clearly ignored Baihu's caution. We saw more and more spirit gates cropping up along our path, which left me with a deepening sense of intertwined dread and guilt, so that I could barely look at the corpses littered on the forest floor, much less the still-writhing ones, alive but not for long.

How many had successfully made the transition? How many had emerged as spirit summoners, glorifying in their newfound power and awareness? How many already regretted their bargain? How many had begun to sense the insidious pull of corruption?

In the woods, we stumbled upon two crying children—a rare sight in these parts. I wished to avoid them, but Lei insisted on investigating.

Standing at the bank of a dried creek bed were two young girls, the older one around Rouha's age. Though distressed, they appeared unharmed.

"What happened?" Lei asked, crouching in front of the older one.

"Ma," she whimpered, pointing toward the creek bed. "She went through that . . . that pocket. She didn't come out."

The pocket was a spirit gate. It shimmered against the forest shadows, its surface rippling like an ocean tide. Even from a distance, I felt the luxurious heat radiating from it, the way its lixia tugged at me, calling me closer. But to Lei, it meant nothing.

"You," said the younger girl, her huge eyes locking on me. "*Help.*"

Her expectant gaze unsettled me. Somehow, she knew I could help. She knew I could cross into the spirit realm and search for their missing mother.

"I-I'm sorry," I whispered, backing away. "I can't."

The older girl grabbed my hand. "You can!" she insisted. "I know you can. Please."

I yanked my hand free, too forcefully, and the girl stumbled back, landing on her bottom. "Why?" she cried out. "Why won't you help us?"

I shook my head, as if swatting away an angry bee. Why must I help? Hadn't I done enough? I had saved my kingdom during the war, only to be slandered for it. That was when I'd learned: selfishness was survival.

I had done my part; I had warned Kuro to stop. If the veil between realms tore, let the rest of the world solve its own problems. I would not lift a finger to help.

"Rui? Sisi?" A man crashed through the underbrush, sweeping his daughters into his arms when he saw us.

"Who are you?" he demanded. "What do you want?"

"She's here to save Ma!" the older girl said confidently. "She's the one from the stories!"

The man's eyes settled on me, afraid and assessing. I took a step back. Always, I would be found lacking.

"Are you?" he asked, suspicion in his voice. "Are you the one we've been waiting for?"

In the silence, I felt Lei's wordless gaze slide toward me, a gaze like a lit match.

"N-no," I stammered. Then I turned and ran.

AFTER THAT, I TRIED TO AVOID ALL SPIRIT GATES. IT WAS NOT NECESsary to steer clear of them—Lei was immune to the lure of lixia, and I could come and go freely between realms—but my guilt was intensifying to the point of pain. Every portal was a reminder of the violence I'd inflicted, the high cost of my hubris. And yet Lei would not allow us to deviate from our path. He made a point of passing every gate, looking into the faces of those lost to our world.

He did not try to convince me of any side or stance, but his silence conveyed more than words ever could. After all, I reminded myself, the Ximing prince always had his own agenda.

Only once did we run into bandits along the way. Instinctively, I reached for my irons, but Lei recognized my intent and stopped me. "No," he said.

"But—"

"You know it's not worth it," he said darkly, and I recalled that it was Lei who'd held me as I'd suffered from lixia withdrawal, shaking through the odd hours of the night.

Before I could answer, he'd thrown a series of daggers, and within moments all the bandits lay wounded or dead.

We left without making a scene.

I found a semblance of peace in our near-total isolation, in the lack of demands and directions and desires thrown at me. Lei and I learned to read each other's thoughts by gesture alone, until we could determine when the other wanted to rest or press on by a simple look or pause. Knowing he was immune to the dragon's influence, I took comfort in his steady, even-keeled presence, trusting that even if I were to lose myself, he could keep me sane.

But the peace of our journey was short-lived, and by the time we reached the base of the Red Mountains, I sensed that confrontation with Sky was inevitable. Only one path led up to First Crossing from the northern outpost of Kuntian, and from the rumors swirling around town, the Anlai prince and his men had set up camp just beyond the Kuntian city limits. Kuntian was the last outpost before the five-day mountain trek to First Crossing. On the Red

Mountains, which lacked abundant vegetation or prey, we would have to carry our own provisions.

So that evening, as Lei set out to purchase supplies for our journey, I feigned exhaustion and told him I would sleep early. I did not know if he believed me, but he said nothing.

As soon as he'd departed from our campsite, I doused the fire and strapped my sword to my back. Then, as I was about to leave, I noticed a stray shadow a little way from the fire.

Lei's best moon dagger. He'd known—and left it for me.

A lump in my throat, I secured the trusted dagger against my thigh. I glanced at the moon, brilliant in its fullness. A line from *The Classic of Poetry* came to me: *And if I ever write "Tonight the moonlight is strong," I am trying to say that I miss you.*

I hate you.

I miss you.

Ignoring reason, I crept into the dark.

ALL I WANTED WAS TO SEE HIM ONE MORE TIME. NOT EVEN TO SPEAK TO him—I would be satisfied with just a glance. I wanted to see his face, the familiar lines around his eyes and mouth, the cowlick at the back of his head. Our relationship was over, and we could never go back to the way things used to be. But I would pretend, just for one last night.

Then I would move on.

His camp was hard to miss. The Anlai warlord and his heir had traveled with over five hundred men for the signing of the Three Kingdoms Treaty, and now they pitched their tents just outside the city limits of Kuntian. Climbing up the roof of the temple building, which was the highest vantage point in Kuntian, I surveyed the expansive night sky and the sleeping camp below it. Patrol soldiers circled the perimeter, their metal armor flashing against the dark. Others, off duty, stumbled sleepily to the latrine or stayed up late chatting around the firepits. They looked so close I felt as though I could reach out and touch them. But I was not afraid; I knew no one ever bothered to look up.

One soldier ignoring protocol caught my eye; he drifted away from the center of camp, into the surrounding darkness, with only an oil lamp to guide him. How presumptuous, to think himself above the law. If I had ever dared wander alone at night, Sky would have rebuked me to no end. But here he was, doing what he would advise no other to do.

The field was fallow, littered with cut sorghum stalks and stubble, like a young man's beard. Setting his lamp down, Sky drew his sword against the dark, and as he wove his blade back and forth in a rising crane formation, the moonlight reflected against the steel, casting the planes of his face in stark relief.

His face was so dear to me it hurt.

I hated him. I hated him for making me care for him. For making me want him. And then, with the same breath, behaving in such a way that I could never be with him again.

His blade hesitated, then lowered. Sky raised his head to gaze up at the moon, which was merciless, baring what was best left hidden in shadow. I watched the lines of his neck and shoulders, the tapering of his waist, the hair at the back of his head that would not lie flat. I watched him and I said goodbye.

Then he turned.

Impossibly, his eyes searched the temple eaves. I froze, caught between fear and desire. Did I wish to be known? To be found?

He found me. There was a single breath, a moment between moments, when I believed it might be possible to suspend reality. Then the moment passed. Sky took a single step.

My chest seized with fear. I recognized the lunacy of my actions and leapt up from my crouch. Sky started to run. Heart racing, I sprinted across the temple eaves and threw myself across the gap toward the next building. And then the next.

I felt him before I heard him. The thud of his body landing on the temple roof, sending vibrations across the wood. He was close behind me and gaining still. I pushed myself faster, faster; I could not let him catch me. I could not let him undo weeks and weeks of running from him, the palace, imperial life at court. I flew from roof to roof, until I'd reached the end of the village. In a moment of weakness I glanced over my shoulder—and gasped. He was nearly upon me.

Running was futile. I spun and hurled a throwing star I'd taken from the Leyuan rebels. He dodged but kept advancing.

"I don't want to fight you!" he shouted, and his voice sent shivers of terror and happiness coursing through me.

"Then stay away from me!" I shouted back. But he ignored me, approaching with his usual stubbornness.

I had no choice; I drew my sword. His jaw tightened but he responded in kind, raising his own. I attacked first, launching at him and spinning across the low-hanging eaves. He parried, distracted, his attention lingering on my face rather than my sword. My anger unfurled within me, long-buried resentment resurfacing beneath the moonlight. This time, I struck without restraint, and my blow landed with such force that he stumbled, his sword slipping from his grasp and tumbling off the roof into the shadows below.

Unaccustomed to the terrain, he tripped on a loose tile, falling dangerously close to the edge. I didn't give him a chance to recover. Seizing my opening, I pinned him down, my blade pressed to his throat.

"If I beat you in single combat," I said, and he stilled beneath me. I saw it in his eyes—he was remembering, just as I was, the first time we'd fought with lethal intent. "If I beat you in single combat, then you leave."

"I thought winning meant staying," he whispered, the knot at his throat rising and falling.

"That was when I wished to stay." How young I'd been in those army days, thinking everything I wanted could be won with glory.

"And now?"

"And now I'll never return." I started to rise. "Let me go, Sky."

His face darkened. He reached out and grabbed me by my tunic, pulling me down. Furiously I struggled against him, and in our frantic tussle we slid farther down the edge. We cared less about living than about fighting, and perhaps that was why the moment we tipped, we only saw each other.

TWENTY-NINE

Everything reminds me of you.
—LIU SKY, IN A PRIVATE MISSIVE, UNDELIVERED

THE MOMENT WAS FAST YET BRUTAL. SKY WRAPPED HIS ARMS around me, positioning himself beneath me to take the brunt of the fall. Still, when we slammed into the hard earth, the impact drove the breath from my lungs with such force that I couldn't inhale, couldn't move. I lay sprawled in the dirt, my vision flickering at the edges. I could hear the gentle susurrations of a bamboo grove around us, the clack of bamboo poles and the ominous shushing of leaves whistling in the wind.

Gradually, I felt Sky stir beside me, and I forced myself upright despite my aching bones.

Sky groaned and crawled toward me. I tensed at his proximity, reaching for my blade, but then saw the grudging mirth in his eyes. As if against his will, he began to laugh, and it was then that the absurdity of our situation struck me. He smiled at me, and without meaning to, I smiled back. It was like muscle memory; I couldn't help it.

His eyes softened as his hands searched for me in the half dark. I didn't know if he was trying to strangle me or to kiss me. Still, I let him. I was weak and I let him.

His hand slid up my throat to cup the back of my neck. This was madness, I thought, but I did not pull away as he lowered his mouth to mine, gently, tenderly, with none of his former violence.

I let my blade clatter to the ground as I breathed out a sigh of inexorable pleasure, relaxing against him. He tasted like nostalgia, like the blinking stars on a warm summer night. He tasted like the golden haze of all my long-held dreams.

I had wanted him so badly, for so long. He had been mine, and then I had let him go. Why had I let him go? Why had I believed this couldn't work between us? What if we could try again—what if we truly stood a chance at happiness?

He ran skillful fingers across my shoulders, massaging my neck where I liked, knowing which places were my weakness. I hummed like a cat, leaning into his touch. I let him deepen the kiss, giving in to the present moment.

And then—I heard it. The quiet drag of rope. It was barely discernible against the murmuring bamboo, but my ears were attuned to the threat like the sound of my own name. My eyes flew open as I caught sight of the coil of rope in his left hand, long enough to bind an unsuspecting prisoner.

Anger returned to me like summer rain, needing no preamble. I shoved him back before grabbing my sword, which had fallen in the dirt. Furious, I swung recklessly at him. He ducked out of the way, but my sword caught the trunks of several bamboo poles, slicing them in half so that they fell like beheaded men.

Sky's gaze went from my sword to the sliced bamboo. "I don't know what else to do, Meilin," he said, his voice wretched. "I don't know how else to keep you safe."

"The difference between me and you," I bit out, "is that I've never tried to own you."

He tried to speak but I was done talking. I feinted left, then struck out with the hilt of my blade, connecting my steel to his temple. Sky crumpled to the ground, the coil of rope abandoned beside him like a lifeless snake. For a cruel moment, I considered tying him up, to teach him what it was like, to remind him of what he'd done to me.

But my gaze drifted above the bamboo grove to the moon, scintillating in its fullness.

"When I look at the moon," Xiuying had told me, *"I think of you."*

My stepmother would have loathed tonight's violence. It would have reminded her of my father.

My father, who I hated to emulate. My father, whose inheritance I'd tried so hard to run from, every day for the past nineteen years of my life.

An inheritance of addiction and violence.

I checked Sky's pulse—stable—then gathered my belongings and went on my way, the full moon my witness behind me. As I climbed again onto the rooftop eaves, this time, I resisted the urge to look back.

LEI WAS WAITING BY THE FIRE WHEN I RETURNED, SHARPENING HIS blades. At the sound of my approach, his gaze traveled over me in silent, exacting assessment. When I winced as I sat beside him, he said, "You're hurt."

"Only bruised."

He stared into the fire. "I thought you might go with him."

I swallowed. "Our time is over. I'm sure of that now."

The even strokes of his whetting filled the quiet mountain hush, until the stars above seemed to blink in time with the rhythmic sounds. The hour was late, but I couldn't sleep, not on a night like this. In the thin air, I could smell the subtle fragrance of wildflowers, of bamboo groves, of cold running water. Chuang Ning and the Forbidden City felt far, far away. Yet somehow, on a night like this, its memories felt so very close.

"Let me look over your wounds," said Lei some time later, after he'd put away his weapons.

Reluctantly, I unbuttoned my tunic and lowered it from my shoulders, exposing my back, which had taken the brunt of my fall, to him. The night air chilled my bare skin, but I embraced the cold, feeling as if I deserved some punishment for the stupidity of the night. Yet Lei's hands were warm as he assessed the cuts and bruises littered across my back.

"This one may need disinfecting," said Lei, uncorking the last of his wine supply.

As the alcohol met my open wound, I hissed at the pain, though I had endured far worse. In fact, it was nothing, nothing more than a scrape. Nothing more than a boy, a boy I'd known for barely a year, really, a boy that I'd thought I'd spend my entire life with.

Instead, we'd tried to kill each other. More than once.

Was this who I was? Incapable of love, engendering violence and hate in those I tried to cherish?

The dragon had chosen me for a reason. Because I was filled with greed, never satisfied, always craving more than I deserved. That was the darkness within me, the hunger that could never be sated.

My eyes ached at the corners. I felt a single tear roll down my cheek, then another.

Silently, Lei dressed my wounds. When he was done and I'd re-tied my tunic, he handed me a handkerchief. It was a women's handkerchief, embroidered with yellow and pink peonies in bloom. Briefly, I wondered who had given it to him.

"Have the rest," he said, offering me the remnants of his last bottle of baijiu. "We'll need to pick up more supplies in First Crossing anyway—I couldn't find much in Kuntian."

I took a generous gulp, grimacing as the liquor burned my throat. "It was stupid," I said, answering a question he hadn't asked. "I was stupid."

He shrugged, passing no judgment. He was unusually reticent on the subject, I noted. Almost as if he didn't want to influence me. I offered the bottle to him, and to my surprise, he hesitated.

Considering him in the half dark, I asked, "You knew where I was going tonight." Aloud, it sounded less like a question than a statement. "Why did you let me?"

A different prince certainly would have stopped me.

"You're allowed to make your own stupid decisions," he said, voice light and teasing. Then he took the bottle and drained it. Without his usual confidence, he said, "But next time, let me come with you."

I shook my head at this. I didn't need a chaperone, especially not one to bear the brunt of my mistakes. "I can handle myself," I told him. "And if I can't, it's my problem."

A memory from the war surfaced, and a bitter smile tugged at my lips. *"You're a good fighter, Ren, but you're a terrible soldier,"* Sky had told me. *"You think for yourself. You don't obey orders. And you look out for your own agenda over your platoon's."*

He'd been right, all along. I had never followed orders particularly well. Not in my father's house, not in the army, and certainly not in the imperial palace. I had never worked well with others. I had never known how to see them as equals and partners in my plans.

"I know you're strong," said Lei, his eyes ruminative in the firelight, "but being strong doesn't mean you don't deserve to be protected and taken care of."

I couldn't meet his gaze. Looking away, I swallowed the sudden emotion rising in my throat. "Who gave you that handkerchief?" I asked, changing the subject. "Lady Tang Liqing?"

"She had little reason to make me cry," he said, in his mocking way.

"Then who?" I asked, wondering just how busy he'd been around the palace.

He appeared ready to crack another joke, but at my warning look, he said instead, "My sister."

I hadn't even known he'd had a sister.

That was when I remembered—Zihuan, Lei's brother, had once mentioned another girl. "Rea," I recalled, and Lei nodded reluctantly. "Where is she now?"

"Tzu Wan." A pause, and then, "She was married this past month."

"I'm sorry you missed the occasion," I said, and I meant it. "Did you approve of the match?"

He nodded with a certain arrogance. I would've bet money he'd orchestrated the entire affair himself.

At his reserve, I asked, "What's she like?"

He sighed, reaching for the bottle before finding it empty. "I'm not drunk enough for this."

I shook my head at him. "I need you clearheaded, Lei."

"I know," he said with a sigh. "But it doesn't make me miss the taste."

He spun the empty bottle against the dirt. "What is she like?" he wondered aloud. "Rea . . . Rea is insatiably curious. She asks more questions than a constable, and solves more cases than one too.

People come to her with all sorts of problems, and she loves to help them, no matter how small the issue."

I watched his face, the way his eyes grew soft as he spoke of his sister. He looked young then, and I was reminded of the fact that he'd been a boy not too long ago. We had all been children, once—before this war had consumed us.

"She had these pet dogs that she used to bring with her everywhere. She loved them, probably more than she loves anyone. She'd feed them before she ate her own supper. Her teachers all disapproved, of course, but against their wishes she trained them—until they could perform truly marvelous tricks. Feats even humans couldn't manage." He smiled at an unknown memory, his expression far away.

"You love her," I said, for it was plain to see.

His eyes cleared. He stretched out his legs, feigning tiredness. But I waited, not letting him evade the question. At last, he replied, "Yes."

"Why do you never speak of her?"

He rolled his jaw. "It is a weakness," he replied. "And it can be used against me. I am not so foolish as to wear my vulnerabilities on my sleeve." And he had once cautioned me against doing the same.

His own brother had used this weakness against him.

"Yes," he said, and I wondered if I had accidentally spoken aloud. "But Rea is safe from him, for now."

"Do you think your brother was the one who had you poisoned, during the Spring Festival?"

Grimly, Lei nodded. "Zihuan had my father assassinated in a similar manner."

I hadn't even known his father was dead. Theirs was a strained relationship, and yet he was still his father. "I'm sorry."

He shrugged. "Ours is a family only on paper."

I watched him toy with the empty bottle, struck by how little he had. Vilified by the official reports, treated as a demon in Anlai, and dismissed as a frivolous, empty-headed prince in Ximing. Neglected by his family, hunted by his own brother. And yet, despite it all, he cared more than I did. He still believed the world was worth saving.

Compared to him, I had so much. I thought of Xiuying, Rouha, and Plum—my family, who had been kept from me for months. I'd seen them only for a few precious moments before fleeing Chuang Ning, and now there was a very real chance I would never see them again.

"I have a sister too," I blurted out before I could stop myself. "Well, more than one."

Lei's eyes flickered like moonlight on water. "Did you visit them in Chuang Ning?"

"The Imperial Commander forbade me from seeing them. For over a year I didn't see them." I clasped my arms around myself, thinking of how much I'd sacrificed in the palace. I'd had no friends and no family in the Forbidden City—so that Sky had become my everything. And I had fostered that dependence.

"I saw them before I left the capital. Only for a few minutes, but... they've grown so much. I could hardly recognize Rouha and Plum."

"You've grown too," said Lei.

I returned his gaze. It was true; I wasn't the same girl who'd fled my father's house a year ago. I was more calloused, more scarred, more angry, more afraid. I had more to lose now.

I leaned back on my forearms, gazing up at the night sky. "When do children stop being children?" I asked.

"In war?" said Lei lazily. "Yesterday."

At my lack of understanding, he said, "There's no hope for children in times of war. You either grow up or become another casualty."

I remembered Plum jumping into the ring of dragon dances, Rouha stuffing her face with mooncakes. I thought of Lei's sister, Rea, training her many dogs. I imagined Ming Lei as a little boy, watching his mother's beheaded corpse dragged in the dirt. I recalled myself at eleven, covering my ears late at night to shut out my father's violent tirades. I remembered a bloated purple foot slipping free from the shroud, the last trace of my mother that I'd ever seen.

I thought of a young woman training late into the night, who'd believed it was courage and hard work that would make others recognize her.

She'd believed the world to be a fair and kind place.

"I want something better for them," I said, thinking aloud. "I want a different sort of childhood for them. Not like the kind we had."

Lei's eyes bored into mine. When he spoke, his words sounded like an oath. "Then we make it happen."

The bamboo leaves murmured in foreboding. In that moment, I missed my mother more than anything in the world.

I shook my head, drawing my knees into my chest. The world was broken, but so was I. This was a job for someone else, another great warrior, or a hero that could be sung about in ballads to come. It wasn't a problem for someone like me, someone damaged, someone who couldn't afford to care for others while my own life hung so precariously by a thread. I had to be selfish. I had to save myself.

But how will I be remembered? a voice whispered in the back of my mind. Would history vilify me? Would they call me selfish? Would they ask why, when the world was falling apart, Hai Meilin stood by and did nothing?

It did not matter. Like my mother, I was running out of time.

"I-I can't, Lei." I didn't know what he wanted from me, but I couldn't take any more responsibility. "Don't push me on this."

He released a hard breath, which fogged in the cold air. To my surprise, he let it go. "I'll take first watch. You should get some rest."

THIRTY

I advise the use of erxin berries. Even those trained in poison cannot develop resistance to them, making them an effective and discreet option.
—MINISTER HUI, IN A PRIVATE MISSIVE TO CAO ZIHUAN, 924

First Crossing had descended into total chaos. Despite the flood of newcomers here for the Three Kingdoms Treaty, most trading stores had been closed and boarded up, so that basic supplies like rice and salt were selling for ten times the market rate. Spirit gates had appeared along the edges of the city, making it even more challenging for travelers to enter. As if this weren't enough, the inclement weather made it so the mornings were frigid with icy rain, while the afternoons blazed hot as a furnace, the lack of vegetation on the mountain peak making for scarce shade.

Lei's expression was grim as we crossed yet another spirit gate, this one so small only a child could squeeze in. And by the looks of it, a child had. Her head was facedown in a puddle of water, her little hands clenched into fists. When Lei turned her body over, I gasped in fright to see her face—inky black veins extending out of her eyes across her cheeks.

Lei grimaced, closing her eyes and moving her body out of the main road. Was Kuro responsible for this? For surely the Black Scarves had reached First Crossing weeks before we had, with their many horses and supplies.

As we entered the crowded thoroughfare of First Crossing, my neck crept with anxiety. Road-weary travelers surrounded us, some looking to trade, others looking to steal. In the houses overhead, I scanned the boarded-up windows and doors, unable to shake the suspicion that we were being watched.

Lei had stolen from the bandits we'd encountered, so that we had a reasonable amount of coin on hand. The trouble was, we hadn't anticipated how high the demand would be, and how limited the supply. With the surging prices, we wouldn't be able to afford even a week's worth of provisions, and the trek across the Red Mountains purportedly took months, if you lived to see it through.

"We'll need to sell some of our jewelry," I muttered, looking around the thoroughfare for vendors.

"Not here," Lei cautioned. "It's too public."

Abruptly, he turned and jerked me into a nearby alleyway off the main road. Caught off guard, I nearly tripped over a sleeping man in the corner of the longtang, who'd curled up in the shade of the wall. "I'm sorry!" I said, before looking more closely at the old man. He was barely a skeleton, his skin hanging off his bones in ragged folds.

"Food," he croaked, reaching for me. "Please."

Overhead, a light rain began to fall. I hesitated, wondering what I could spare, but Lei dragged me away.

"I only—" I protested.

He covered my mouth with his hand, pressing me into the shadows. Confused, I tried to shake him off, before he jerked his head toward the roof.

Over two dozen soldiers were crouched on the rooftop, scanning the thoroughfare below. Most puzzlingly—they did not wear Anlai colors.

They wore Ximing uniforms.

"But," I tried to say, into Lei's hand. He tightened his grip.

The old man looked from us to the soldiers. Then he grinned, revealing several missing teeth. "Over here!" he shouted, above the growing rain. "They're over here!"

Lei swore. "We could've given you coin, old man."

"Not as much as they can," the man replied cheerfully.

Lei pushed me forward to run, but it was too late. The soldiers had spotted us and begun rappelling into the alleyway. We both drew our swords, but the space was too narrow, and we were outnumbered fifteen to one.

Hands shaking, I reached for the key to my irons. The rain was thickening now, and it would become my instrument.

"No," said Lei immediately, his hand closing around my wrist. "I won't steal more of your life force." He stepped forward and sheathed his sword. "I'm the one that you want," he said to the soldiers, making his voice heard above the rain. "Let her go."

This had to be Zihuan's doing, I realized. He saw his younger brother as a formidable threat and was determined to eliminate him before he could rise to power. In that way, we were in agreement: Ming Lei was a formidable threat.

"Lei," I ground out. "Don't do this."

"You paid your debt," he told me lowly. "You don't owe me anything."

"Then not out of debt," I decided, "but friendship." And I slid the key into its lock.

But before I could act, an arrow whizzed past me, embedding itself in the shoulder of a Ximing soldier.

The soldiers, lulled by our apparent defeat, were slow to react. In the time it took for them to draw their weapons, Lei cleaved one of them in two. I wondered if he'd known the soldier.

A girl with a black scarf yelled as she swung down into the longtang, skewering another soldier with a long spear. Could it be the Black Scarves? But the rebels had abandoned us, and there was no love lost between their leader and me.

"Friends of yours?" Lei asked, as he took down another soldier who'd come at me from behind. Before I could respond, I saw the knife whizzing toward me and ducked, tripping the soldier to my side so that he took the brunt of the blade.

More and more Black Scarves joined the fray, fighting with shoddily made spears, cheap throwing stars, and even rocks. But one girl—I recognized her by her gap-toothed grin.

"Lily?" I gasped, astonishment surging through me, closely tailed by fear. "What are you doing here?"

"The rebellion!" she shouted. "It's begun!"

A migraine pounded at my temples. I squinted against it as I struck, dodged, slashed. It was a numbers game now, and this time, we had the advantage. As the rain cleared, the remaining Ximing soldiers began to retreat, and then run.

"After them!" a rebel cried out.

"No!" said Lily. "Remember Kuro's orders!"

"Kuro?" I tensed, the sting of betrayal sharper than any battle wound. "You're working for him now?"

"He's the one who sent reinforcements. He's been looking all over for you, Phoenix-Slayer." She yanked off her drenched scarf impatiently. Her face had tanned from time spent outside the palace, and she seemed to have grown even taller in the past few months. Lily was so young, no more than sixteen. And already she was out here, killing in the name of the rebellion.

"*I want a different sort of childhood for them,*" I'd said to Lei the night before. "*Not like the kind we had.*"

And yet, what was I willing to do about it? Nothing.

"Come with me, my lady," said Lily, before laughing. "I mean, Meilin. I'll bring you two to meet him." She grinned conspiratorially. "We're planning something monumental. A way to take down every tyrant at once. Now that they're all gathered at First Crossing, they've made it so easy . . ."

But when the other rebels surrounded us, I pulled away uneasily. "I don't think I should go with you, Lily," I said, taking Lei's hand. If they were targeting monarchs, then Lei would also be in their sights. "You see, we didn't exactly end things on good terms."

"Nonsense," said Lily. She leaned in, lowering her voice. "I think you'll find Kuro's much changed."

I frowned. "It's only been a month since we last saw him."

"A lot can happen in a month."

KURO'S BLACK SCARVES HAD SET UP THEIR OWN CAMP IN THE NETWORK of secret catacombs running beneath the city. I hadn't known about them, but Lei clearly had. I watched his face as we descended, and I could see the mental calculation in his gaze as he tallied up the hidden tunnels and their capacities.

Inside, the air was dank and chilly, an ever-present drip-drop of water coming from far away. Without warning, Kuro appeared in a tunnel doorway like a ghost. I jumped in fright as his giant body leered over us, the top of his head nearly skimming the ceiling.

"Phoenix-Slayer!" he exclaimed, lumbering forward with a limp he hadn't had a month ago. He made as if to reach for me, but I drew my sword, creating distance between us.

"No, no," he said, waving a hand in the air. "I mean no disrespect. Come in. *Please.*"

Lily was right—Kuro *had* changed. His previous confidence and charisma had been replaced with nervous twitching. His complexion, once tawny and vigorous, was now sapped of color. Most strikingly, his eyes, formerly a vivid gold, had darkened in hue, with streaks of black now threading through the brilliance.

He motioned for us to sit, but when I refused, he sat first, anxiously. He cleared his throat, but the words wouldn't come.

I was the first to break the silence. "What happened to you?" I asked bluntly.

"I-I . . ." He swallowed and licked his dry lips. The rebels standing guard looked pained. I examined their faces. Jinya was nowhere to be found.

The back of my neck tingled in a sudden premonition. I glanced at Lei, his eyes steely with understanding. He'd guessed too.

Kuro cleared his throat again. "I lost Jinya," he said, his voice breaking at her name. All at once, the words poured out of him. "She disappeared eleven days ago. There's no trace of her anywhere."

"The spirit realm," I guessed. "Have you tried the spirit realm?"

"I've tried every day. I've walked the forests and the plateaus and the mountains. But it's too slow. If you help me—"

His choice of words was strange. "You've *walked*? Have you not tried impulsion?" I asked, recalling how I'd located Chancellor Sima in the spirit realm, during the war.

"What's that?" Kuro asked, and I raised a brow.

He flushed crimson. "Apologies for not being as learned as you, my lady," he bit out. "Not everyone had the privilege of growing up in the imperial palace."

"I didn't grow up in the palace," I snapped, though I understood to

Kuro, it hardly made a difference. I'd grown up a noble, and he'd grown up a commoner.

"Impulsion is a way of infiltrating the emotions and thoughts of another," I said. "If you use your spirit power—"

At this, he seemed to deflate. When he spoke, his voice was small. "It's no use, then. I've tried to call on Baihu, but she does not answer."

"That's impossible," I said, astonished. Even when the dragon and I were feuding, he had never been able to restrict my powers before.

"We are bound to each other. If she stops using her powers, so must I." He exhaled sharply. "I think she's gone into hibernation. Before she left, she told me she had no desire to play any part in the veil's destruction."

My mouth fell open. How selfish of her, then, to abandon us to our own ruination. If she was truly so noble, why didn't she help us? Why didn't she intervene with her great power?

But in fleeing to the eternal spring, wasn't I doing the very same thing?

"Y-you were right," Kuro said brokenly. "I opened too many gates. I should have been more careful. Jinya... Jinya didn't want to make a bargain with a spirit. She had no interest in lixia. But... you know how hard it is to resist."

I narrowed my eyes. "To resist what?"

He swallowed again. "The lure of power."

"Are you blaming her?" I asked.

"N-no!" he cried out, gesticulating wildly. "I-I only... You of all people must understand. When I accepted Baihu's seal, she fed on my pride. She nurtured it within me—like a pig for slaughter." He let out a broken laugh. "I changed. I thought I could do no wrong. I refused to listen to anyone who disagreed with me. Even when Baihu and I started clashing, when I began tearing more rifts in the veil, even then I believed I no longer needed her. I-I changed," he said again. "I don't know how to go back."

"You can't go back," I said harshly.

"Please." He stood, reaching for me. I tightened my grip on my blade, intimidated by his stature despite the frail, pleading emotion in his eyes. "Please, my friend, help me. I'll do anything—give you anything. I just—I need to find her. I need to make things right."

Then, to everyone's shock, he got down on one knee, and then the other. Trembling, he kowtowed before me. I could almost imagine Baihu's presence in the room with us, bristling with humiliation and affront. The spirit of the Ivory Tiger, the West Wind, who drew upon pride and arrogance for power . . . and here was her human vessel, fighting against her very nature.

Kuro stood a chance, I realized. He was not subsumed yet. Indeed, when he raised his eyes to meet mine, I could see the natural shades of black within them, flickering against the gold. The realization was followed by piercing jealousy. Was his willpower stronger than my own, or was it his sheer desire to live?

But if Kuro could do it, if Kuro could stand against his master—so could I. I was not lost either. Not yet.

If I used my lixia, I would upset my already depleted life force. And yet Kuro had saved Lei's life. He'd twice spared me. It was true I had only a few months left to live as a free person. But if Jinya was lost in the spirit realm, she had none.

"All right," I said, and the tension seemed to ease from the room. Lily smiled, the other rebels sighed, and Kuro, to my infinite astonishment, began to weep. Only Lei appraised me in his impassive way, a knowing glint in his eyes.

I wondered if he could read my thoughts. Because there was another, more selfish motive I had in mind: I wanted to see my mother again.

"Thank you, my friend." Kuro rose to his feet unsteadily. "You won't regret this."

I thought of the last time I'd tried to enter the spirit realm with another summoner. It had not ended the way I'd planned, with Chancellor Sima and I somehow falling into a third realm, the space between realms.

"The safest way to enter together," I said, thinking aloud, "would be through a physical gate."

Kuro nodded, glancing down at his arm, which I saw was covered in cuts. Rather than entering through a gate, he'd been drawing his own blood to enter. For efficiency, perhaps. And because up there, with the imperial families congregating in First Crossing, he was a wanted man.

"Lei," I said, turning to him. "Will you stand guard? My body will be . . . unprotected."

He nodded curtly, and I made to leave before he caught my wrist. "Are you sure about this?" he asked lowly, his familiar scent enveloping me in a cloud of cedar and jasmine. "You know the cost."

His gaze held mine. For a moment, he let his mask slip. Worry, concern, fear, and understanding all flashed through the luminous amber of his eyes. I did not know the full extent of his Ruan abilities, and I guessed I'd never know, but I understood then that he could not truly predict the future. That he was as vulnerable and ignorant to fate as the rest of us, living day to day with nothing more than our feeble hopes and prayers to keep us from sinking underwater.

"I know the cost" was all I said.

THIRTY-ONE

If a man dies in the realm of light, his spirit can pass on. But if he dies in the realm of dark, his spirit is destined to wander forever.
—WINTER AND SPRING ANNALS, 483

We left at dusk, under cover of growing night. Our enemies were myriad: the Ximing warlord, the Anlai warlord, and everyone who hated the Black Scarves.

When we neared the spirit gate, I refused to let Lily venture any farther. She claimed to have resisted the lure before, but I was not taking chances. I allowed only Lei to accompany us, and even Kuro's eyes went wide at the casual and effortless way the Ximing prince approached the gate, undaunted by the whisperings of the spirit realm or the teasing wind scented with lixia. The gate lay directly within a small pond, which was so clear it looked like a mirror, reflecting the darkening sky. The surface of the water shimmered, seeming to wink at us. *Come in*, the waters murmured. *We've been waiting for you.*

I shivered with want, with need.

Lei helped me unfasten my manacles, his hand lingering on my wrist a moment too long before letting go. I gave him a questioning look, but he only responded with a smile that didn't quite reach his eyes.

"This isn't goodbye," I said sternly.

"I know," he said, though I couldn't help but notice the way his gaze strayed to the many bodies lining the lake, some writhing, others still. All unable to enter the spirit realm, yet lost to our world. That this had become commonplace was the most disturbing fact of our new reality. No one had come to clean up the bodies. No one had dared.

Kuro and I locked eyes. His guilt was unequivocal, scarred into the drooping lines of his face. "We'll find her," I told him.

We stepped through together.

THE IMMEDIATE CALM OF THE SPIRIT REALM WASHED OVER ME, THE tension of the past few weeks melting from my limbs. For the first time in what felt like ages, I took a deep, unburdened breath.

The glittering lights seemed to welcome me home. I looked wonderingly from the stirring bamboo groves to the glimmering mirror lake, which reflected the golden stars in the sky. It was a world so beautiful I wanted to weep.

It was a world so beautiful I could not bear to give it up.

"I've already searched all the bamboo forests," said Kuro. "I heard that spirits like to congregate there."

I tensed as an aimless wind drifted through the bamboo grove, so that the leaves murmured around us. Was the dragon nearing? No, I could not sense him anywhere. We were safe, for now.

"Come with me," I said, taking Kuro's hand.

I pulled him with me as I began to listen and search, sifting through the medley of noise to find the voice I was looking for.

Time and space moved differently here, and within seconds or days we journeyed through alpine forests, rolling grasslands and salt lakes, hot springs and humid marshes and cold, high plateaus.

We heard the cries of lost children, the ramblings of madmen, the screams of terrified prey, and occasionally, the gleeful exultations of spirit summoners, reveling in their newfound power. Still Jinya was nowhere to be found.

It was in a thicket of cherry blossoms on a high mountaintop that I heard a familiar voice, but not one I had been searching for. She was sobbing profusely, clawing at the trunk of a cherry blossom tree and leaving red streaks in the wood. Her once perfect nails were now cracked and bleeding, and her pale skin marred with spidery black veins.

I went still. "Princess Ruihua."

The composure I once admired in her had vanished. Now she reminded me of a thinly frozen pond, fragile and on the precipice of shattering.

When she turned to me, I saw that her irises had gone white.

"My children!" she screamed. "Where are my children?"

With sinking dread, I recalled how young her children had been. "How did you end up here?"

Her unseeing eyes finally landed on me. "*You—*" she said. "*You* brought me here. *You* stole everything from me."

She rushed at me, but her limbs moved like those of a puppet, jerky and awkward, as if she lacked full control of her body. I sidestepped her, a knot of unease tightening in my throat.

"Ruihua," I began.

"Who?" she giggled, her eyes slowly turning from white to yellow. "I don't recognize that name—" Her mouth opened and closed, and I could feel the woman she'd once been, fighting it. Fighting her new master.

"You know what?" she announced, still giggling. "I will go back. Her children can be next. Her qi is delightfully strong. I have no doubt her children will—"

She struck her head so violently against the tree, a cascade of petals broke from their branches. "No!" Her mouth contorted in a soundless scream.

I stood frozen, not knowing what to do. I watched as Ruihua grabbed a fistful of petals, then, implausibly, stuffed them into her mouth. She choked, gagging, struggling to speak. Then she ran at me, so fast I could hardly defend myself, but I was not her target. Rushing past me, she ran straight for the edge of the mountain, and then, without hesitation, dove off the cliff.

I stared in shock at the empty cliffside where she had stood just moments ago. The wind stirred, sending more cherry blossoms fluttering from the trees, gathering in soft pink mounds along the forest floor. From where I stood, they resembled the shape of a corpse.

"Meilin," said Kuro, startling me. "Let's keep going. There's nothing you can do for her."

"But..."

"She's gone," he said.

I knew he was right, but the choky feeling in my throat wouldn't subside. I was responsible for her demotion, for her madness, and now for her death. Her children would grow up never knowing their mother, who'd become another casualty of war. Once, I'd believed Prince Yuchen had no reason to hate me. But now I understood that he did.

"Meilin?"

I nodded, swallowing the ache in my chest. "Let's keep looking."

"She's near," said Kuro unexpectedly. "I can sense her."

This time, I let him guide our path. He led us across the Red Mountains, into Leyuan. From there we went north, toward the Runong Desert, where even spirits slept under the hot sun.

"Jinya?" called Kuro softly, the hope in his voice almost too painful to bear. "Jinya, it's me. I'm here. I said I'd find you." He ventured farther into the sand. "I said I'd always find you."

But there was nothing alive here. I couldn't sense any spark of qi, of human vitality. *"But don't you know?"* a line from a lixia text came to mind. *"Mortality is what makes the taste of life so sweet. That is why all spirits crave the taste of human blood."*

Blood. Sinister foreboding slid down my spine as a speck of red drew my eye. I followed the trail of crimson, scattered like freckles against the sand.

"Kuro," I said, as he continued to circle the same place. I crouched and pressed my finger against the red sand, which was wet, then sniffed my finger. Blood.

His gaze followed mine, before his expression contorted with terror. He began to dig, sheer desperation lending him an inhuman strength. The ground slid out from under us as we tunneled deeper and deeper into the earth. Only once the sky was blotted out, and the air stale and unmoving, did we hear a sound.

A soft whimper, like a hungry dog. Kuro went still. "Jinya?" he whispered.

The sound ceased.

"Jinya?" he shouted, and his voice echoed through the earth. *Jinya, Jinya, Jinya.*

But I could sense her too now—a thin, dimming light.

Kuro stumbled through the half dark, his hands outstretched. I followed behind him, my heart pounding in my throat. *You did this,* the voice in my head whispered. *You started this.*

I watched the rebel leader fall to his knees, a sound of devastation tearing from his throat. Beside him, a small creature lay prone, convulsing on the ground.

"Jinya," he tried to say, but his voice cracked. "I-I'm going to save you. I'm going to bring you home. I promised we'd go back, once the rebellion is over. I promised we'd go home."

Jinya's spirit was unrecognizable. Like a dying fire, embers emitting a faint hiss. She twitched once, twice, and then—her eyes flew open.

Her irises were white and unseeing. "The spirits wanted me," she whispered, her voice as dry as sand. "I buried myself here to hide, like we used to do, but . . . they found me in the end."

"N-no," said Kuro, shaking his head. "I'm going to save you. I'm going to bring you home."

She exhaled slowly. Despite our proximity, I couldn't sense her qi. The spirit energy was too strong in this place, ever hungry and pressing closer.

Kuro shook her by her shoulders. "Jinya, stay with me. You can't go yet. Wait for me." Clenching his jaw with sudden resolve, he took out a knife and slit his palm. Fresh blood gushed forth, and the spirits above and below seemed to pause in their whispering, before drawing nearer: eager, curious.

Without any regard for his own pain, Kuro pressed his wound to Jinya's cracked lips. "Drink," he ordered.

But here in the spirit realm, it was not Jinya who drank, only a shadow of who she'd once been. She drank, and drank, and drank, until the light revived in her eyes. But those were not her eyes.

"Kuro," I said uneasily. "You're only luring spirits with—"

Jinya began to convulse, before letting out an earsplitting shriek. We both jumped. Her skin was turning deathly pale, as white as parchment.

My panic rose. "She doesn't have enough spirit affinity—"

Her body spasmed, and then she screamed again, a sound of

pure agony. It was so wretched I could not stand it. I, who did not even call her a friend. No one deserved to suffer like this.

"I'm sorry," I said, swallowing hard as I drew my sword. "You know what I must do."

Black tears were streaming down her cheeks. Her body contorted at an unnatural angle as she screamed again, seizing.

"No," said Kuro, raising a hand to stop me. I tensed, preparing to fight, but he said, "I-I'll do it. It's my—" His voice broke. "It's my responsibility."

He knelt beside her, cradling her face in his hands. He tried to speak, but only a strangled sound emerged from his throat. He tried again; still nothing came. Jinya's body twitched like a trapped animal, unable to escape. My eyes stung with tears, but I couldn't look away. With trembling hands, Kuro pressed his knife to her neck. He was shaking so hard the knife would not stay still.

Jinya was writhing again. "Kuro—" I began.

He slit her throat.

It was not cleanly done. Blood spurted everywhere as he hit an artery, and Jinya bucked, her eyes rolling back in her head. Kuro held her as Jinya's spirit released a final defiant hiss, before surrendering at last, fading into oblivion. The sudden silence in her absence felt like condemnation.

You did this. You started this.

Numbly, Kuro got to his feet, staring at his bloody knife. I struggled for breath, but the thick grief and guilt hanging over us seemed to suck all air from this place.

Without warning, Kuro let out a bellow of pure rage, and the spirits hovering near us dispersed like flies.

"Kuro—" I tried.

"Leave me!" he roared.

"It's not your—"

He swung toward me with murderous intent. "Get out of my sight!"

I ran. I ran as far as I could, but still I could not escape my guilt, which followed me as a shadow. My throat closed and I wheezed for breath, trying to draw air. The lixia swarmed in my bones, my veins, seeking an outlet, a release. The war had not ended with Chancellor Sima's death, as I'd once foolishly believed. No, the war was ongoing, and the death toll only rising as the beasts we'd let out to play stole more and more from the lives we'd once deemed commonplace.

I had hated my former life. I had been so ready to give it up, to trade it for six months of freedom and a roll of the dice. But I had not realized then what a luxury it was to trust your own mind, to know that your loved ones slept soundly beside you, to know that the days would go on and that you were not responsible for the destruction of the world.

I had always sought to prove myself, to become the best, to have my name recorded in the annals of history. But I had never considered the possibility that it might be as a villain.

All at once, I found myself standing before the Wen River. The place my mother had drowned. White plum blossoms drifted down from the overhanging branches into the river. From above, it looked as though the trees were crying.

It was spring, I saw. It was spring, and the world was weeping.

"I don't know if I can do this anymore," I said.

A cold, slender hand slid into mine. Kuro? No.

"Ma?"

She searched my gaze, as I searched hers. How young she looked, younger even than my own reflection. "I don't know what to do," I admitted to her. "You know I was searching for the eternal spring. To save myself. To finish what you began."

She did not speak.

"But now . . . now I wonder if I shouldn't go. If I give up my power . . . who will stop the dragon? Will the world as we know it be forever changed?" I thought of Princess Ruihua dragging her broken nails across a tree, Jinya burying herself deep in the sand. "*You can't go back*," I had told Kuro. Had the rebellion been worth it to him? If he could change the past, would he do it all over again?

"Why did we give up so much for the sake of power? Why did we make such a bargain, thinking it a worthy trade? Why didn't we suspect we'd lose ourselves in the process? And why must I feel this guilt now—why can't I run and save myself?"

I was beginning to cry, so I nearly missed her answer. "You could run and save yourself," she said, voice level, calm. "But what would be the world you returned to?"

I trembled, crying harder.

"You sought the dragon's power, and the power corrupted you. Now you wish to forsake it, and return to who you once were. But the world itself is irrevocably changed. Even if you find the spring, qinaide, and even if you succeed in relinquishing your powers, do you really think you can go back to the person you once were? You will live with what you have done, for the rest of your life."

I shook my head in desperation. "All I wanted was power for myself," I said in a small voice. "Not to hurt others. I just . . . I didn't want to be hurt again."

But my mind, the traitor, conjured memories of irrefutable violence. The way I'd laughed as I'd tortured Red, my own squad member; the way I'd brutalized and maimed a rebel from the Black Scarves, because he'd reminded me of a certain general from the war. The way I'd even tried my best to make Sky suffer.

My mother seemed to read my thoughts. "But then, with your

power," she said softly, "you hurt others. You became what you once feared."

I breathed in the fragrance of plum blossoms as they floated in the air for a few precious seconds before drowning in the water below. For how could a flower petal stand against the river?

How had I ever believed this world would not corrupt me?

"Shh," she said. "It's okay. There's still time. Remember: history is always being rewritten."

"Ma," I cried, reaching for her. "I-I need you."

She did not let me cling to her. She had never been one for physical affection, even when I was a child. Instead, she drew back, disentangling her hand from mine. "You must go," she said, and I fought against the sharp sting of disappointment. "Why do you think the dragon has not noticed your presence in the spirit realm?"

I hiccupped. If his attention wasn't on the spirit realm... "He's found a way into the human realm?" I asked in astonishment. My mother did not answer. The river below stirred with fallen petals, and I was, once again, alone.

THIRTY-TWO

Where are you? They claim you've gone home, but I cannot believe it. You of all people would never abandon our cause. Did you hear me when I called your name in the woods? Did you see me weeping, broken and terrified without you? I'm sorry. It was my damned pride, as you warned me. What I meant to say was, I need you. The rebellion needs you. The Black Scarves follow me in name only. The true leader is you.

—TAN KURO, IN A PRIVATE MISSIVE TO LÜ JINYA, UNDATED

I BURST THROUGH THE PORTAL GASPING FOR BREATH. ALL THE FALSE calm of the spirit realm deserted me, and in the human realm, I was struck by the full force of my anxiety.

Lei caught me by the shoulders as I started to hyperventilate.

"Kuro—" I choked out, for I could not see his body anywhere.

"He returned already. He . . . he didn't want to talk."

He'd been forced to kill Jinya with his own hands. Would I one day be forced to do the same?

I gasped for breath but couldn't seem to draw air. The sky was darkening, the air rife with the odor of rotting flesh. A dragonfly buzzed by my ear and I shrieked with alarm.

"Breathe," said Lei, as he looked me over. "Are you hurt?"

Jinya's writhing body sprang to mind. I shook my head, trying to clear the blood-coated memory. It refused to release me, its grip on my mind like weeds in still water. I could see Jinya's ink-black blood oozing onto the sand, the hovering spirits whispering above us, their hunger as palpable as the warm, cloying wind.

"Meilin," said Lei, voice low with authority. "Look at me."

Slowly, the memory faded, the stirring lake faded, even the corpses of the fallen faded. I met Lei's implacable gaze, his luminous eyes that always seemed to see straight through my masks and lies. *Lei knew me*, I realized. He knew the ugly parts of me that I tried so hard to hide. He was always one step ahead of me, too clever, too devious, too good at reading and manipulating others. In captivity, I'd feared this ability of his. But now, I found myself seeking comfort from it. For in some perverse way, it made me feel seen. Despite knowing me, despite knowing my selfishness, my greed, my fits of hysteria and madness—still, he'd stayed. He'd stayed and protected me.

Why?

Perhaps he truly did care for me. But with the Ximing prince, there was always more than one motive.

I thought of how he'd approached every spirit gate on our journey, how he'd made sure to honor the dead—even though I'd never known him to be sentimental.

It had been another of his schemes, I saw. And the truth was, it had worked.

Because every death had eaten at me. The corpses littered along the road, the children too young to even enlist in war. Despite my best efforts, I had seen them, and I had thought: *You did this. You started this.*

Then Princess Ruihua. Then Jinya. *Who else? Who else must I cross paths with in the spirit realm—who else must I recognize with dread?*

It was said that spirits were drawn to those with darkness within them. And yet, in the aftermath of war, who had not been tainted by darkness?

What if Xiuying was the next body I discovered along the river?

"I told you plainly I was going to the eternal spring," I said, increasingly upset. "I told you I wasn't getting involved in the rebellion, or the thinning of the veil, or any of this!"

"I know," he said.

"You agreed! You said you'd come with me to the spring!"

"And I will," he said, his hands tightening on my shoulders. "I gave you my word."

"But..." My jaw quivered. *If I leave for the spring now...* "But..." My voice dropped. "Lei, I don't want to care for this world."

"I know." His eyes looked so very sad.

"I wish I didn't care for this world."

His calloused hands slid down my arms, before he took my hands in his.

"But..." Pressure built at the backs of my eyes. I was so tired of crying. "But..."

"But you do," he finished. "You do care."

"Yes." I relented, my shoulders slumping forward. He caught me, steadying me against him.

"I can't give it up," I admitted into his chest. "Even though I can feel my qi thinning. Even though I only have a few months left to live. If I go now, and seek the spring, the world may not have even that."

Lei said nothing. I raised my head and watched his jaw pulse, the knot at his throat lifting. After all his tricks and mind games, his silence now frustrated me to no end.

"Say something!" I snapped. "Wasn't this what you wanted? Wasn't this your plan all along? Wasn't this the choice you manipulated me into making?"

"Sweetheart..."

"No!" I cut him off. "Now you'll just twist my words. You'll make me think this was all my doing. But I know you—I know you have an agenda. You always do." Tears leaked from my eyes, running unabated down my cheeks. My jaw was trembling so violently it was hard for me to speak. "I'm not the kind of person people think I am," I gasped, through my tears. "I don't work well with others. I hurt people. I-I'm selfish—I'm selfish to my core—"

"You're not selfish, Meilin."

"I am! You've seen what I've done. I opened the spirit gates. I killed innocent people. I-I ruined Sky." In a softer voice: "I ruin everyone I love."

He took me by my chin then, forcing me to meet his gaze. "We're human, each of us." The warmth from his hand seeped into my ice-cold skin. "But I believe we're more than our worst moments," he told me, his voice quiet yet thrumming with authority. "It's our best moments that have the power to define us."

His gaze seared into mine, and suddenly I saw myself laughing with Autumn, my clothes dripping wet but my eyes bright with mirth. I saw myself from afar, stopping a zuqiu ball from rolling into the pond, then throwing it back to the boys who'd been playing in the palace courtyard. I saw myself teaching Lily how to defend herself. I watched myself stumble after a particularly grueling practice session, my body flagging before Lily asked if we could duel once more. Despite my fatigue, I nodded, forcing myself upright. *"One more time,"* I agreed, because I didn't know how much time I had left to teach her.

I surfaced from these memories with a gasp. For a moment, I was too startled to speak. My surprise was so great even my tears had ceased. "Lei." I cleared my throat. "Did you just ... compel me?"

His lips twitched. "I think you'd know if I suddenly became a spirit summoner," he said wryly.

"Then ... what was that?" All those memories, I realized, they hadn't been from my perspective. *They were from his.*

"Sometimes, when the Ruan form a particular bond with someone, they can endeavor to communicate in more ways than one." He hesitated, before explaining, "It began after you saved my life, back on Mount Fuxi."

"Since Mount Fuxi?" I exclaimed. "You could read my mind since Mount Fuxi? Have you done it before?"

"No," he replied, before amending reluctantly, "Well, perhaps once or twice."

Outraged beyond words, I could only glare at him.

"It's only when the thought is aimed at me," he clarified. "Then it's rather like you're shouting in my head."

I flushed indignantly. "It's not fair," I said. "It's not fair that you can know what I'm thinking, that you can even speak into my mind, and I can't do any of that."

"But you can," said Lei, surprised into laughter. "Sweetheart, you're the summoner of a Cardinal Spirit."

I shook my head. "It doesn't matter. Your mind is like a locked door to me. I can't read you. Believe me, I've tried."

He considered this, trying and failing to conceal his gratification. "How about . . . now?"

I blinked at him. His smile was as playful and unknowable as ever. But this time, when I looked into his eyes, I felt a soft wave of feeling overcome me. A crack in the doorway, left open just for me.

I stepped closer to him instinctively. His emotions were like a gentle summer wind, enveloping me in their warmth. He was proud of me; I could feel the strength of his pride. He believed in me; he believed I could change the world. But still, he was afraid for me. He was afraid for my safety, for my well-being, for how little I slept at night. He knew how many people wanted things from me; he was guilt-ridden for wanting more. That was why he hadn't asked outright—he'd wanted the choice to be mine.

"*I promised you—I will go with you to the eternal spring.*" Lei's voice in my head was like a warm caress, nothing like Qinglong's icy brutality. *"The moment you decide to leave, I will go with you. Just say the word."*

I looked up at him. How strange that I had once hated this man, that I had once wished him dead. Now I trusted his promise. I trusted it with my life.

It was my responsibility to fix this; I understood that now. I was not my father, who destroyed but never mended. I would not leave behind a legacy of ruin; I would not let my memory be one of cowardice. All my life, I had been taught selfish ambition. My father had modeled how to fend for yourself, how to consider your own desires before the needs of others. After all, how else could you survive in a society as harsh as ours? Without a sober father and a sane mother, how else could you thrive in a world this unforgiving?

But there was another way to live. I had seen it in Xiuying; I had even glimpsed it in Sky and Lei. Those who sought to change the world for the better, who believed not only in the goodness of the world but also in their own inherent goodness. Those who trusted that their actions would not corrupt, but heal.

"I will," I thought to Lei, and I caught the flicker of recognition in his eyes. Aloud, I said, "Were you spying on me? Back in the Forbidden City." At his crooked smirk, I asked, "How? I never saw you." And I had made certain there were no bystanders at our illegal practice sessions. If anyone had known I'd been training the palace servant girls, it would have been a criminal offense.

Lei's eyes crinkled. "I can't give up all my secrets," he said. "Where's the fun in that?"

"Where did Kuro go?" I asked, as we returned to the city.

"He came back from the spirit realm hours before you," said Lei. "He wasn't really in the mood to chat."

I shot him a sardonic look. "I gather you suspect what happened," I said.

Lei nodded. "It's unfortunate for the Black Scarves. Lü Jinya was their linchpin."

"Really?" I asked, not because I hadn't respected her, but because she'd always seemed secondary to Kuro.

"Kuro relied on her for all their logistics coordination, offense strategy, and supply operations."

"No wonder he took it so hard," I said.

"It seems there may have been other reasons for his grief," said Lei. "They grew up together on the outskirts of Xianju, near the Runong Desert. That's where the rebellion began, as you may have heard."

"How do you know all this?" I demanded.

"Soldiers talk."

I sighed, resigned to the fact that Lei would always know more than me. "We'll need Kuro eventually, to restore the veil," I said. "I can't do it alone."

Lei nodded.

"I'll give you the task of convincing him," I said. "Since that seems to be your specialty."

"Yes, sir," replied Lei, smirking.

I ignored this, thinking. I had read all of Sky's books on the practice of lixia, but I was still no more enlightened as to how to repair the veil between realms. Sima Yi would most likely have been our best bet, given his extensive studies on the subject, but now that he was no longer an option...

"I may need to seek out Winter," I told Lei. "Sky's brother." I hesitated. "Is that okay with you?"

He lifted a brow. "Why would that not be? I've always liked him."

"*But you know who he'll be with,*" I thought to him.

"Whether or not I like him has little to do with the situation at hand."

I nodded, gratified. My question had been a test—and he had passed.

"Right now," I continued, thinking aloud, "the spirit gates are many, but the veil still stands in place. I know this because no spirits walk among us. Not in their corporeal form, at least. They still require human vessels to enter the physical realm. Once the veil collapses . . ." I shivered at the thought. Then Qinglong would no longer need me. "Anyway, we won't let that happen. We'll seal the veil before it collapses.

"Do you think you could get a message back to the New Quanlixia scholars?" I asked Lei. "I want to understand the fundamentals of how the veil works. We can make a plan from there, and perhaps find a way to evacuate the—"

I gasped, my chest caving inward from impact. My hands went to my sternum, which felt as if it had been cracked into pieces.

"What is it?" demanded Lei.

I couldn't speak from pain. I folded into myself, and Lei seized me before I keeled over. My throat was closing, my breaths turning short and shallow. The world blurred before me, the streets and people and animals turning into shapes and sounds and monsters.

"The dragon," I gasped. "He's—he's coming for me."

I could not say how I knew. But I knew—I knew it in my bones.

There was a loud boom in the distance, followed by deep reverberations in the earth. My knees shook as I felt the vibrations thrumming across the mountains. Then the screams began.

We were too late.

PART III

THIRTY-THREE

Baihu is a guardian of the old order. To her, balance is key, and any change—whether for gain or loss—is a disturbance to be resisted. While some chronicles revere her as a protector of tradition, others cast her as an enemy of progress.

—A HISTORY OF LIXIA, 762

THE FIRST SPIRIT BEAST TO REACH THE AIR WAS A GREAT HAWK with wings of steel. It shrieked as it took flight, flying higher and higher as if trying to reach the sun. Then it dived.

Its shadow disappeared behind the city gates. But by the screams that followed, I had no doubt it found its mark.

"We need to get you out of here," said Lei urgently. "Does he know where you are? Does Qing—"

"Don't say his name," I gasped, my superstitions emerging. "I-I don't know."

Would Qinglong come for me now? And yet, with the dragon free to move between realms, what need did he have for a human vessel anymore?

"Kuro," I croaked out, pressing my hand to my sternum as if to hold the bones intact. "We need to find Kuro."

"Let's get back to the rebel base," suggested Lei. "Can you walk?"

I nodded, though my insides ached. The lixia in my bloodstream was like a living thing, clamoring to escape. There was lixia in the air too, so heady and rich that breathing felt like sipping wine. The sky had darkened, but the stars loomed too close for comfort. As if the world were tipping on its axis, as if the realms were merging into one.

The reverberations deepened, until the mountains started to shake. A colossal oak tree groaned as its gnarled roots split the earth, and then, seconds later, the tree plummeted. Lei shouted and seized me, throwing us both to the side before the tree could careen into us. I heard the splintering of wood and stone, and then a loud crack, followed by another.

"Earthquake," said Lei grimly. "I hope they evacuated the tunnels."

More spirits were appearing in the sky, glowing more brilliantly than the stars. They were all headed for the city.

"Qi," I rasped. "They feed on qi."

The brilliant life force of the city and its throngs of people called to them, just as their lixia called to us. And yet, was that inherent hunger meant to be sated? What happened when we got the thing that we so desperately wanted, when we held it within the palm of our hand? Did it cease to be a thing of want? Or did we simply want more, and more, until the mere idea of balance became an impossibility?

Even my craving for lixia had lessened, the near constant migraines and nausea abating in intensity. But one problem had simply been replaced by another.

"Where are you, my little rat?"

I froze, ice creeping into my lungs.

"You can't hide forever."

I don't need forever, I thought before gathering my qi. I imagined that willow tree by the Wen River, its long leafy branches, the way it shut out the sun, protecting the cool air within its expansive shade. I would be that shade.

I could feel Qinglong's frustration, his mounting anger. It was barely a muted whisper, and then it was gone.

I smiled in grim victory.

My father had not given me much, but this he had given me. An ability to read emotions, and to guard my own. Living with his temper had necessitated it, and at the time, I had resented his mercurial nature. But now, I understood it to be a boon. This was why impulsion came naturally to me, as it did not to Kuro or even Sima. Because I was a woman, and I had grown up powerless. From this I had found my power.

"Is the dragon . . . ?" Lei began.

"He can't find me," I said. "Not through impulsion, at least." I straightened. "The rebel base—we'll have to enter the city."

Grimly, I surveyed the traffic leading up to Meridian Gate, which was backed up with overturned wagons and swarming masses of people. Some were trying to get out; others were trying to get in. It was total pandemonium.

"I know another way into the city," said Lei.

"Of course you do," I muttered.

We took a roundabout way through the woods, then scaled a low fence that led to an outdoor trading post teeming with people. In the frenzied, panic-stricken crowd, Lei and I went unnoticed. Although the air was feverish, we were far enough from the city center that the chaos had not reached here—not yet.

"I'll give you a tael of silver for your mule! My son needs to see a physician, please—"

The bearded trader shook his head. "The hospitals will be flooded, miss. They won't take any new patients. Not unless you have imperial connections."

The mother was crying. "But . . ."

"Believe me, they won't take your son when Warlord Liu himself barely has a bed."

"What happened to Warlord Liu?" I interrupted, nearly tripping over a crate of barley in my haste to eavesdrop.

The trader turned a distasteful eye toward me. "Where have you been? They declared an official state of emergency a few hours ago."

"Before the earthquake?" I asked.

He shot me an exasperated look. "Are you here to buy something or not?"

I reached into my pockets, which were, of course, empty. Thankfully, Lei slid a coin into the man's hand. "We're from out of town," he explained.

The trader hefted the coin in his palm, then smiled. "Our dear heads of state fell ill at the signing of the Three Kingdoms Treaty. Official reports called it a minor case of spoiled food, nothing serious. But no one's seen them in public since. If you ask me, I think it was poison."

As the merchant turned away, I glanced with alarm at Lei. It was not the first time poison had been used on a prince.

And yet who would target *all* the royals? Someone who didn't bear allegiance to any kingdom, surely; someone who wanted *all* of them disposed of.

The Black Scarves. "*Tan Kuro is a poison master,*" his healer had told me.

"Kuro," I breathed.

"He's been busy, it seems," said Lei dryly.

I was opening my mouth to reply when Lei pointedly glanced toward the entrance of the trading post. Two imperial messengers rode down the street, stopping in front of the gate.

"Any citizens caught harboring black magic practitioners will be put to death, alongside their families!" the younger messenger shouted. From his garb, he looked to be a Leyuan representative from the old regime.

"They're united in their enmity, at least," Lei muttered.

Even though it shouldn't bother me, not at a time like this, still I felt deeply wronged. "They're targeting the very people they should be helping!" I whispered angrily.

Lei took my arm, deftly positioning himself in front of me by pretending to investigate the barley prices. I felt the messenger's attention drift toward us, before Lei struck up another conversation with the bearded trader, who looked positively gleeful in the chaos. At least there was money to be made in a crisis.

Meanwhile I was shaking with barely concealed anger. Our rulers were useless, as always. The veil had collapsed and all they thought to do was round up available spirit summoners? They would destroy all of Tianjia if they had their way.

Someone beyond the trading post cried out in warning. I peered around Lei as a young girl ran down the dirt road toward us, barefooted and clothed in worn rags. An orphan girl, who likely survived by begging on the streets. Who was she running from? I moved out from behind Lei to scan the road.

"You—" The older messenger, an Anlai soldier, caught sight of me. He dismounted from his steed, withdrawing a pair of iron handcuffs. "The princess is looking for you."

I tried to back away, but the crowd had pressed closer in curiosity. The orphan girl approached the Anlai messenger with little regard for his personal space. When he reprimanded her, drawing his sword, she did not run away. Instead, she closed the distance between them and—*sank her teeth* into his stomach. She was so small she only reached his torso. But when she bit him, she had such strength that she ripped chunks of flesh from his bones.

The crying mother stopped crying. The smiling trader stopped smiling. Even I forgot to breathe as the messenger's organs dangled from his torn stomach.

Who was this child?

Teeth gleaming red, she tilted her head toward the sky, licking blood from her lips. Then she turned to us.

Her eyes were colored gold.

"Run," I whispered to Lei, who did not need a second warning. He took my hand and shoved his way through the panicking crowd, steering us not toward the outer gate but instead into an adjoining shop. To my surprise he led us up three flights of winding stairs, then down a narrow hallway, which deposited us onto an open-air balcony connected to another via dangling laundry lines.

"Climb!" he shouted, as the maelstrom began in earnest below.

But from this vantage point, I saw it. That shimmering black haze at the center of the city, a haze like a ripple of heat, only there was no sunlight and it should not exist. Beneath the haze was a deep crevice in the earth, like a fault line, its depths shrouded in darkness. Here was the epicenter, I saw, the heart of the torn veil.

"We'll have to go there." I pointed, trying to summon the resolve needed. "To close the tear in the veil."

"Not now," hissed Lei. "Now we take cover and formulate a plan."

I opened my mouth to argue, before realizing the depths of my exhaustion. My lixia had never felt more alive, but my qi was terribly depleted, so that I felt hardly more human than spirit.

I conceded his point. "All right—" I began before my breath left me. All reason faded as I cried out, "Sky!"

He could not hear me from up here. Of course he could not. But I could see him, and I could see what were perhaps his final breaths in this life. There was a great bird of prey that had pinned him to the ground, her shimmering talon around his throat, a glowing bead of jade poised in her razor-sharp beak. Sky's face paled as he struggled for breath, his bare hands scrabbling in the dirt as he sought a weapon. But his sword glinted just out of reach.

Sky's hands twitched—once, twice—before going limp.

THIRTY-FOUR

There is none more jealous than a spiteful spirit, for even a spirit wishing to be free of its human vessel will still be reluctant to share it with another. Never enter into a bargain with a spirit lightly, for once you choose one, you can never choose another.
—A COMPREHENSIVE OVERVIEW OF LIXIA-INDUCED DISORDERS, 910

"SKY!" I SCREAMED AGAIN, BEFORE EYEING THE DISTANCE BETWEEN us, wondering if I could make the jump from a three-story building.

But Lei read my intention and held me back. Quick as a thief, he withdrew a throwing star from his sleeve and threw it into the wind in the opposite direction.

"What are you—"

The miniature blade caught the gale and curved, reversing course and striking the great bird directly in the back of her neck.

She shrieked in pain, her wings rising involuntarily. Sky seized her moment of distraction to crawl away in search of his sword. But the spirit seemed to steel herself, falling upon Sky once more. Both of them went still. From this high up, I could not see Sky's expression, but I could sense the surrender of his posture.

Was she speaking into his mind? I wondered. Was she offering him a bargain he could not refuse?

I could not abandon him to this fate.

Remembering the lixia texts I'd read, I withdrew my knife. I didn't even pause to draw a breath—I simply sliced open my arm.

"What are you doing?" Lei roared, grabbing the knife from me.

I faltered as blood dripped liberally down my arm. Lei grabbed me, bracing me against him, before ripping a piece of his cloak to stanch the flow. But before he could bandage the wound, I stopped him.

"No," I said. Was blood always this black, or was mine so tainted with lixia that it resembled ink? "Like flies to honey," I recited, "so too are spirits to qi."

Lei swore under his breath but left me to my madness. He withdrew both curved blades from his back, moving into a fighting stance. Far below, the giant spirit bird raised her head and shrieked, before lifting her wings and soaring into the sky.

Toward me. The way she flew was overconfident, as if she believed me to be easy prey. Keeping my gaze fixed on her, I took a few steps back, anchoring my energy.

"What in the twelve skies—" began Lei. As the bird loomed closer, I took a running leap—and crashed onto her.

My momentum lent me more force than I'd intended, and I collided into her with such impact that we both plummeted from the sky. Scrambling to hold on for dear life, I grasped at her feathers as she squawked and tried to shove me off. Desperate, I found her neck and clung to her like a child to a mother, so close I breathed in the particular scent of her lixia. How strange that she was corporeal, this spirit that did not yet belong to the human realm. It weakened her, I could tell, being here in this foreign place. And that was why I stood a chance.

We landed hard in the dirt, though her wings involuntarily cushioned my fall. I skidded off her, rolling into a crouch. I winced at the trail of blood I left in my wake, quickly tying a makeshift bandage.

"Meilin!"

I looked behind me at the heap of rubble, remnants of a fallen building that had not survived the quake.

"Here!" The flash of movement caught my eye; it was Sky, half-hidden in debris. He gestured for me to come hide with him. I shook my head. The spirits had already scented my blood.

But I'd forgotten the one I should fear. In my distraction, he'd broken through my mental shields.

"There you are," said Qinglong.

I'd never before heard his voice like this—both in mind and body. I covered my ears with my hands but it did nothing to stop the sheer impact from racking through my bones, the vibrations of his voice seizing me like a fly in a spider's web. I fell to my knees, shaking at the reverberations of his words. *There you are. There you are. There you are.*

The Azure Dragon was so colossal he towered over the nearby trading posts. The air around him seemed to freeze as he descended, and even the great bird of prey went silent at his suffocating, exhilarating presence. Despite my terror, it was impossible to deny his beauty. The radiance of his gold-flecked eyes, like stars; the impossibility of his cobalt scales, which captured and held the light, so that gazing at him felt like staring into the heart of the sun. I was drawn to him, just as he was drawn to me. Like two mirrors searching each other's reflections, unable to find the other, our combined ambition knew no limits. Just as I could not accomplish my goals without him, he could not accomplish his without me.

But he no longer had need for me, now that he could freely enter the human realm. And so I was reduced to an obstacle in his path.

He laughed coldly. "*I do not view you as my enemy, Hai Meilin,*" said the dragon. "*On the contrary, I view you as my kin.*"

I shook my head repeatedly as his voice burned into my bones. *He lies*, I told myself. *He lies.*

"*I am doing this for the both of us,*" he continued, and this close, his voice hurt me like a gong sounding in my ears.

"I don't want to die," I whimpered, like a child in my fear.

"*Then don't,*" he said. "*There is another way. You can live forever—through my power. But you must give your will to me.*"

Which would you choose? A long, easy life without agency, or a short, difficult one—with freedom?

I recalled the young woman who had endeavored to change her fate—who had joined the war simply for a chance at independence. And I knew my answer, always.

"Never," I said aloud, before my eyes darted to the bird of prey, who cowered beside me beneath the Cardinal Spirit's aura. Before she could guess my intent, I whirled toward her and seized her beak with my bare hands. I felt her resistance but forced her beak open, never mind that her razor-sharp jaws cut into my palms. The blood drove her into a frenzy, so that she could not protect herself when I reached into her mouth and withdrew her pulsating jade seal.

"*Look how she dares defy you,*" I said to the dragon, but this time, I spoke with compulsion. "*You would let her take me from you?*"

My instincts had not led me astray: both the bird and the dragon flew into an uproar. The dragon's jealousy swept through the air like a tidal wave. Even if he was enraged at my disobedience, I would belong to no other spirit. He bellowed and lunged for the bird, who escaped in the nick of time, flapping her wings and soaring into the air. Qinglong followed in hot pursuit, as I'd suspected.

The bird's frantic cries resounded in my mind. "*Help me, help me, help me—*"

Gritting my teeth, I focused my qi and returned silence to my thoughts. Then I crawled toward the rubble, searching for Sky in the shadows.

"Sky?" I hissed. "Where are you?"

I shoved aside a wooden plank and caught sight of a pale face crouched behind the debris. It was like seeing a ghost from the dead.

"Tao?" I said hoarsely, incredulous. I had not seen him since the day I'd been thrown in jail.

Firm hands grabbed me from behind. I screamed.

"It's me!" said Sky, as I tried to wrestle free from his grasp. Twisting, I saw that it was indeed him—his sharp jaw, his messy hair, his scarred palms. But my heart still raced wildly.

"I thought I saw . . ." I glanced back; there was no one there.

Shaking my head, I let Sky guide me to the entrance of a partially caved-in bunker.

"Is it safe?" I asked, eyeing the murky opening dubiously.

Sky nodded. "The bunkers were built during the Wu Dynasty to ward off spirits—they're reinforced with iron." He urged me forward. "Winter is down there already."

I took a tentative step into the bunker. Still dazed from the dragon's brilliance, I tripped on a shard of rubble, but Sky caught me before I fell.

"What you did," he said, clearing his throat, "that was incredibly foolish."

"The usual compliments from you," I retorted, before glancing back at him, remembering the state in which we'd left things. As if he was following my train of thought, his hands tightened around me, and I wondered if I'd inadvertently made myself his prisoner again.

How easy it was to slip into former habits.

"*Lei?*" I asked silently, searching for him in my mind's eye. I felt silly, not quite knowing what I was doing. "*Can you find me?*"

Silence, and then: "*Yes. I'm coming.*"

It was, unmistakably, the feeling of him. I felt relief crash through me, followed by terrible fatigue. If Sky brought me to the Anlai warlord now, there was nothing I could do to protect myself. And if I tried to run from him in my current state, Sky would most certainly catch me.

"Don't," said Sky, and the catch in his voice surprised me. It was hard to recognize his expression in the half-light. "Don't look at me like that."

"Like what?"

His voice dropped. "Like you're afraid of me."

I met his eyes then, flickering against the dark. I understood how I'd hurt him, just as he'd hurt me. Foolishly, I wished there were a way to erase this broken history between us. How was it that we hurt the ones we loved the most?

"*But then, with your power,*" my mother had said, "*you hurt others. You became what you once feared.*"

"Sky," I said, overtaken with weariness. "I don't want to be your prisoner."

He swallowed thickly. I could feel him struggling to rein in his emotions, his insistence that he was right, that his way was the right way. He had imagined a future for us, and in doing so could not conceive of a different path beyond that one. And how could he—when everything had always gone as planned before?

But perhaps people could change, for he released me and said, "Then what about a friend?"

I exhaled, cruel hope surging in my chest. "I would like that very much," I whispered.

His eyes were pained. He hated this, I could tell. He did not want this conciliation. But he hated my fear more, and so he would give me this.

"All right," he said, more to himself than to me. "All right."

Walking in silence, we listened to the intermittent screams overhead, which were all the more jarring because of their sporadicity. The aftershocks from the quake had mostly ceased, though the earth still shuddered with a sort of restless agitation, as if struggling to find its balance once more. The longer we walked, the more frequent my stumbling grew. At last Sky stopped me.

"Get on my back," he said.

I squinted through a migraine, its intensity sharpened by the oppressive weight of iron. "But—"

"Meilin," he said. "You can hardly walk." Then he checked my bandaged arm and swore. "You tied this yourself? I thought I taught you better than that."

Grumbling under his breath, he redid my tourniquet. Then he crouched and I silently climbed onto his back, too tired to argue, letting my head loll onto his shoulder. I was exhausted, and everything about this night felt surreal, as if we were only acting in a theater production of nightmares.

"Sleep," he said. "You're safe with me."

Sky had never been one to lie. Still, I couldn't understand why he was being so kind to me, after everything that had transpired between us. How could he have forgotten all his prior animosity toward me?

"Why?" I asked, closing my eyes at the pressing fatigue. I had humiliated him, dishonored him—even tried to kill him. "I-I've—wronged you."

He did not answer for so long that I began to drift into sleep. "I love you," he said at last. Then, so quietly I wondered if I was dreaming: "I wish I didn't."

THIRTY-FIVE

I do not care if he is integral to the new treaty accords. As long as he lives, he remains a threat to me and the kingdom. Eliminate him without fail, no matter the cost.

—CAO ZIHUAN, IN A PRIVATE MISSIVE TO MINISTER HUI, 924

I WOKE TO A BURNING SENSATION AGAINST MY ABDOMEN. SHOOTING upright, I would have struck my forehead against rock if not for Sky's strategically placed hand. I blinked at my surroundings; we were in a dimly lit cavern, torchlight pooling against the iron walls like fiery dancers. I felt the burning sensation again and reached into my tunic pocket, groping for the bird spirit's seal. To my surprise, I could not find it. Instead, my hand came away with nothing but fine powder, still hot to the touch. She had not succeeded in making a bargain, I realized. And now—Qinglong had destroyed her.

Perhaps he would come for me next. But beneath the iron walls, I could no longer feel him—not the weight of his lixia, nor the strength of his will. All my senses felt dulled, cast in shadow. When I tried to take a step, the world tilted as if I were trying to walk on water.

"Easy," said Sky. "You've lost a lot of blood."

"Does the dragon know where you are?" said someone else.

I whirled around. Winter stood in the cavern entrance, a fresh cut marring his beautiful face. My eyes widened at the wound; never had I seen him with any physical imperfection.

Winter's hand went reflexively to the cut. "It seems the spirits, like humans, prefer some over others," he explained.

"His qi draws them," said Sky, shaking his head. "As does yours."

Because we both had greater spirit affinity than most—which was why Winter could walk the realm between worlds, even without a seal. I had seen him there once, during the Three Kingdoms War.

Could we use this to our advantage now?

"You're both alive," I said. "I heard—poison—"

"Yes," said Sky grimly. "And I think I know who is to blame."

"Would that be me?" someone asked.

We all turned as the newcomer ambled inside.

"Tan Kuro," he said, smirking. "Leader of the Black Scarves." He bowed low in mock deference. "What an honor this is—I get to finish the job myself."

SKY DREW HIS SWORD AT ONCE. SHAKING, I FOLLOWED SUIT, THOUGH I did not quite know who I was defending. Kuro raised a taunting brow at me, and I saw then that his eyes were back to their brilliant golden hue.

Baihu has returned.

"So you're back to being the empire's pawn?" Kuro asked me. "I wonder what that must be like . . . to have such low self-esteem that you'd let yourself be clapped in irons."

Sky hissed. "She's not a—"

As he raised his blade, I threw myself between them. "We need him, Sky!" I interrupted. "I can't seal the rift alone."

"She's right," said Winter, though he too eyed Kuro apprehensively. Kuro met his gaze, and held it.

"You're the sixth prince, aren't you?" the rebel leader said, a challenge in his voice. "I've heard about you. You circumvented my poison. How?"

Winter smiled, a smile that I suspected sent stronger men to their knees. Kuro considered him with an air of curiosity, but before he could speak, Sky interrupted: "How did you find us?"

"Why, the Ximing prince, of course," said Kuro easily. "I never knew royalty to be so helpful."

Sky's lip curled as his eyes sought the shadows. "Is he here now?"

"I was sent ahead," said Kuro, inspecting the iron walls with a shudder. "He's dispatching a few messages above, but he'll come."

Sky smiled now, a smile that promised violence.

"Sky . . ." I said quietly. "Don't make this harder than it needs to be."

"What does that mean, Meilin?" Sky rounded on me, his former fury resurrecting. His eyes flashed dangerously, like lightning before a storm. "Are you so desperate to seek a new bedfellow?"

I gasped. "How dare you?"

"It seems a whore never forgets her ways—"

I struck him across the face. Hard enough that his head snapped back. Meanwhile, Kuro began to laugh.

I faltered, backing away as I stared at the red mark on Sky's cheek. A mark left by my hand. I had struck him in the same way my father had once enjoyed hitting me.

Tears pricked my eyes as I considered the depths of my own monstrosity. Was it all my fault—because I cared for Sky, and in the same breath, cared for another? How could my heart be so duplicitous—and how could my feelings be so fickle? Was I the only one who kept hurting those I loved? Was it my love itself that was so damaging, like a poison that corrupted at the core?

"So," drawled a new voice, "it seems the cat has left the bag, and my, it's not a very sweet cat."

Lei appeared in the cavern entrance, windswept and pale, but largely unharmed. His words, directed at Sky, seemed to drain the very air from the room.

Sky's voice was like a growl. "*You—*"

"I do have a name," said Lei pleasantly.

Sky spat. "It was a mistake to let you live."

"A very foolish mistake," agreed Lei. "Though some seem to take pleasure in my company, I can't understand why. Perhaps it's simply that, compared to a few others, my company is slightly less foul." He raised a brow at Sky, who bared his teeth at him.

They brought out the very worst in each other, and it pained me to see it. "Stop," I said. "Stop this."

Sky ignored me. "It's a mistake we can remedy," he said, advancing with his sword drawn.

"Di Di," said Winter quietly. "We can't kill him."

"I don't intend to kill him," said Sky, his expression a mask of brutality. "I only intend to ruin that pretty face. Without it, he's nothing."

Lei smiled mockingly. "You think I'm pretty?"

There was no bluster in Sky's demeanor, and it frightened me. "I'll give you a face to match what you really are inside."

"A *very* pretty face, then."

"Please," I said. "Stop."

No one paid me any heed, as if I hadn't spoken at all. I felt a wave of fatigue buckle my knees. I could've resisted it, I could've fortified my qi and straightened, but instead, as a last resort, I let myself collapse.

The effect was immediate: Sky lowered his sword and went to me. I let my eyelids flutter shut as I heard his distress. "Meilin?" He said my name over and over again. "Are you all right?"

Why do you only come to me when I'm in pain? I wanted to ask. *Why is this the only way I can get your attention?*

I felt him lift me, checking my pulse, then my wounds.

Silently, I called to Lei. *"Stop your bickering. Please."*

"A convincing performance," replied Lei in my mind. *"You should consider a future as an actress."*

I did not respond; I was too vexed with him. Opening my eyes, I found Sky above me, his face familiar with concern.

"Forgive me," he said quietly, and I could feel his hands shaking.

"It seems a whore never forgets her ways."

I pushed myself upright, saying nothing. If I addressed this now, I would let the ocean of my guilt and anger flood this place.

It was not the first time I had been called a whore.

"While that was certainly entertaining, we do have bigger problems on our hands," said Kuro.

I rose to my feet, ignoring Sky's proffered arm. Focusing my qi, I guarded my mind not only against Qinglong but also against Lei, against my own emotions. I shut them all out, contending only with the external.

"I'm going to find a way to seal the rift in the veil." I addressed Kuro, my voice echoing across the cavern walls. "Will you stand in my way, or will you join me?"

Kuro swallowed, his eyes meeting mine in recognition. Here we were, back at that same crossroads—but last time, we had both made different choices.

And yet, back then, Jinya had still been alive. The Ivory Tiger had not turned her back on her own vessel. The Azure Dragon had not broken free of the spirit realm. And I had naïvely believed I could escape the consequences of my own actions.

"You sought the dragon's power, and the power corrupted you. Now

you wish to forsake it, and return to who you once were. But the world itself is irrevocably changed. Even if you find the spring, qinaide, and even if you succeed in relinquishing your powers, do you really think you can go back to the person you once were? You will live with what you have done, for the rest of your life."

Kuro glared at me, then at the other princes. I bit my lip, wondering if he would choose defiance just for the sheer sake of it. But then I heard the guilt in his voice: "Jinya wouldn't have wanted this."

I capitalized on that guilt. "Do it for her, then. For her memory."

Kuro sighed. "What's the damn point?" he asked. "You know we'll be remembered as the villains of this story. Their fathers"—he pointed at the princes—"will make sure of that."

I shook my head. I did not know if it was naïveté or stubbornness that drove me, but I truly believed there could be another ending to our story.

I would make it so.

"There's still time," I said, repeating my mother's words to him. "Remember—history is always being rewritten."

"You won't be alone," said Winter. "Let us set aside our differences and support one another." He paused, looking around the cave. "*All* of us."

With another sigh, Kuro nodded, as did Lei. We all turned toward Sky. His mouth twisted, his eyes scornful. I could feel the unhappiness radiating off him. But slowly, meeting my gaze, Sky too nodded.

"A Three Kingdoms truce," said Lei, eyes glinting with mirth. "A real one, this time."

THIRTY-SIX

Only twice in known history have the pacifist southern monks interfered in military conflicts of any nature. The first recorded instance occurred during the Great Floods of the Quan Dynasty, when the harmony of the natural world was threatened. The second occurred nearly five centuries later, when a prophecy was made regarding a half-Ruan prince. Because of the prophecy, the monks swore an oath. When the prince called for their aid, they would come.

—CHRONICLES OF THE THREE KINGDOMS, 954

"I HAVE AN IDEA," I BEGAN, AS WE GATHERED NEAR THE TORCHLIGHT. A wave of déjà vu crested through me as I regarded their familiar faces, lit by flame. "I stole another spirit's seal today. It drove the dragon mad."

"Jealousy," commented Kuro. "All the spirits are prone to it."

"It gave me power too," I said. "I wonder if we could somehow use that to seal the veil."

"Where is that jade now?" asked Lei.

I reached into my pocket and showed them the ash remains. "I think Qinglong got rid of her."

Lei raised a brow at this. "What power did her seal lend you? Lixia?" he asked.

"Yes."

"Then that won't work," said Lei. "Excess lixia was what created the spirit gates in the first place. It won't be lixia that closes the rift. It will be qi."

Our life force. What spirits craved, just as we humans sought lixia. That push and pull was fragile, but it had never splintered, not until now.

Winter nodded. "He's right. The counterpart of lixia is qi, which no spirit possesses. To restore the balance between realms, one would need to return qi to the veil."

"So," said Kuro, "which gate do we target? You know there are gates all over the Three Kingdoms by now."

"Is it feasible to close all of them?" I asked.

"You don't have time," said Sky brusquely. I met his eyes—and felt that familiar snarl of rage and remorse. His gaze held mine before I turned away; I could not surrender to my emotions, not at a time like this.

"Then what?" said Kuro unhelpfully.

Lei gestured toward Kuro's bow. "Do you mind if I borrow this?"

Kuro removed the weapon and handed it to him without objection. The two seemed to have made their peace in the aftermath of the quake.

Lei gathered a few rocks from the ground, then crouched and set the bow on the dirt. Pinning the bow against the ground, he pulled the bowstring taut, then positioned it there against the dirt.

"Hold this for me, will you?" he asked Kuro, who shrugged and complied, gripping the bow in place with one hand, and the taut string with the other.

We all watched silently as Lei placed a few pebbles and rocks along the string, weighting it down, then added a massive stone on top of the nocking point.

"You can let go now," said Lei. Kuro released the string; it stayed in place.

"The deepest tear in the veil," said Lei. "Where is that?"

"The chasm at the center of First Crossing," said Kuro with grim confidence. "As far as I know, that's the only gate through which spirits have crossed."

Lei nodded, expecting this answer. "Say this is the gate at First Crossing," he said, pointing at the massive rock at the center. "We seal this one and—" He removed it from the bowstring.

Not seconds later, the bowstring bounced back into place, scattering the smaller rocks everywhere. Winter winced as dust billowed up, smearing his robes.

"Is it that simple?" asked Kuro skeptically.

Winter tilted his head. "Balance seeks itself. That which was once in balance will seek to return to balance," he said thoughtfully. "Prince Cao has a point. Once you close the deepest tear and restore the veil to equilibrium, the other spirit gates will naturally decline as lixia fades from the human realm."

Kuro shrugged. "All right," he said. "Then how do we feed our life force into the veil?"

I was beginning to understand just how much of the leadership Jinya had contributed to the Black Scarves.

"I have a way," Winter volunteered, before glancing at his younger brother. "But you won't like this."

Sky said nothing.

"What is it?" I asked.

"Blood," said Winter. "Qi concentrates within blood."

My own went cold. *The spirits demand blood,* my mother had told me. Back then, I hadn't understood what she'd meant.

"So we give ourselves up?" asked Kuro, torn between outrage and amusement. "As human sacrifices?"

"No," said Sky. His jaw had gone as taut as the bowstring.

Lei's expression was inscrutable. "Excess blood will only lure more spirits out."

I thought of how I'd cut myself to draw the bird spirit away from Sky. "It does drive them into a frenzy," I admitted.

"Which is the opposite of what we want," said Lei. Sky nodded emphatically. For once, they were in agreement.

"Then how else do we end this?" asked Kuro.

Winter said nothing, only folded his lips into a flat line.

Kuro shot me a sidelong glance. His face was ragged with weariness, but there was a spark of levity in his eyes. I was reminded of all life had thrown at him, how often he'd fallen down—and how often he'd gotten back up again. And yet this time, the rebel leader looked ready to let go. In fact, at the thought of certain suicide, he looked almost *relieved*.

"Phoenix-Slayer," he said to me, with a certain tone of reluctant camaraderie. "Are you ready to die?"

OUR MOMENTARY CIVILITY ENDED AFTER THAT. SKY FIERCELY OBJECTED to Winter's plan, Lei tried to brainstorm alternatives, and Kuro began to laugh, his mind teetering on the brink of sanity. He had lost Jinya only a day ago, I reminded myself. If not for the iron walls surrounding us, I would've peered into his mind, which felt volatile, like flames dancing with oil.

After a few more minutes of pointless dispute, Winter asked if we shouldn't break for food. This of course raised further debate.

Kuro suggested the rebel base, which Sky disapproved of. Winter proposed the Anlai camp, which Kuro protested against.

"What if we split up?" I asked.

Kuro shoved a finger in Sky's direction. "How do I know you won't simply go back to your troops and turn us in?" Kuro demanded.

"How do I know you won't do the same?" said Sky.

"None of us separates from the group," Lei decided. "We stick together, until the veil is restored."

"Then the cease-fire's off," finished Kuro. "Am I right?"

At the ensuing silence, I guessed he was.

For the issue of sustenance, Lei suggested a nearby pleasure-house, which was known for being discreet regarding delicate matters.

As it turned out, there was little need for delicacy. The pleasure-house, along with all other businesses, was shuttered, its residents having fled the city in the hours following the quake. Now those less fortunate, who hadn't managed to escape, would never leave at all.

The streets of First Crossing, once bustling, were now eerily silent but for the creaking of trees in the wind or the errant moan of a casualty. Apart from bandits and other foolhardy opportunists, few roamed the open streets.

It was a strange party then that we comprised: Sky in the front, his sword at the ready; Kuro at the rear; and Winter and I in the middle. Lei kept toward the back, occasionally breaking away to tinker with the locks on various stores.

"This one," he said at last, and we followed him to an abandoned noodle house. We gathered around Lei as he inserted a hairpin into the lock.

A stray motion caught my eye; I glanced over my shoulder to see a corporeal rabbit spirit peering at us from around the corner. Sky stepped in front of me, lifting his sword.

"Wait!" Kuro and I exclaimed in unison. In our indecision, the rabbit turned and hopped away.

"Not all spirits are violent," explained Kuro. "They're like us; they vary in disposition and temperament."

"How do you know that?" I asked, turning back to the noodle shop as the lock clicked and Lei pushed the door open, ushering us inside. Kuro and I entered first, followed by Winter.

"Baihu once told me," Kuro replied, and I felt a twinge of surprise, followed by jealousy. Baihu was nothing like Qinglong. She had always sought to maintain balance between realms, and even now, with the veil torn, she hadn't attempted to cross into the human realm. Was it our ban on black magic that had first cast spirits as beings of malice and evil? And in perceiving them that way, had we somehow made it a reality?

I cleared my throat. "The Ivory Tiger seems—"

"Liu Sky!" Lei shouted. "Get down!"

I whirled around just as a seemingly dead corpse picked himself off the street and, with supernatural strength, proceeded to pitch an axe at Sky. Sky, standing outside the noodle shop, ducked just in time, the axe barely grazing his shoulder. The old man's hair had gone to gray, and his face was as wrinkled as a dried prune. And yet, when he saw the axe had not met its mark, he charged at Sky, sprinting as if he were a boy in his prime.

Sky anchored his stance, raising his sword, but Lei beat him to it. With practiced aim, Lei hurled a dual-sided knife at the man, who choked as the blade sliced cleanly across his throat. The blood that trickled out was the color of black tar.

The old man fell to his knees, chortling. I couldn't tell if he was choking or laughing, or both. His yellow irises fixed on mine as he died. As if he saw me, and knew what I was.

Someone like him.

Someone ready to die.

"Get in," ordered Lei, shaking me from my stupor. He bolted the door behind us.

NONE OF US, IT TURNED OUT, KNEW HOW TO COOK. THERE WAS NOODLE dough sitting on the kitchen counter, yet no one who knew how to knead it. Then there were chicken eggs in the basket by the fire, and no one who knew how to cook them. Laughing at our incompetence, Lei endeavored to learn.

Meanwhile, I escaped to the storage room, craving solitude. Being in Lei and Sky's combined presence grated on my nerves like the shrill whine of a whistle, leaving me agitated and on edge. I shut the storage room door and sat in the dark, seeking focus and calm. An idea was simmering in the back of my mind, like a pot left over a low flame.

"*We're human, each of us,*" Lei had told me. "*But I believe we're more than our worst moments. It's our best moments that have the power to define us.*"

"*Remember yourself.*" My mother's advice had enabled me to escape the spirit realm. "*Remember your humanness, and you will be able to return.*"

What was humanness? Was it a condition of being, or was it inherent somehow? Was it possible to lose one's humanity, or was that like water losing its wetness? How then did human vessels die? It was when we lost our qi, yes, but more than that, it was when we lost our will to live.

What gave us our will to live, then? Joy, perhaps, and hope. Where did those feelings stem from?

"*The future is always a source of comfort,*" Lei had once told me. "*It's the past I despise.*"

I found now that I did not agree. It was my memories that offered the essence of me, that brought me invaluable comfort, that reminded me of who I was. I thought of my mother in her moments of lucidity, teaching me how to swim. Xiuying braiding my hair. Rouha and Plum stuffing their faces with dumplings, asking me to tell them the same story over and over.

"*What happened to the cowherd and the weaver girl?*"

"*They lived happily ever after,*" I said, having changed the story for them.

"*What happens after happily ever after?*"

"*Every day, they wake up and choose happiness.*"

"*Like us,*" said Rouha, her mouth full. "*We do that too.*"

The door burst open, yanking me from my thoughts. Sky leaned against it, panting, his face stricken and white.

"What is it?" I asked him, reaching for my sword.

"Nothing," he said, color slowly returning to his face. "Don't go off alone," he added roughly. "We thought you'd been taken."

I've been in here for all of five minutes, I wanted to argue. But I saw the strain on his face, which likely matched my own. Holding my tongue, I strode past him to the kitchen.

Dinner was boiled eggs—underboiled—and noodles—overcooked. Still, after life in the army, I was not one to refuse food.

"Look what I found!" announced Kuro, emerging from the cellar with a bottle of sorghum wine. "It's a proper meal now."

All of us accepted a glass. All of us—except Lei, who opted for barley tea instead. I glanced at him curiously, before remembering that I was upset with him.

"To those who make history," said Kuro, toasting us.

"And to those who live to write about it," said Winter, smiling.

The sorghum wine warmed me, calming my nerves and settling my thoughts. Over the dining table I scrutinized Kuro, thinking hard.

"What is it?" the rebel leader asked, after he'd eaten twice as much as the rest of us.

"Nothing," I said.

"*You look like you're scheming.*" Lei spoke into my mind.

"*Go away,*" I replied. I felt the weight of his gaze but studied my chopsticks instead.

"*Are you upset with me?*"

I said nothing.

"*We'll find another way. Did you think I'd consent to Winter's plan?*"

Now I did look up, the anger I'd been holding back threatening to emerge in a way I could not control. "*You think that's what I'm angry about?*"

A long pause, and then: "*Is this about Sky?*"

For a mind reader, he was awfully slow on the uptake. "*You antagonized him.*" I thought back to the violent and hateful way they'd fought. The way I'd hidden in the corner, useless, helpless, angry with them, angry with myself.

"*He hurt you, Meilin. Is it not permissible for me to loathe him for it?*"

I rose abruptly from the table and went to the fire, stoking the flames with a bit too much aggression. Although the air had warmed considerably, gooseflesh still lined my skin. On second thought, it most likely had less to do with the temperature and more to do with the iron Lei had barricaded against the door.

"*I feel like this is all my fault,*" I finally answered. "*I poisoned you, both of you, I corrupted you—*"

"*No, sweetheart.*" The thought he sent me was so forceful it quieted all other noise in my head. "*If I am corrupted, it is because of the world, not you. Never you. You who have been a balm to my soul.*"

Those words . . . they were familiar. Because he'd heard my thoughts before. I had spoken to him in my mind, before I'd known he could hear me.

Now I raised my face from the fire and sought his gaze across the room. He was so beautiful to me; that much was unchanged. From the moment I'd met him, I'd thought him lovely. Then my impression had shifted—as I'd witnessed his monstrosity, his cruelty, the lengths to which he would go to obtain what he wanted. It had frightened me, but at the same time, it had drawn me to him.

For I'd recognized parts of myself in him—the part of me that longed for love and trust but thought myself unworthy. The part of me that blamed myself for my mother's passing, yet still—foolishly, perhaps—sought redemption. The part of me—however small—that decided it was less important to be remembered as a hero than to do what was right and good for those I loved. For no one would ever know that Lei had tried to stop Chancellor Sima on his path of vengeance. History would not remember him as anything more than a vain, self-serving prince who had lied and cheated his way to victory. But I would remember. I and Autumn and perhaps his sister, whom he spoke of with light in his eyes. Would that be enough?

And more importantly, was that enough for me?

KURO AND I TOOK FIRST WATCH TOGETHER, THE TWO OF US SITTING BY the door as the others slept by the fire. Sky, who I knew had trouble sleeping, kept rising to double- and triple-check the locks.

"I saw some dried jujube tea in the storage room," I said in a low whisper, as Sky sat up yet again, woken by an errant scream in the distance. From our time in the army, I knew he often brewed jujube tea to help him sleep through the night.

Sky studied me in the dim light. I could not make out his expression in the shadows, but I could trace the planes of his face: hard and smooth as marble.

"I'm fine," he said at last, but there was a note of pain in his voice. Had I hurt him again, unwittingly? But how could I pretend distance between us, when once we had been so much more than strangers?

"You royals are an amusing bunch," whispered Kuro, as Sky stalked into the storage room.

"I'm not a royal," I hissed.

"Not yet," said Kuro with a wink. "If you ask me, my dear, my vote is for the Ximing prince. Much better temper."

"I didn't ask you," I snapped. Kuro chuckled, though I noted the smile did not reach his eyes. Ever since we'd returned from the spirit realm, the rebel leader hadn't been the same.

"It's not your fault, you know. What happened to Jinya."

Kuro didn't look at me. "It is, and you know it."

I shook my head. "You once asked me to destroy the foundations of the old world with you, and build a new one from its ashes. Remember that? These are its ashes, Kuro. The new world is ready for the taking." I sat up. "Imagine how much good you can do. You can create that world you envisioned—a world for *all* people. Wouldn't Jinya have wanted that?"

"Jinya wanted to live," he snarled. He withdrew his seal from beneath his shirt, thumbing the smooth jade for comfort. More quietly, he said, "I'm ready to move on, to tell the truth. I'm ready to go to her."

"Don't say that," I said, alarmed. "The people need you."

Kuro laughed. "They don't need *me*. They need a hero they can adore—and shunt responsibility to." He shook his head. "Plenty of those to choose from."

Jinya's death had changed him, irrevocably. He was no longer the same man I'd met in a Canyuan cellar: charismatic, confident, effervescent with energy. Now he was losing his will to live, which, if my suspicions were correct, was exactly what we needed to succeed.

"Is anyone out there?"

Kuro and I both turned toward the door, though neither of us made a move to rise. The speaker sounded like a young woman, her voice panicked and near tears.

"Please—please save us!"

We'd covered all the windows and doors, and now we could not risk looking outside without alerting the spirits to our presence. "It's likely a trap," I said, through gritted teeth.

Kuro nodded. With a stray stick, he began to draw a sketch in the dirt.

"No—no!" There was a sound like a baby's wail, and I winced, a hollowness expanding in my chest. Then abruptly, the screams stopped, replaced by the whistling of the wind.

You did this. You started this.

"Kuro," I asked, forcibly changing the subject. "How did you open your gates?"

"What do you mean?" He yawned. I saw he'd drawn a rudimentary picture of a smiling girl with pigtails.

"The spirit gates you created—how did you do it?"

He sat back, frowning as he tried to remember. "It happened naturally. I didn't think much about it. I used my power..."

"What power?"

"Lixia, of course."

"And how did you draw on your lixia?" I asked, knowing my own answer.

His frown deepened. "I called on my belief—that I was worth more than this. That I deserved to be known, known and remembered..."

I nodded. Kuro had drawn on his pride, the pride that the Ivory Tiger fed and bolstered. It was the same way I accessed the dragon's power. Through my greed.

These emotions drew the spirits to us, who then fed and nurtured these desires, until we became nothing but shells of our former selves. But there was more to us too. We were more than our pride and greed and our desire for vengeance; we were joy, and kindness, and wonder too. Perhaps more than blood, our qi existed in this inherent state of humanness.

I thought of how I'd managed to escape the spirit realm last time, when Qinglong had come for me. I'd drawn on my memories, and they had enabled my escape. Perhaps those same memories could fuel the qi needed to restore the veil. A reverse impulsion, a process of giving rather than taking.

Slowly, I explained my plan to Kuro.

"The veil *is* a living thing, of sorts," Kuro said, when I was done. "I don't see why it wouldn't take impulsion, just as other beings do. But have you ever tried to manipulate a spirit?"

"I've shielded my mind against the dragon," I said. "But I don't know if I've ever compelled him. Perhaps . . . once," I amended, remembering how I'd distracted Qinglong with the bird spirit.

"*Look how she dares defy you,*" I'd told the dragon. "*You would let her take me from you?*"

Had it been the fact that his vessel had taken another spirit's seal that had driven him into a frenzy? Or had it been more than that—had my compulsion actually worked on him?

If spirits could indeed transfer some of their abilities to their human vessels, then was it so far-fetched to believe that humans could usurp their spirit masters? I could believe it. If this ability of mine led to the dragon's demise, then only he was to blame. By nurturing my ambition, Qinglong had taught me to dream greater dreams, to aspire to a greatness beyond even what he had bestowed upon me.

"Have you ever tried to compel the tiger before?" I asked Kuro.

"No," said Kuro, wrinkling his brow. "But anyway, I don't need to. We have the same goals."

Because Baihu wanted the veil restored, I remembered. She wanted the realms to remain in balance. I'd forgotten that just because the dragon wished for chaos did not mean the tiger wanted the same.

"Not all spirits are violent. They're like us; they vary in disposition and temperament."

"Should we split up and target different gates?" Kuro asked. "That way, if one of us is intercepted, the other can still go on."

I understood the logic, but my last conversation with the dragon made me reconsider.

"*Humans are weak-blooded creatures,*" Qinglong had said. "*Their only real strength lies in their numbers. Fortunately, they rarely agree on anything, so even that advantage is inaccessible to them.*"

Perhaps the dragon had inadvertently shown me his hand.

My gaze drifted to Kuro's sketch in the dirt, which reminded me of the drawings of another.

"*Long, long ago, in a time before ours, spirits and men walked the earth together. They say it was an era of chaos and instability, because the spirits were capricious and fickle, and the emperor a weak and corrupt man.*"

Consort Caihong's story spoke of remnants of old gods, fossilized pieces of amber left on the caverns of the Red Mountains.

"*Only, the emperor's bones had fossilized into amber, and just as the father had once shared qi with his son, now this amber could be used to bridge qi from person to person. Understanding his father's last gift to him, the prince gave the amber to his people. Together, they joined hands and shared their qi across the land, and thus with their great numbers the first veil between spirits and men was formed.*"

Her tale differed from the versions I'd heard, but they all shared a belief in the bones of old gods, used to form a veil between realms. What if? I wondered. It wouldn't be the most outrageous story that had turned out to hold some grain of truth.

Still mulling it over, I shared the story with Kuro. "You wouldn't happen to know which caves the story is referring to, would you?" I asked.

He hesitated. "It's not exactly the same, but in Leyuan, we tell a different tale. Have you heard of the Reed Flute Caves? They're a few li from First Crossing."

I shook my head.

"Legend has it their stalagmites are the fossilized amber remains of mythical creatures, back when they freely roamed our world."

My mouth fell open as an old memory resurfaced. Sky had actually intended to visit those caves, until I'd derailed his plans: *A seer told my father he could find a powerful weapon in the Reed Flute Caves.*

I scrutinized Kuro. "You think it's the same amber?"

"I'd take our chances," he said.

If we joined our powers as one, Kuro's qi would become mine, and mine his. I shuddered but nodded. Once our life forces were intertwined, we could likely never disentangle them.

"So we pay a visit to the Reed Flute Caves, join our powers together, and then use impulsion to restore qi to the veil," continued Kuro, settling on his haunches. "Instead of bleeding ourselves to death like jiangshi. I like it. More respectable."

"It will take time," I cautioned. "And the more violent spirits are bound to cause trouble."

Kuro grimaced, but I wasn't finished.

"We'll likely lose ourselves during the process," I continued, recalling my previous attempts at mental manipulation. "As our minds wander, our bodies will be left vulnerable and undefended."

"You won't be undefended," said Sky from the fire, startling me—I hadn't realized he was still awake. "When the time comes, I'll guard you."

He got up and motioned for me to switch places with him.

Blearily, I saw that my shift was over. The night was bleeding into early morning.

"What about me?" asked Kuro jokingly.

"Both of you," Sky amended, though his jaw twitched. "I'll muster my best men for the job."

"How can I trust they won't turn traitor and off us in our sleep?" asked Kuro suspiciously. "Particularly after your father spread all that propaganda about us being black magic practitioners."

"I'll convince them," said Winter, who apparently was also awake. "And I'll make sure we choose soldiers who can be trusted."

I nodded, counting on Winter's emotional intelligence in this regard.

Lei too rose to swap places with Kuro. It seemed no one had truly been sleeping. "I'll be able to lure the violent spirits away from the site of the chasm," said Lei.

"How?" I asked. Even though Lei lacked a spirit disposition, and was not at risk for being corrupted, there was no way he could take on that many spirits on his own. "Don't forget your brother wants you dead."

"Zihuan will have his own problems to deal with," said Lei, with a ruthless smile that almost made me pity his brother. "As for the spirits, I can ask for the aid of the Ruan monks."

"The southern monks?" repeated Winter, with a certain awe.

"They can harness lixia without relying on spirit summoning," explained Lei. "And they owe me a favor or two."

I nodded, trusting the others to play their parts. Though suspicion still lingered between us, I also sensed something vital and intrinsic binding us together. Despite our differences, we were alike in our shared imperatives and, perhaps, in our mutual desperation—to right the many wrongs that had led us here: to this abandoned noodle shop, to this desecrated city, to these wounded and terrified people. To our loved ones—and the hungry ghosts we left behind.

As I surveyed the weary yet watchful faces of my companions, illuminated by the pale blue glow of dawn, I thought: *How lovely all of you are. How lovely this little life of mine. How dearly I will miss each of you, and how deeply I will loathe to give it all up.*

THIRTY-SEVEN

It is said that the Reed Flute Caves were once home to mythical creatures of ancient legend. One day, the dragon spirit, jealous of their earthly home, flooded the cavern with a magical torrent, turning the creatures into pillars of stone. Although most of these stone formations have been eroded with time, an astute explorer may still make out the shapes of the creatures that once were.

—TALES OF THE EASTERN STEPPES, 612

SKY AND WINTER LEFT US TO MUSTER THEIR TROOPS, SETTING OUT for the Anlai base camp just outside First Crossing. Winter wanted more time to prepare, but Kuro was adamant we act before the spirits could wreak greater havoc. I, worried about my diminishing days, agreed to make haste.

We would move the very next day, striking at dawn—when the nocturnal spirits would be resting. That left us less than twenty-four hours to prepare.

Sky and Winter departed promptly, without even saying goodbye. Lei was next, leaving to liaise with the Ruan monks. Despite the distance he had to traverse, he promised to return by sundown. We would reconvene at the noodle shop, and if the noodle shop was no longer standing, then at the entrance to the bunkers.

"You'll be safe on your own?" I asked Lei, thinking of the many people who wanted him dead.

"I'll be fine," he said, his mouth curving in an insolent smirk.

Come to think of it, I'd seen Lei perform, seen him feign weakness, but I'd never truly seen him do battle, as if his life depended upon it. I did not know the full extent of his abilities.

So quickly I didn't have time to react, Lei cupped the back of my neck and drew me to him, kissing me on the crown of my head. He released me before I could argue or turn away. Taken aback, I was quiet.

"Worried for me?" he asked. "I'm flattered."

"Don't get yourself killed," I said roughly.

He arched a brow at me. "Sweetheart, I may not be a spirit summoner, but I *can* wield a sword."

As Kuro approached, Lei shot me a look. *"Be careful around that one,"* he said into my mind.

I bristled, defensive of anyone questioning a spirit summoner's sanity. *"His intentions are in the right place."*

"And I don't doubt that," he told me. *"But there's something off about him."* He narrowed his eyes, thinking. *"There's a certain air a man has."*

"What do you mean?"

His eyes cut to the rebel leader's back. *"The air of a man ready to die."*

ALTHOUGH IT HAD ONLY BEEN HOME FOR A SINGLE NIGHT, I FELT A TAD forlorn leaving behind the safety of the noodle shop. Kuro and I departed last for the rebel base, where he needed to attend to the leadership duties he'd been neglecting for some time. With Jinya's absence, his neglect had become all the more evident within the Black Scarves.

Kuro and I agreed to reconvene at high noon to head to the Reed Flute Caves together. To pass the time, I ate, practiced qi gong, and pored over a few lixia scrolls the rebels had stolen from Leyuan. At noon I sharpened my blades and went out to meet Kuro at our appointed rendezvous point. He was not there.

I waited for a minute, then several more, growing increasingly impatient as the sun reached its highest point in the sky. We had one day to prepare; did Kuro not understand the urgency of the matter? Outside, spirits were running amok, people were dying, and the balance of the world had been thrown off kilter. And still Kuro was late.

I forced myself to exhale. Perhaps he was simply tied up in meetings. I thought of my time in the war, when Sky had certainly had his fair share of council meetings—most of which he hadn't been able to escape. Kuro was the military leader of the largest rebel group across the Three Kingdoms—and we were reliant on him to mobilize his troops for our cause.

Somewhat mollified, I returned to the catacombs to search for him. But when I reached his rooms, the response from his guards left me more than a little uneasy.

"He's not . . . himself right now," said his personal guard. "I'd recommend staying away for a day."

"A day?" I balked. "We don't have a day!" I shoved him out of the way. "Let me see him."

"Suit yourself," said the guard, who looked as though he were throwing me to the wolves.

I marched inside to find the room smoky and airless, and Kuro himself lying on the floor, staring up at the ceiling as if it were the most beautiful thing he'd ever seen. His eyes were as wide as saucers, but his irises were so constricted his eyes looked almost white.

"Kuro!" I cried out, rushing to him. "What's wrong?"

I touched his skin—cool and clammy. I was about to ask if he'd been poisoned when I saw the opium pipe in his left hand. It was poison—but he'd done it to himself.

"You're smoking *now?*" I demanded.

With great effort he focused his gaze on me. "Phoenix-Slayer," he said slowly, his lips curving into a vacuous smile.

I stifled the urge for violence. "Kuro," I said. "Get up. We have to go now. Do you remember the plan?"

"I can't," he replied, his voice slurring. "I'm tired. I'll stay here."

"You'll *stay* here?" I repeated. Now I couldn't restrain myself; I grabbed him by his shoulders and shook him, hard. He let himself sway like an overgrown rag doll, limp and defenseless. "As if that's an option—" In my indignation, I knocked over a liquor bottle on the floor. It fell on its side, but nothing came out.

"I can't do this without her," he told me, his voice threadbare. He closed his eyes, and seconds later, fell asleep in front of me. I swore. There was nothing I despised more than this—this waste and indulgence. Others told me my father had once been a clearheaded man, but I had never known him as such—because the opium had changed him. And now Kuro, smart, charismatic Kuro, had fallen prey to the pipe.

I got to my feet, assessing the damage. It was already afternoon, and we needed to get back before dusk—when the spirits came out to play. Sky and Lei were both occupied with their own equally important tasks. I could ask a few rebels to accompany me to the caves, but they could sooner become liabilities if possessed by a wayward spirit. No, better to go alone and leave less of a trail.

I scratched out a note and gave it to Kuro's personal guard. I considered requesting a horse, then decided it was better to ask for forgiveness. Stealing a mare, I left the rebel base and galloped out of the city. The woods lay deceptively empty, though the air was far from calm. There was a tense stillness like the hush before a storm: no birdsong, no animals rustling in the grasses, not even the buzz of mosquitoes to disturb the uncanny quiet. In some places, the lixia was so thick in the air it felt like breathing in a drug. The aftermath of this violence would surely leave its mark for years to come. But would there ever be a day when the horrors of this war dissipated like dandelion fluff on the wind, scattering into fragments too small to see?

The future was always so hard for me to imagine. It brought me no comfort, as it did to others. If I were to die, I did not wish to think of it. But if I were to live, that too seemed impossible in its complexity. Others would move on. Others like Rouha and Plum would grow up and go to school and get married and perhaps even have children of their own. But I would not move on. I could feel it in my bones—that I lacked the normalcy that brought others happiness. It was why I ran away from home. Why I accepted the dragon's seal. Why I *desired*.

Without the usual foot traffic, I was able to make it out of the city roads in a quarter of the time. Dismounting before the Reed Flute Caves, I tied my mare to a nearby tree and left her to graze, listening for the sound of whispering spirits.

The lixia did feel thinner here; I did not know why. Perhaps they despised the dark, having spent too long in the spirit realm. Or perhaps the caves, devoid of people, were simply of little interest to them.

"Hello?" I whispered into the cavern, without quite knowing why I was whispering. Although we had passed the caves on our way into First Crossing, we had not stopped to venture inside. Beneath the low rays of golden sunlight, the stalagmites within seemed to sparkle like jewels. Like the Leyuan legend said, they did appear like mythical creatures, their sharp crags reminiscent of faces and bodies. The rock below was as smooth as polished marble and bore the rippling discoloration of a long-ago ocean floor. How peculiar, then, that these caverns now stood on a mountain peak far from the sea. How the world changed—and how it stayed the same.

My disquiet growing, I entered hesitantly, the sun's rays at my back. I reached for a thin stalagmite and felt my vital energy pulse in response. As I gripped the stalagmite, my qi began to expand, spreading beyond the caves to the rivers and the mountains. I heard voices, laughter; I felt the beating hearts of people near and far. Gasping, I released the stalagmite and withdrew my knife, sawing at the fossil.

The dull thud of a boot startled me. I turned instinctively, just as a blur of movement flickered before me. That was when I realized—I'd made a mistake.

If I hadn't shielded Qinglong from my mind, perhaps he would've warned me. Or perhaps he merely would have laughed. But by the time I turned, it was too late.

The last thing I saw was a finely dressed woman, her red-tinted lips parted in a wide, open-mouthed smile. A dark cloth suddenly covered my face, choking me. My training kicked in—I held my breath, twisting to drive my elbow into my captor's stomach. But before I could summon the dragon's power, nimble fingers struck my qi points with a precision few could match. I gasped, and my body went limp as I breathed in the cloth's poison, my mind rejecting what my body already knew: I had walked into a trap.

I WOKE TO A SPLITTING HEADACHE, THE LIXIA WITHDRAWAL SO BRUTAL I felt on the precipice of death. I tugged weakly at my hands, before realizing they were secured by what must be iron manacles. *This again.*

Despite my many injuries, the lixia in the aftermath of the quake had been enough to buoy me, lending me a false strength that resulted in overconfidence and conceit. Now, stripped of lixia, I felt like nothing more than an animated corpse. I ached everywhere; there was no muscle in my body that did not throb; my skin hurt as if stretched too tight; and beneath it all, ever present, coursed an undercurrent of violent lack. My body had grown to depend on spirit power, like a warped tree that requires a stake to stand. I needed Qinglong's power now to breathe, to live, to even *wish to live*. Belatedly, I understood that the only thing keeping me from keeling over was my chains. Without them, I would be fetal on the floor.

It was in this moment of weakness that Sky's long-ago admonition came to mind: *"You're a good fighter, Ren, but you're a terrible soldier. You think for yourself. You don't obey orders. And you look out for your own agenda over your platoon's."*

He was right, of course. It was my instinct to act alone that had led me straight into this trap.

"How weak you are," said a new voice. "I always wondered—however did you last in the Three Kingdoms War?"

With effort, I forced my eyes open. I was chained to a tapering column rising from the floor of the cave, my arms tied behind me and an iron collar fastened around my throat, which felt excessive. *Because my captives are afraid of me*, I saw. They were afraid of the power I possessed.

I raised my head and met the smiling gaze of Princess Yifeng. *Of course.* The Anlai messenger had even warned me at the trading post, but distracted as I'd been, I had ignored the threat.

"Hello again, Lady Hai."

"Come to finish the job?" I rasped, remembering the last time she'd tried to kill me. I squinted at her. "Why are you even here? Were you banished from the Forbidden City?"

"Of course not," she scoffed, though I could tell I'd offended her at the suggestion. "The crown prince is sick. I was simply accompanying him to the treaty signing to ensure his health and well-being."

"If you're speaking of your husband, you know he's no longer the crown prince."

Her neck flushed. "He will be once I bring your severed head to the Imperial Commander!"

I was so tired. "And how will that help anything?"

"You are a black magic practitioner," she spat. "There's no point in denying it. I have proof."

And then, to my utter horror, she beckoned forward none other than Luo Tao, Sky's former personal guard. I remembered glimpsing his face amid the wreckage after the veil's collapse, and it struck me—he must have been spying on me for days.

"Your prince banished him under threat of death, but he returned after recognizing the danger your existence posed."

Looking into the familiar lines of his face brought memories of the war flooding back to me. I recalled the sheer dread I'd felt, kneeling before the Imperial Commander's throne as I awaited my sentence. I recalled guards dragging me below ground into the dungeons, losing the warmth of sun on my skin, the scent of pine trees, the song of morning larks. Losing my sense of self, my will to live.

"If only I had killed you at the end of the war—instead of leaving you to the justice of the throne," Tao spat. "But now I see that you are too dangerous to be left to live."

I was struck by the force of his animosity. It was true that if he had killed me then, perhaps the veil between realms never would have torn. And yet I had tried to save the Three Kingdoms then, just as I was trying to now. I had *always* been trying to save the Three Kingdoms. Couldn't they see that? Was intention not worth something? Or was it only the echoes of your mistakes that history remembered?

I drew a ragged breath, trying for calm. "If you kill me now, you are ruining our last chance at closing the spirit gates," I said. "I am trying to *restore* the veil."

"The audacity of your lies," he snarled. "You were the one who opened the gates in the first place."

Desperate, I shifted tactics, appealing to his sense of duty as a soldier. "Do you think Sky will forgive you for this?" I asked.

"That boy is lost in his romantic delusions," Princess Yifeng interrupted. "But he will understand and step aside when the Imperial Commander selects Keyan as his successor." Her expression was one of pride. "My heroism will ensure that."

Tao had backed away in disgust, but Princess Yifeng, conversely, drew near, lowering her voice as if sharing a juicy morsel of gossip. "You know, Lady Hai, as *deviant* as it is, I think I rather understand you. We women do tend to draw the short end of the stick, do we not? We do all the dirty work, and the men get to claim the reward. But you know what your mistake was? You got too greedy. You should've learned from me and pulled the strings backstage." She clucked her tongue like a scolding schoolteacher. "You could've had a good thing going. And we could've been friends." She shook her head. "But that time has passed now."

THIRTY-EIGHT

Humble apologies for the sudden inquiry, but might you know the current residence of Yu Xiuying? I heard she moved to the capital, and was hoping to pay her a visit before I left town for good.
—PRIVATE CORRESPONDENCE FROM WANG SPARROW, 924

"WAIT," I SAID, STRUGGLING AGAINST MY CHAINS. SURELY Kuro had read my note by now, and figured out where I'd gone. Were they on their way? I had to stall Princess Yifeng. But the sun had already set, and she too was anxious to be gone.

The princess gestured for Tao, who drew his sword.

Qinglong, I thought. *Please. Help me. Lei? Can you hear me? Please. Anyone! Can anyone help me?*

"I have a secret," I said. "A secret you should know."

The princess frowned. "What is it now?"

I reached for something clever to say, but my body ached with pain, and my mind, craving lixia, refused to cooperate. "Prince Keyan," I began. "He has an illegitimate child."

Princess Yifeng threw her head back with laughter. "Is that all?"

"No," I said. "The prince—"

The sun was gone, the only light emanating from the lit torches the soldiers carried. So we all recoiled as a shadow moved and a guard came sprinting inside. He whispered something to Tao, who scowled in consternation and followed him out of the caves, his strides long and urgent.

I held my breath, afraid to hope.

A rat skittered in the distance, fleeing toward the shadows. Princess Yifeng peered into the cavern depths, at all the various tunnels snaking into the mountainside.

"Keep her quiet," she ordered the nearest soldier. "And extinguish the torches."

The guards stationed outside must've sensed an approaching threat. Realizing this was my chance, I let out a high-pitched shriek, my voice echoing across the cavern walls. I only had time to scream once more before the guard struck me across the face. My cheek slammed into the stalagmite I was bound to and I choked on my own blood. Then a guard stuffed a gag into my mouth, silencing me.

The torches went out, leaving us shrouded in hazy darkness, breathing in smoke. I could make out the faintest glimmer of moonlight at the cave's opening, which rippled as a shadow moved, as fluid as ink spreading through water. Only one person I knew could move like that.

The first scream cut the silence like a knife. My eyes took time to adjust as screams split the air, followed by the ring of steel against steel, the tang of freshly spilled blood, and the low thud of falling bodies. Then that dark shadow was upon us, whirling through the air like a sword dancer, dispersing smoke, light, sound, his twin blades like blinking stars against the night.

He was beautiful—and monstrous. I recoiled as blood sprayed everywhere, coating my face, my hair, my clothes. Death hung like a miasma in the air, bodies falling like stalks of wheat beneath a scythe.

In the shadows I saw Princess Yifeng trying to run, but her expensive robes gave her away as the ivory silk drew the moonlight.

She didn't stand a chance. His speed was unnatural as he caught her from behind and slit her throat, the movement so swift it made me believe in the legends of old, that perhaps mythical creatures *had* once lived here, and that they'd remained as ghosts. Ghosts that returned in the dead of the night, beckoned by blood and violence. For surely this was not the work of a man.

But I caught sight of his face, distinctly human in his anger as he sensed the threat I'd overlooked. Mesmerized as I'd been, I'd missed the closer danger—and only now I saw Tao was still alive. He bore a fatal stomach wound, leaving a trail of blood in his wake as he limped toward me, determined to finish one last job. He raised his blade in the air, but the Ximing prince was faster. Lei stabbed him so viciously Tao moaned in anguish, his organs spilling from his flesh. Then he withdrew his blade and stabbed him again, and again. By the time he was done, the Anlai soldier was unrecognizable.

Chilled to the bone, I could not speak. There were monsters in all of us, I told myself. But the monster in him was *terrifying*.

At last, when everyone was dead and the reek of blood hung in the air like a dense fog, Lei dropped his curved blades. They clattered against the stone like a discordant melody. Instead of coming to me as I'd expected, he leaned heavily against the cavern wall, positively falling against it. Was he injured? I tried to speak but could not through my gag. The language of his body, the way he pressed himself against the wall—it spoke of utter defeat. He said nothing for a time, then let out a broken sound of unadulterated rage—rage and sorrow and grief.

My concern growing, I struggled against my bonds. His face was partially turned from me, but I could see something there—something in his expression that unnerved me to my core. He looked... *inhuman*.

A beautiful monster, I'd once thought him.

"Lei?" I tried to say. "What's wrong?"

Only a muffled sound emerged from my gag, but it was enough. He rose, shaking as he turned in my direction.

"*Lei?*" I thought to him.

In a few long strides, he'd crossed the cavern floor. He ripped the gag from my mouth, then held my blood-splattered face in his hands. His touch was so very cold.

"Skies, Meilin," he breathed, his voice coming out hoarse and gravelly, as if he hadn't spoken in days. "You—you're alive. I thought... I thought I'd lost you."

Then, to my utter amazement, he pressed his forehead against mine and began to cry. Broken sobs that reminded me of his humanity.

"Shh," I said. "It's okay." I tried to wrap my arms around him, forgetting I couldn't move. My shoulders squirmed uncomfortably in their sockets. "Could you ...?"

He roused himself then, lighting a torch to search the dead bodies. He found the key on Tao's person. He unlocked my collar first, and I gasped for breath as the suffocating iron came off me. The resulting lightness was exhilarating.

I started to fall as he unlocked my remaining chains. Lei caught me in his arms, expecting this. Instead of setting me down, he buried his face in the crook of my neck, breathing me in, not seeming to mind the blood and filth soaking my skin.

This time, I let myself embrace him. In response he drew me closer, until no space remained between us, until our shadows merged as one.

"I was thinking of everything I'd done to you," he said quietly. "All the torture and grief and unhappiness you'd undergone because of me. And that was my greatest regret—that I hadn't been able to make things right for you."

His voice broke beneath the weight of his regret. *It's okay*, I wanted to say, but my throat was constricting, and I too could not speak.

He spoke into my mind. *"I promised myself I would make it up to you—even if it took every damn day of the rest of my life."*

"You've already saved me countless times," I answered. *"You don't owe me anything."*

"Then not out of debt." A pause. *"But out of—love."*

I raised my face to look at him. He swallowed, the knot at his throat lifting. He looked so vulnerable then, as if I had the power to save or destroy him.

"I told you—I don't know if I'm capable of love anymore."

Lei brushed a stray hair from my face. *"What is love—if not care for one another? Pride in all that you've done. Belief in what you will continue to do. And hope—hope that we will grow together, as one."*

"Is that what your love is?" I asked him.

He considered this for a long time. Warring emotions crossed his face—guilt, desperation, sadness, longing. I recalled that he too had been a child of loss, bearing the weight of his mother's passing from far too young an age.

"It is how I try to love," he answered at last. And somehow, this liberated me. This simple admission of imperfection. For I too was fallible, bad at loving. It did not come naturally to me as it seemingly did to others. My instincts, so trustworthy in battle, led me astray in matters of the heart. And yet, if love meant the act of *trying*, then I loved. I loved with all my being.

"I love you," he told me, his eyes flickering beneath the weak torchlight. In a cavern drenched with blood, with hands cold as ice, he said this. "I am a monster but I love you."

It was as if the words had been stolen from my mouth. "If you are a monster, then so am I," I said quietly, and his eyes shone as falling stars. "*I find I am suited for a monster's love,*" I added.

I reached up to bring his face down to mine, and then I kissed him, softly this time. I could taste the blood on him. I had witnessed him murdering an entire platoon of soldiers to get to me. I knew his violent tendencies, his scheming ways, his penchant for drink. I knew his flaws, and yet he knew mine. He saw me; he saw past my deceit for who I really was. He knew the lies I told myself at night and the weaknesses I tried so hard to hide in the dark. He knew them, and still, he loved me. He believed in me, more even than I believed in myself.

"Lei," I said, wanting to tell him how I felt. "I-I . . ." No sound emerged from my throat. I could not say it.

"It's okay," he said, pressing his lips to my forehead.

A tear snaked down my cheek. *There must be something broken within me*, I thought. Gently, he wiped the tear with his thumb.

"Thank you for coming for me," I said instead.

There was no hesitation in his voice. "I will always come for you."

The pounding of hoofbeats made us separate. I stiffened, but Lei assured me it was the others. "When you weren't back by sundown, I went to look for you. I saw the note you'd left, and wrote one of my own."

"Why did you come alone?" I demanded. "Do you know how dangerous that is?"

"And if I had been a minute slower, I might've been too late," he said, with a self-assurance I found vexing. "So no, I won't apologize for it."

I was too tired to argue, and besides, I likely would have done the same. I stooped to gather the fossils I'd come to collect, but when I tried to rise, I lost my balance. Lei caught me and supported me as we left the caverns, and he was so warm and steady and solid that I couldn't even find it in me to be upset.

The moonlight outside was blinding. To my astonishment, two moons hung in the night sky. Both were nearly full.

"The tides will be thrown into chaos," remarked Lei, who seemed to be taking this all in stride. "I pity the sailors aiming to set sail tonight."

Balance was integral in everything—in the tides, in the seasons, in the directions of the wind. In Anlai, we believed balance was key to life itself. For the first time, I understood the extent of the havoc we'd wrought. There was no coming back from this. No matter what I did or did not do tomorrow, I would be etched into memory as the villain who tore the veil.

"Unless you surrender yourself to me." The dragon's voice was friendly, sympathetic. *"Only then can you rise as a legend."*

My sanity, already teetering on the edge, threatened to collapse. The weight of my choices felt insurmountable, as if I could swim and swim with every fiber of my being and still never reach the surface.

"Breathe," Lei said lowly.

I forced air into my lungs, trying to ignore the wild, erratic pulse of the dragon's seal, or was that the beating of my own heart?

"Meilin!"

I lifted my head as Sky leapt off his horse and ran toward us. He took in our blood-soaked robes and faces with dual horror and relief. Behind him, Captain Tong and Winter dismounted in a more orderly manner, while Kuro followed at the rear, his steps weighed down with obvious reluctance. He winced at the state of us.

"I should've gone with you," Kuro said gruffly, scratching the back of his neck. By the way he swayed, I could tell he was still intoxicated.

"Apologize to her," said Sky, with all the imperiousness of a future warlord. Kuro stiffened with anger, and I saw that he would not receive such an order from a monarch. We did not need more discord between us, not on the eve of battle.

I intervened. "What's past is past. Just don't do it again. I need you clearheaded, Kuro."

It was not the first time I'd said this. Lei, who was still holding me, squeezed my hand.

"It won't happen again," said Kuro, keeping his distance.

Sky, meanwhile, closed the gap between us. "Who was it?" he asked. His voice, a low growl, was a promise of violence.

"Princess Yifeng, wife of Liu Keyan," answered Lei.

Sky's face had gone white. "Where is she?"

"Dead."

I thought Sky would react poorly to this, but he simply nodded. He regarded me, eyes hard, and I wondered if he would admonish me for my stupidity, if he would tell me again what a terrible soldier I was. Instead, he only lifted the back of his hand to my face, brushing his knuckles against the newly formed bruise on my cheek.

"Sky..."

He dropped his hand, turning away. Without another word he mounted his horse and rode off into the dark.

THIRTY-NINE

Meeting you was like glimpsing the sea for the first time.
All rivers and streams faded; only you remained.
— THE CLASSIC OF POETRY, 532

WITHIN THE IMPERIAL BUNKERS, I LISTENED TO THE RHYTHmic plink of water echoing through the walls, counting the seconds until I could count no longer. I could hear Kuro in the adjoining room to my right, his snores deep and unbroken.

Only a few hours remained before daybreak, and I knew sleep was vital for restoring qi. And yet, no matter how much I tossed and turned, sleep would not come to me.

At last I rose and tiptoed out of my room, hesitating outside the door across from mine. *"Are you awake?"* I asked him silently.

I felt him before I heard him, a tentative question in my mind like the brush of a hand against your arm. There was a rustling of blankets, before a bare-chested Lei opened the door.

"What's wrong?" he asked, his voice raspy with sleep. My gaze skipped down to his shoulders, the broadness of them, the hue of his skin, like fresh honey.

Blushing, I returned my gaze to his face. Perhaps this was a bad idea. "I can't sleep."

"Come in," he said, holding the door for me, then letting his hand drop to my lower back as he saw me inside. His touch, although light, sent invisible tremors down to my toes.

His room was smaller than mine, barely the size of a storage closet. There was space for one pallet and a weapons rack. I gathered that imperial soldiers had once bunkered here during the Wu Dynasty, before the empire had splintered.

I sat on his pallet, pulling my knees up to my chest. "I can't sleep. Or," I amended, "I don't want to sleep."

"Why not?" he asked, settling beside me.

"I'm . . . afraid," I admitted, keeping my voice low so as to not wake Kuro next door. "I can't stop thinking about tomorrow. About all the ways we could fail."

"Do you want to talk about it?" he asked, and his voice was as warm as a crackling fire. It was hard to believe this was the same man who had once spoken to me with such coldness I believed he would not care if I lived or died.

"Not really," I said, and my eyes wandered again to his bare chest, the hollows and ridges of it, the heat that emanated from his skin, and with it, the scent of him, like jasmine and cedar and something else now, something distinctly male.

"Well . . ." he said, his voice teasing. "We don't need to sleep."

I cocked my head at him. "Do you think we should set out early?"

"Not really, no."

"Then what do you mean?"

"There are a few other things I can think of doing," he said, his smile amused and rakish. "Besides sleeping."

And now I understood. "Kuro's in the other room," I hissed, smacking him lightly on the arm. Quick as a snake, he grabbed my wrist, pulling me to him. I lost my balance and he caught me, scooping me into his lap. My heart jumped into my throat as I was overwhelmed by the sheer presence of him: the texture of his exposed skin, the prominence of his veins, the strength of his arms, the intimacy of it all. Capturing me by my waist, he grinned at me lazily, a predator surveying a well-laid trap.

"I can be quiet if you can," he said, and it sounded like a dare.

I rolled my eyes, feigning nonchalance even as my stomach turned somersaults. "It's not me I'm concerned about."

Lei's smile grew wolfish. "Is that a challenge, my love?"

I blushed down to my neck. When he called me that, it dragged my mind back to the Reed Flute Caves: the metallic stench of blood in the air, the caress of death down my spine, the coldness in his eyes as he'd butchered and slaughtered. That animal sound of pure, unadulterated rage. Beneath his pretty smiles and arch flirtations lurked a monster in the dark.

"How can you be like this?" I whispered.

He had not released my sword hand. Now he toyed with it, tracing each of my calluses. "Like what?"

"You're so ... flippant." At the quirk in his lips, I added, "And you keep smiling."

His answering smile was even more crooked. "Am I not allowed to smile?"

I took a breath, not sure who I was trying to remind here. "Earlier today I saw you murder a dozen men in the time it takes most soldiers to draw their swords. I saw you kill a princess faster than she could scream. And I saw you so thoroughly butcher a man he surely cannot enter the afterlife whole."

"He betrayed you," said Lei lowly, the gleam of violence back in his eyes. "I remembered him."

My voice hitched. "And now here you are, flirting with me as if you haven't a care in the world." *And here I am*, I added silently, *flirting back as if I'm not to blame for all of this.*

And now I wondered who I was truly upset with.

"*You're entitled to your happiness.*" He spoke into my mind, and I flinched, forgetting he could do that. At my change in mood, he released me, and I edged away from him, hating this tendency of mine and yet unable to take a different path. When someone offered their love, I returned it with distance. When someone showed me their vulnerabilities, I repaid them with spikes and sharp edges.

"Are you afraid of me?" he asked quietly.

"No," I said, but I could not meet his gaze. "I just . . . I've never seen anyone kill like that."

The silence was back, and along with it, the uneven plink of water droplets. I started counting them, hating that sound, hating my inability to communicate. I was a mess of contradictions. I craved intimacy, and yet, when offered it, I found myself unworthy. I wanted affection, and yet, when someone showed me how much they cared, I shrank from that trust, as if it were a collar around my throat. I did not know what I desired anymore. *I* had been the one to come here late at night, to wake him from his rest, to demand his attention, and now I was the one pulling away, trying to hurt him, trying to hide from him. And still there was a part of me that longed to be known, that begged him to forgive me, to understand me, to not let me push him away.

Unable to look at him, I rose to my feet. "I should go," I said. "It's late, and you should rest."

I reached for the doorknob, but before I could open it, he was behind me, caging me in, his arms planted firmly against the door.

"I told you what I am," he said, his voice a low rasp. "But what I didn't tell you is this—if they had taken your life today, I would have hunted down every last one of them. I would have scoured the

Three Kingdoms for every soul responsible—and I would have given each of them a slow, slow death. And then, once I was finished, I would have followed you to the afterlife. I would have found you, and dragged you back from the hands of Death itself."

I shook my head, avoiding his gaze. "Have you been drinking again?"

"No," he answered, sounding, for once, affronted. He sighed, reaching for me. "I meant what I said. I told you, I protect what's mine."

Backed against the door, I had no choice but to look up at him. His eyes smoldered, no longer softened by amusement. I recognized that he feigned frivolity to hide the immensity of his feeling. *"Don't wear your insecurities on your sleeve,"* he'd once warned me. *"Then scoundrels like me can use them all too easily against you."*

His vulnerabilities were not on his sleeve. They were not even in his heart. They were buried so deep within him that they were hibernating seeds planted in the depths of winter. And yet in his eyes now were signs of early life, green seedlings that had emerged from the coldest of seasons.

I rose on the balls of my feet and kissed him on the cheek. I frowned at the bruise beneath his ear, where the hilt of a sword had caught him earlier today. I kissed this too, the soft underside of his jaw, and then the hollow of his throat, which rose and fell beneath my touch.

"You are nothing like the stories say," I whispered. "You are nothing like I thought you were."

"And what did you think I was?" The mischievous crook of his smile had returned.

"A handsome yet vain fool."

"And now?"

"Now I know you're even more vain than I supposed."

He laughed as he kissed me, the sound catching low in his throat. "As long as you still find me handsome."

I deepened the kiss in answer, and he drew us closer together, until I could feel evidence of his want against me. Guiding my arms around his neck, he began to lift me.

"Your injuries—" I protested, but he picked me up anyway.

"Don't you worry about me," he said wickedly. "It's you who will suffer tonight."

"What do you mean?" I asked, as he deposited me on his pallet.

"Lie back," he ordered. "I'm going to make you stop thinking."

Tentatively, I lay down. Leisurely, he unbuttoned my robes, then studied me in my nakedness. Beneath his possessive gaze, gooseflesh pricked my skin.

He cupped my breasts, which ached with his touch, then traced his way down my stomach. One hand went around my hip, as the other stroked the inside of my thigh, slowly parting my legs.

At last, he dragged my undergarments away, and I closed my eyes, bracing myself, guessing what was to come. Instead of the painful intrusion I had been warned of, I felt a single finger slip inside me. I jumped at the unexpected nature of it, my eyes flying open.

"Aren't you supposed to use . . ." I flushed crimson. "Something else?"

He laughed under his breath, his face intent with focus. "That'll come later, sweetheart."

His finger slowly circled me, moving in foreign motions that made strange things happen to my body. To my mortification I felt a new wetness welling from between my thighs, and I moved to close my legs, to hide myself, but he would not let me. He did not appear embarrassed, only pleased. With wicked patience he slid a second finger inside, stretching me. I gasped from the shock of it—

and the resulting pain and pleasure. They were so intertwined my senses grew completely overwhelmed, and as his fingers plunged deeper inside, I cried out reflexively.

"Quiet, my love," he said, his tone arch. "What did we say about not waking our neighbor?"

I reached for him, needing to cling to something for balance as wave after wave of sensation rolled through me. "Lei," I gasped, taken captive by the feeling he'd wrought over me. "What—what are you doing to me?" I asked, panting with exertion.

"I'm pleasuring you, sweetheart," he said, steadying me against him as my hips bucked. "No one's done this for you before?"

At the shake of my head, he was quiet for a moment, thinking, before saying, "Then let me show you."

I was already soaking wet, but still Lei parted my thighs farther, guiding me into sensations I had never dreamed of experiencing. I was biting my tongue so as not to scream, my hands twisting the bedding into knots. Just when I thought I could take no more, I felt his tongue where it had never been before. I thought surely I must be dreaming, surely this could not be real. But then he found my apex, tasting me, and I knew I was awake. I had never been more awake. A crest of feeling flooded through me and I cried out, so loudly Lei covered my mouth with his hand. I shuddered beneath him, feeling like the tide caught beneath two moons, roiling with a perfect gratification I had never known before.

"How sweet you are," he murmured. His eyes were glazed with desire.

"Come here," I said, and he obeyed, bringing his face close to mine. He held himself up by his forearms so as to not crush me, but I could still feel the strength of his lust against me.

"Do you have protection?" he asked.

It took me a moment to grasp his meaning. After my betrothal,

Xiuying had mentioned methods to prevent pregnancy, but I hadn't pressed her for details at the time—I hadn't thought it would matter for me.

I shook my head.

He sighed, shifting away from me. With a soft groan he fell onto the pallet beside me, then drew me into his arms so that I rested atop him.

"Is that okay?" I asked into his chest. I did not understand the nuances of physical gratification, but I'd heard the stories of men transformed into beasts in their passion. Every Anlai woman had heard them, as a warning and as a threat.

"I'll wait," he said, brushing my mussed hair from my eyes. "We have all the time in the world, my love."

Ming Lei always did know how to lie. He knew how to make false words taste like candied hawthorn, so that they went down smooth and sweet. And I, the most hopeless of them all, believed him.

FORTY

The sword of Liu Zhuo was known as the dragon's sword, for there was no blade as tremendous or as costly. Forged by the famed blacksmiths of the Runong Desert, it was said to be made of the finest diamond and steel. Its blade was three mi long, and its weight over twenty jin. Indeed, it was said that to even lift his sword was a feat of considerable strength.
—CHRONICLES OF THE THREE KINGDOMS, 954

THE NEXT MORNING, I AWOKE TO AN EMPTY BED; LEI WAS GONE.

At the sound of rumbling wheels beyond, I hurriedly returned to my room, but not before Kuro caught me in the corridor, shouting good morning with a cheery wink. I ignored him.

In my room I dressed and armed myself to the teeth, then touched my jade for good luck. I could no longer feel Qinglong's attention, but that did not mean he had given up on me. Just as I'd been biding my time, so too had he.

Just like the moons in the sky, the two of us cannot exist in this world, I told myself. *One of us has to go. And it won't be me.*

"Phoenix-Slayer, are you ready?" At the sound of a young woman's voice, I threw open the door. But it was not Lily.

"Where's Duan Lily?" I asked, for I'd expected her to come see me before I departed.

"She left yesterday to gather provisions outside the city," replied the Leyuan rebel. "She still hasn't returned."

My frown deepened. "Shouldn't you send someone after her—"

"We can't spare the manpower right now."

I saw the reality of it in the woman's eyes; they were stretched too thin as it was. I prayed Lily had simply been taken captive by the Anlai army. At least in the brig, she stood a chance at escape. If she'd been possessed by a spirit, there was no going back.

I felt it was my responsibility to find her, as I had been the one to teach her how to fight. But there was simply no time. I thought of her gap-toothed smile, her sincere delight in swordplay. If she had been taken, it was my fault.

Another item to add to my long list of crimes.

Sky was waiting for us aboveground. He too was heavily armed, surrounded by a platoon of veteran soldiers on horseback. To my surprise, Winter was beside Captain Tong, mounted on a white stallion.

"You're coming too?" I asked Winter, who had never been known to fight.

Winter nodded, and Sky looked away, tight-jawed. I had the feeling I'd walked in on the tail end of an argument.

Kuro, who was taller than any man I knew, could only ride his own horse, which he'd brought with him from Leyuan. The rebels had tried to find me a suitable mount, but they were all too skittish and untrained. So Sky had decided to lend me his stallion, which he never parted with. Now he held the reins as I mounted his steed, and I tried not to listen as he whispered words of comfort to his faithful companion. I was trying and failing not to think of the worst-case scenario—that every person and animal we brought with us to the chasm might never return.

Kuro's soldiers gathered around him as we prepared to depart. Though a few had deserted after Jinya's passing, the majority had remained, pledging their allegiances until death. Now, most of the rebels would aid Lei and the southern monks in staging their diversion, to lead the more violent spirits away from the site of the rift.

Knowing Kuro, we all expected a grand speech. Instead, he only lifted one fist in the air, his face unexpectedly grave. "My life for the rebellion," he said. His voice, though low and somber, boomed through the crowd.

"Everyone wants change," he'd once told me, *"but no one wants to pay the price of revolution."*

If he knew the true price, I wondered, *would he still be willing to pay it?*

"My life for the rebellion!" they echoed. Out of curiosity I glanced at Sky to catch his reaction; he was acting as though he couldn't hear them. This cease-fire was makeshift at best, and would end the moment the veil was restored. If we lived that long, anyway.

There were so many things that could go wrong, I thought, not for the first time. So many ways this could end in bloodshed and suffering. But I was a gambler's daughter, and I had inherited my father's penchant for risk.

"Move out!" shouted Sky, and he was once again every ounce the commander I knew him to be. His men surrounded us in perfect synchronization as we rode out toward the city center.

Leaving the tunnels, I could tell Lei had already made his move. The streets and skies were deserted, but I could sense traces of a fight brewing elsewhere, just beyond First Crossing's southern border. Although the battle was too far for its sound to carry, I could feel its reverberations in the earth, the way the mountains seemed to shake with every meeting of qi and lixia.

Lei would be okay, I told myself. He was immune to spirit corruption, and his qi was strong.

But what if his brother had recovered from his poisoning? What if the monks turned on him? What if—

"There's nothing you can do for him now," said Kuro knowingly. "He chose this path for himself."

I tightened my grip on my reins. "And are you afraid?" I asked the rebel leader, looking at him astride his stallion, his face turned up to the sun.

He grinned. "Mark my words," he said, answering a question I hadn't asked, "history is being written today."

I tried to smile back, but my skin felt stretched too tight. A tinny, high-pitched ringing filled my ears, just soft enough that its source remained unidentifiable. As we neared the site of the veil's collapse, the air grew swampy and choked with lixia. The horses turned fearful, their soldiers having to urge them forward with shouts and even switches. Sky's stallion nickered nervously beneath me, before spotting Sky ahead of us as he moved confidently toward the chasm.

The air turned viscous, and I felt as though I were breathing in syrup, or a gossamer spiderweb that clung to my every sense. Everything dimmed: my vision, my hearing, my sense of the ground beneath me and the sky above. The world could have been inverted, floating, and I would not have been able to tell.

One thing remained: lixia. It was everywhere, screaming at me for attention. I could smell it, taste it, even *hear* it, as if it truly were a living organism.

Slowly, my eyes adjusted to the absence of light. We were closer to the chasm than I'd expected, as if time moved slowly and then all at once. The chasm was so much larger than any other spirit gate I'd seen. It was a rift between worlds, and it felt like one, truly, like a crime of the highest order. The imbalance of it all rang in my bloodstream, in my bones, in the way the mountains rumbled and the tides shifted. The world had tilted. Now it was in free fall.

"Stop!" Sky shouted. For he had perceived what I was just now noticing—a subtle, gravitational force drawing us in. Tempting us, luring us closer. *Fall*, it seemed to say. *Fall in.*

Kuro's horse bucked with agitation. The rebel leader tried to calm him, but the animal clearly wished to run. We'd planned to remain on horseback as we worked, to enable a quick getaway. But now I wondered if a getaway was simply wishful thinking.

"We should dismount," I told Kuro, as he lurched forward on his horse. "We'll need our concentration."

Sky looked furious at this, but he had the sense not to argue. "Don't go any closer to the edge," he warned me.

I dismounted clumsily, landing on one foot. Sky's horse was much taller than I was used to, and gravity did not seem to function properly here, as if up and down had somehow reversed. A wave of déjà vu washed over me. Were we nearing the in-between realm, the place where I'd fought Chancellor Sima at the end of the war? Could that have been the start of the rift, when we'd begun to blur the borders between realms?

Lost in thought, I barely noticed the saber-toothed bird that flew from the chasm, her wings slicing through the air as she dove toward me. At her vicious screech, I threw my arms over my head—but the blow never came. Sky's iron-tipped arrow had already struck, lodging deep in the bird's side.

I gaped at Sky. "Thank you," I said breathlessly.

He nodded, fitting another arrow in place. "Do what you need to do."

Another boom shook the earth from afar. What was Lei up to? But I could not afford to think about him right now. Closing my eyes, I channeled my qi through my core, releasing any errant worries. When I opened my eyes, Sky's soldiers had formed a small clearing around us.

Only Kuro was left beside me.

Tentatively, I held out a spirit fossil from the Reed Flute Caves. "Ready?" I asked him.

Kuro grinned, positively buzzing with anticipation. He wrapped his hand around mine, so that we both grasped the spirit fossil. At once, I felt our life forces merge, the essence of him bleeding into me.

"See you on the other side, Phoenix-Slayer."

As one, we left behind our bodies, our spirits entering the site of the rift like petals floating along a river current. I recognized the feeling of the in-between realm now, the way it entrapped qi and lixia, the way it allowed for both human emotion and spirit detachment.

Kuro's qi centered me like an effusive embrace. Perhaps he *was* a reincarnation of the Great Warrior, for his qi was like nothing I'd ever known. I could not feel the limits of it; I could not sense where his life force ended and Baihu's lixia began. The first embers of hope stirred within me. With my gift for compulsion and Kuro's boundless qi, perhaps we stood a chance.

Perhaps there could be a happy ending to our story.

I intertwined our energies together. Just as I was deficient in earth and wood, Kuro lacked water and fire. Our metal was the strongest, both of us surging with excess. Together we cycled through our combined elements—*wood, fire, earth, metal, water*—and then I began to impel.

I drew on my own memories at first, finding comfort in the familiar. "*Remember yourself,*" my mother had told me. "*Remember your humanness, and you will be able to return.*"

Remember what you have to live for.

I was five years old again, spying on my mother instead of practicing my penmanship. Through the rice paper screen I watched as my mother bathed with her best friend, a woman she'd known since girlhood. The two were lovely together, contradictions of sharp angles and soft curves.

"Let me braid your hair," said my mother, kissing the back of her neck. Her friend said something in reply, and my mother laughed, a sound like silver bells. Even in those early days, I rarely heard my mother laugh.

"You have a talent for kung fu," Uncle Zhou was saying. I was thirteen and training with him in the woods behind our house. *"Yours is a rare, extraordinary gift."*

My penmanship was crude, my embroidery an embarrassment, and my ability to play the erhu nonexistent. This was the first time I'd been told I was good at something.

I reached for my first meeting with Xiuying, but Kuro's memories pressed at the edges of my consciousness. I let him in, and together we directed his memories toward the veil.

I felt his exhilaration as if it were my own, watching as he beat up the town bully, despite being the shortest boy in his class. Watching as he celebrated his thirteenth birthday, and at last began to grow. *And grow.*

"What do you feed him?" the neighbors asked his grandmother, as he grew five inches each year.

"He's destined for greatness, that one," his grandmother replied, puffing out her chest with pride.

I watched the day he met Jinya, when she beat him in a game of cuju, despite being half his size. His initial scorn shifted into unwavering admiration. From then on he followed her everywhere like a lost puppy, though she would not give him the time of day. Even when other girls flirted with him, even when he won the affection of her sisters and brother, still she ignored him.

Late one evening Kuro was returning home from the fields

when he heard sounds of a commotion. Never one to run from danger, he hurried toward the raised voices and caught sight of Jinya arguing with a big-city constable.

"If you're hiding her here, you know that's illegal," the constable warned.

"It's illegal for someone to hide in their own household?" Jinya shot back.

"You know very well she no longer belongs to that family. She is the property of the Rao clan now."

"Then tell them to feed her! Even the pigs eat better than she—"

The constable tried to slap her, but she ducked, sidestepping him. "Why, you insolent child—"

Kuro darted between them, causing the constable to recoil. "My good man, how are you?" Kuro said jovially. Though he was only fifteen, his considerable stature often led others to mistake him for a grown man.

The constable sized Kuro up. "I'm looking for a runaway bride," the constable explained stiffly.

"No runaway brides around here," said Kuro, making exaggerated searching motions. Jinya rolled her eyes, her expression unapologetic. The constable glared at her, and she glared right back. Before things could escalate, Kuro stepped between them again.

"Sorry about my—my wife," he invented, taking her hand.

He winced as Jinya dug her nails into his palm, hard enough to draw blood.

"Control your woman," said the constable, "or the law will intervene."

"Yes, sir," said Kuro. "Best of luck with your search."

Once the constable was gone, Jinya ripped her hand out of his. "Mind your own business," she snapped.

"Why are you so angry all the time?"

"Why am *I* so angry all the time?" she demanded. "Why are you *not*?"

"What do you mean?"

She stared at him, her chest heaving with exertion. In the silence that followed, she waited for him to interrupt, to contradict her, to make a joke at her expense. He only stared. There was something about her that drew him in, like a reckless moth mesmerized by flame. No matter how destructive she would prove to be, he knew he needed to be near her. To admire her, to draw warmth from her, and eventually, to burn with her.

"Do you actually want to know?" she asked, her voice tentative now, shy.

He nodded.

She took a step closer, pushing him into the shadows of the alleyway.

"The system is broken," she told him, a clarity in her eyes he'd never known before. "They tell us *anyone* can rise through the ranks and become a jinshi scholar, but that's a lie they use to placate us. No boy from our backwater town will ever pass the imperial exams, because our schools are simply not good enough. Meanwhile, some noble's son with half a brain will rise through the ranks to become magistrate—and claim the system is fair. He'll go to the capital, while you and your brothers toil over the fields for the rest of your damned lives, sowing the crops but never reaping the harvest. The nobles will take your grain and your profit, and you will never make more than just enough to scrape by.

"As for us women, our only hope is to marry well. The better we marry, the farther away we'll go. If our husbands are generous, they'll let us return home once a year for the Spring Festival. Then we'll see our families, and we'll weep, seeing them old and withered, knowing we won't be there to hold their hands as they pass.

Knowing we belong to our husbands' households now. That is the best we can hope for—to be a servant in another's home. And you ask me why I am angry."

All this I channeled into the chasm—Kuro's awe, his curiosity, his will to live another day, and another, and another. Even his grief-tainted memories I fed to the rift, knowing this too was a deeply human emotion. I gave the veil my delight at my mother's delight, my pride and happiness at Uncle Zhou's praise. My first inklings that I could be *good* at something, that I could aspire to something more in this life.

I assumed the impulsion would be like water pouring from a breach in a dam; at first the memories might trickle in slowly, but gradually, the pace would increase, until no spirit could stop its momentum.

Instead, the veil welcomed our human memories, absorbing our qi like a long-lost friend. It took and took and took, and still came back for more. But as our qi slowly began to supplant its lixia, the veil began to resist us, as if not knowing how to balance itself against the changing composition of our realms. I fortified my impulsion, drawing strength from my memories. *"Remember,"* I heard my mother's voice say in my ears, *"there is so much to live for."*

Beyond, I was distantly aware of fighting that had broken out in the human realm. Yet the sounds of bloodshed were like the cries of birds in the sky, and we were submerged deep in the sea. Only when I felt Kuro's corporeal hand rip from mine did my concentration waver.

"Guard him!" Sky's infuriated voice broke through the haze of the in-between realm. I felt as though I were peering up at my former commander from a great distance, trying to make sense of a world that was not my own. My body had been left unattended in the clearing, though I appeared at ease, merely sleeping. Kuro lay beside me, one hand still joined with mine. There was blood trickling down his chin. *Blood?*

Had Lei's diversion failed? And yet these were not spirits fighting Sky's soldiers, but other men. Adding to the confusion were their uniforms—which also bore the Anlai colors.

"Commander—behind you!" Captain Tong threw his spear at Sky's attacker, grimacing as the soldier dropped. He seemed to recognize the fallen man.

And then a gray-haired warlord on horseback broke through the clearing, and I understood: Liu Zhuo had found us out.

The Anlai warlord dismounted and drew his sword, striding toward my defenseless body. "My greatest mistake was letting you go," he snarled, as if he somehow knew I could hear him. "This ends now."

But before he could get within a few feet of me, his son barred his path.

"Father," said Sky. "This is my last warning. Call off your men."

"You fool!" Liu Zhuo spat. "You think I'll still name you my successor after this?"

Sky raised his sword. "I couldn't care less what you name me anymore."

His father had been an accomplished warrior in his time, but the years had not been kind to him. His movements were sluggish and predictable, and his health was failing. Beads of sweat rolled down his face as his sword clattered against his son's, his two arms shaking against one of Sky's. Deftly, Sky drove his sword up to his father's hilt, so that Liu Zhuo had no choice but to disengage. That was his mistake. As he pulled his blade back, Sky disarmed him with a swift chopping motion.

His once-famous sword clattered to the ground, rendered useless despite all its former glory.

"Call off your men," commanded Sky. "This is no longer your war to fight."

His father glared at him, unmoving.

"For the sake of your honor I will not kill you," said Sky, sword still raised. "But know—"

"Too bad I don't particularly care about honor," said a high-pitched voice from behind him. My calm shattered as I recognized Lily's small figure. With the sword Lei had given her, and with the flying crane maneuver I'd taught her, she leapt across the clearing, a blur of light, and stabbed the Anlai warlord through the chest.

Sky faltered as if stabbed himself. He stared open-mouthed as his father fell to his knees, coughing up blood. Lily smiled down at the warlord, surveying her work. "Mingze was my brother," she told him. My mind reeled, recalling the spirit summoner executed at the palace gates. "And I promised him I would not die until you did."

Assured in her victory, she lowered her arm so that her blade dragged in the dirt. *Never drop your guard on the battlefield!* I wanted to scream at her, but I could not move. Still choking on his own blood, Liu Zhuo seized her sword and wrested it out of her hand. She tried to fight him but his sheer size overwhelmed her. In one breath, he'd stolen her blade and beheaded her.

"*Lily!*" I screamed, or tried to, as her severed head hit the ground. The rest of her body lay crushed beneath Liu Zhuo's massive corpse. He was so much larger than her that I could not see her in the fray.

Blood pooled on the ground, the silent marker of a life stolen.

How could Lily be gone? How could she be dead after everything—after scheming with me against the princes, after training with me every morning, after helping me escape the palace? I owed her so much. Now I would never be able to fulfill those promises; I would never be able to watch her grow up, to witness the woman she would become. *She was sixteen.* I had wanted more for her—a lifetime of freedom and dreaming, not one shaped by confinement and revenge.

I felt tears gather behind my eyes, tears that had no place to go. Thus the veil became my outlet, so that I fed it my sorrow, my grief, and my rage.

"Did you really think you could hide from me?"

Qinglong's voice cut through me like a blade of burning ice. Connected as we were, I felt my panic lance through Kuro, disrupting the flow of his qi. I tried to calm us both, to continue channeling our life force into the veil, but the closer we came to sealing the rift, the more fiercely it resisted us.

"I'm coming for you." It was a threat and a promise.

"We have to hurry," I told Kuro in the in-between realm. "Qinglong's realized it's a diversion."

"It's not enough," said Kuro. "*We're* not enough."

"But . . ."

I looked down at our joined hands and realized he was right. Here in this liminal space made of shadows, the two of us had become just another silhouette. Our life forces were nearly depleted, and our spirits fading. Still the rift gaped over us, its mouth open as if laughing. Were all our efforts in vain?

My knees buckled; I was so weak already. I would give all of myself, and still it would not be enough. It wasn't supposed to end like this; I wasn't meant to sacrifice myself for nothing. Deep down, I had foolishly believed there could only be two outcomes—the selfish one, where I sacrificed the world and saved myself, or the selfless one—where I sacrificed myself and saved the world. But even after choosing the latter, my sacrifice had meant nothing.

A part of me died then—the part that believed the world could still be fair and kind.

This was how it would end. Our lives lost. Our stories forgotten.

We had given so much, fought so bravely, and still no one would be saved. No one would remember.

"Neither of us wants it enough," said Kuro bleakly. "Our will to live—it's not strong enough."

The war, it had altered us both. Our hope was not enough; our belief in this world and its people was not enough.

My vision darkening, I began to release Kuro's hand.

"Then take mine."

We both turned at the force of his qi; Liu Winter had joined us in the in-between realm. *Impossible.* How could a human without a spirit seal find his way here? And yet I recalled seeing Winter in my dreams, though I hadn't known it at the time. He'd always possessed a remarkable spirit affinity; even Sima Yi had known it. He out of all of us was certainly destined to become a summoner of a Cardinal Spirit. Even so, he'd refused the offer, because he'd loved his life as it was.

"Use me," said Winter. "I know the cost, and still, I choose to pay it."

There was no time to argue. I extended my hand, and he took it with grim trepidation. He understood the cost would be great.

I thought I did too. But in truth, perhaps none of us fully understood the price we were about to pay. If we had known, would we still have done what we did?

The three of us stood in a circle beneath the flickering light, as if peering up from the bottom of the ocean. Winter's qi, untarnished by lixia, was like a flowing river to our stagnating bodies of water. Together we connected our elements, our spirits merging as one, and our combined qi blossomed into a force so immense, it rivaled that of a Cardinal Spirit.

FORTY-ONE

Ma—perhaps this is not goodbye, and yet I feel a strange certainty that this journey will be my last. I do not wish to leave you alone, but I cannot go on in a world where my brothers' murderer lives. Know that my death will not be in vain. Whether it takes a hundred years or a thousand, I will find you in every lifetime. And in another life, when we meet again, I hope to be the one to care for you—as you have cared for me.
—DUAN LILY IN A PRIVATE CORRESPONDENCE TO DUAN YAJING, 924

A TWELVE-YEAR-OLD WINTER STOOD BEFORE AN AUDIENCE OF Anlai nobles, who studied him like a pinned butterfly beneath glass. With an awkward, nervous bow, he went to his instrument, a seven-string guqin. Then, with a deep breath, he began to play.

The melody that emanated from his instrument was so lovely it brought the audience to its knees. Although this was a social occasion, no one dared speak as music flowed from Winter's dexterous hands, eloquent and exquisite and entirely bewitching. Listening to his song felt like being cast under a spell, one even the magician himself was lost in. For when Winter played his guqin, only then was he truly happy.

"*Why do you toil for hours at your useless instrument?*" demanded his father. "*Your tutors tell me you are ludicrous with a sword. How they laugh at me—a warlord with a musician for a son! What happens if we go to war?*"

"I have no interest in war," said Winter.

"*Will you stay at home like a girl, then? Play your little music while your brothers go off to fight for their country?*"

"*There are other ways to fight,*" said Winter.

"*Do you really think you can entrance your enemies with your music?*" Liu Zhuo laughed. "*Let me show you—this is what they'll do.*"

With little ceremony, he stepped on Winter's prized guqin, an heirloom made from the finest zimu trees of Mount Fuxi. Beneath his father's boot, the instrument splintered in half, its strings clanging together in protest.

Years later. The Three Kingdoms War raged on, but Winter spent most of his time in his tent, reading poetry and composing songs. He missed his guqin, but it would have been impractical to transport.

"Why won't you look at me?" he asked Lieutenant Tong Peilun, late one night as the rest of the camp slumbered on.

"Your Highness," he said, staring at his boots, "it isn't proper."

"Is it because I'm a prince?" he asked. "I've seen you meet my brother's eyes."

Peilun swallowed, his cheeks flushing beneath Winter's regard. "It's because you make me nervous," he admitted.

Winter tilted his head at him, baring the long line of his neck. "And why do I make you nervous?"

His anxiety gave way to frustration. "I can't do my job properly around you," he said angrily.

"I don't need you to do your job, then." Winter rose from his chair, and Peilun's gaze drifted to him like a fly to honey. "I have other jobs for you, Peilun."

The sound of his name was like a release. Peilun strode across the tent, closing the distance between them. Winter extinguished the lamp, but even in the dark, they found each other.

"You must learn to wield the sword!" Peilun snapped, wiping sweat from his brow. Their practice blades lay discarded on the mat after another failed bout. "What if I'm not there to protect you one day? What then?"

"Will that day come?" asked Winter, raising a brow.

"I don't know," Peilun replied, exasperated, "but I for one am not willing to risk losing you. Take this seriously, *please*!"

The prince sighed. "I told you when we first met," he said calmly, "I have no taste for violence."

"Then why did you agree to receive instruction?" Peilun growled, his patience wearing thin.

Winter held his gaze. "To spend more time with you, of course."

Peilun let out an aggravated breath. "Your Highness—"

"I told you to stop calling me that."

He clenched his jaw. "You're infuriating."

The prince grinned, leaning forward to wipe a drop of sweat from Peilun's brow. "Do go on."

―

"WHY DO YOU ACT LIKE A GIRL?" ASKED A TEN-YEAR-OLD SKY. AN older memory then, from childhood. "*You know the others make fun of you for it.*"

"*There are worse things than being made fun of,*" said Winter.

Sky wrinkled his nose. "*Like what?*"

"*Like not knowing yourself,*" said Winter. "*Like being ashamed of who you are.*"

And Winter's sense of self *was* that strong. It was so strong he recognized he did not need immense power to make others fear and respect him. He did not need lixia to feel satisfied with his life. His contentment and self-acceptance were like poison to the spirits, who picked at any insecurity they could find to tempt him. *We can give you eternal beauty. We can offer a life without pain. We can provide fame and consequence and glory beyond your imagination.*

"*I don't need any of that,*" answered Winter.

Their voices were drowned out by his will to live. His belief in this life, and his desire for it. His qi poured into the rift, a sea with no shore, filling and filling the chasm until the wayward spirits began to shriek, desperate to return home before the rift sealed shut.

THE GROUND BENEATH US TREMBLED. OUR JOINED HANDS TIGHTENED, each of our attentions fixed inward as we directed our remaining qi into the rift.

"*Hold on,*" said a once-familiar voice in my head. As if emerging from a hundred-year sleep, I remembered vaguely that I knew that voice. Ming Lei.

"*Don't give it everything. Leave enough to come back.*"

The reminder was a jolt to my consciousness.

"Hold back!" I shouted to the others, just as the earth began to tilt, and the chasm sink. "We have to be able to get out!"

They could not hear me. Winter's music had reached its climax: strings swelling, applause ringing. Kuro's blade clashed against his brother's, and the reverberations were felt through the field, so that stalks of sorghum swayed in answer. Rouha and Plum stamped their feet to the beat of the dragon dances, the drums pounding faster and faster. All the memories that made us who we were—we fed them into the veil. Only I kept something back. And now, as I tried to swim to the surface, dragging Kuro and Winter with me, I found their hands slipping through mine, turning translucent and spectral.

"Liu Winter!" I screamed. "Tan Kuro!"

The balance of our world was reasserting itself, and now nothing could stop its passage. I fought the current, struggling to tow Winter and Kuro with me. I was almost to the surface. A single beam of light emanated from above, fracturing as it struck the restless waves.

But I'd forgotten that my enemies existed on both sides of the veil. Before I could plunge my hand through the opening, a massive shadow obscured the light. He peered down at me, and smiled.

Qinglong.

He'd come for me at last.

FORTY-TWO

Of the four Cardinal Spirits, none are more elusive than the Onyx Tortoise, who sleeps through the passing seasons and stirs but once in a hundred years. Only the arrival of a vessel worthy of his power can draw him from the depths of his lair.

—A HISTORY OF LIXIA, 762

I UNDERESTIMATED YOU," SAID QINGLONG. "I UNDERESTIMATED your ambition."

I smiled at him, shielding my fear. "There comes a time when the master must bow to the pupil. For it was you who trained me well." With those words, I called upon my hunger, my want, and the sea rose to meet it.

Qinglong roared as the churning tides swept him from the air. The moons doubled in my vision as he sent haixiao waves whirling toward me, pulling me under. We both fell, through oceans and realms and worlds within worlds. My mother had warned me: the two of us were connected at our core.

We surfaced at the mouth of the Dian River. Where this had all begun—where I'd accepted his bargain and taken his power as my own. It was my insecurity that he'd capitalized on, to make me depend upon his power. But just as I needed him, so too did he need me.

Now I looked into his yellow eyes and saw his vulnerability. I saw his jealousy, his lack, the way he always hungered for more.

"*You don't belong here,*" I told him. "*You will never belong here.*"

He laughed at me, at my paltry attempts at compulsion. "*You think you can compel the Azure Dragon?*" he asked, still roaring with laughter.

He set upon me as I dove away, rolling into a crouch. Before he could turn, I jumped onto his back and clung to his scales. Outraged, he tried to shake me off, but I held on with maniacal stubbornness. He leapt into flight, thinking to frighten me, but instead I used the opportunity to scrabble up to his head. Gritting my teeth against the fierce wind in my face, I withdrew a dagger from my belt and stabbed him through the eye.

He roared in agony, flinging me off his back with a violent twist. I tumbled through the air, not knowing up from down, before I summoned my power and called upon the sea to cushion my fall.

"How dare you?" the dragon snarled. "*You think you can slay a dragon? Don't you know your life is tied to mine?*"

He was right in that I could not kill him, for his death would destroy me. In the same way, Qinglong did not want me dead, only ensnared and under his control.

"I don't need to slay you," I said. "I only need to make you see reason. Our worlds depend upon balance. It was your greed that tempted you to disrupt the equilibrium of all living things. But this time, you went too far.

"Look around," I said, gesturing to the roaring Dian River rapids beneath us. "Your hubris is your undoing. In this realm, I have the upper hand. And you are not what you once were in your world."

He lunged for me, but his immense size made him slow. I slashed at his side with my sword, black ink pouring from the open wound. He bellowed and smashed his tail into me, so that I went careening off the riverbank.

Wood, fire, earth, metal, water. I forced calm through my thoughts and directed a wave to ease my descent. The wave brought me back to the mouth of the river, where I sent knives of ice spinning toward him. He dissolved the blades in a single breath, turning them into a dense fog that obscured my vision.

"*It was you who agreed to the bargain,*" hissed Qinglong. "*You who decided my power was worth its price.*"

"You deceived me," I said. "You tried to use me as your puppet."

"Funny," he growled. "*Your mother said the same thing. But even she accepted her fate.*"

My anger knew no end. I screamed, throwing open my arms, and the fog dissipated, revealing the dragon once more.

"*Leave this world behind,*" I said, staring into his punctured eye. "*Leave.*"

And the Azure Dragon went still, unblinking, and I thought—perhaps my compulsion had worked. Perhaps I had truly overpowered a Cardinal Spirit.

But then I tried to step back, and I could not. I tried to blink, and I could not. Rather than him falling into my trap, I had fallen into his.

His eye seized me, captured me whole. I fell into his will, a bottomless pit with no end. My own will stolen, I could not move as ice crystallized around my limbs, locking me in place. Cold, I was so cold.

"Now you are mine," promised Qinglong. "*For you, my slippery little rat, I will put on a show.*"

The ice fogged my breath, my sight, so that when Qinglong's vision infiltrated my mind, it was the only thing I saw.

Diaochan was running, her long hair loose over her shoulders, her feet bare and her robes open. Her robes were her downfall; she tripped over their long hem and went tumbling, so that the soldier fell upon her, slitting her throat. Her last thought was of her sisters and the promise she would never fulfill for them. For she had promised them she would return home one day.

Little did she know her sisters were already dead.

"*No,*" I tried to say. "*No!*"

Qinglong brought me next to Chuang Ning, to my childhood home in Willow District. Dread flooded my being as I heard Xiuying's familiar cry.

A stranger with yellow eyes had pinned Xiuying against the wall. "*My vessel is weak,*" said the man, his voice echoing with the boom of another. "*I am tired of this broken shell. I want you, Yu Xiuying. You will be my rightful vessel.*"

The man was trying to press a glowing jade seal into her hand, but she resisted him with improbable strength. "Never," she spat out. "You will never have me."

But then the door creaked open. "Ma?" said Plum, his eyes as round as his nickname. "What's wrong?"

The vessel smiled. "*If you do not accept my bargain,*" he said, "*I will make your boy take it.*"

Xiuying's shoulders slumped forward, her surrender reflected in the hollowness of her gaze. "I'll accept it," she said softly. "Don't take him. I'll accept your bargain."

"Please," I tried to say. This was my breaking point. This was what I could no longer survive.

I had failed her; I had failed my family. Rouha and Plum would grow up without a mother, as I once had. With time they would forget the sound of her laugh, the neatness of her stitches, the resourcefulness she could conjure in any situation. They would never know how much she loved them, and how much she had tried to stay.

Qinglong showed no pity. Without delay he forced upon me his next vision—bringing us to the outskirts of First Crossing.

Lei's forces were dwindling. Both hungry spirits and Ximing soldiers converged upon them, hemming them in from all sides. It was a trap, I wanted to tell him, but he already knew. Perhaps he'd known from the start. Still he'd walked straight into it, because he'd hoped to give me a fighting chance.

On the blood-soaked battlefield, his brother rode out to meet him. Zihuan had waited until Lei's best men were dead, until Lei was exhausted and alone. Still Lei fought, the monster I'd witnessed at the Reed Flute Caves once again released, so that there was no feeling or emotion in his eyes.

Zihuan hung back, waiting, watching. Only when Lei flagged, taking a dagger to his side, did Zihuan come forward. And that was when I noticed his changed eyes—now the color of spun gold.

Zihuan had accepted a spirit bargain. That was how he'd survived the poisoning.

"So it's come to this," shouted Lei, breathing hard, one hand clutching his bleeding side. "I always knew it would be me and you."

"Oh, I'm not interested in fighting you in combat," said Zihuan, smirking. "I learned from you, Di." Dismounting from his steed, he raised a hand in signal. "Two can play at this game."

And the emotion returned to Lei's face as Zihuan's guard brought forth a thrashing woman bound in rope. With near theatrical flair, Zihuan removed the cloth bag from her head.

"It's a little family reunion," said Zihuan. "Hi, Rea. Miss me?"

Rea glared at the new warlord of Ximing, a brewing storm in her eyes. "Kill me," she said, like it was a dare. "Kill me and my hungry ghost will haunt you for the rest of your days—and when you're awake I'll follow you, and when you're asleep I'll follow you, and when you eat I will curse every morsel of food that you touch, and when you drink—"

He slapped her, hard enough that her head snapped to one side. Lei looked murderous.

Zihuan patted Rea on the head, his attention fixed on her. "That's enough, dear—"

Lei seized on his distraction and threw a knife at him, but Zihuan simply snapped his fingers and the blade crumbled into dust.

"Pity you could never accept a spirit bargain," said Zihuan. "But I guess you can't help your blood."

He held his blade to his sister's throat. "Surrender, or she dies."

"Ge, no!" Rea shouted, fear sluicing through her eyes.

Lei did not hesitate; he dropped his sword.

"Kneel before me."

Lei fell to his knees.

"Put your head to the ground."

Lei kowtowed.

Zihuan began to laugh.

"Lei!" I screamed, but this was a memory Qinglong had shown me, and Lei was perhaps already dead. And yet would I not have felt our connection sever? How could he be dead when I still lived? How could Xiuying be gone when I still survived? How could this be my curse—to remain behind even as everyone I loved perished?

The vision disappeared. Now we were in Tzu Wan, in the castle on the cliff. The Black Sea roared beneath us, disturbed by the two moons in the sky. From the open-air balcony, Autumn turned and ran, sprinting down the corridor.

She'd cut her hair short since I'd last seen her, and now her braids slapped against her cheeks as she rounded the corner. Breathlessly, she threw open the door to the nursery room. But Rea was gone.

"It can't be," she breathed, scanning the empty room. Even her dogs had gone.

Rea's husband appeared in the doorway, panting with exertion. "Where is she?" he asked, his voice cracking in fear. "How could he take her?"

He seized Autumn by the shoulders, shaking her. "How could he take his own sister?" he demanded. "How?"

Autumn shook her head. "I don't—" Her words were lost in the quake. She screamed as the ground slid out from beneath her, and the room split in two. The Tzu Wan palace, built on the cliffside, began to surrender to gravity.

"Take my hand!" he shouted, reaching for Autumn. But she was already slipping off the edge, the sea roaring hungrily beneath her.

"*Meilin.*"

That voice. It was one I never thought I'd hear again.

"*Meilin. Tell me where you are.*"

His command burned me to my core, waking me from a long winter of hibernation. I felt the ice around me thaw, the chains I'd perceived as immovable dissolving into dust. My will was my own.

You have so much to live for.

With every ounce of willpower I possessed, I tried to answer. My mind, sluggish and cold, struggled beneath the dragon's claws. But I thought of my mother, seeking the eternal spring. It had been too late for her.

Let it not be too late for me.

"The Dian River," I gasped. "*I'm at the Dian River.*"

The dragon reached for Lei but found he could not touch him. With a snarl of frustration, he satisfied himself with my anguish instead. Relentlessly, he hurled loss after loss, death after death. Every sorrow, every despair, every torment—it was all my fault. There could be no redemption for someone like me.

And yet Lei's voice had broken Qinglong's grip on my mind. It was not reality he was showing me, I realized, merely a distorted reflection of one. Just as I had compelled so many others, so too had he compelled me.

Ours was a two-way street, and what he did to me, I could do to him. I began channeling his core elements—matching his water and metal—in order to penetrate the crevices of his mind.

Qinglong's mind was like no human's. He was at once everywhere and nowhere. His memories were multitudinous yet shallow, without human emotion and depth.

I saw Diaochan's sisters searching for her, interrogating soldiers, putting up posters, sending out letters. I saw them praying every night at her shrine.

I saw Xiuying backed against the wall of our sitting room, surrendering to the spirit's demands. "I'll accept it," she was saying. "Don't take him. I'll accept your bargain."

But behind Plum, a tall figure burst into the sitting room. Xiuying gasped—looking up at her childhood friend from Huang Ju.

"Yu Xiuying!" Sparrow shouted, using her maiden name. His first love, he'd once told me. I had forgotten—forgotten that he had lived a life before, one beyond the bitter final acts that had shaped my hatred for him.

He grabbed the possessed man by the shoulder. "Take me," he said. "Take me instead."

"Sparrow—" Xiuying began, but Sparrow did not heed her. He seized the glowing jade, and the spirit subsumed him.

I did not know if he lived or died.

I followed the trail of blood to the outskirts of First Crossing, where Lei battled men and spirits alike. Amid the bloodshed and violence, he was backed into a corner, alone, kneeling without sword or spirit power to call upon.

"Kowtow," Zihuan was saying.

Lei obeyed.

Zihuan signaled to his guard, who came forward with an executioner's blade, long and slender. Rea thrashed wildly, sobbing, her movements berserk as she fought against Zihuan. With helpless rage she flung her head back and screamed, and perhaps it was this sound that called her dogs to her. They came. Tearing through the streets, all two dozen of them, fur soiled and matted, paws raw and bloodied. Zihuan eyed the approaching horde with contempt, until one—the smallest of them—bit him in the leg.

Zihuan howled with pain as Rea wrenched free from his grasp. One dog gnawed through the ropes binding her, while the others attacked at her command. And then she was free, and sprinting toward Lei, and he was on his feet, fighting, mowing through Zihuan's guards in an effort to reach him.

He wanted to deliver the killing blow, but Rea's dogs got there first. Zihuan tried to call upon his spirit power, but the dogs were myriad, and they were hungry for blood. Just as Lei's mother had once been dragged by dogs, so too was Zihuan's corpse.

I left First Crossing, searching for Autumn, for the memory at the Tzu Wan palace, but Qinglong ripped his consciousness from my grasp. I surfaced at the Dian River as Qinglong breathed a dense fog over me. In the mist, I went still, listening for him.

There. I whirled around, only for him to catch me first. I tried to strike him, but he ripped my sword from my hands and pinned me to the rock, trapping my neck between razor-sharp claws.

"There is always a cost to power," he hissed. *"This is yours."*

I grasped in vain at his claws, reaching for my qi and finding nothing. "I will never—"

A thunderous boom shook the earth as the dragon's claws were ripped from me. Gasping, I crawled away, seeking a hiding place. But the earth was moving.

Before my eyes the riverbank reshaped itself into a mountain, and the Dian River, which I had believed as enduring as the seasons, began to reverse course, its currents flowing *away* from the sea.

I knew of only one creature who had the power to make mountains.

"*Baihu*," said Qinglong, but there was a new note in his voice. Was it fear? "*I warned you to stay out of this.*"

"*You've gone too far.*" The Ivory Tiger's presence was like the sand of the Runong Desert, ancient and forbidding and vast. "*It's time we ended things.*"

And as she roared, the earth itself trembled with awe. Lightning flashed through the sky as Qinglong rose to meet her, their cardinal forces to be the ruination of our world. I clambered back, certain this was how the human realm would meet its end. But Baihu had not come here to fight. Instead the wind stirred around us with a different kind of power, animals scurrying for cover, leaves blustering in the gale, the scent of autumn and harvest all around us, in the air itself.

The thought struck me—how had Baihu known to find us here?

Then it clicked: Lei. I had told him I was at the Dian River. Could he have passed that on to Kuro, who then told Baihu? If they were in contact, it could only mean one thing—they were still alive.

I scrambled upright, elation surging through me, as the mountains once again began to ripple like water. Baihu flickered, like an ember about to burn out. So too did the dragon, despite his desire to remain. She was returning them to the spirit realm, I saw. They would leave me alone, and at last, I too could return.

The thought brought tears of relief to my eyes. I hauled my aching body forward, seeking refuge from the gale. But I should not have underestimated the dragon's spite. For at the last second, just before they vanished, the dragon seized me within his claws—and dragged me back into the spirit realm.

FORTY-THREE

By the emperor's decree, all my hard-won achievements were cast to the winds, like dust upon a worn path.
—RECORDS OF THE GRAND HISTORIAN, 489

I FAINTED WITH FATIGUE, BUT MY RELIEF WAS MOMENTARY. CHITtering fireflies woke me, buzzing in my ears with equal parts awe and fear. All around us, the lights of the spirit realm wobbled and shivered, their pulse frenetic and faltering. It seemed as if the world itself was holding its breath.

But the Cardinal Spirits did not care. A hair-raising snarl ripped from the sky as the Ivory Tiger struck out at the Azure Dragon, and the two of them went spinning through the air.

Their violence knew no bounds. Ancient trees were ripped from their roots, tremendous rivers ran dry, tidal waves flooded forests, the sky rained ash. Bruised, bleeding, and exhausted beyond belief, I simply hugged my knees to my chest and covered my head with my arms, trying to remain as small as possible. Trying to be forgotten. Trying to forget myself.

It was hard to tell how much time had passed. The sky burned overhead, so that no sunlight was visible from where I hid. I could see shadows pooling at my feet, but I did not know if that meant dawn or dusk.

It was only when Baihu landed hard beside me, skidding into the earth with a growl, that my hiding place was uncovered.

"*You,*" she snarled, and I flinched instinctively. "*You need to get out,*" she warned. "*Don't you realize the rift is closing? If you do not leave now, you will lose your way back to your world.*"

I stared at her open-mouthed, uncomprehending. Then she was gone, their fight moved elsewhere, and hot panic sluiced through me.

The spirit realm had a way of erasing the passage of time, severing your ties to the world you once knew. And I, foolishly, had allowed myself to sink into a dreamless sleep.

But now, my memories swept over me like a frigid wind, and I began to run. I ran like I'd never run before, and then I was no longer running, but flying, keeping pace with the birds, who were guiding me home. I'd forgotten that not all spirits were hostile, that just like humans, no two were alike. Yet the first spirits to cross the chasm had been driven by greed and conquest, leaving behind a damaging legacy that shaped how all were perceived.

Shadows loomed above and below. Day seeped into night, or night into day. How much time had I wasted down here? Was I too late? Was there still a way out?

"Lei!" I called, but there was no response.

The birds dove, and I followed them, trusting their instincts. They took me through a hilly desert, until I spotted a familiar hulking silhouette sleeping beneath the stars.

"Kuro?" I could not tell if it had been days or years since we'd seen each other last. And yet I knew him. I knew his fondest memories, his dreaded nightmares, the last words he'd spoken to Jinya. I knew the scars along his hands and the limp in his left foot and even the way his joints ached when it rained.

Slowly, he woke from a deep slumber. "*You . . .*" he said, his voice hoarse and rasping, as if he'd forgotten how to form syllables.

I offered him a hand, and he stumbled toward it, his body clumsy and imbalanced. "Come with me," I ordered. "Now."

And then we were running, the sand dunes blurring past us. A cliff rose up in our path, but we didn't hesitate; we jumped. The light was closing fast, the shadows growing longer with every passing second.

We swam through the currents, fighting turbulent waves. Disoriented, I sought the surface of the ocean, forgetting how to tell up from down. There—I could see that solitary beam of light in the distance, blinking at us as if beckoning us closer. I gave a shout of triumph—we weren't too late!—and swam with fervor.

But Kuro was tiring, his focus waning. The currents played cruelly with us. With every stroke I made, the waves drove us back twice as far. The attack felt personal—this was how I had lost Zilong during the war.

"It's too late for us," said Kuro.

"No," I gasped, fighting the currents. "We can't—give up—"

"We had a good run," said Kuro, disentangling his fingers from mine. "But I'm ready. I'm ready to move on."

I reached for his hand, but the waves were too strong. Borne by the currents, he disappeared into the depths of the dark sea.

"Kuro!" I screamed, treading water. But the pale beam of light was fading, and I was out of time. I surged forward, lighter and more buoyant without him. Still the light narrowed, the chasm that had once been so vast now barely wide enough for me to slip into.

Through the opening I could see the clear expanse of sky, only one moon hanging from above. I could see people and horses and even my own body, which I'd abandoned, and next to it—Sky, my first love, who I never thought I'd see again.

As if sensing my desperation, he turned toward the fissure and peered through it.

"Sky!" I screamed. Somehow, he heard me. He reached a hand through the crack, and I was reminded of another night long ago, a Ximing cliff, waves crashing far below me. He had saved my life then, despite the impossibility of it, and perhaps because of that memory, that moment, I found myself imbued with false confidence. I trusted Sky; I trusted him to save me. His touch would return me to the human realm. It would be my bridge back to myself.

I reached for Sky's hand, that solitary source of light against a world of darkness. But my fingers, like a ghost's, slipped through his. He fumbled for me, his hand meeting nothingness.

My will, already threadbare, unraveled into dust. I surrendered to the currents. I let go.

"Meilin!" he screamed.

The last thing I saw was Sky, plunging into the darkness after me.

FORTY-FOUR

*And do not the birds, weary from far-flung flights,
still know to find their way home?*
—THE CLASSIC OF POETRY, 532

TIME PASSED LIKE THE UNSPOOLING OF THREAD, SLOWLY, THEN all at once. In the darkness I wandered, neither alive nor dead. At times I heard stories, stories of great heroes and terrible villains, stories of war and adventure and chaos. And I thought, *I wonder what that must be like.*

Gradually, I forgot my name. I forgot my life before. I wandered the trees and the rivers and the mountains, knowing I liked warmth, knowing I gravitated toward light, though I could not recall why. I migrated with the seasons, finding solace in the habits of birds, who knew how to make a home anywhere.

It was early in the spring when the plum trees had blossomed, and I was sitting beneath their shade, gossiping with the fireflies. A young human woman approached me, hesitantly at first, then with a boldness that made me uncomfortable. I was not afraid, of course, for true emotion in the spirit realm was a rare thing. But I was not accustomed to boldness; most of the human wanderers in this place bore only a vague sort of aim about them.

"Qinaide," she said. *Beloved.* "I've been looking for you."

What a peculiar word—*beloved*. For there was no such thing as love and affection here, or any emotion that required intensity of feeling.

I observed her as she drew near. Her shoulders were strong and straight—swimmer's shoulders—and the apples on her cheeks high and pronounced. She looked young, but there was a certain depth of experience in her eyes that only came with age.

"Do you know my name?" she asked me. I shook my head.

"Do you know your name?" she asked me, and this I pondered for a beat longer, before shaking my head.

"You really did give it all to the veil, then."

I did not understand her, so I said nothing. This did not frighten me, that I did not understand. There were many things about this world that I did not understand. For example, why did the water feel cold when you first stepped in, but warm when you left it? Why did the stars seem brighter on cold winter nights? Why did some birds always sing, even with no one to return their song?

She sighed and sat beside me, picking a fallen plum blossom and tucking it behind my ear. "Let me tell you a story," she said. Under her breath: "Where should I begin?"

"At the beginning, of course," I said, and she laughed.

"Why, yes," she said, settling back on the grass. "Let's see. This is a story about a girl, a girl named Hai Meilin."

BY THE TIME MY MOTHER WAS DONE, THE SEASONS HAD SHIFTED AND it was winter once more. Day fell into night with swift alacrity, and the shadows liked to linger, making friends with the morning hours.

Still, my mother waited. When Meilin's story ended, she told me hers, and when her story ended, she told me her grandmother's.

On and on, as the world changed and stayed the same around us. Until one day, I understood what she'd been waiting for.

On a clear autumn day, a man on a winged lion flew into the meadow. He landed too quickly, tumbling in the grass, but he recovered with the skill of a seasoned warrior. He did not appear as I'd imagined him from my mother's stories. He did not have his boyish vigor, that plumpness to his pale cheeks, and he did not walk with any bounce to his step, as if he believed the world would part at his command. But it was his eyes that most surprised me, that induced a pale shadow of fear, if fear could exist in this world.

From my mother's stories, his eyes had been the color of dark chestnuts. Yet now they were unmistakably the color of ripe wheat.

"My name is Liu Sky," he said. "I've been looking for you. I'm an... old friend of yours."

He smiled, not because he was happy to see me, but because it was the polite thing to do.

"Come with me," he said. "I can bring you home."

Home? But I was home. And yet... my mother had told me stories. Stories of another world. Of a place of beauty and wonder and terror.

I found, for the first time in a long time, that I was frightened. I was frightened and exhilarated. I thought of that girl in the story, who had loved adventure and risk and possibility. And I thought, *I wonder if I can be like her too.*

I looked back at my mother, sitting beneath the plum tree where we'd first met. "Are you coming?" I asked.

She shook her head. "I have no place there anymore," she answered. "But it's not too late for you, qinaide."

"Thank you," Liu Sky told her, bowing. I laughed, finding the gesture comical here, in the world of spirits.

"For what?" I asked him, as we left the meadow.

"She made sure you held on," he replied. "Otherwise, I never could have found you."

"And why were you looking for me?" I asked curiously.

He considered me, a furrow between his brows. "I couldn't leave you behind," he said at last. Then he called upon his spirit, a beautiful lion with wings of light, helping me onto the beast's back. The journey was both long and short, familiar and strange. I did not know if I was happy or sad, inspired or indifferent. I only knew that something was about to change. That the calm and distant peace I'd felt here in this land of shadows was about to be replaced . . . by what, I did not know.

***

LIU SKY'S BLOOD EASED OUR PASSAGE INTO THE HUMAN REALM, SO that we emerged without trouble or delay. And yet there was nothing that could have made the transition easy—nothing that could have assuaged the pain that besieged me as the weight of nineteen years of grief and rage and suffering came crashing down upon me. I screamed, clutching my head, as my mother's stories connected with reality, as the truth of them lodged in my throat, as I learned I was the girl in those tales, I was the girl who'd disobeyed her father and joined the army and sought the glory and honor of war, and instead found the brutal reality of it. *There are no easy choices in war.* I had chosen what I'd thought best at the time. I had tried to protect those I loved. And above all, I had tried to honor the part of myself that had dared to dream of more, that had known I was just as capable, strong, and clever as the rest of them—and that I could prove it.

The onslaught did not slow, but it grew more manageable. Buried within moments of suffering were moments of joy and resilience, like precious stones within bedrock. Lifting my head, I found Sky watching me. He looked just as he had the last time I'd seen him, and I recognized that while we both had aged what felt like centuries in the spirit realm, little to no time had passed in the human world.

And yet his eyes—they were still gold.

"What happened?" I asked him. "How could you?"

His gaze was as hard as steel. "It needed to be done."

"It needed to be . . . ?" I trailed off as I recalled how he'd dived into the spirit realm after me, even as the rift was closing. He'd accepted a spirit bargain to find me, I realized, to save me.

I closed my eyes, guilt like a suffocating collar around my throat. "I'm so—so sorry—"

"Meilin," he said, cutting me off. He made to reach for me, before holding himself back. "Don't blame yourself. It's okay." Straightening and assuming a businesslike demeanor, he said, "I've prepared supplies for your journey. I wasn't sure what you'd need to pack, but . . . I had help."

I swallowed repeatedly, trying to speak through the lump in my throat. "What journey?" I said hoarsely. "I can't leave you now."

He shook his head. "My spirit isn't like yours." He scrubbed the back of his head, considering how to articulate his thoughts. "Let's just say he's less of the troublemaking sort." He shrugged. "Less powerful too, but perhaps there's a reason for that."

I could hardly hear what he was saying. I looked into his golden irises and felt my own eyes well with tears. Sky, the purest man I knew, the most honorable and duty bound . . . I had reduced him to a fate his father would never condone.

His father, who was no longer alive.

Sky was the new Imperial Commander of Anlai.

There was too much happening at once, and I did not have the mental capacity to process it. My tears collected faster, blurring my vision.

Sky rummaged for a handkerchief he did not have, before looking helplessly at me. "Don't stay out of pity," he said. In a softer voice: "You owe me that much." Hesitantly, he put his hand on my shoulder. When I did not recoil, he drew me to him and pressed his lips to my forehead. Then, just as quickly, he released me, creating deliberate distance between us.

We'd been through so much together. He had been the first man to ever hold me, to save me, to love me. He had been the first one to believe in me, to tell me I could succeed in a man's world. But in the stories of our lives, we were not each other's happy ending.

I wished with all my heart he would find his.

I began to cry in earnest now, great, shoulder-racking sobs. Sky looked past me with an imploring air, and then a new embrace caused me to break down completely.

"Mei Mei," said Xiuying, patting me on the back. "Don't cry so hard. It's unbecoming."

I snorted through my tears, and she laughed with me, holding me as she used to. We clung to each other, feeling for scars old and new. It was hard to say what could have dragged us apart if not for Rouha and Plum diving into our midst, trying to worm themselves between us. I looked for Uncle Zhou beyond them, but Xiuying told me quietly he had passed during the Day of Terror, when the veil between realms had split in two. Father too was gone, though I could not quite bring myself to mourn him. "He was much more docile," said Xiuying generously, "toward the end of his days."

"Did a spirit kill him?" I asked. "Or a soldier?"

"Neither," she laughed, but there was no resentment to it. "He passed in his sleep. So it goes," she said with a shrug.

Talk of death reminded me of other matters. I spun toward Sky, who stood with his men. "Did you get Kuro out?" I asked, recalling the haunted, faraway look in his eyes toward the end. *"We had a good run,"* he'd told me. *"But I'm ready to move on."*

Sky shook his head, his expression strained. "I couldn't find him," he said. He paused, glancing at a tall, brown-haired soldier behind him and adding, "I looked for him, and Winter too."

"Winter?" I repeated in confusion, before the truth sank into me like a stone in water. How could I have forgotten? Winter had joined us in the in-between realm, though it had not been part of the plan. It had been his qi we'd required to seal the rift, his boundless, uncorrupted qi that had given us the life force needed to rebalance the veil to equilibrium.

I would never fully understand why he'd done it.

"Winter—is gone?"

Out of all of us, Winter was the one I most believed would survive. He had never sought battle, never chased glory or honor in war. He had no need to make a name for himself, nor would he let pride or greed lure him into a reckless bargain with a spirit. Winter had cherished his life, had desired nothing more. He had taught me what it meant to live with contentment.

I had imagined Liu Winter outlasting the rest of us—growing old with Captain Tong, playing his guqin to the delight of the flowers, the trees, the moon, and the stars. He would have been someone who brought gentleness and beauty no matter where he went.

But that life, as lovely as it could have been, was gone. He, who had never made a pact with a spirit, who bore no blame for the veil's collapse, had given his own life to restore it. And now he was gone.

There was no justice in war.

Sky nodded. "He's gone," he repeated quietly.

"Sky..."

At the tightness around his eyes, I wanted so badly to hold him, to comfort him, to say anything that could ease his suffering. But with my happy memories of him came other, less happy ones. And I knew that my comfort was not what Sky needed.

"You should go," he said, turning away. "Only a few days have passed, but you don't have much time left. It could take weeks to find the eternal spring, if not months."

Zhuque's eternal spring. Meilin—I—had been seeking that spring. To sever my connection to the spirit realm, and to heal my corrupted qi. I grasped my jade, which pulsed hot against my palm. Qinglong had not sought me out, neither here nor in the spirit realm. I did not know what had happened to him, and I did not particularly care to find out.

"Your qi *is* weak," said Xiuying gently. "You should make haste." She restrained Rouha and Plum, preventing them from using me as a climbing frame. "What did I tell you?" she chided them.

Rouha spoke as if reciting a command: "We need to let Jie Jie go."

"But when will we see her again?" asked Plum, pouting.

"She'll come back, when she's ready," said Xiuying.

"If you take too long," said Rouha to me, "I'll come and find you."

Xiuying scowled in disapprobation, but I only smiled, squeezing Rouha's little hand. Her bright eyes and gap-toothed grin brought memories of another, bittersweet ones, for Lily had passed. I told myself it was what she wanted—to learn how to fight. I had given those girls swords and trained them for battle, and now the world would live with the consequences. Already the Black Scarves were composed of one-third women. But that meant those young women would live and die by the sword. That they would assimilate into a man's world, rather than carve out a place of their own.

I tugged on Rouha's braids. "You're growing up so fast, little one."

Rouha grinned up at me. "Just you wait. I'm going to become the best swordswoman the Three Kingdoms have ever known. And then I'm going to become a jinshi scholar."

My mouth twitched at this last remark. "Oh?" I said. "And how are your grades?"

Her chest swelled with pride. "Master Shen says I'm the brightest pupil he's ever taught."

"More like the only pupil he's ever taught," huffed Plum.

At my look of confusion, Xiuying explained, "He's a new teacher."

Rouha rolled her eyes. She was only seven, yet her self-assurance and faith in the world far surpassed mine at that age.

"I'll make you a promise," I said to Rouha, crouching before her. "If you pass the imperial exams—" Sky raised a brow at this, for women were not eligible for the exams. Not yet. "I'll come home to congratulate you. And I'll bring you an enormous gift," I added, knowing Rouha was a natural bargainer.

"Even if you're in another kingdom?"

"Even if I'm in another kingdom."

"Even if you're off at war?"

I swallowed at this, but nodded. "Even if I'm off at war."

"Skies forbid," murmured Xiuying.

Rouha's face shone, a challenge in her eyes. "See you there," she said.

"But we're so, so proud of you—no matter your accomplishments," Xiuying broke in, shooting me a warning glance. I hurriedly echoed her sentiments.

"Now, go," said Xiuying, ushering me toward the waiting horse and supplies Sky had prepared, most likely with her help. When she saw me still dawdling, she added, under her breath, "If you want to keep your word to Rouha, you best hurry now."

But I was dragging my feet for another reason. Someone had

once promised me he would accompany me to the eternal spring, and I had believed him. In my mind's eye, I hadn't intended to go alone.

"Looks like rain's coming," said Sky, peering up at the clouds and the Red Mountains beyond us, their jagged peaks like giants' teeth piercing the sky. I shivered despite myself. "Storm's heading west."

I nodded reluctantly. It was best to depart the city now and make haste up the mountain before the storm arrived in earnest. I looked down at my veins—charcoal black—and sensed the weakness of my qi, a ghost of what it once was.

It was time to go.

Trying to ignore the heaviness in my heart, I said my final goodbyes and prepared to depart. It was only when a light rain had begun overhead that another mare skidded into the clearing.

The Ximing prince leapt from his saddle, windswept and out of breath. "Sorry I'm late," he said, not mincing words for once in his life.

As he crossed the clearing toward me, I examined him in the rain. His damp hair was plastered to his face, which was marred by a new gash below his ear. To my relief he walked with no visible injuries, his broad shoulders straight, his long-legged strides confident and easy.

Just as I studied him, he studied me. His eyes traced over every detail of my body with such attention that I blushed beneath his gaze. It felt as though years had passed since we'd last seen each other, and yet he was familiar to me in a way I could not explain, like a verse from a childhood lullaby, one you never forgot.

"*You look well, my love,*" he thought to me, a crooked grin lifting his lips.

"*I feared you'd forgotten your promise,*" I told him.

In his eyes was his answer. He reached me at last and slid his arms around my waist, bringing me to him as if he'd been holding his breath all this time, and at last he could finally draw air.

"Never," he whispered.

FORTY-FIVE

The snow flowers have bloomed again, as you said they would. You once told me that you had no taste for violence, and I called you a fool, certain that violence would find you regardless of your inclinations. But now I see that I was the fool, for not daring to believe in a world beyond our kingdom's ceaseless wars. Wherever you are now, I hope you have found that place.
—TONG PEILUN, IN A PRIVATE MISSIVE TO LIU WINTER, UNDATED

THE JOURNEY WAS LONG AND BRUTAL. THE RED MOUNTAINS WERE notoriously impassable, with their labyrinthine slopes and narrow, crumbling rock ledges. To make matters worse, the air was thin and cold, often permeated by dense mists that obscured our path ahead. In the mist, we could only make out vague silhouettes, and what looked like fierce predators were often just dense forests of twisted pines. Their gnarled roots jutted out of the rocky soil, creating countless opportunities for tripping and falling to our deaths.

We could only bring our horses partway to the summit before we had to abandon them because of the rough terrain. Lei had paid an astronomical sum for an antique map drawn by a famed Wu Dynasty scholar who claimed to know the approximate location of the spring. The trouble was, the map was over a century old, and the mountains only bore a vague resemblance to what was depicted on paper.

Every day I grew weaker, until some nights I could not lie down without wheezing. On those nights Lei fed me his qi, so that his life force was the only thing keeping me from total collapse. Still we did not stop. Each day we climbed dozens of li, our conversations growing sparse as the pain in my body intensified and the strain on Lei's face deepened. Again and again he told me that I would make it. But secretly, I had begun to wonder if perhaps I wouldn't.

When I thought I would collapse from exhaustion, desperation drove me to ask the dragon for help. I reached into the abyss, wondering if he could hear me still, from wherever he lay hiding in the spirit realm. It was clear from the aftermath of the Day of Terror that Baihu had won their fight, and I guessed that the dragon was now hibernating somewhere, biding his time, waiting for another window of opportunity to strike again. Thus the cycles continued, the immortal spirits caught in their endless feuds.

"Qinglong," I thought. "*Can you hear me? Can you help me—just this one last time?*"

Spiteful to the end, he did not deign to answer. He would watch me go mad and die, I thought. And he would watch gleefully.

But perhaps the other spirits were not quite so vengeful. On the fifteenth day we came upon a mountain trail that surely had not been there days before. The path was smooth and groomed, rare for these parts, and there was even shade from a grove of pine trees to ease our way. But it was the sound of rushing water that most excited me. Turning to Lei, I saw the painful spark of hope in his eyes, which mirrored my own. But before I could follow the path, he seized my arm. "Wait," he said. "Let me take your sword."

Bemused but impatient, I pushed it toward him without thinking, relieved to be free of the weight. To my surprise, he plucked my dagger from me too, and even the hidden knife I kept in my boot. Too distracted to argue, I listened only to the sound of running water and at last began to run.

It was more like stumbling, but I moved my legs as fast as they could carry me, chasing that sound—that sound that I now realized had always echoed through my dreams. And when I came upon the spring, the strangest wave of déjà vu crested over me, as though I had been here before. But of course. In the spirit realm, the golden pool where my mother had loved to swim—it had always been Zhuque's spring.

She had been trying to show me all along.

It was a lovely sight to behold—the water crystalline and sparkling, fracturing the late sun's rays into diamond schisms that danced across the mountain peaks. The scent of magnolia blossoms permeated the air from a nearby tree, its colorful branches drooping lazily toward the water as if hoping to steal a sip. Wildflowers and moss-covered rocks lined the bank of the spring, their cool, damp surfaces providing respite for sleepy dragonflies.

I made haste down the rocky slope to the bank of the spring, ignoring Lei's proffered hand—I was determined to do this on my own. But as I neared the edge of the water, its rippling surface lost its appeal. Up close, it seemed the surface of the pool was simmering, and that if I were to step in, the waters would burn me alive.

I hesitated, caught between fear and anticipation. All at once, my spirit power surged through me, reminding me how much I'd come to depend upon it. I'd made a name for myself with my lixia. I'd ended the Three Kingdoms War with my lixia, and I'd saved my family with it. It was a power both terrible and lovely. With it, I'd been able to do anything, be anything. I'd grown into my truest self—ambitious, attention-seeking, and power-hungry.

The Ruan seer had foretold this.

"Have you heard of the myth of Zhuque's eternal spring? Legend says the spring waters can heal lixia corruption by severing the connection between spirit and vessel. If you journey to the Red Mountains, Meilin, you will find it. Its healing waters can save you, but only if you choose to go in."

"Why would I choose not to?"

"It is a difficult choice, one only the strongest can make. For in order to be cleansed, you must give up that which is most precious to you. I do not know what your decision will be; I cannot See it."

I had believed with conviction that I would go in. Why else would I journey hundreds of li and endure days and nights of unspeakable suffering just to give up? And yet, as I considered my predicament now, I realized I had not thought through all the factors at play.

If I severed my connection to the dragon, I would lose all my power. I would no longer be free to come and go as I pleased, to know that I could defend myself in any situation, against any man. All the respect and recognition I'd earned as a warrior would fade, for who would celebrate a powerless hero?

Wouldn't death be a kinder fate?

But perhaps I needn't die. Perhaps I need only bargain with the dragon; perhaps there was a way to tether myself to his immortality. I could accept his offer, let him take these impossible choices from me. At last I could rest, the weight of responsibility lifted from my shoulders.

But, Meilin, you've always fought for your independence.

What was independence anyway? What was the value of freedom without the power to use it? I was thinking logically now, and I knew that going into the spring was not a logical decision.

Calmly, I turned to Lei, my chin lifted high. "I've fought hard for my power," I told him. "And it's made me who I am today. I've decided—I'm not going to give it up."

Lei regarded me, his expression impenetrable.

"I will never live again as a person without power," I told him, resolve in my voice. I moved to brush past him.

But he barred my path.

Now I shot him my fiercest glare. "I thought you of all people would respect my agency in this matter, and allow me to make my own decisions."

He shook his head. "You're not being rational, sweetheart. It's the lure of power that's corrupted you."

"Because I'm a woman?" I snapped. "You think because I'm a woman I can't be rational?"

"No," he said, his eyes darkening. "I meant—"

"I'm done here," I said, shoving out of his grasp.

"*No*," he said again, but with a different tone of voice this time. Then, to my astonishment, he drew his sword. "I thought it would come to this," he said grimly. And I remembered with horror how he'd made me discard my weapons at the top of the mountain.

I shifted tactics as swiftly as a monsoon storm. "Don't get angry," I pleaded, reaching out to embrace him. I leaned in to press my lips against his, but he shoved me away, and not gently. As I stumbled, he pressed his blade to my back, prodding me forward.

"Move," he ordered, his tone lethal. My heart began to thunder in my chest.

When I didn't budge, he pressed his sword harder against my back, hard enough to draw blood. "I won't ask twice," he said, his voice now at its most dangerous—soft as silk.

"You of all people I never expected to betray me," I rasped. "How can I trust you after this?"

He did not speak, but I felt his blade against me.

"I will despise you forever," I threatened, choosing words that I knew would cut. "I will call you a monster with my dying breath. You are a fool if you think I will ever forgive you for this."

"I won't ask for forgiveness, then," said Lei, and I was reminded of how cruel he could be.

I felt a sickening twist of fear in my belly. Lei took a step forward, and I was forced to yield or be cut open by his blade. I glanced back at him over my shoulder, but his face was a cold mask, nothing like the man who'd held me at night when I couldn't sleep, who'd given me his qi rather than let me suffer. That man was gone; before me was a stranger.

As we approached the pool's edge, I could see the water simmering, spitting, its slow ripples seeming to reach for me with hungry arms. I tripped on a rock; still he did not pause. The water was so near. And I was so afraid.

"*I am a dragon.*" Qinglong's confession returned to me now. "*I must desire more. It is simply the way of things.*"

Just as the dragon could not exist without his greed, I could not live without my power. How could Lei make me go against my true nature? How could he ask me to ruin myself?

"Please," I said, tears clogging my throat. "Don't make me do this."

I searched his face pleadingly, but there was no emotion there, and he had always been impossible to read.

"I-I can't, Lei. I'm begging you. If you've ever loved me, if you've ever felt anything for me, please"—my voice broke—"please don't make me—"

Doing what I never thought I'd do again, I knelt on the ground before him, ignoring the sharp rocks pressing into my legs. Heart throbbing in my chest, I prostrated myself before him.

"Please," I said to the earth, humbling myself to the highest degree. "Please."

I glanced at him through my parted hair, catching the fleeting moment when his eyes softened with pain. It lasted only a second, but a second was all I needed.

I sprang up and tackled him to the ground. His blade flew from his grasp as we tumbled together in the dirt, both struggling for dominance. Though his strength surpassed mine, my advantage lay in my refusal to hold back. I scratched, clawed, and struck like a wild animal, driven by an unthinking fear. All I knew was that he was trying to take my power from me. And I would let no one stand in the way of my power.

Lei fought not to harm but to restrain, and this was his undoing. He tried to pin down my wrists, but I refused to be taken prisoner. I smashed my head into his with such force that we both began to bleed. Black blood dripped into my eyes as I clawed at his throat, scrambling for a choke hold.

"Meilin!" he shouted hoarsely. "Wake up—this isn't you!"

But I could not hear him. All I could think about was my power, my power, my power. I could not give it up. Not when it had made me who I was today. Not when I was nothing without it.

My gaze lit upon the telltale glint of steel in his tunic. I lunged for it, and Lei tried to twist away, but then his eyes widened as he saw the protruding rock between us. He covered its jagged edge with his hand mere moments before my forehead collided with it. Stunned, I recognized that he had just saved me from a potentially fatal head wound. And yet the thought passed through me like mist, leaving no trace. I saw his vulnerability and dived for the dagger, wrestling it from his grip.

"Put the blade down," he said warily. I gripped the dagger, wondering if I had the nerve to use it. But then his eyes narrowed on my necklace, my jade, and my heart hardened against him.

"The jade," he said lowly. "It's changed you."

My jade throbbed against my skin. I wrapped my fingers around it, and in response, I felt the waters stir at my feet. I couldn't explain how, but I knew then: if I walked away now, Hai Meilin would become a living legend, my name enduring through the centuries. The people would follow me, adore me, revere me. I would be the woman warrior who disguised herself as a man to join the army, who saved the Three Kingdoms, who brought the world to its knees.

The pull of the tides grew stronger, more insistent.

But if I entered the spring, if I let the waters take me, my story would be lost forever. History would forget my name and erase my great deeds from memory. When I died, it would be as if I'd never existed. Everything I'd fought for, everything I'd sacrificed. For nothing.

"Meilin," warned Lei.

I smiled at him, then attacked. This time he fought to win, shoving me to the ground and capturing me with his superior strength. But he underestimated me. They always did.

Tightening my grip on his dagger, I aimed upward and plunged it into his chest. His eyes went wide in shock as my blade met flesh. He coughed, and blood sprayed from his mouth.

"Qinaide," he gasped. *Beloved.*

My mother used to call me that. My mother, who sought the eternal spring. My mother, who had been too late.

I stared in shock, consumed by the horror of what I had done. Lei's face was growing pale from blood loss, his fingers pressing against the wound, slick with crimson. And yet, beneath the haze of pain in his eyes, his love for me endured, unbroken. He loved me, even now. And this was how I repaid him.

My hunger for power poisoned everything it touched, driving me to destroy the very things that mattered most.

It struck me then how foolish I'd been. All along, I'd had a life outside my power. Those who loved me loved me regardless of my strength. When I died, and we would all die, it did not matter if I was remembered as a hero or as a villain, or if I was remembered at all. This was the true price of power—that no matter how pure your intentions, relinquishing it was the hardest thing in the world.

So I didn't think about it. I didn't try to make the rational decision, or kneel and beg, or fight and inflict pain. I simply seized Lei, and then, as he'd once done, I threw us both into the water.

I WAS BURNING, BURNING AND FREEZING ALL AT ONCE. SENSATIONS crashed over me, too manifold to isolate. I felt my jade splinter, and my bones unravel. I heard the dragon's hoarse screams in my ears, his childlike pleas for relief as he curled deeper upon himself, trying to hide from the pain of severance. I screamed until I could not scream any longer. All the while, my memories blazed through me like falling stars.

"*You're a sharp one, aren't you? Remember, beauty is the wisdom of women. You have a pretty face. Be grateful to the gods. Your mouth will be prettier if you keep it shut.*"

"*We're going to war tomorrow. And I'll be damned if I die because one of the soldiers who was supposed to have my back was off getting smashed instead. You can sabotage yourself in your own time. But don't bring the rest of us into this.*"

"*Then you should have died an honorable death, instead of shaming your family name. There is no mercy for those who forsake their duty.*"

"*Winter told me to look after you. That you could become Anlai's most important weapon one day.*"

"*You hate me, but you're the only one who understands me. Do you know—the greatest injustice the warlord did to me was not in murdering my family? It was in letting me live. Do you know what agony it is to live at the expense of others? No? I will show you.*"

"*Everyone wants change, but no one wants to pay the price of revolution.*"

"*I told you what I am. But what I didn't tell you is this—if they had taken your life today, I would have hunted down every last one of them. I would have scoured the Three Kingdoms for every soul responsible—and I would have given each of them a slow, slow death. And then, once I was finished, I would have followed you to the afterlife. I would have found you, and dragged you back from the hands of Death itself."*

I felt myself descend deeper and deeper into myself. I saw myself in the Forbidden City, wondering if I could use Sky as my means to the throne. I saw myself in the Three Kingdoms War, wondering if I could save all of Anlai to prove myself a hero. And I saw myself as a little girl, wondering what it felt like for the entire world to surrender at your feet. That little girl had been the first to aspire for more. To crave, deep down, fame and respect and power. It had been her voice that had called to the dragon, that had felt his greed—and matched it.

Since then, my ambition had lifted me to soaring heights—and plunged me into the blackest depths. It had once been just a part of me, but now, under the dragon's influence, who was I without it? Could I be more than my ambition again? Could I be my kindness, my loyalty, my fondness for the sun? Could I be the little girl who once loved freely, who gave without expecting anything in return?

I plummeted into the depths of the spring, which ran so deep it blurred into the spirit realm. Blinking awake at the flickering lights around me, I understood that I would miss this place. It was beautiful and terrifying, gentle and unknowable. Never again would I return to this realm of shadow and light, this realm that knew all my secrets and still treasured them, hid them, guarded them with all the secrecy of a jealous mistress.

At the mountain's peak, I came upon a pool of golden water. A young woman was swimming within it.

And I would never see my mother again.

She emerged from the water, her skin glistening like polished stone. When she saw me, she smiled, slicking her damp hair back.

Her face, forever youthful in this world, now appeared younger than mine.

I would age. I would age and grow old and die, and still she would remain here, separated from time.

And I would never see her again.

"Qinaide," she said. "So you've come to say goodbye."

She was both the mother I'd known and the young woman I never knew. She was wise and loving but also reckless and fickle. There was still so much I did not know about her. There was so much I would never know.

"I don't want to go," I told her imploringly. "I don't want to say goodbye."

"Everything has its time, Meilin," my mother said, and I remembered how stern she could be, even when I only wished for comfort. "It's time for you to let go."

"But how can I live without my power? How can I live without you?"

She pushed herself up to sit beside me on the bank, our legs dangling in the golden water. Here in the spirit world, the pool was a warped reflection of its twin in the human realm. Like yin to yang, the two would touch, but never cross.

"It's time to find another way to live," she said to me. "One that does not draw strength from the weakness of others."

I gazed at the spindly trees clinging to the mountain peaks, their branches buffeted by the wind. "There is no other way to live," I protested. "That's just the way the world works."

Her fierce eyes caught mine. "Then imagine a new world."

EPILOGUE

Dear brother, you wrote to me about the woman warrior as the woman you loved, and so I have thought of her in this way alone. But lately I have begun to hear stories apart from you, stories of her adventure and courage and cunning. It has made me wonder... why don't I too learn to fight?
—CAO REA, IN A PRIVATE MISSIVE TO CAO LEI, 924

I SURFACED FROM THE SPRING WITH A RAGGED GASP, MY BODY thrumming with adrenaline. In the distance the sun was setting behind the Red Mountains, casting a soft, plum-colored haze across the sky. The world was somehow both more and less lovely without the shadow of the spirit realm behind it. For without spirit power, I knew this life was fleeting. I was born and I would one day die, but that only made today more precious in its transience. My time here was short. But it was enough.

I wished to share these thoughts with another. And that made me realize he was not here.

"Lei?" I called, pushing myself out of the water. "Ming Lei?"

I scrambled upright, finding his discarded knife on the sandy bank, which was still tainted with his red, uncorrupted blood. "Lei?" I cried out, trying to keep the panic from rising in my voice.

"Took you long enough."

I whirled around to find him striding down the hill, carrying our supplies and drying his wet hair with a spare tunic. My eyes skipped down to his bare chest, which was unmarked, as if we'd never fought at all.

"Zhuque was always my favorite," he remarked, and I laughed, running toward him, feeling alive in a way I hadn't for a very, very long time. That was the danger with addiction, wasn't it? It crept up on you, slowly, until you began to forget what life before was like. But this was how it felt—to breathe freely, to laugh with abandon, to hold someone in your arms and tell him you loved him, without restraint.

Lei dropped our supplies and swung me in the air, ignoring my protests as my braids came loose and my hair spilled out of its ties. Setting me down on the grass, he ran his fingers through my wet hair.

"What's my name?" he asked suddenly.

I rolled my eyes. "As if I didn't just call it for the whole mountain to hear, Cao Ming Lei."

He sighed with relief, crushing me to him. "You still have your memories," he said. "What did the spring take from you?" he asked, as I'd told him the Ruan seer's prophecy.

"My name," I answered, with only a touch of sadness. I tried to shrug. "I guess history will forget me."

Lei said nothing, a tendon in his neck rising as he swallowed. "I'll remember," he said at last, his voice low yet thrumming with power. "For as long as I live."

I met his gaze, and it threatened to consume me whole. Whether the world remembered me or not, this was the legacy I'd leave behind: one of strength and weakness, vengeance and forgiveness. A girl who'd strived with all her might to obtain immense power, and then, rather than live and die by it, decided to give it all up.

I would have to find a new way to live now.

I touched his bare chest, perfect and unblemished. "I thought

I'd lost you," I told him, tears pricking the backs of my eyes. "I thought you were gone, and I'd never told you—I love you."

His hands cradled my face, his thumbs caressing the arches of my cheekbones.

"My love," he whispered. And then I kissed him.

I kissed him like I never had before—with nothing held back. With the certainty that my love was no longer a curse, that it would not poison him. That beyond ruin, there was hope. Beyond redemption, there was forgiveness.

As the sun dipped below the horizon, reluctantly, I pulled away.

"Will you come with me?" Lei asked, his finger idly tracing the shell of my ear. This close to him, I could track the rise and fall of his throat—his only tell. "To Tzu Wan?"

My smile slipped. I took his hands in mine, and at my expression, his own shuttered. No matter how guarded I was, he always could read me like an open book. "In the last moments before our connection was severed," I told him, "I think the dragon was trying to tell me something."

Through our connection, I'd felt a pang of unequivocal regret. I could not tell if the regret was directed at me, or at him, or at how things had ended between us. Yet with it, he'd sent me a final vision. A little girl, living in the wastelands of the Runong Desert. At her feet in the sand glowed the final cardinal seal, the Onyx Tortoise, the North Wind. I watched as she admired the flickering jade, tilting the stone to let it catch the light. *"I'm going to keep you safe,"* she told it, and the once-buried jade hummed happily in answer, lost no more.

"You promised me you would come with me to the eternal spring, and you did," I told Lei. "I'm promising you now—I'll come find you one day, wherever you are. This isn't goodbye."

Lei said nothing.

I took a breath. "The dragon showed me the fourth summoner, a little girl living in Leyuan. I need to find her, and I need to teach her how to control her power, before it controls her." I thought back to the start of the war—how easily my mother's necklace had seduced me. How recklessly I'd flung myself into something far beyond my understanding. *"I won't let history repeat itself,"* I told Lei silently.

He did not speak. I think it was too hard for him then. Instead he drew me against his chest, and I pressed my cheek against the solidity of him, taking comfort in his warmth, his beating heart, the familiar strength of his presence, like a balm to my soul. I would return to him—I knew this in my bones—but my journey was not yet over.

I love you, I told him silently, reveling in the words I'd never before been able to say. *I'll come back to you.* I hesitated, knowing it was selfish, asking it anyway. *Don't forget about me, okay?*

I won't, he answered, holding me to him. *I can't.*

―

IN THE DAYS TO COME, I WOULD RIDE ALONE TO THE RUNONG DESERT. I would cross the border into a kingdom I had never known, and I would meet new people and see new places beyond anything I had ever imagined. But in the rising of the sun and the fall of the moon, I would remember those who had touched my life, and I would carry their memories with me, even when the world moved on, even when history forgot their names, and mine. This was the legacy my mother had left me: her story, and the stories of all who'd come before. In truth, I had never been alone.

Imagine a new world, my mother had told me. She had gone, but now I answered the moon, the stars, the mountains beyond it.

"I will," I said.

I will.

LEGACY OF THE THREE KINGDOMS PERIOD, 974:

In the aftermath of the Day of Terror, qi was restored to the land and the spirit gates gradually dwindled in number until they became subjects of mere legend. Following the war, Imperial Commander Liu Sky enacted perhaps his most influential edict—an act that would come to shape the course of the Kaiming Period. By reforming the eligibility requirements for jinshi scholars, he authorized anyone, regardless of class or gender, to sit for the imperial exam. Six months later, he introduced the anonymous grading system, which soon proved so effective that it was widely adopted across all of Tianjia.

The ensuing era was one of peace and prosperity. Some credit the fair and equitable treaty accords following the Three Kingdoms War as the cause of the sustained order. Others credit a fabled woman warrior, who allegedly brokered the peace agreements between the warring kingdoms and initiated the modernization of the jinshi scholar system. However, historians are divided over this account, as there is little evidence today for such a notable figure. If she did exist, her name has long been forgotten in history.

ACKNOWLEDGMENTS

Endless thanks to my agent, Peter Knapp, for believing from the very beginning, and to my editor, Anne Sowards, for guiding me through every step of the journey with patience and insight.

Immense gratitude to the brilliantly talented team at PRH—especially Adam Auerbach, Megan Elmore, Christine Legon, Daniel Brount, Kristin Cipolla, Stephanie Felty, Jessica Plummer, and Elisha Katz. And to my fierce champions at Park & Fine, including Danielle Barthel, Kathryn Toolan, Abigail Koons, Ben Kaslow-Zieve, and Olivia Valcarce, thank you for your unwavering support.

To my UK agent, Claire Wilson; my UK editor, Molly Powell; and the entire team at Hodderscape—particularly Sophie Judge, Laura Bartholomew, Kate Keehan, and Daisy Woods—for bringing *The Night Ends with Fire* to the UK with such tremendous energy and vision.

To Anissa and the entire Fairyloot team, for making my London book launch a dream come true.

To Victo Ngai, for the breathtaking cover, and Natalie Naudus,

ACKNOWLEDGMENTS

for bringing the audiobook to life. To Carissa Susilo, for the stunning character art.

To all the authors who generously read and blurbed my book—Thea Guanzon, Amélie Wen Zhao, Patricia Briggs, Grace D. Li, Nalini Singh, India Holton, Peter Tieryas, and Axie Oh—your kindness and encouragement meant the world.

To designer Veronica Zhai, whose styling genius is responsible for every outfit compliment I received on tour.

I was blown away by the enthusiasm and support of the booksellers, bloggers, authors, librarians, and readers whom I met on tour. Amani, Ramishah, Daphne, Katrina, Nikki, David, and so many others—you all made me feel at home no matter where I was. I'm so glad *The Night Ends with Fire* has found readers like you.

To my fellow writers and creatives—Grace, Chloe, Ann, Amélie, Hairol, Aleese, Gloria, Heather, Yuqi, Lucy, Yixuan, Michelle, and Evelyn—your work inspires me every day. (We got this.)

Writing a book while in school is its own brand of chaos, and I couldn't have done it without the friends and family who kept me sane. To Michelle, Sea, Akshatha, Marc-Aurele, Mehek, Quinn, Sadiki, Shikhar, and many others—whether it was cooking food for me when I hadn't eaten all day, tracking down my lost phone on the streets of Manhattan, or asking every bookstore across the globe if they carried my book, your consideration, humor, and thoughtfulness sustained me.

Finally, to my family, always—for everything. 致我的家人，感谢你们给予的一切。

WANT MORE?

If you enjoyed this and would like to find out about similar books we publish, we'd love you to join our online Sci-Fi, Fantasy and Horror community, Hodderscape.

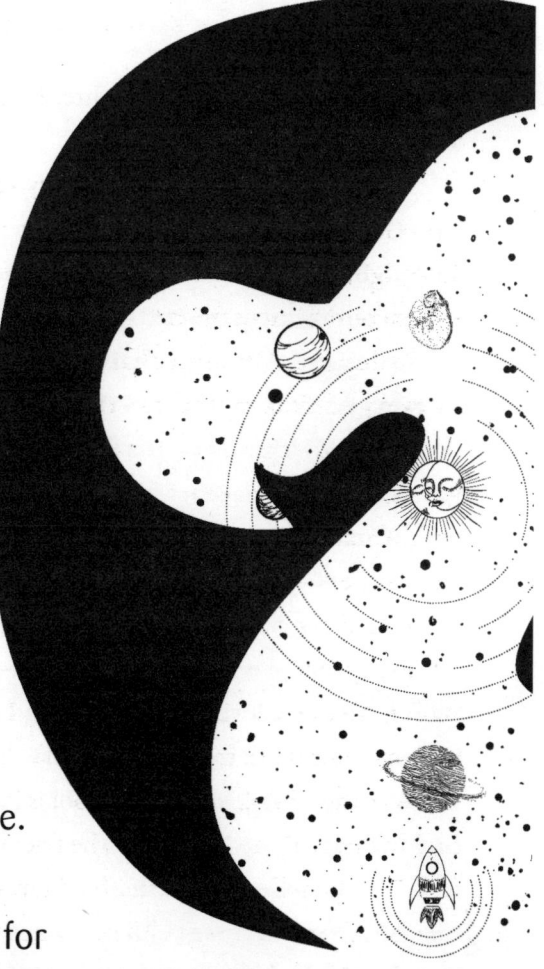

Visit hodderscape.co.uk for exclusive content from our authors, news, competitions and general musings, and feel free to comment, contribute or just keep an eye on what we are up to.

See you there!

HODDERSCAPE
NEVER AFRAID TO BE OUT OF THIS WORLD

@HODDERSCAPE   HODDERSCAPE.CO.UK